D0869779

HIDDEN

CSI REILLY STEEL #3

CASEY HILL

2nd Edition
First published in Great Britain
by Simon & Schuster, 2012.

Copyright © Casey Hill 2011

The right of Casey Hill to be identified as the Author of the Work has been asserted by her in accordance with the Copyright, Designs and Patents Act 1988.

All rights reserved. No part of this publication may be reproduced, stored in a retrieval system, or transmitted, in any form or by any means without the prior written permission of the author. You must not circulate this book in any format.

All characters in this publication are fictitious and any resemblance to real persons, living or dead is purely coincidental.

HIDDEN

CSI REILLY STEEL #3

PROLOGUE

*How can this tainted world contain us, how can it contain our
dreams?*
*At night, in the freedom of my mind, the shackles of this mortal realm
fall away as I soar above the fields and the farms, over forests and
hills.*
*I have always dreamed of flying — dreams like this are where the
spirit comes alive, where we create our own rules, our own reality.
Why should we let other people tell us how to live, or what is right
and what is wrong? Flex your wings and soar with me, my little ones.
Do you see our land below us? Is it not beautiful? The lake and the
fields, the river and the trees, the horses running free beneath the sun.
This is our world, our home, our sanctuary, and within it we are safe.
Is that a dream? No, it is our reality. And so I know that when I
awake, when the rooster calls me to another day, that my eyes will
open onto our own paradise.*

1

C olin O'Dea was trying to figure out the fastest way to murder his wife. Dark hedgerows rushed past the windows as he sped along the narrow country road.

'Will you please slow the hell down?' Fiona grunted. 'Your work buddies may be impressed by your new car, but I'm not.'

He responded by speeding up, unable to resist the urge to do the opposite of what she asked.

Just a few minutes until they were home. Then she could go off and have one of her herbal baths, or whatever it was she called them, and he could watch the Chelsea game he had recorded earlier. What sort of people had dinner parties on shaggin' Thursday nights? At least he'd escaped reasonably early.

'Colin!'

His wife's sharp scream pulled him out of his reverie just in time for him to spot something lying in the road — a white bundle. Rubbish from a truck, or a dead sheep maybe? Without thinking, he swerved around it, feeling the BMW's anti-lock brakes push back against his foot with a faint shudder.

He tried to fight the slide — dammit, that's what traction

control was supposed to do — but it wasn't enough. The car was going too fast, the road was damp from the rain shower earlier, and Colin wasn't as good a driver as he liked to think.

They spun 360 degrees, fields and fences, trees and ditches racing past in a blur as the headlights threw everything into sharp relief for a split second, then back into blackness. Then, as suddenly as it had started, the car was still once more. The only movement was the smoke and steam pouring past the headlights' beams.

Colin was rigid, his knuckles white where he had gripped the steering wheel, his heart pounding in his chest, while beside him Fiona sat in shocked silence. The engine continued to purr quietly.

Finally Colin unpeeled his hands from the steering wheel and glanced around. They were sideways across the road, the front corner of his precious new car dangling over a ditch.

'Fuck!'

He slammed his hands on the wheel, threw the door open and stepped into the chilly evening air.

Colin studied the front of the car. The headlights shone on the grassy bank at the side of the road and the reflected light was enough to show the damage. The front spoiler was crunched up beneath the car, the plastic split. Damn ... It was almost as if he himself had been violated — his new car was supposed to be perfect, a tonic for his midlife crisis.

The sound of Fiona opening the passenger door made him look up. 'What was that?' she asked, looking back down the road, her voice trembling. 'What did we...?'

He stood up and peered in the same direction. 'Dead sheep I think.'

'It didn't look like—'

Colin sighed in exasperation. 'What else would it be? Stupid animals are always wandering out into the road around here. Farmers ought to take better care of them.' He removed his glasses and wiped the drizzle off them. 'Jimmy hit one last month in his Land Rover. Made a right bloody mess of the front end, I can tell you.' He put his glasses back on. 'Where are you going?'

Fiona was already stumbling up the road on her high heels. 'It didn't look like a sheep to me,' she continued doggedly. 'Even if it was, we need to get it out of the road before somebody else hits it.'

'Forget about the bloody sheep,' he growled. 'How are we supposed to get the car out of this ditch?'

He crouched down again and examined the spoiler. It was already pretty messed up so, really, backing the car up could hardly do it any more damage ...

'Oh, God, shit!'

Colin stood up again and stared down the road to where Fiona stood, her green dress almost ghostly against the dark hedgerows. 'What now?' he called out irritably.

His wife said nothing, she just stood with her hands clamped to her mouth.

Colin squinted at her face as he approached, suddenly disconcerted by how pale she looked against the beams of the car's headlights.

'What is ...' The words froze before he could finish his sentence, and his eyes locked on to what lay at her feet.

'Fuck ...'

For a moment neither of them moved, then Colin turned and vomited on to the road, the viscous liquid splattering his expensive shoes and the leg of his designer suit.

The body of a young woman lay on the road. Even in the darkness they could see that she was barefoot and wearing nothing but a pale nightdress and the only burst of color came from her thick, red, curly hair. There were cuts and scrapes all over her body, a deep gash in her head, and a bone sticking out of her ankle at an unnatural angle. For a horrible moment,

Colin worried that he had caused that, but then he remembered he'd swerved in time to avoid hitting her.

Or had he?

'Is she...'

'Dead ...?' Fiona whispered, tears brimming in her eyes. 'Without a doubt.'

The girl's skin was pale, and she had an almost ethereal look as she lay on the dark road, her red hair framing her face, her body and white clothing seeming to glow against the darkness around them.

'On this road, at this time of night, she could have been here hours without anyone seeing her...'

Fiona snapped open her handbag. 'I'll call 999.'

Colin glanced around. 'Should we move her or ...?'

'Better not.' She glanced at him, her voice full of meaning. 'Just in case.'

'Oh Christ.' Colin's chest tightened. Surely nobody would think they'd run her over? He knew he hadn't hit her, and despite the damage to the front of the car that should be easy to prove, shouldn't it?

Bending down, he hovered over the girl's body. As he glanced again at the extent of her injuries, he frowned, noticing something.

Her long hair was splayed across to one side, revealing the base of her neck. On the skin Colin could make out a strange pattern disappearing beneath the nightgown.

His eyes narrowed as he tried to process what he was looking at.

'Holy Christ,' he muttered. 'What the hell is that?'

2

The small kitchen was dark with just the ghostly orange glow of the street lights to illuminate the gloom.

Reilly Steel's flashlight played across the room. At first a cursory glance around, then a more orderly scan. First impressions, then the methodical search.

The flashlight's beam revealed the details of what had happened here and the lives that had been played out: an overturned chair; a dark pool of blood on the torn linoleum floor; an overflowing ashtray on the table beside a baby's bottle; the sink overflowing with dirty dishes.

Reilly hated domestic violence cases — the hidden years of tension, the secret beatings, the lies, the cover-ups. There were no winners, only losers, just another generation of damaged children growing up to believe that this was what relationships were like and how people treated each other.

This one was worse than most — the wife was currently in hospital, her stomach held together by a hundred staples after her husband had stabbed her with a broken bottle.

The Garda Forensic Unit wasn't usually called in on these

cases, as they were generally cut and dried, but this one was different. Not only had the woman nearly died — the bottle had nicked her superior mesenteric artery — but the husband denied doing it and the wife was now insisting she'd simply fallen on broken glass.

The saddest part, Reilly mused, was that the poor woman feared further wrath from her demonic husband far more than she trusted the system to bring her justice and protection.

Her jaw clenched as she snapped on a pair of latex gloves. Attacking a defenseless woman with a broken bottle, stabbing her in the gut, then running off and leaving her lying in a pool of blood and claiming that he wasn't even *there*? What kind of man would do that? The kind that she was determined to see convicted.

She brushed aside a lock of her blond hair, tucking it in place behind her ear. Not for the first time, she wondered if she should get a short, functional haircut, something that would look sharp, professional and most importantly would never get in her way. Still, she liked the sensation of quite literally letting her hair down on her admittedly few days off.

She scanned the kitchen once again. The alleged attacker, Brian McGavin, had been thorough — he'd fled the scene, established an alibi with friends, taken the weapon with him. If Reilly couldn't find anything to place him at the scene at the time of the attack, there was a good chance that he would get away with it.

She was not prepared to let that happen.

She had seen McGavin when the detectives brought him in for questioning. He had a cocky, brutal face — a life-long bully who challenged any man with his eyes — and a rap sheet as long as his Neanderthal arms.

She was of course supposed to be impartial, simply gathering the evidence that presented itself, but there were times when it was impossible not to get involved, not to have a personal investment in nailing someone.

The kitchen table told its own story. An ashtray full of cigarette butts, yesterday's copy of *The Sun* open at the horse racing pages, and an empty can of Heineken. There were traces of McGavin everywhere, but could Reilly place him here at the house when the attack took place?

Sudden noises spooked her — kids outside shouting at each other, an empty can being kicked, the roar of a car — but just as quickly the street fell quiet once more and Reilly's focus was back on the job.

She enjoyed working late in the evenings, liked the way the darkness naturally forced her to focus on nothing other than the small pool of light thrown up by the flashlight. With nothing to distract her, she was forced to focus on the minutiae and look for the little details that might otherwise be missed.

She aimed the flashlight on the floor and crouched down to look closer at the bloody pool. Reaching out with a gloved hand — the deeper parts were still slightly sticky — she realized that there was something else there. A faint glint of light caught the beam as it skipped across the floor.

She reached out with her tweezers and slowly lifted up a shard of blood-covered glass. A fragment of the weapon? Something to go on at least.

She looked closer at the immediate surroundings. The floor hadn't been mopped in years, the once-white lino now stained a motley gray. And there, under the edge of the sink unit, was another thin sliver. Once again she picked it up and slipped it into an evidence bag. Taken alone, the pieces of glass meant nothing, but it was possible that they might have picked up the slightest glimpse of a fingerprint or a tiny piece of skin, anything that might link them to McGavin.

Reilly stood up, closed her eyes and took in a few deep breaths through her nose as she tried to imagine exactly what had happened here. Her sharp sense of smell filtered out individual odors from a cacophony of stench. She slowly edged forward toward the blood-stained couch, the metallic smell breaking through the more pungent whiff of baby vomit.

Why had the row gone from verbal to physical? Perhaps the wife had stood up to him, goaded him from behind the perceived shield of his child suckling on a bottle.

The reason didn't matter; what did matter was hard conclusive evidence that would put this animal behind bars where he belonged.

She looked at the floor, the bottle of baby formula on its side, and a dried pool of milk around it where it had fallen. A white muslin cloth close by was covered in blood and yellow milky reflux. Reilly closed her eyes again, this time as an involuntary gesture, and she hoped the baby had done the same rather than witness the full horror of what had happened here.

She held up her camera and pressed the shutter button, the harsh flashlight briefly illuminating the room.

OK, so McGavin had flipped, she thought, continuing her inner monologue. He'd grabbed the bottle, smashed it across the table like he was in a barroom fight, and stabbed his wife in the stomach while the baby was still in her arms.

It was a parting shot; he wouldn't have hung around, and he'd left the injured woman slumped on the floor, desperately trying to stem the flow of blood with her hands while her baby, *their* baby, screamed in fear. Reilly could almost hear echoes of the infant's desperate cries, and she tried to block it out and focus on the here and now. She glanced across at the kitchen door. It led out to a tiny back garden, a low fence separating it from an area of wasteland. The perfect escape route if you didn't want to be seen. Or if you were carrying a blood-covered broken bottle …

She reached the back door. It was still open, revealing a patch of scrubby lawn, a rotary clothes line draped in tiny clothes, and an overturned rubbish bin, with its contents strewn across the dirt by local foxes.

She paused in the doorway, flashlight scanning up and down, following the doorframe ... and then she saw it. It was small, easy to miss, but to Reilly's trained eye it was unmistakable — a bloody partial.

As McGavin had barged out the door and fled the house, leaving his wife lying bleeding on the floor, his hand had glanced against the doorframe.

Reilly swung her camera around and took shot after shot of the incriminating print. She had him.

A small smile of satisfaction stole across her face as she pressed a thin film of tape on to the print, before gently easing a sample of the blood onto a cotton bud.

The shrill ring of her mobile phone startled her. Slipping the sample into its container, she slid her phone from her pocket and glanced at it.

Chris Delaney.

'Chris. What's up?' She knew the detective wouldn't be calling her at this time if it wasn't urgent.

'Hope I'm not disturbing you. I tried the lab first.' He knew her habits — they had worked together for long enough. Still, there was a faint coolness in his tone. They might have been good friends once, but there was a definite distance between them now.

Despite herself Reilly felt wounded by it. Since her arrival at the GFU almost a year and a half ago, she and Chris had been to hell and back together in the course of the job, and until lately she would have considered him her closest friend.

But that was before he'd started hiding things from her.

It made it even more apparent that the longer Reilly lived in Dublin the fewer friends she seemed to have, such was the imbalance between her always hectic work schedule and non-existent social life. A sharp contrast to back home in California, where the work–life scales were generally tipped in the opposite direction with after work drinks and parties on the beach a common occurrence.

'Not a problem,' she said, her tone neutral and professional. 'I'm just at the McGavin house in Ballyfermot – the wife-beater?'

'Not the best area to run a scene at this time of night,' he commented, sounding like an overprotective father.

'It's fine. There's a uniform stationed here in case one of his firefly cronies shows up to do a job on the place.'

'So did you find anything to incriminate him?'

She mentally crossed her fingers. 'I think so. We'll have to have a chat with the wife when she's able, let her know there's a good chance we can put him away if she'll testify.'

'Chance would be a fine thing,' Chris said ruefully, making Reilly suspect that her efforts might well be in vain.

Well, that would be his department. As far as forensics was concerned, her job was done.

'So, I'm guessing this isn't a social call,' she said. 'What's up?'

'Suspected fatal hit and run,' Chris said flatly. 'Rural area near Roundwood in County Wicklow. Just took the call from HQ. Not a lot of detail but by all accounts the locals seem a bit spooked.'

'Spooked?' Reilly repeated, frowning.

'Like I said, few details so far. But seems there's definitely something about this victim that needs a closer look.'

3

Detective Pete Kennedy climbed slowly out of the silver Ford Mondeo and looked around. 'A lonely place to be wandering around at night,' he said to no one in particular.

A younger cop hurried over to meet him. 'Davis,' he informed Kennedy. 'We were first on the scene.'

Kennedy nodded and pulled a packet of John Player Blue cigarettes from his pocket. He opened it and popped one between his lips. 'Hit and run, we were told.' The cigarette dangled as he talked. The driver's side door opened and Delaney jumped out, slipping his arms into a crumpled waterproof jacket with 'Garda' written on the back of it.

'Certainly looks that way,' Davis replied. 'Body's just over here. You should take a look at … well, it's just weird,' he mumbled, leading them towards the scene of the accident, as the detectives exchanged glances.

They approached the body that was lying on the road. Chris bent down to look more closely at the dead girl, while Kennedy finished his cigarette, steeling himself for yet another look at death in the face.

'Where do you think she might have come from?' he asked Davis.

The other man shrugged. 'Not much around here, apart from a couple of farms. Roundwood village isn't too far away.'

'Are there ever any parties, raves, whatever you call them, out this direction?'

Davis couldn't keep the smile from his face. 'No, sir. Nothing like that out here.'

Kennedy nodded and puffed on his cigarette. 'Well, this is your home turf. Got any ideas?'

Davis wanted to say something insightful — it wasn't every day that a city detective asked him for an opinion — but in truth he was as puzzled as anyone else. 'To be honest, I don't. The couple who found her say it was like she just appeared out of nowhere.'

Kennedy grunted. 'Of course they did.' Carefully quenching his cigarette with his thumb and forefinger, he placed the half-smoked butt back into the pack. 'If there's one thing we can be sure of,' he said, standing straight and pulling up his trousers, 'it's that she didn't fall out of the sky.' He bent down to where his partner crouched beside the body. 'Well, any ideas?'

Chris replied without looking up. 'She may not have fallen from the sky but she sure did have wings,' he said, gently pulling back the clothing on the dead girl's shoulders to reveal a large, intricate tattoo. 'I'm guessing this is what you meant by weird,' he said to Davis, who nodded.

'Christ, that's a lot of ink.' Kennedy's gaze followed the beam of light from the other cop's torch, revealing artwork which completely covered the girl's upper back. The blueish tinged lines were fine, sweeping the wings upwards from near the base of her spine to fan outwards as they reached her waist, eventually covering almost the whole of her upper back. 'An out-and-out fallen angel.'

'She certainly got hit by somebody,' Chris commented,

pointing out the contusions, tarmac burns and dirt etched into her skin. 'The question is, was she alive or dead when she was hit?'

'We'll have to wait for the ME before we know that.' Kennedy groaned as he got up from his haunches. 'So did she walk here or was she dumped?'

Chris directed his flashlight down to the girl's ankles, careful to touch nothing. As the light played across her bare feet it revealed a layer of mud and gravel smeared across the soles, blades of grass sticking in places. 'She's certainly walked some way,' he observed.

Kennedy was still gazing around. 'Is there a hospital around here, a residential home, anything like that?' he asked Davis.

The officer nodded. 'There's a sheltered housing place over near Newtownmountkennedy. I think it's a sort of respite facility for special needs people, Down's Syndrome and the like.'

They all gazed at the dead girl's face. There was no sign of the typical physical characteristics of Down's – the flatter face, the upward slanting eyes. In fact she had elfin features, a small mouth, a dainty nose, chiseled cheekbones. Combined with her flowing red hair you would have thought her quite beautiful had you seen her in any other circumstance. What would lead such a young woman to be wandering a lonely country road in the middle of the night in nothing but a thin cotton dress? Her delicate features bore a look of deep sadness; it was hard to imagine that events leading up to her death had been anything other than tragic.

'That would still be quite a walk,' observed Kennedy. 'Even cross country it's got to be what … five miles or more?'

'And barefoot.' Chris gently touched the edge of her night-dress and rubbed it between finger and thumb. 'It'—s pretty damp — she must have been out in the rain for quite some time.'

He looked out across the dark fields. Before she was hit, the dead girl could have come from anywhere, a hundred yards or five miles away. Out in the darkness lay hundreds of solitary houses, dozens of farms, several villages ... and that was assuming she had walked here. If she had been dumped then their search area expanded almost infinitely.

'The ground is more damp than wet though, and it's a mountain mist in the air rather than rain.'

Chris looked at Davis. 'Better check out the local houses. Some parent might wake in the morning not realizing their kid has gone sleep-walking in the night.'

But something told him this was no accident.

Kennedy pulled out his unfinished cigarette again and tapped it thoughtfully against the packet. 'So what now?'

'Better talk to the couple who found her, then wait for Thompson to give us a COD. Forensics are on their way too so let's see if Reilly and the crew come up with anything.'

Kennedy gave a deep sigh. 'Is that what it's come down to now? We just sit on our hands and wait for the science guys to throw us crumbs?'

Chris shrugged. His partner was old-school, and increasingly apprehensive about the more scientific bent to police investigation these days. He could understand his frustration, but there was no denying that developments in forensics and crime scene investigation helped considerably.

'For the moment it would also be worth our while calling at houses within a couple of miles of here, to see if they saw or heard anything unusual while it's still fresh in the memory. Like I said, maybe there's a simple explanation.'

Kennedy gave him a disbelieving look. 'You're not serious about the sleep walking thing.'

'There's only one way to find out: some good old-fashioned detective work. Aren't you the one constantly complaining about the lack of it?'

'Let the locals handle that; at least they will know the neighbors. We roll up to some farmhouse at this hour in an unmarked car and we'll be running the gauntlet of guard dogs and farmers with shotguns. People don't live out here in the sticks because they want to be disturbed in the middle of the night, you know.'

Chris wrinkled his nose. 'Fair point. But for the moment, the tattoo seems like the only decent lead we've got in terms of ID. Let the GFU in to take a photo, upload it to the lab, and within a few minutes one of the techs will be comparing it with every known piece of ink from Ballymun to Bangkok.'

Kennedy might decry the GFU's 'toys', but an interactive device Reilly had been beta-testing for one of her old Quantico workmates had proven its worth on recent cases. The device, called iSPI, enabled fast and accurate re-enactment of crime scene details with 3D imagery, and provided a mine of information that sped up the investigative process. iSPI would almost certainly be able to indicate in which direction the girl was traveling at the time she was hit, and exactly where on the road the fatal impact had occurred. If she had indeed been killed this way.

It was merely one of many nifty gadgets the GFU had at their disposal. Now almost three years in existence, and with a propensity for in-depth analysis and, more importantly, fast results, the purpose-built forensic unit headed by Reilly Steel had improved the force's abilities no end.

It wasn't appreciated by everyone, however.

Kennedy pulled his cigarette out of his mouth and stuffed it back into his pocket. So much for trying to quit. 'We're becoming bloody errand boys you know, gofers for the scientists, that's what we are,' he grunted. 'They'll be training monkeys to do our jobs soon, the way things are going ...'

Chris watched him out the corner of his eye as they walked towards the couple who'd discovered the body. In the four years or so that they had worked together he knew Kennedy's moods well and was pretty sure that something other than 'the scientists' was bothering him.

The detectives briefly interviewed the couple who'd discovered the body before sending them to the local police station with Davis's partner to obtain more detailed statements.

'So are you going to tell me what's got you so fired up today?' he asked Kennedy eventually as they made their way back towards the body.

The detective said nothing, just took out the same cigarette and tapped it against the packet again. Chris was experienced enough as an interviewer and friend to allow him the space and time to organize his thoughts and answer when he was ready.

Kennedy relit the cigarette this time, took a puff and let out a deep sigh. 'Ah it's nothing...'

Again Chris let the silence do its job, looking sideways at his partner as he fiddled with the filter of his cigarette.

'It's Josie.'

Josie was Kennedy's wife, the bedrock upon which he rested, his safe haven after a day amongst the detritus of society. A few years older than her husband, she had taken early retirement, and seemed happy to potter around the house and be there with a warm dinner and a pair of slippers when Kennedy came home from work more often than not drained and exhausted.

'What's up?'

'She's been having some stomach problems, they ran some tests...there's something not right...' He looked sideways at Chris, worry etched across his features. 'You always fear the worst, though, don't you?'

Chris nodded. 'Human nature. And the more the person means to you...'

Kennedy stared out across the dark field once more for a

few moments, before turning abruptly back to Chris. 'You hear that?'

Chris listened. He could hear the faint sound of another vehicle approaching. 'Car? So what?'

'That's not just a car, that's a gearshift cranking one-eighty.' He reached over and started straightening Chris's leather jacket. 'Miss Baywatch is on the way. Here, let me smarten you up a bit.'

'Give it a rest.' Chris immediately recognized the sharp switch in mood as a cue to drop the subject. It was characteristic of Kennedy to not let his guard drop for very long. Still, Chris made a mental note to keep an eye on his partner. Such concerns were potentially a dangerous distraction from the job, something he himself knew only too well.

'I keep telling you,' Kennedy was saying, 'one of these days you might catch her in a weak moment, when she's desperate and lowers her standards...'

Unlikely, Chris thought, especially now. Right from the beginning, he and Reilly had had some kind of connection, and while at one point there might have been something brewing between them, he'd done something which disappointed her, and he knew it.

Back to his usual blustery self, Kennedy guffawed as the headlights swept around the curves and Reilly Steel approached the scene. 'Here comes trouble.'

4

Reilly's eyes widened. 'Angel wings?'

'Impressive, eh?' Chris crouched down beside her as they studied the extensive tattoo on the dead girl's body.

'It's beautiful…and so intricate.' She pulled out her own flashlight and ran it slowly up and down the corpse. 'So what do we know?'

'We thought you were going to pull out that iPad thing of yours and tell us.' True to form, Kennedy was always the smartass.

'Ah, don't mind him,' Chris chipped in lightly. 'He's having one of those days — must be his time of the month.' But Reilly noticed the subtle yet meaningful look Chris gave her, suggesting that something else was at play with the older detective. She wondered what it might be. 'She was spotted by passing motorists, they called the emergency services and a local patrol car was first on the scene. Seems she was already dead,' Kennedy told Reilly. 'No ID as yet, and as you can see she's barefoot and in her nightgown.'

'But her skin … it seems very wet?'

'Well, it's been drizzling most of the evening.'

'I know. But her clothes feel soaked right through.' Reilly leaned down and sniffed at the hem of the dress.

Kennedy looked at Chris. 'Here we go,' he groaned. 'She's going all weird on us again.'

Ignoring him, she straightened up. 'There's something … I'm not sure but I don't think it's just rain.' She stood up as the lights of another approaching vehicle illuminated the scene.

The drive out on the quiet country roads that evening had been her first chance to unwind after an already hectic day — and with another scene to process, it was likely to be the only time to herself before collapsing into bed some time after midnight. If she was lucky.

Unwinding for Reilly meant something different than it did for most. She had opened the windows of the van, allowed the cool, damp air to rush past and given her mind the freedom to wander. It gave her a tiny window of opportunity to dwell on things other than work. Random thoughts and promises. The organized nature of her brain would not allow for too much pointless daydreaming though; inevitably she would start to make mental to-do lists, like inviting her dad and his new partner over for dinner, or finding time to get out for a run before her ass got any bigger. Recently, the thing that loomed largest during a moment of quiet was a dull ache, a growing loss that she attributed to the absence of her sister.

Lately, though, it was becoming apparent that it was something more than that and once again her thoughts drifted to home.

Moving to Dublin had been an easy choice initially: the promise of a new challenge. Her father had already made the move and she had nothing to lose — or so she'd thought.

Now things had changed. The truth was that Reilly missed the US. It had taken her a while to recognize the fact, mostly because the workload left little time for California dreaming.

'That'll be Thompson or your crew,' said Chris, looking into the headlights.

Another white van parked behind the police car. The doors opened and two GFU technicians in boiler suits emerged.

Temporarily setting aside all thoughts unrelated to the here and now, Reilly sprung into action. 'OK, let's get this scene cleared – I'll need all these cars backed up, and all non-essential personnel out of the way.'

Chris smiled, by now well used to her direct manner. He turned to the watching officers. 'That means you lot — get your cars moved back at least a hundred yards either end of the road, and stay back there with them until she calls you.'

'Who's that and how come she's in charge all of a sudden?' grumbled Davis.

'Reilly Steel from the GFU,' Chris informed him, 'and she's the one who's going to figure out what happened to our fallen angel over there.'

Reilly strode over to the advancing techs. 'We're going to need to move the van back at least a hundred yards, then we can start to have a proper look at what we've got going on here.'

Gary had an open friendly face with a scruffy half-beard that made him look far younger than his thirty years. 'Will do, boss,' he said, in a typically upbeat manner. He turned on his heel and headed back to the van, the keys jangling in his hand.

Lucy, the other tech, was in her mid-twenties. Her blond hair was cut into a stylish bob, and she wore dark-framed glasses — an attempt, Reilly always thought, to make herself look older. But despite her best efforts at promoting a more serious persona, Lucy was the energetic, enthusiastic member of the team, the spark plug who kept them going over long shifts when energies were flagging and spirits were falling.

Lucy hurried over to Reilly, who noticed she couldn't keep

her eyes from the body lying in the road. 'Where do you want to start?'

'Someone hit that girl, and we need to try and figure out who. Let's concentrate on the area immediately around the body for starters.'

Lucy's eyes remained on the dead girl. 'Do they have any idea who she is?'

Reilly shook her head. 'We'll deal with that later. Right now let's focus on trying to figure out what happened here.'

Lucy reluctantly tore her eyes away from the body. 'Sure.'

While they were talking, the surrounding vehicles were moving away. As their headlights receded, the scene took on a different air, the fainter lighting giving it an almost artistic look — a fine, misty rain falling through the beams of the police cars' headlights, the girl lying on her side, almost peaceful looking, the angel wings visible through her thin nightgown.

It almost looked as though she could get up at any moment and fly away.

With the area cleared, the forensic techs set to work, combing the road for anything that might be of interest, like road debris that could have come from the vehicle that hit the girl or any sign of recent skid marks.

It was painstaking work, crouched over scanning the road with a flashlight, trying to ignore the damp that settled on the back of their necks. Every time one of them found something of interest — a scrap of forensic trace that might be relevant — they put down a numbered marker, took a photo of the item they'd found in situ, then bagged and tagged it, the number on the evidence bag corresponding with the number on the yellow plastic markers.

Before long, the road on either side of the girl's body was littered with markers, but Reilly paid little attention to what her team were doing — she was focused on the body, her flash-light moving at a snail's pace up and down the corpse.

Every so often she would stop, and try to order her thoughts, before continuing her search. So engrossed was she that she didn't notice the approach of Karen Thompson, the Medical Examiner. The older woman gave a little cough. 'Reilly, OK for me to do my initial exam on the body now?'

Reilly looked up, surprised. 'I didn't hear you pull up. That would be great, thank you.' She stood up and moved a respectful few paces back to allow her the space to conduct her examination.

A tall imposing woman in her late forties, Thompson lowered herself slowly to her knees and hunched over the corpse. She had a distinctive way of leaning over the bodies she examined, almost as though she needed to get close enough to them to hear their stories.

Reilly was aware of the doctor talking to herself, almost as if she was cross examining the victim in a witness box, her latex-gloved hands gently turning the limbs, checking under the hairline at the base of the girl's skull, feeling for broken bones, crushed muscles, ligaments and tendons torn apart by the impact of whatever had hit her.

After a minute or two she climbed to her feet.

Reilly eagerly awaited her verdict, but Karen wasn't done, simply changing position. She moved to the other side of the body, knelt down once more and resumed the examination.

Reilly already had a fair idea of what she was going to say. She had enough training and experience to know the differ-ence between injuries that directly caused death and those that had occurred post-mortem, but she knew better than to say anything — it was protocol and politeness to defer to the ME, even when the cause of death seemed obvious.

Finally, Karen Thompson finished her examination and called the detectives back over.

'Hit and run. Killed on impact,' she stated sympathetically, turning her wide eyes on the three of them. 'But I'm sure you already knew that.' She nodded towards the body. 'See here...' Reilly and the detectives crouched down over the body together. 'Impact was right here.' Karen pointed to the back of the girl's legs. 'She was struck from behind, just above the knees. But there's also impact here.' She gently lifted the girl's nightdress to reveal contusions on her lower back.

Chris frowned. 'So more likely a van than a car?'

'Correct. A car would have rolled her up across the bonnet, causing a different pattern of injuries. So yes, a slightly larger vehicle with a flatter, non-aerodynamic front end.'

'And the official cause of death?'

Thompson crouched down again, and indicated that the others should do the same. She gently prodded the back of the dead girl's skull — it gave slightly under the pressure of her fingers. 'Secondary impact. All these other injuries' — she indicated the grazes and abrasions to her arms and legs — 'are primary, arising from contact with the vehicle itself, but the secondary injury — blunt force of impact to the head — would have killed her, after the collision threw her into the air and back onto the tarmac.'

'So we should be looking for a van with damage to the front and probably a cracked windshield,' Chris stated flatly.

'I'll be able to tell you more after full autopsy of course. I've called to arrange transport and will try to schedule the exam for tomorrow afternoon. All going well you can expect the full report by teatime tomorrow, but you might have to wait a little longer for the toxicology report.'

'Thanks, doc,' Kennedy said. 'So our angel didn't jump or get pushed out of a moving vehicle then.'

'Definitely not. Such a scenario would cause a completely different injury pattern.'

Reilly scanned the array of cones that were laid out across

the road. A single set of spray-paint marks suggested that Colin O'Dea's car had been the only vehicle in the immediate area that had recently tried to slow down.

So was the collision that killed the girl accidental or intentional?

She slipped the iSPI device out of her kitbag. Although she still preferred time-honored forensic skills for much of her work, she was always willing to use new technology when it might be deemed useful.

3D crime-scene reconstruction using CAD software was nothing new — it had been around since the mid-1980s — but it had always been something carried out after the event, in the lab. The beauty of this new software app was that it worked on a portable device such as an iPhone, and thus could now be used in the field.

She input some basic parameters into the program — the victim's gender, direction she'd been facing, nature and physical location of injuries. Then, using the integrated camera, she filmed the road, the exact location of the body and the injuries themselves. Once she had done that, the pathologist's office was given the green light to remove the girl.

Although she had seen it dozens of times, Reilly still found the finality of a corpse being zipped up in a body bag emotional — the lifeless limbs, the pale skin, the cold staring eyes.

She understood why they closed the victim's eyes in movies. The majority died with them open, and Reilly always found it disconcerting, almost accusative, the way those dead eyes almost seemed to follow her around. She wondered how many sets of lifeless eyes she had already seen, and how many more were to come. She knew if she thought long and hard enough she could remember them all. But she tried only to forget, not remember — especially not the pair that haunted her the most; the cold dead eyes of her own mother. Reilly remembered that day like it was yesterday, her first crime scene — except she wasn't working it; she was part of it.

She watched them lift the body bag onto a stretcher. As there was minimal damage to the girl's face, at least her family would be able to say goodbye, something she'd never had the chance to do with her mother.

Small mercies.

Once the corpse had been removed, Reilly was ready to let the software do its job. Standing over the site in the exact location where the girl had been found, she held the iSPI device up. After a moment of processing, it projected a re-enaction of the accident, using GPS data to show where on the road the actual collision was likely to have occurred.

Chris and Kennedy crowded round, and the younger techs came over for a look too — and not just for the gimmick of it. Knowing where the impact was likely to have taken place would enable them to more effectively target their search for relevant forensic trace.

Reilly extended the device at arm's length so everybody gathered could see. The screen was blank with a small circular arrow rotating in an anti-clockwise direction indicating that the sequence was loading. She tilted the screen slightly downwards to stop the heavy mist landing on it as the wind started to pick up. Finally the 3D re-enactment started to play, showing first a lone female figure walking along a road, then a vehicle coming round the corner and hitting her from behind.

Her body sailed through the air, limbs flailing, before finally landing in a similar position to the one they had found the girl in, her skull hitting the surface of the road violently with what seemed like a heavy thud, even though the device emitted no sound. Finally, the screen flashed 'Estimated Impact Speed: 43 MPH.'

Nobody said a word. The simulation was almost too good, rendering the events that had taken place on this lonely road even more tragic. The sequence began to replay from the start, but Reilly put the device away, having seen enough. They could witness it again and again as it happened, but now the focus needed to be on finding the culprit rather than wishing they could intervene to save the victim. As real as the sequence was, it could never be stopped or reversed.

'It gives me the creeps every bloody time,' Kennedy muttered.

'I notice it's suggesting a white van for the vehicle,' Chris commented, looking at Reilly. 'It must know a thing or two about Irish drivers.'

'Give it a second and it will go one better than that,' she told them. 'Based on the injury pattern, and depending on the trace we find, it will give us a list of potential vehicles we can cross-check.'

Kennedy gave an appreciative look. Maybe technology was not so bad after all... He might well be home in time for the football highlights.

'But for now, let's take a closer look at where the impact occurred in real life.'

Holding the phone out in front of her, Reilly walked back up the road, taking care to avoid any yellow markers on her route. As she moved, the device constantly updated their position using its GPS connection. They'd walked about twenty yards when iSPI beeped to indicate the calculated impact area. It was on a curve, the road narrow, a minimal grassy verge and a ditch on either side.

Gary looked back up the road. 'If you were coming round that bend, you'd barely have any time to notice anyone.'

'Especially if you weren't expecting them to be there,' Lucy added. She thought for a moment. 'I'll bet the driver lives locally.'

Reilly looked at her with interest. 'Why do you say that?'

'Locals drive faster. We tend to relax when we're close to

home, we know the roads, think we know all the hazards — that's one reason why most accidents occur within three miles of your own home. A stranger would proceed much slower on a road like this.'

'Good point. But the injuries indicate that she was hit from behind and iSPI concurs. On a dark night like this, even with the bends you'd think she'd have seen the headlights or heard the engine...' Reilly's train of thought was momentarily distracted by something on the road surface.

'What have you got?' Lucy asked.

'Looks like paint fragments — or chips more like.' She waited while Lucy photographed the area and put down another marker. Then, using tweezers, she carefully lifted the fragments and examined them under the floodlights.

'From our vehicle?'

'Well, whatever vehicle it came from, it has a bit of history. It's not just paint, there's some kind of hardened resin here too. Looks like it could be a crash repair,' Reilly said, placing it carefully into an evidence bag. 'When a previously crashed car is damaged a second time all the fillers and resins from the repair are far less flexible than fresh metal, and so they tend to sheer off. Kind of like disturbing layers of snow on a fence.' This was good; if the van that hit the girl had already crashed, then this taken with iSPI's calculations should make it easier to narrow down its identification.

She looked around. 'We'll need to go through this area with a fine-toothed comb. If there was any damage to the van after the collision, anything snapped off or broken, this is where we'll most likely find it.'

Lucy peered dolefully into the murky soup that lay at the bottom of the ditch. 'Looks like fun.'

5

When first I saw it moving across the waves I readied myself, stood steadfast, armed for the battle ahead. But then as she stood before me, the past no longer mattered. I was entranced.

Her beauty held me captive, banished the demons that tormented me.

Her words gave me strength; I knew what I must do.

We had to be together, together in a place free from the pain and misery that had surrounded me for so long. We must find our sanctuary, a place fit for eternal beauty, somewhere the pain and sorrow of this world had no place.

A land where I will be king and we will protect the righteousness of youth. The cruelty of this world casts a spell on the innocents, and together we will punish those who do not know the beauty that lies beneath their nostrils, and who don't deserve the blessings that have been bestowed upon them.

I will revoke those blessings and bring them to a place where they belong — beside me in paradise.

. . .

REILLY ENTERED the darkened morgue and flicked on the lights. The bright glow of the fluorescents bounced back off the gleaming aluminum worktables, the harsh light emphasizing the shadows around her eyes. She glanced up at the clock – 01:20 – and gave a snort of self-derision. Why would anyone in their right mind be working at this hour of the night if they didn't have to?

But she knew the answer, knew it as well as she knew herself. Leaving her examination of the girl's body until the morning would simply be a waste of time — she couldn't sleep knowing that Lucy and Gary were still out on that lonely stretch of road searching for clues in the muddy ditches before the rain washed everything away. She couldn't sleep without figuring out what it was about the corpse that bothered her, what the faint aroma that she had smelled on the girl's skin was.

Reilly's heightened sense of smell had always been one of her best assets and had served her well throughout the course of many investigations. As such, she knew better than to ever discount it.

She had called ahead, and the body was ready and waiting for her on a mortuary slab; pale, almost ethereal on the examination table. Reilly slipped on her latex gloves and allowed herself to simply observe.

She walked slowly round the table. In the brightness she could now see that the girl wore no make-up and her ears were not pierced. In fact, there was no indication of jewelry of any kind. Unusual for a teenager in this day and age.

Reilly examined her face more closely. Her skin was flawless, eyes a cold shade of pale blue — these things and her vivid red curls indicated Celtic origins.

Reilly gently parted the hair — no colorants used there either; the lush red was completely natural. She leaned over and softly inhaled. There was the smell again. It wasn't unpleasant, and definitely not a synthetic or chemical scent; no, it was natural. She was also almost certain she recognized it, but couldn't quite place it — it was lurking at the back of her mind, something from childhood, a deep-seated memory of warm summer days, picnics in the park with her folks and Jess...

Pushing it aside for the moment, she continued her examination.

She selected a comb from a nearby tray of equipment and began to tease through the girl's hair for debris. As she did so, she watched what came out onto the sample dish. The hair was remarkably clean — just some small fragments of debris from the road, and then something else ... Some kind of plant matter?

Reilly checked the area of the hair she had been working on — tangled in amongst the thick curls were indeed some fine strands of greenery. She gently freed it from the hair, laid it in the palm of her gloved hand, and sniffed.

Definitely the same smell again. But maddeningly, whatever it was still eluded her. She put the samples in the dish for analysis and moved on.

Her gaze ran down the girl's cold bare arms to her hands. No nail polish on her fingers — no surprise there — but the skin on her hands seemed rather rough. This was a girl who was evidently used to manual work ... a farm girl maybe?

She'd been found in a rural area so that fitted. Yet, the preternatural paleness of her skin didn't indicate much time spent outdoors. Reilly sighed. It was all too easy to jump to conclusions.

Of course, Reilly thought as she rolled the girl onto her stomach, any assumptions she might make about the girl's background based on her immediate appearance needed to be tempered by the one unmissable feature that now stared out at her.

The wing tattoo was, in its own way, quite beautiful. Each feather was elegantly drawn with tiny, delicate lines — it was a work of art, a labor of love. With the help of the bright lights she could see now that the ink was not black, but rather a blueish shade that hinted at hidden depths of color.

She was always struck by how much more vivid a tattoo was on a corpse. Reilly's thoughts automatically turned towards Jess and the day she'd come home from school with the DIY crucifix tattoo on her upper arm. Her sister had been so proud of it, and so surprised by Reilly's horror when she showed it to her.

Jess and a classmate, bored at the back of math class, had used a compass and some pen ink to brand themselves. Jess had pleaded with Reilly not to tell Mike, but there was little point in alerting their father as by then the damage was already done, and thankfully far enough up Jess's arm to be easily concealed. Unlike dim Dom, whose three-inch crucifix was no doubt today still visible on the back of his hand. Instantly, a memory of that same tattoo on her sister's death-cold flesh crept into Reilly's consciousness and banishing the image, she focused once again on the corpse lying in front of her.

Reilly took photos of the wings close up from both sides, trying to capture every detail, every nuance. She knew that the tattoo represented the best chance of identifying the girl, so it was essential that she captured it properly.

By the time she had finished her examination it was almost 3 a.m.

She shook her head wryly. There was a time when seeing 3 a.m. on the clock meant a great night out in the company of friends, but these days it only signified nights like this in the company of the dead. Lately, she had more interaction with them than the living, especially since Mike had gotten all loved up and Chris had turned cold.

Carefully packing her things away, Reilly called down to the duty guard to let him know she was finished. She had done everything she could for now; next it was up to Karen to see if a post mortem could uncover anything else of interest.

She flicked off the lights and massaged her neck to try and relieve the tension in her shoulders. She was tired — exhausted in fact — but she knew that at least she might actually be able to sleep now. She had done enough to allow her mind to switch off and grab an hour or two before starting all over again in the morning.

In the morning? It was already morning, she reminded herself. By the time she reached home and got into bed it would be well after four. No matter, a couple of hours' sleep would have to do. By now, Reilly was used to running on empty.

TOO FEW HOURS LATER, Reilly was at the GFU lab, finalizing a report on her findings from the McGavin house. She then turned her attentions to processing the evidence from the hit and run scene, and from the victim herself.

Lucy greeted her arrival in the main lab with a groan. 'You owe us big time,' she complained, as Reilly entered the main lab, buttoning her lab coat as she walked.

'I always do,' she replied, 'but why today in particular?'

'Those ditches,' the younger girl groaned. 'Cold, wet and nasty.'

Gary nodded. 'They weren't a lot of fun.'

'Perks of the job. Did you find anything?'

'Quite a lot actually,' Lucy told her, indicating the workstation. 'Whether or not it's of any use I can't say yet.'

Reilly looked at the items spread out across Lucy's bench, a collection of broken plastic, empty soft drink cans, a coffee cup, all the kinds of detritus that inevitably collected in a roadside ditch. Gary's table was also covered, but with smaller items. Among them were several bits of plastic that looked like they might have come from a car's side lights and indicators, plus numerous glass and paint fragments.

'Certainly looks like the debris from a collision of some sort.'

Gary nodded. 'I'm going to analyze it now, and see if any of it comes from the same vehicle. Did you get anything from the body?'

'Mostly what you would expect — gravel, traces of oil and so on. But there is one thing that is interesting…'

She reached for the dish containing the fine green fronds she'd picked out of the dead girl's hair, and held it out for them to sniff.

'You don't smell it?' she asked when neither reacted.

'We don't have your keen nose, boss.'

'I picked this up on her right from the start, but I just can't place it. Something about it reminds me of family picnics by the lake back home…' Then she shrugged. 'It might not even be relevant, who knows? But there is definitely something strange about this girl.'

'Besides the massive tattoo of a pair of wings on her back?' Lucy put in sardonically.

'Not just that. How many teenagers do you know who wear no make-up, have no piercings, jewelry, or use hair coloring?'

Lucy pretended to think hard. 'Let me see — none?'

'Exactly. Apart from the tattoo, this girl looks like she could have just stepped out of the nineteenth century.'

Gary looked confused. 'Because of the nightdress, and the fact that she wasn't made-up to the nines?'

'Lots of girls out my way walking the streets in their PJs, but usually with plenty of make-up and bling to boot,' Lucy put in.

'Perhaps, but I'll bet you've never seen one in an ankle-length nightdress that wouldn't seem out of place in a Jane Austen novel.'

But in truth it was difficult for Reilly to put her finger on what it was about this girl that had given her that sense. Perhaps it was the calm, almost ethereal aura about her.

For the next hour or more the lab was silent as the small team worked on the physical evidence they'd gathered. They all knew each other well, and each was familiar with the working style of the others.

All three wore earbuds, each listening to background music while they worked. Lucy listened to the radio, liking the company the chatty DJ gave her; Gary had dance music on, his head bobbing to the beat as he went; while Reilly usually played classical music – Bach for his calm, methodical style, Mozart when she needed something to lift her mood, or Beethoven to stir her emotions and keep her engaged if she was working late into the night.

She was so caught up in her work that it wasn't until the other two came and stood in front of her that she noticed that they had been trying to get her attention. She slipped her headphones off and looked up, a sheepish smile on her face.

She followed them back over to their respective benches.

'Like we said, most of it is just junk,' Lucy explained. 'It's either been there way too long to be connected with our crime,' she picked up the faded soft drink cans, 'or it's completely random and unidentifiable. These, however, might be of interest.'

The objects she pointed to were a relatively clean Mega-Coffee branded coffee cup and some small pieces of black plastic.

Lucy indicated the cup. 'This was the first thing I saw — it was floating in the water. It's very new, and the coffee dregs inside are quite fresh.'

'Any saliva traces on the rim?'

Lucy nodded. 'Fortunately, yes. First and foremost we'll have to check that the couple that found her weren't the source, but if they're not and we find a suspect, it could tie them to the scene.'

'How do you reckon it got there, though?'

'I was thinking about that. *My* guess is that it was maybe rolling around on the floor of the vehicle that hit her, maybe the driver stopped and got out to see what he'd hit and it fell out and into the ditch.'

'And these?' Reilly pointed to the pieces of black plastic.

'These look like they might have come off the front end of a vehicle — again, they weren't covered in mud which suggests they'd not been in the ditch for very long.'

Reilly looked closely at the plastic scraps. 'If we find the vehicle these could well be critical.' She turned to Gary. 'Anything from your end?'

He shook his head. 'Mostly junk, and the majority of it irrelevant.'

'Hey, you have to kiss a lot of frogs to find a princess.'

'No kidding. There was a whole army of frogs on that road. But I did pick up these close to where iSPI reckons the impact would have happened.' Neatly arranged on the bench was a handful of safety glass, tiny crystal nuggets.

'Fortunately for us, different motor companies use different types of glass. These, believe it or not, come from the front headlights of a commercial vehicle manufactured by Ford sometime between 1991 and 1997.'

'Wow, that specific?'

Gary shrugged. 'According to the database anyway.'

'Good work. I'll get this information to the detectives right away,' Reilly said.

'Any luck with the green goo, boss?'

'Actually yes.' She held up a printout of the chemical analysis of the mysterious greenery. 'It's algae,' she told him, still kicking herself for not figuring it out. 'At some point before our victim was hit by the van, she must have been in a pond or a lake.'

'BIZARRE,' Kennedy said when later that morning, Reilly arrived at Harcourt Street station to update him on the findings. 'Why would a girl in a nightdress be swimming in a lake in the middle of the night?'

'Why would she be wandering around *anywhere* in the middle of the night in bare feet and a thin nightdress?' she countered.

'Good point. Did I already mention that you look terrible?' he teased, studying her.

'Yes,' she replied archly, 'but the difference between you and me is that I only look this bad when I've had no sleep.'

'Touché.' Kennedy pulled a chair across from his cubbyhole for her.

She sat back, and crossed her legs. 'Where's Chris?'

'Meeting with the boss. Can I get you a coffee?'

'I'd kill for one, thanks. So what's he talking to O'Brien about?'

'Statement to the press. We're going to need help getting an ID on the girl.'

'You've already canvassed the local area?'

He nodded. 'Local boys have been on it since the early hours. Nothing to report so far, but here's hoping they turn up something that leads to an identification. At least then we can concentrate on catching the scumbag who left her dead in the road.'

'I presume they're going to —'

'Widen the area?' he finished for her. 'Yeah. But you and I both know that just makes things harder.' There was a mathematical relationship involved in widening a search area, and all too often the numbers quickly became unmanageable with so many personnel and subsequently much more information in the mix.

Chris arrived while they were talking, and Reilly immediately sat up on alert. She hated the way they both now always seemed so uncomfortable around one another.

The current rift stemmed from a major difference of agreement. Chris was covering up something from his superiors — something important, which he'd reluctantly confided to Reilly in order to enlist her help. At the time, she'd assumed they had an understanding: she'd help him get to the bottom of the issue, and he'd deal with the implications. As far as Reilly was concerned, she'd held up her end of the deal, but he had not, and in refusing to come clean was potentially putting himself and others on the force at risk. She couldn't condone that, no matter how much she liked him. She'd always believed Chris Delaney to be an honest and decent guy, someone to trust with her life. Now she knew he wasn't as upstanding or truthful as she'd believed.

And the realization had hit her much harder than she'd expected.

'So what news from on high?' Kennedy asked Chris.

'We've got the go ahead,' he said, nodded a brief greeting to Reilly. 'We'll put out a standard press release to all the local and national media, say it's a hit and run, ask for help in identifying the girl, and appeal for possible witnesses.'

'What about the tattoo?'

'We should keep that to ourselves for now,' replied Chris quickly, and Reilly could tell by his tone that this was a point of argument between them. 'O'Brien agrees.'

Kennedy scowled. 'For Christ's sake … it's so distinctive — if you'd ever seen it you wouldn't forget it. I'm telling you, we *have* to use it.'

'I agree with Chris actually,' Reilly said tentatively. 'If we can get an ID without revealing it, well, it's a pretty personal thing...'

'And if we mention it too soon but *don't* get an ID, it's the kind of thing the press will be all over,' Chris pointed out. 'Before we know it we'll have another hyped-up circus on our hands like we did with the Dante thing last year.'

'Still...'

'We'll know soon enough anyway,' he continued. 'Press release is scheduled to go out soon, so it'll be on the lunchtime news.' He picked up Reilly's preliminary evidence report and scanned it. 'I'll pass the information about the Ford along to the locals. There are lots of farms, workshops, all sorts out there where someone might have a Transit van — we'll just have to hope something shows up. We'll add the details to the press release too.'

'That will just tip the guy off,' Kennedy grumbled.

'Maybe, but we're damned if we do, damned if we don't.'

'Your call,' his partner retorted grumpily, burying his face in his coffee cup.

Reilly glanced at Chris, wondering again what was up with Kennedy, but he was concertedly avoiding her gaze. 'So what direction do you want to take with this lake information?' she asked after a beat. 'It seems strange that—'

He cut her off. 'There are lakes, ponds and bogs for miles around in that particular area. It may not be that significant.'

'Fine,' Reilly said, feeling wounded by his attitude. He was normally so receptive to her findings and willing to discuss options that the stone-walling made her feel like she was back at day one on the job, hoping to prove her worth to a suspicious, mostly hostile police force.

Back then Chris had been her biggest champion — why now had everything changed?

6

State Pathologist

DATE and HOUR AUTOPSY PERFORMED:

15/03/2012; 8:30 A.M. by Karen Thompson, Chief Medical Examiner

Assistant:

Victoria O'Neill, MD

Full Autopsy Performed

SUMMARY REPORT OF AUTOPSY

Name:

Jane Doe

Coroner's Case #:

1398-277

Date of Birth:

N/A

Age:

N/A

Race:

White

Sex:

Female

Date of Death:

14/03/2012

Body Identified by:

N/A

Case #

001294-23E-2012

Investigative Agency:

GFU

<u>EVIDENCE OF TREATMENT:</u>

N/A

EXTERNAL EXAMINATION:

The autopsy is begun at 8:30 A.M. on March 15, 2012. The body is presented in a black cadaver pouch. The victim is wearing a white cotton dress.

The body is that of a normally developed white female measuring 67 inches and weighing 118 pounds, and appearing generally consistent with that of an individual in their late teens or early twenties. The body is cold and unembalmed. Lividity is fixed in the distal portions of the limbs. The eyes are open. The irises are blue/green and corneas are cloudy. Petechial hemorrhaging is present in the conjunctival surfaces of the eyes. The pupils measure 0.3 cm. The hair is red, untreated and approximately 26 inches in length at the longest point.

Initial visual examination of the body shows clear blunt force trauma, with several cuts, lesions and extensive bruising visible on exposed skin of arms, legs and face. There appears minimal bleeding which suggests the victim's heart stopped beating soon after receiving visible injuries.

Upon removal of the victim's clothing, an odor of damp vegetation was detected. Areas of the body were swabbed and submitted for detection. Several more cuts and bruising were clearly visible along with signs of internal bleeding. Several items of trace were removed from the lesions and have been sent for analysis. Swabs and scrapings also taken from fingernails.

The genitalia are that of an adult female and there is no evidence of injury. Limbs are equal, symmetrically developed and show no evidence of injury. The fingernails are short in length and fingernail beds are blue. There are no residual scars. The victim's back is approximately 80 percent covered with a tattoo of a pair of wings. Several tissue samples have been taken along with further trace from wounds including glass and metallic fragments.

INTERNAL EXAMINATION:

HEAD--CENTRAL NERVOUS SYSTEM: Subsequent autopsy shows a fractured skull and jaw bone. The brain weighs 1,303 grams and within normal limits.

SKELETAL SYSTEM: Compound fractures to left and right tibia. Pelvic fractures. Several simple fractures to right ribs 3 & 7, left rib 2. There are simple fractures in the radius and ulna of both arms along with several fingers. The amount of trauma appears consistent with an RTA.

RESPIRATORY SYSTEM--THROAT STRUCTURES: The oral cavity shows no lesions and there are no injuries to the lips, teeth or gums.

There is no obstruction of the airway. The mucosa of the epiglottis, glottis, piriform sinuses, trachea and major bronchi are anatomic. No injuries are seen and there are no mucosal lesions.

The lungs weigh: right 355 grams; left 362 grams. Both lungs showed significant and unusual signs of inflammation. Swabs and tissue samples have been sent for further testing.

CARDIOVASCULAR SYSTEM: The heart weighs 253 grams, and has a normal size and configuration. No evidence of atherosclerosis is present.

GASTROINTESTINAL SYSTEM: The mucosa and wall of the esophagus are intact and gray-pink, without lesions or injuries. The gastric mucosa is intact and pink without injury. Approximately 125 ml of partially digested semisolid food is found in the stomach. The mucosa of the duodenum, jejunum, ileum, colon and rectum are intact.

URINARY SYSTEM: The kidneys weigh: left 115 grams;

right 113 grams. The kidneys are anatomic in size, shape and location and are without lesions.

FEMALE GENITAL SYSTEM: The structures are within normal limits. Examination of the pelvic area indicates the victim had not given birth. The victim was however pregnant in second trimester at the time of death. There is no evidence of recent sexual activity. Fetus was removed, measured, weighed and tissue samples taken before being returned to the uterus. Age has been verified at eighteen weeks. Vaginal fluid samples have been removed for analysis.

TOXICOLOGY: Sample of right pleural blood and bile are submitted for toxicologic analysis. Stomach contents are saved.

LABORATORY DATA:

Cerebrospinal fluid culture and sensitivity:
    Gram stain: Unremarkable
    Culture: No growth after 72 hours
    Cerebrospinal fluid bacterial antigens:
    Hemophilus influenza B: Negative
    Streptococcus pneumoniae: Negative
    N. Meningitidis: Negative
    Neiserria meningitidis B/E. Coli K1: Negative

Drug Screen Results:

Urine screen {Immunoassay} was NEGATIVE.
    Ethanol: 0 gm/dl, Blood (Heart)
    Ethanol: 0 gm/dl, Vitreous

EVIDENCE COLLECTED:

1. One (1) white cotton dress, size Small.

2. Samples of Blood (type O+), Bile, and Tissue (heart, lung, brain, kidney, liver, spleen).

3. Twenty three (23) swabs from various body locations, to be tested.

4. Eleven (11) autopsy photographs.

8. One post mortem CT scan.

9. One post mortem MRI.

OPINION

Time of Death: Body temperature, rigor and livor mortis, and stomach contents approximate the time of death between 9:00 and 11:00 P.M. on 14/03/2012.

Immediate Cause of Death: Blunt force trauma due to high-speed impact.

Manner of Death: Vehicle strike.

Remarks: Decedent originally presented to this office as hit-and-run victim. The injuries present indicate this as most likely cause of death. There are no wounds inflicted post mortem, which suggest the victim was only struck once. GFU and case detectives were notified of these findings immediately upon conclusion of examination.

'You are kidding me,' Reilly said, partly in shock but also annoyance. It was later that evening and she was back at the city morgue, discussing the autopsy findings with Karen Thompson.

She had examined the girl carefully; there had been no outwards sign of pregnancy, nothing showing at all. 'How did I not spot it?'

The ME shrugged. 'Some women, especially younger first-time mothers, or first-time pregnancies rather,' she corrected herself quickly, 'don't show until seven, maybe even eight months.'

'I know, I guess ...' Reilly paused, searching for the right words to explain her surprise. 'It just doesn't fit my image of her. She seems so young, so innocent — beyond innocent even, otherworldly. When I examined the body it almost felt like I was handling a china doll.'

'I know what you mean. I try to view the bodies I examine as dispassionately as possible too, but I agree — this girl does have an unusual air about her.' She picked up her case notes. 'Based on bone growth I'd place her at around seventeen or eighteen years of age. Oh, and here's another strange thing...'

Karen paused, and Reilly raised her eyebrows in anticipation.

'Dental records.'

'Helpful?'

'Non-existent. The girl has no fillings, orthodontics — nothing.'

Dental records were often a last resort in trying to identify unnamed victims. Without them they were back to square one.

Reilly sighed. 'Damn.'

'I've ordered hair analysis,' Karen continued, 'which should give us a clear picture as to what she was, or indeed wasn't doing before she ended up out there.' Hair analysis was an extremely effective way of testing for drugs in the system and would in essence give them a six-month pharmacology record for the girl.

'Again, I'm not picturing her as a good-time girl,' Reilly stated, but knew from experience that appearances could be deceptive.

'In any case, somebody, somewhere knows who this girl is,' Karen said. 'And sooner or later they'll come forward to report her missing.'

'Let's hope so.' Reilly's gaze rested on the comments in the respiratory section. 'Any thoughts on the lung inflammation?'

'That's a strange one,' the doctor replied. 'She was suffering from silicosis — unusual at her age — it is typically associated with somebody much older. It can often be an occupational disease, hence its other names: miner's phthisis, grinder's asthma, potter's rot, to name a few.'

'Any idea at this stage what could have caused it?'

'Exposure to some form of silica dust for starters, but further analysis should tell us more. Anything else on the tattoo?'

Reilly shook her head. 'Not yet. We've sent a sample of the ink for analysis. We should have something back in a few days.'

'Well, you don't need any advice from me of course, but if I were you, I'd be focusing my search on that tattoo.'

'Our next port of call. Thanks, Karen, I appreciate it.' As she headed through the door the doctor's next words sailed after her.

'Not now, I hope.'

'What?' She paused and looked back.

'I meant that I hope you're not going off to chase it down this minute, the tattoo I mean.' She looked at her watch. 'It's after six on a Friday evening, Reilly, and if you're anything like me you've been on the go all day. Head home, get some rest and try and leave the detective work to the detectives.'

Reilly smiled. Karen knew as well as Reilly did that this job was far from a nine-to-five. 'Don't worry, home is exactly where I'm going now. Believe it or not,' she added mischievously, 'I have a date.'

7

T he city center was buzzing with after-work revelers as Chris and Kennedy crossed the Ha'penny bridge.

Taking in the surrounding landscape Chris noticed a group of seagulls occasionally dipping into the dark water for a tasty titbit and emerging with weeds on their beaks. It immediately reminded him of the algae found on the hit-and-run victim. Where had it come from and what did it mean? Happy as he was to have some trace material that might help with identifying the girl's origins, right now it simply remained another enigma. Like her.

So for the moment, they'd decided to investigate a different aspect instead.

Continuing on over the bridge they passed through the archway that led to the cobbled streets of Temple Bar. They eventually saw the sign they were looking for. 'Tiger Tattoos.' Kennedy pushed open the door and they stepped inside.

It was a small store, the walls covered in various tattoo designs — gothic, Celtic, skulls, almost any style was available. In racks in front of the wall was book after book of even more designs, everything from puppy dogs to roses, death-metal logos to elegant flowing scripts.

'Hello there. What can I do you for you two gentlemen?' A thin man in his forties had emerged from the back and was looking at them with interest. He had a shaved head and thick, dark eyebrows, his arms covered in a maze of richly colored tattoos.

'Are you the boss?' Kennedy asked.

He nodded. 'Yep. Jimmy Tiger. And I'm guessing you're not here for a tattoo.'

They were both dressed in dark slacks, tieless shirts and light windbreaker jackets which screamed law enforcement to anybody with an ounce of street wisdom.

'How did you guess?' Chris flashed Jimmy his badge. 'Detectives Delaney and Kennedy,' he informed him. 'I wonder if you could look at a few photographs for us, see if you might recognize the work?'

He nodded. 'I'll give it a go.'

Chris took the photos of the angel wings out of his inside pocket and spread them out on the counter. The tattooist slipped on a pair of black plastic framed glasses, and studied the images for a moment. 'That's good work...' he murmured. He ran his finger across the lines. 'And judging by the skin I'm guessing it's a woman. She dead or something?'

'We can't comment on that,' Kennedy told him.

'I understand.' He peered at the pictures again and moved closer to the doorway for some more natural light. 'There's only so much I can tell you without seeing it firsthand, but whoever did this has a pretty distinctive style — a lefty too, which is unusual.'

Chris looked up, interested. 'You can tell something like that from the photo?'

'Yep, from the direction the ink is going.' He slid his glasses down to the end of his nose and looked from one detective to the other. 'Don't think it's by anyone I know though. I've not seen this work before, and I'm familiar with the style of most artists around here.'

Chris nodded. He knew it was too much to hope that they would strike lucky straight away. 'Well, thanks for looking.' He slid the photos back into his pocket and turned towards the door.

'But I'm probably not the person you need to be talking to,' Jimmy added.

They stopped and looked at him inquiringly.

'If I were you, I'd talk to Rasher,' he said. 'If there's anyone who can identify these for you, it's him. He's a lefty too, only one I know.'

'And where would we find this ... Rasher?'

'Well, let's just say he doesn't have a shop with a sign out front like this,' he said. 'He works by invitation only.'

Chris raised an eyebrow. 'All sounds very underground ...'

'Last I heard he was down in Bray,' the tattooist went on. 'Just ask around at any of the pubs on the seafront and they'll tell you where to find him.'

8

'Sorry, I got held up.' Reilly had the apology out of her mouth before she opened the door of the car.

'No worries, sweetheart, just got here myself. Here, let me help you with those.' Mike Steel took the grocery bags out of her arms as they walked up the path towards an imposing redbrick Georgian house.

Situated on a quiet Ranelagh residential street, yet within walking distance to the lively village center, like many similar houses in the area it had been subdivided into flats. One of those was the place Reilly now called home.

'I hope you're hungry,' she told her father. 'I'm making shrimp fajitas.'

'Nice one.'

Reilly thought back to when they were living in California. Back in the days before their mother left, and well before he'd started hitting the bottle, Mike used to make that very dish for the family every Friday night without fail. There was truly nothing on earth like the scent of fresh chili and lime mingling with the warm Californian air.

Opening the door to her flat, she punched in her alarm code

and flicked on the lights before making her way straight to the kitchen.

'How's Maura?' she asked, referring to her father's girl-friend as he set the bags down on the worktop. 'You should have asked her to come along.'

Reilly had met Maura, a pleasant woman in her early sixties, a couple of times, but didn't know her terribly well, nor understand what she and her father could possibly have in common. Mike was a recovering alcoholic with a checkered — to put it mildly — family history, whereas Maura was a kindly widow who by all accounts lived a staid and uneventful life. The complete and utter opposite of her mother, Cassandra. Then again, Reilly thought sadly, maybe that was a good thing...

'She's grand. She meets up with the girls on Friday nights.' He took some avocados out of the bag and gave them each a little squeeze to test for ripeness. 'Actually I'm surprised you didn't cancel on me again this time,' he added, eyeing her. 'Not working late tonight?'

She sighed. 'Dad, you know that in this job you don't get much control over the workload ...' she began, but it was a well worn argument at this stage. 'And actually yes, I probably should have stayed on at the lab tonight, but I wanted to see you.'

'You spend way too much time in that damn place if you ask me. Work is like an addiction for you but then again,' he said with a rueful smile, 'I guess we're an addictive kind of family.'

She knew the comment was lighthearted, but still his words got to her.

'Actually, I've got lots of things going on besides work,' Reilly lied. 'I've really started getting back into the running. I'm thinking about training for a marathon this year...'

'You sure know how to let your hair down.'

This time she smiled. 'Ah, spare me the lectures — and enough about my life,' she said, starting to peel and deseed the avocados. 'How're things with you? Still all loved up with Maura?'

'Don't change the subject. But speaking of loved up, how's that fancy man of yours?' When she looked blank, he continued, 'The tall fella I met before.'

'You mean Chris? We're just workmates, Dad, you know that.'

'Are you sure?' Mike's voice grew serious for a moment. 'I really wish you had someone to take care of you, sweetheart, the way you're always taking care of everyone else. I can't help but feel guilty about how you gave up so much for me, moving all the way over here to look after me when I couldn't look after myself.' He emptied a bag of nachos into a large bowl. 'I was a mess, I know that, but still ...'

'Dad, coming here was a *choice* I made, and it wasn't just about you. I wanted a new challenge.'

And she'd certainly got that with the GFU. In all her time in law enforcement she didn't think she'd ever worked so hard or been so busy.

'It's just ... well, you've always had everybody else's best interests at heart, and now that the worst of our troubles are in the past, I just want to make sure you're happy.'

'I will be if you put those tortillas in the oven and set the table.'

Mike reached across and gave her shoulder a squeeze before kissing the top of her head. As Reilly scooped the flesh from the avocados into the mixing bowl, she realized how great it felt to see her dad so happy. He was clean, sober and seemed content with life for the first time she could truly remember.

She proceeded to chop onions, chili peppers, tomatoes and coriander, then piled them into the bowl with the avocados and started to mash them all together. Next, she sliced open a couple of limes and squeezed the juice into the bowl, the fresh citrus smell hitting her delicate nose. If there was one smell guaranteed to transport her right back to California, to a different time and place, it was this.

Reilly finished mixing the guacamole and carried it over to the table where Mike was now sitting.

'Here you go — the famous Steel 'mole. Get stuck in,' she said, digging a generous portion onto a tortilla chip and popping the whole thing into her mouth. The kitchen was soon alive with the sizzling smells of a Mexican cantina as she blackened the fresh shrimp along with sliced onion and mixed peppers; the chilies making her eyes water.

Reilly grabbed two glasses and a bottle of virgin margarita from the cupboard. She set them down on the table and grabbed another chip.

'You want to finish these before I bring on the fajitas?'

'Why not, these beauties deserve to be savored.' He looked hesitantly at the margarita bottle. 'Is this...?'

'Of course.'

'Go ahead and spice your own up if you want.'

'No alcohol for me tonight either; I've got an early start tomorrow,' Reilly said, returning to the table after placing the shrimps in the oven.

'This 'mole is awesome, sweetheart, takes me right back to those Friday night fiestas we used to have back home.'

She smiled. 'I know exactly what you mean. Funny, though, isn't it, the way we still call it home? After all, we've both been in Dublin for a couple of years now.'

'Yep. I used to call Ireland home when we were in California and now I'm here it's the other way round.' He chuckled. 'Hey, you remember that time back home you all came to see me marching with the fire trucks at the big Paddy's Day Parade in the city?'

Reilly gave a bittersweet smile. 'Of course! Jess looked so cute in her little leprechaun outfit, she'd been so excited about it for weeks beforehand.' She paused; they rarely mentioned Jess – it was almost as if she'd been airbrushed out of their lives.

Never out of their past though.

Mike was too lost in his own memories to notice. 'Yeah, and your mother wearing her green wig and that "Kiss me I'm Irish" T-shirt. Seems like a lifetime ago now...' He looked into the distance, a wistful expression on his face.

Reilly realized with some regret that the edges of those precious happy family memories — especially the ones featuring Jess – were starting to blur.

She felt as though certain aspects of her life had always been on hold. With their mother's absence, the fun and innocence of childhood had ended too soon certainly, but now something else concerned her: the lack of any new happy memories.

She'd grown up all too fast, focusing on Jess and making sure she was OK and then after that completely on work, which was the only thing that seemed to bring her solace. Her obsessive nature didn't leave much room to be swept along on life's great roller-coaster ride.

Still, Reilly felt safest in situations she could control, and if not risking the highs also meant bypassing the lows, she could live with that, she thought as she loaded another tortilla chip.

She and Mike both ate in silence, sipping on their decidedly non-potent cocktails. Talk soon returned to everyday matters about work and life in general. Much to his disappointment, and not for the want of trying, he hadn't managed to pick up a job in Dublin. A retired fire officer by profession, he was too old for anything in a similar field, and given that Ireland was suffering a major economic downturn, work was hard to come by for any man, let alone one of his age. While his fireman's pension was supplemented by Irish State welfare, he was the kind of man who needed a reason other than financial to get up in the mornings.

When the chips were almost finished, she fetched the fajitas from the oven, and they both began to expertly load them onto warm tortillas.

'Got a phone call the other day from Todd Dempsey actually,' Mike said between mouthfuls.

'Todd from Sausalito?'she said, recognising the name of one of his old co-workers from the fire department. 'What was the wife's name again?'

'Sally. Yeah, they called to invite me to this big retirement bash he's having next month.'

'You should go. It'd be great to see all the guys again, wouldn't it?' Reilly drew a line of salsa and sour cream across a tortilla before loading it with shrimp and vegetables and folding it into a cone.

'I'm thinking I might, and Maura's keen to go too.'

Reilly grinned. 'I'll bet she is ... Californian sunshine for a few days instead of this.' She indicated the damp weather outside.

'We were actually thinking we might stay a while — like you say, miss some of the bad weather.'

Reilly stopped chewing. What did he mean 'a while'? Just how long was he planning to stay?

'Since neither of us has much going on here,' he continued, 'and I thought it would be great to see the place again, especially given the ... cloud I left under.'

She smiled tightly. 'Sounds like a good idea, most appealing actually.'

The very idea of home, of bright sunshine and great surf appealed to Reilly just as much as the evocative scent of fresh lime earlier. In truth, she felt an ache of homesickness just thinking about it.

'Shit, honey, I never even thought … you should come too, we could make a holiday out of it.'

She shook her head. 'Even if I wanted to, I don't think I could get the time off from work,' Reilly lied, the prospect of playing gooseberry to her dad and his girlfriend outweighing the prospect of a vacation. 'Maybe some other time. But yes, you and Maura should definitely go. And enjoy.'

Still, Reilly had a niggling worry in the back of her mind. She was really only here in the first place because she'd followed her father back to his homeland to keep an eye on him. Now, he no longer needed her, was way past needing her. If he returned to California would he be tempted to stay?

And if he did, what was left in Ireland – other than work — for her?

9

My dreams are restless, the past rising up to haunt me or delight me by turn. The dark dreams take me back to that place, that hole I was in, the pit of despair. I left that place behind, never to return, but even though my conscious will refuses to go back there, at night it returns to remind me of whence I came. I will not go back ...

But the past also brings back happier times, and lately my dreams have been filled with her, the moment I realized that she was my future, that there was another way, another path that would lead to great happiness.

She was skipping at the time, those flaming curls bouncing with every step. She looked so sweet, untouched, but with a quiet maturity that shone through her sadness like sunshine on a rainy day.

He didn't appreciate her, I knew, didn't know what he had, an angel sent down in human form. And as I watched her I knew, knew what I must do, knew that with me the flame of youth that burned so brightly within her would last for ever, and all fear and suffering would be banished.

When I freed her she seemed almost to be expecting it. There was *no fear, no reluctance ... she had been waiting for me, as though she knew the earthly paradise we would create together.*

She was the beginning, the foundation, the bedrock on which our world was built, and now she is gone. We must continue, but how?

'PIG'S BLOOD?' Reilly repeated in some disbelief as the following morning, she read through the lab report Lucy had just given her.

'Don't forget soot,' Lucy reminded her. 'Pig's blood, soot and some form of pure alcohol.'

From her rudimentary knowledge of tattoos Reilly knew that most professional tattoo artists used inks that were pre-made — pre-dispersed they called it. Whereas this one seemed like a homemade concoction. With luck, an artist that took a more organic approach might stand out and be remembered within the tattooist community.

'And since different types of pure alcohol are difficult to individuate,' Lucy went on, 'we're going to test that further in order to narrow it down.'

In any case, what was it that had forced a pregnant young girl out onto a solitary country road so late at night?

Later that morning, Reilly received a call from Chris.

'Looks like we might have struck lucky on the van for the hit and run,' he said. 'Body shop in Ballymount, a company van brought in for work after a supposed "animal strike". Our media release set off some alarm bells and the owner called it in. We're on our way now, but could do with one of your crew to give it the once-over.'

'No problem, I'll send Gary,' she said, and he noticed the same coolness in her tone that had been there for the last few weeks. He was tempted to just come right out and ask if she was going to squeal on him, but it wasn't the time or the place.

And to be truthful, Chris wasn't sure he wanted to know the answer.

'Thanks,' he said, his tone equally clipped. 'Will let you know how it goes.'

The auto-repair shop was tucked away on an anonymous industrial estate on the outskirts of the city along with a couple of lockups, a delivery company, furniture shop, the usual fare.

The premises was easy to spot; the tarmac out front had taken on a pale color from the fine mist of dust and spray paint, and several cars with various windows and lights covered with newspaper and tape awaited a new paint job.

Chris and Kennedy sought out the owner in the main building. Kennedy got straight to the point. 'You called in with the van tip-off, Mr Danson?'

Danson nodded. 'Yeah, a guy brought it in this morning, wanted a quote to fix up the front end and put a new windshield in. I remembered the news report about that hit and run, so I thought, better be safe than sorry.' He filled them in on the details of the van's owner, a courier. 'I've got a mobile number somewhere.'

Back in the car, Chris punched in the number and held the receiver to his ear.

'Hello, Connolly and Sons; Shane speaking,' a man answered in a business-like tone.

'Mr Connolly, my name is Detective Chris Delaney. I wonder if you could confirm that are you the registered owner of a white Ford Transit van, registration number 08-MH-3457?' He used a direct yes or no question, to not give Connolly any time to think.

'Yes, yes, that's my van,' was the nervous reply.

'Mr Connolly,' Chris said, his tone ominous, 'I think you and I need to have a little chat.'

10

Rory sat hunched over his computer screen. There was a vast amount of information in the Central Database. New cases existed in both physical and digital form, which made searching for information or cross referencing with older cases much easier, especially for somebody with his analytical brain.

His friends nicknamed him 'Data', after the android on *Star Trek TNG*, one of his all-time favorite TV shows, due to the fact that he shared the uncanny ability to sift through and locate information, and also had a terrific memory for detail.

He quickly scanned through the older digital case file, hoping for something to jump out.

And when two hours later it did just that, Rory smiled.

'Bingo,' he grinned, getting to his feet.

State Pathologist
DATE and HOUR AUTOPSY PERFORMED:
24/10/1993; 10:00 A.M. by
John Harris, ME

Assistant:

James O'Neill, MD

Full Autopsy Performed

SUMMARY REPORT OF AUTOPSY

Name:

Jane Doe

Coroner's Case #:

7634-311

Date of Birth:

N/A

Age:

N/A

Race:

White

Sex:

Female

Date of Death:

Unknown

Body Identified by:

N/A

Case #

000453-4S-1993

Investigative Agency:

SCU

EXTERNAL EXAMINATION:

Autopsy at 10:00 A.M. on October 24, 1993. The body is presented in standard body bag. The victim is wearing a light cotton jacket, polyester blend shirt and denim jeans with worn leather shoes.

The body is that of a young adult female of small build measuring 63 inches and weighing 98 pounds, estimated age of 16-18. Blue eyes. Long red hair 30 inches approx.

Rigor mortis has passed and liver mortis is fully developed.

Visual examination of the body shows no sign of trauma.

Alger mortis test carried out rectally which results slightly above ambient temp proving inconclusive for TOD.

Victim's clothing and footwear removed and stored for evidence.

The victim has an elaborate and extensive tattoo across a large portion of her back, which should aid with identification. Six (6) photographs taken.

Abdomen is slightly inflated suggesting decay. Multiple blowfly larvae present.

Swabs and scrapings taken from fingernails.

Genital exam reveals no sign of sexual activity or trauma.

INTERNAL EXAMINATION:

Skeletal system is fully intact and normal.

Brain showing signs of decomposition — weight 978 grams, samples taken.

Respiratory system and throat system are normal but also showing initial signs of decay, larvae collected for dating. Lungs samples taken, signs of tissue damage as well as decay.

Heart of normal size, no signs of coronary disease.

Stomach contains high levels of gases indicating decay, no semi-digested food present.

The Urinary and female Genital system are normal but showing signs of decay. Swabs and tissue samples removed for analysis.

TOXICOLOGY: Sample blood and bile submitted for toxicologic analysis.

Drug Screen Results:

Urine screen {Immunoassay} NEGATIVE.

Ethanol: 0 gm/dl, Blood (Heart)

Ethanol: 0 gm/dl, Vitreous

EVIDENCE COLLECTED:

One (1) cotton jacket, pale colored, size Small.

One (1) denim jeans, size 10.

One (1) T-shirt (brand unknown).

One (1) pair of worn leather lace-up shoes.

Blood samples (type A+); Tissue samples — brain, heart, lungs, liver, kidney.

Eighteen (18) swabs to be tested.

OPINION

Time of Death: Body temperature, livor mortis, gastric bloating and the presence of blowfly larvae approximate time of death at more than four days (but less than seven) taking into account recorded weather conditions in localized area.

Cause of Death: Exposure to low temperatures below the metabolic rate.

Remarks: The victim was healthy and without signs of trauma or disease. The prevailing frost and absence of warm clothing may have led to death.

11

'The wings design has cropped up before?' Reilly scanned through the cold case file Rory had just handed her.

Right off the bat there were a few similarities between their case and this older one — both girls had been redheads, both were unidentified, and most strikingly, both had remarkably similar tattoos on their backs.

She then compared the photographs of the tattoo from the cold case to the ones they'd taken of the hit-and-run victim.

'I'm no expert,' Rory said, looking at both sets of photos, 'but the tattoos look very similar to me.'

Reilly exhaled. 'Well, they're similar but not identical, though we're not comparing like with like either,' she pointed out.

'What do you mean?'

'According to the autopsy report, the girl in this older case died of exposure; she'd been out in the open for at least four days before she was discovered. That's clear from the photos, and while the tattoo looks the same from the outset, I can see some differences in the detail.'

She arranged the photos side by side. 'This tattoo is missing some of the finer detail of our more recent one.' Using a pen, she circled an area near the shoulder blade of the hit-and-run victim's photo. There did indeed seem more detail in the individual feather renderings of the latter tattoo.

'There are plenty of things that could cause that,' Rory offered. 'The age of the tattoos for one, not to mention the age of the girls themselves when they were inked.'

She shook her head. 'Neither tattoo looks that fresh though. They both look faded on the skin, so could have been done a while ago, leading to a loss of definition.'

She placed the photos back on the desk. 'Let's not over-analyze the obvious here. Anything else stand out about this cold case?'

Rory picked another file out of the box. 'No dental work for this girl either. I don't know about you, but pretty much everyone in Ireland these days has at least a filling.'

'Well, not to brag, but where I come from fillings aren't so common.' Reilly grimaced, revealing her perfectly maintained orthodontics.

'Fair enough, but these two Celtic redheads were a million miles from Californian girls,' he replied archly.

Notwithstanding the tattoos and both girls' appearance, the similarities were starting to become uncomfortable and she knew she needed to advise the detectives about this new slant to the investigation.

But this second unidentified girl had been found nine years before. What possible connection could she have to their 'Angel'?

12

'Can't deny the similarities, that's for sure,' said Kennedy when they called to the GFU on their return from the auto-repair shop.

'I don't think we should rule out the fact that these two girls may have originated if not from the same place then certainly from a similar background,' Reilly said.

Chris frowned. 'I don't follow ...'

She tried to explain her train of thought. 'I can't quite put my finger on it yet, call it instinct if you like, but it certainly feels like each of these girls were somewhat at odds with the real world. My guess is that wherever they came from they were cut off from reality, and never had to face any dangers, anything that might hurt them.'

'Overprotective parents?' Chris suggested with obvious skepticism. 'Then why have both remained unidentified for so long, the cold case especially?'

'No. I don't think it's overprotective parents. Problem is I'm not sure what I think. It's just a feeling.'

'Ah, here we go ...' Kennedy said, and while usually Reilly never minded him teasing her about her famed 'instincts', for some reason she felt embarrassed in the face of Chris's blatant cynicism. The last thing she needed was for him to stop trusting her judgement. It made her question herself. The tattoo aside, was she reaching for related similarities in these two cases, grasping at straws?

'Look, it might well be nothing, but in any case, I thought I'd go and take a closer look around the discovery site. I know it's been nine years since she was found but—'

'Well, if there is anything there, no doubt that magic nose of yours will sniff it out,' Kennedy chuckled. 'No harm in our getting the lowdown from this … MacDonald,' he said, reading the name of the cold-case investigating officer from the file. He stretched and groaned. 'I thought we'd caught a break with finding the driver. So much for wrapping this one up quickly. Now, it looks like we've got not just one fallen angel, but two.'

13

The following morning, Gary hurried into the lab with his sample bag over his shoulder and kit under his arm.

'What are you doing in on a Sunday – hungry for overtime?' Lucy teased as she turned away from the microscope.

'I could say the same for you, thought you were away with the girls this weekend?'

'Nah, cancelled due to terminal old age; Debs has no babysitter and Nic would rather stay in with her new man,' she said.

In truth Lucy hadn't been too bothered. Lately it always seemed that when she met up with her friends, she had less and less in common with them. Conversation usually turned to something funny someone had said or done years ago, and she was starting to feel jaded by the endless reminiscing. Spending hours alone in a cold, lonely lab didn't faze her. This was what she'd wanted from the beginning, after all — a chance to make a difference, and get closer to finding answers.

'What about you?' she asked Gary. 'No plans at all for the weekend?'

'Nah. Since I started working here I've lost touch with about half my old mates, they move in different circles. It's funny though, I always thought it would really bother me ... you know, being like Reilly,' he added, taking off his jacket. 'But the longer I work here the more I appreciate it for what it is.'

'And what's that?'

'The perfect job. We don't have to clock in, we don't have some troll of a boss breathing down our necks, our "clients" don't — or can't — answer back and most of the time, as long as we get results we get to do things our way.'

Lucy smiled. 'Which is why you're in here bright and early on a Sunday morning instead of sleeping off a Saturday night ...'

'Yep. I've just been down to the compound at the Phoenix Park to give that van a proper comb-over. I might be getting old and boring, but nailing the evidence on this guy is a much better use of a day than fighting off a hangover,' Gary said as he placed the two bags on top of his workstation.

'Find anything interesting?'

'A couple of samples for DNA to see if I can get a match on that coffee cup from the ditch. There were two other older cups in the door pocket, same MegaCoffee branding on the side, so I bagged those too.'

'Should stand up well in the prosecution — the detectives will be happy.'

'Yep, we caught a break, getting a hit on the vehicle like that. Lots to compare with what we found at the scene.' He indicated the full sample bag on his desk. 'At this stage it's looking like this courier guy is toast – I just need to make sure I cover all the angles so that the evidence is water tight.'

'Or "Walter tight" as Reilly would say,' Lucy said with a grin, referring to Reilly's motto about well-known Dublin defense solicitor Jeffery Walters. He had got a particularly nasty individual off on a forensic technicality once, a loophole that Reilly had not foreseen and which had caused a massive storm in the GFU. Since then, none of them took any chances.

'Yep, so that's about the sum of it. What are you cooking in Pegasus?' Gary nodded towards an elaborate unit that looked part-microwave, part life-support machine. On the left of the device was a large keypad and digital readout that displayed various alpha-numerical keys as well as the periodic symbols. Attached to the top of the unit was a standard LCD computer screen that sat beside a tall attachment with pressure dials and gas hoses coming out of either side. This was one of the GFU's greatest weapons, the gas chromatography-mass spectrometry station. Affectionately nicknamed Pegasus, Gary had once joked that if there was ever a fire in the GFU, the first thing Reilly would do was unplug the machine and drag it out the door.

'Just running the tox from the post mortem on the same case. I'm nearly finished if you need to get in here,' Lucy said as she straightened up a bottle in a sample holder sitting on top of the machine. Several bottles were labeled: *Femoral Blood (s1), Heart Blood (s1), Vitreous Humor Fluid (s1), Liver (s1), Brain (s1)*, as well as other pathological trace contained in small bottles relating to their hit-and-run victim.

'Find anything interesting?'

'Nope, I swear I've never seen such a clean set of results. Not that I was expecting to find anything hardcore like drugs or even alcohol. Even the hair analysis shows up negative for pretty much everything you'd expect — no heavy metals or other airborne pollutants. It's like a corpse from the seventeenth century.'

'What about that stuff in the lungs?'

'There's only trace amounts of silica, and I'm guessing she must have been living or working in a dusty environment.'

'Or in a museum,' Gary said dryly.

Lucy tapped some keys on Pegasus and a humming sound kicked in.

'I don't know,' she sighed, 'usually the more analysis we do the closer we get to an answer, but seems to me that we're getting further away.'

'Patience, Luce, one step at a time. Something is sure to turn up that will flick a switch on this. Like this maybe...' He took out a sealed container from his sample bag and held it up for her to see.

'What is it?' she asked.

'Killer snot.' When she gave him a baffled look, he smiled and continued. 'Seems our courier likes nothing better that a good nasal rummage when he's out on the road,' he said gleefully. 'Followed by wiping his mucus-adorned finger on the edge of his seat — remember that the next time you get a delivery from Amazon.' Gary waved the sample close to her face making her reel back.

'Ewww ...' Lucy exclaimed, enjoying the banter. While she enjoyed and embraced the solitude of the job, it was nice to have a little company on a weekend morning when most of her peers were enjoying time off.

Gary walked back to his desk like a triumphant eight-year-old who'd just dangled a worm in front of his little sister. 'No shortage of DNA in the cab of that van either. Like I said, it will be interesting to hear from Batman and Robin about the owner and what his excuse is.'

Lucy giggled at his description of the detectives but a noise from nearby caused them both to turn around.

'Ah isn't this sweet.' Kennedy stood in the doorway with a cup of coffee in his hand.

Lucy laughed at Gary's reddening facial features.

'Well, Einstein, what have you got for me?' he said to Gary. 'Do we have a definite match with that van yet?'

Gary nodded. 'Looks like it. The damaged areas on the

front are consistent with the injuries the victim sustained. I'm just about to run a test on the glass fragments from the van with the ones we found on the road and the body.'

'Can we place the courier at the scene though?'

'I think so. I'm also going to do a particle analysis on the paintwork and match them with what we've already found. While I'm a hundred percent sure we can put the van at the scene, putting the guy behind the wheel is a tricker one, but I'm putting my faith in the coffee cup to give us a break on that.'

'Nice one.' Kennedy smiled as he took a sip of his own coffee. 'We have our guy in for questioning this morning. Hopefully we'll have him singing like a lark once we put those photos of the dead girl under his nose. Speaking of which …'

Lucy duly got up and walked to the far end of the lab to retrieve an envelope.

'Here you go,' she said, handing it to him. 'You can hold onto them — they're copies.'

'Good stuff. As you were, kiddies, and let me know if anything turns up in the meantime.' Kennedy turned to walk out, but then paused in the doorframe. 'Oh, and by the way, Gary,' he added with a wink, 'I'll say nothing to Chris about you calling him Robin.'

14

A little while later, Kennedy strode up to where Chris was standing outside a room in Harcourt Street station marked 'Interview Room No. 4'.

'Where the hell were you? I thought you said you were only five minutes away,' grumbled Chris, glancing at his watch.

'Bloody hell, I didn't think it was me up for a grilling this morning,' Kennedy replied. 'If you must know I went to pick up these,' he said, waving the envelope he'd just collected from the GFU. 'So who moved your cheese?' he added.

Chris stared at him. 'What are you talking about?'

'Well for one thing, you and Reilly seem a little … off.'

'Well, I'm certainly not "off".' Chris felt uncomfortable. He didn't think the 'atmosphere' or whatever it was between him and Reilly was that obvious. 'I have no idea what you're talking about.'

'Look, all I'm saying is you do seem a little wound up. Just be careful, OK? Take it from an old man who knows, life is short, don't let it pass you by,' Kennedy said in a melancholy tone. 'There has to be more to life than the job, you know. If I didn't have Josie to go home to at night …' His voice cracked a little. 'I'd find it a lot harder to stay balanced... on top of things.'

'How's everything going — with Josie, I mean?' Chris asked gently, struck by the uncharacteristic display of sentimentality from the big man. But he was unsure as to whether or not to broach the subject of his wife's health again when Kennedy had been so reticent about it before.

His partner's face immediately closed. 'Grand,' he replied simply. 'You want to take the lead on this first off and see how we go?' he asked, nodding toward the door of the interview room. Once again the topic was strictly off limits.

The van owner had already been in the interview room for three quarters of an hour. Chris had asked one of the officers to turn up the heating earlier, a favorite tactic of his for making interviewees as uncomfortable as possible by legal means.

'Good idea — see what we get before he clams up.'

Chris entered the room, followed by Kennedy.

It was a typical office that you would expect an accountant or civil servant to work out of. The only difference was the lack of furniture and equipment: just a cheap wood veneer table and three uncomfortable chairs around the desk with two more stacked in the corner. The only other point of note was the white security meshing on the outside of the window, usually used to keep intruders out but in this case to keep people in.

'Mr Connolly, my name is Detective Chris Delaney. You spoke with my partner Detective Kennedy here on the phone yesterday.'

Chris and Kennedy assumed positions on the opposite side of the table to Shane Connolly. The courier sat across from them sporting the tired unshaven look of a man with much on his mind. In front of him sat an empty plastic cup.

'Yes of course. Can you tell me what's going on here, please? Nobody has said anything since the squad car called to my door this morning. Am I under arrest?' His demeanor was non-threatening but he was obviously running out of patience.

'Mr Connolly, we have asked you to come in this morning to answer some questions that may assist us in a serious incident we are investigating. You are not being formally charged of any wrongdoing as yet, but your assistance at this stage will be viewed favorably down the line,' Chris said, trying to encourage as much cooperation as possible.

'OK, but as I told the other officers earlier, I can't tell you much about any accident my van was involved with because I wasn't driving it.'

'Who *was* driving, Mr Connolly?'

'Based on the timeframe, it would have been my son William. He said he was helping a friend move house and he hit an animal. He didn't know what it was because when he got out of the van it had disappeared so he assumed it wasn't killed outright and had just run off into a ditch,' the courier said as he shifted in his chair.

'Have you spoken to your son recently, Mr Connolly?' asked Kennedy.

'I tried his mobile yesterday but there was no answer. He'd left a message on my phone on Friday saying his mate had got tickets to a football game and that he was going to London yesterday morning.'

'We need to talk with him immediately, Mr Connolly. Your vehicle was involved with a fatal hit and run in Wicklow. A young girl is dead. Leaving the scene of an accident is a very serious charge, Mr. Connolly.'

The man's face paled instantly. 'A young girl ... I heard it on the news. Are you sure?'

'Very sure.'

'But that's impossible ... and I can assure you my son would never leave anybody dying on the road.' The man's hands shook and he looked as though he was going to pass out.

'We all make mistakes. Perhaps your son had had a couple of cans at his mate's house, and he didn't want to get in trouble,' Chris suggested.

'I don't know. I don't know what to think to be honest. But I swear, when he gets back I will get him to come in and talk to you straightaway. I'll phone him again as soon as I get out of here.' He looked worriedly at the detectives, the thought striking him. 'I will be getting out of here, won't I?'

Kennedy purposely didn't answer. Instead, he said, '*If* he comes back. At this point we will be seeking a warrant for your son's arrest, and given the fact he may have absconded we might have to get Interpol involved.'

This was mostly showboating, but the man gasped. 'Look, I've said I'll personally escort him down here when he gets back. We have nothing to hide, this is just a simple misunderstanding. I'm sure of it,' he added, trying to convince himself as much as anybody else.

'We'll see, but I must warn you again, these charges are very serious indeed. Someone has had their life wiped out, somebody's daughter left to die on a cold dark road,' Chris said.

'If you have a way to contact William I suggest you do it immediately, and tell him to get his arse back here right away,' Kennedy put in. 'Mr Connolly, if you are trying to protect him in any way you need to tell us now. Because these charges will get more serious with every second that passes. The best option open to William now is one of full cooperation.'

Kennedy paused to let the statement sink in and the room fell silent.

The courier swallowed hard. 'OK, Detectives, I get the message. We're a respectable family and I promise you, this is all a misunderstanding. William would never—'

'Good,' Chris cut him off. 'For the moment then you are free to go, but we expect full lines of communication to be kept open. You'll need to keep us updated regarding your son's movements and whereabouts. Anything less will be viewed as obstructive.'

The courier stood up slowly and picked up his coat from the back of the chair.

'One more thing', Kennedy called out as Shane Connolly walked through the doorway. 'Does your son have a solicitor?'

'Not that I know of.'

'Well, if I were you,' he added ominously, 'it would be my second phone call when you leave here.'

eilly parked her car on the grass verge and locked it with the remote while gazing around. The wind had died down overnight, and it was a perfect spring day — a pale blue sky, the overnight dew almost gone where the bright sun had hit it, the trees a blaze of green from the blossoming leaves and the riot of flowers about to bloom.

She climbed a wooden gate and followed a footpath towards a small hill about half a mile away to her left. The immediate area was covered in budding deciduous trees — oak and sycamore, sweet chestnut and whitebeam. It looked beautiful — but it was exactly here that a young girl's body had been found nine years before.

Reilly stomped along the grassy path, grit crunching beneath her hiking boots, her faded jeans and a fleece making her look more at home on the trail than she did in the lab or in court.

In truth, Reilly was born to be outdoors even though she choose an occupation that involved her spending the majority of her time in windowless labs.

She never talked much about her past any more. The pain

of her family tragedy was now something she tried to lock away in the back of her mind. Thankfully, it was never mentioned at work either. People often asked how Mike, her father, was getting on, but that was the extent of it — luckily all those skeletons had been shoved right back into the closet.

She guessed it was a good thing that for the most part she enjoyed solitude, always had, which meant that it was easier to keep her secrets hidden.

She reached a stile in a fence that seemed to have been put in place to protect an area of seedlings from rabbits and deer. The low spring sunshine almost blinded her as she stopped for a moment, closed her eyes and held her face up toward the sun. She breathed deeply, realizing that she really needed to do this more often.

Sometimes she felt split in two: who she really was, and who she'd needed to become. The move to Ireland hadn't been much of an upheaval; crime and murder was for the most part the same everywhere in the world.

The other half of her though — the fun side, the person who loved the joys of nature, and enjoyed surfing a Pacific wave and the feel of the sun's rays on her skin — was stifled, suffocating and becoming lost. It was almost as if those pleasures had belonged to somebody else, such was the current imbalance in her life here.

Now, being in this place brought some of those pleasures flooding back. It reminded her of going on school trips to Muir Woods, the sprawling acres of Californian redwoods and giant sequoias just beyond Golden Gate Bridge overlooking the Bay.

Realizing that the low throb of homesickness she carried was quickly starting to become an ache, she wondered if being a third wheel to her father and his partner for their jaunt back home next month might not be such a bad idea after all.

Temporarily putting the notion aside, she looked around and checked her location against the map. The footpath continued north around the foot of the hill, but according to the case file, the girl's body had been found in the trees, almost at the top of the hill.

Reilly left the path, and marched across the damp grass towards the trees. It was pock-marked with hoof prints, and liberally decorated with an assortment of deer and wild goat droppings, though the goats themselves were all over on the far side of the fence. Obviously there to try and keep them out, but judging by this side, it was having limited success.

As she entered the tree line, she found it was cool and shady under the canopy of the trees, and even though their leaves were sparse they still blocked out most of the sun. She shivered and zipped up her fleece before beginning to climb.

What did she expect to find after nine years?

Reilly had no idea, but right now she was willing to try almost anything to move the case forward. The fact that all those years ago another girl had been found with a similar tattoo demanded a second look.

She reached the top of the hill and looked around. Through the trees the Wicklow countryside could be seen fading towards the horizon, mostly flat, just the occasional hill to disturb the view. Why had the girl come up here in the first place? Was she seeking shelter? Was she trying to get somewhere or perhaps, Reilly thought, *away* from somewhere? Or someone.

According to the file, the girl's body had been found near the top of the hill, against a large oak tree. Reilly looked around — there was one massive oak tree about twenty yards away, its gnarled roots spreading out from the summit, its vast branches forming a roof overhead. If only trees could talk.

Reilly walked slowly towards the oak tree. The soft ground was uneven with the sheer quantity of decaying acorns it had dropped, intending to propagate, to spread its seed as far and wide as possible.

Why would the girl come here to such a remote, desolate place?

Reilly reached out and touched the thick bark. Then again, if she was lonely, or scared, she might have come here to rest against this tree. Its sheer size and majesty was somehow comforting.

She sat down, ignoring the damp, muddy ground. It looked to be the highest spot on the hill — from here you could see for miles. What was the girl looking for up here all those years ago? Was her gaze drawn back to her home, the place she was from? Maybe one of the nearby villages. Was it visible from here?

Or was it freedom that she saw? The lights of a village, a town, somewhere that looked tempting, interesting, some-where to escape to. Reilly thought again about her theory that both girls seemed to originate from somewhere cut off from reality, away from the modern world.

Reilly stood up. Wherever they came from, the world that the girl could see from this hilltop must have looked vast, a whole world of opportunity, but she had simply curled up, cold and alone, and died.

Of natural exposure according to the file. But why wouldn't she have fought death? Could it have been suicide?

There was still so much they didn't know about her. It was clear that back then (and before Karen Thompson's arrival) things were less rigorous at the then Technical Bureau, long before the creation of the GFU. After the autopsy, the body had been buried in the strangers' lot of St Mary's Cemetery.

A basic toxic screen had been run — and come up negative — and there were no signs of a struggle, no unusual markings or wounds on her body, nothing in fact except a girl in a thin cotton dress and worn sandals who had died of exposure on a lonely hilltop. If someone had wanted to devise a mystifying cold case, they could hardly have done better. A cause of death that could only be construed as accidental, no signs of murder or sexual assault.

And of course, a large, very beautiful and very distinctive tattoo on the girl's back. Reilly sighed. Whatever it took, she was going to find out who these girls were, where they came from, and why they had needed to die so young.

16

'What's that?' Kennedy said looking at the piece of paper Chris had just pushed in front of him having walked up to his desk unannounced.

'Recognize the name?'

'Nope. Should I?'

'Well, you've been around here since the Dark Ages so I thought it might ring a bell. James MacDonald, retired detective. Sure you've never heard of him?'

'I vaguely remember the name, where's he stationed?'

'He was in Bray for years, but has been retired four years now apparently. He was one of the original investigators nine years ago on that cold case.'

'So where's he these days? Please say the south of Spain; I could do with a break.'

'You and me both. He's living in Killiney; not quite Marbella but not bad either. I put in a call, he's expecting us.'

Half an hour later, the detectives pulled into the driveway of a large semi-detached house on a suburban street just off the N11.

'I thought you said he lives in Killiney?' Kennedy

complained. 'I was expecting sea views and a stone's throw from Bono and the gang. This is Ballybrack.'

'Yeah well, we both know there's a very thick line between addresses in this part of town and I guess Killiney sounds better down the golf club,' Chris said, unbuckling his seatbelt and reaching down to grab the case file.

They both got out of the car and their respective doors banged simultaneously. As they did so the front door of the house opened and the tall figure of James MacDonald appeared.

'Detectives Kennedy and Delaney, I presume?' MacDonald called out by way of introduction.

'Yes, sir, thank you for taking the time to see us.' Chris kept his tone deferential, as he always did when addressing ex-force members. He always made sure to play to any egos — especially when raking over old work.

'Come on in. I've been expecting you.'

Chris followed MacDonald into the hallway as the former detective held the door open for them.

'Go straight through to the kitchen.' MacDonald indicated a doorway at the end of the hall. Daylight was streaming through the windows of a large open-plan kitchen which had evidently expensive units and décor. 'Please take a seat.' MacDonald motioned them toward several plush leather swivel stools surrounding a large black granite island.

Chris slipped onto the stool facing the window, which had views out onto tidy raised beds. Kennedy meanwhile looked far less comfortable trying to place his oversized posterior onto the moving target. He finally managed to plant himself cleanly and righted himself with two hands on the cold stone surface, his reddened complexion hinting at the levels of exertion required.

'Tea or coffee?' A slight smile escaped as they both requested coffee. 'Right you are. So on a scale of one to ten how strong do you like it? My little beauty here makes americanos and espressos like you've never tasted.' MacDonald indicated a machine that wouldn't look out of place in the GFU lab.

So this is what retirement looks like, Chris thought with a gulp. Raised flower beds and fancy coffee machines.

He was now able to control the aches and spasms that had become a hallmark of hemochromatosis, his condition, but they were a stark reminder that his life could easily take a turn towards such drudgery. Chris was glad he'd got to the root of his medical problems when he did, before things got out of control. His only regret was that he'd taken Reilly into his confidence about it all, and her subsequent insistence that it was something of which their superiors should be aware. Chris violently disagreed. He knew he'd end up stuck behind a desk for the rest of his career — if not off the job altogether. He should have gone to a private clinic under an assumed name, then he could have rested in the knowledge that nobody else at work would ever find out It had left him in a difficult position — he would do whatever it took to continue to do what he loved best, even if it risked his friendship, or whatever it was he had, with Reilly Steel.

'I'm sure whatever you have will be a massive improvement on the machine at the station anyway,' Kennedy said lightheartedly, rousing Chris from his daydream.

'Very good, two cups of Dulsao do Brasil then.' The older cop smiled as if serving coffee was the highlight of his day. And perhaps it was, Chris thought morosely. 'I must warn you though, you'll never drink the ordinary stuff again.' MacDonald pressed buttons and pulled levers on the coffee machine which gave out a groan and a whine as the intense smell of coffee began to waft around the room. While the magic machine did its thing, MacDonald turned to them and got down to business. 'So I believe you have a few questions for me about an old case of mine?'

'That's right, sir,' Chris said, opening the file. 'A Jane Doe, found down in Wicklow about nine years ago, died of exposure?'

'Yes. I remember it. "Sleeping Beauty" we used to call her.' MacDonald served them each a cup of his famed brew and looked eagerly at them for their reaction. 'Have you had a new break?'

'Mmm, smashing,' said Chris. 'Not exactly. We suspect it might be linked to a recent case.'

'The hit and run up in Roundwood?'

Chris was surprised. 'You're familiar with that case?'

'I may be retired from the force, Detective, but one can't help picking up a paper or watching the news and have the old instincts kick in. I read about that hit and run, but it was the call from the chief about my "Sleeping Beauty" that had me wondering if there might well be something.' MacDonald lifted his cup and breathed in the smell of the coffee with one long inhalation. Thank goodness they hadn't asked him for tea, Chris thought, he'd probably be out picking it fresh from the raised beds.

'Unfortunately we've been unable to identify the hit-and-run victim thus far, but stumbled upon some similar body markings that led to the older case.'

'Ah yes, the tattoo, quite a piece of art as I recall,' MacDonald mused.

Chris pulled a couple of sheets he had marked from the file. 'In your report you seem to have had a strong interest in a group of New Age Travelers.'

'Well yes, if you want to be all politically correct about it,' MacDonald scoffed. 'There was a group living in the woods near Greystones at the time; tree huggers.'

Chris remembered something about a stand-off between local authorities and these 'eco-warriors' as they'd been described by national media.

'You suspected she may have been one of them?'

'It seemed a good bet at the time, we turned over a lot of rocks trying to identify her, we knew she wasn't local.'

'You asked around at the campsite?' Kennedy asked.

'Yes, a few times. But they weren't very…how shall I put it… very cooperative with law enforcement. We were the enemy as far as they were concerned.'

'So nothing ever came of it?'

MacDonald shrugged. 'We thought she might have been a runaway, although at the time nothing corresponded with any missing person reports. Of course, there were many different accents amongst that group; if she was one of them, she could have come from anywhere.'

'Autopsy reports "exposure" as cause of death, yet in your own report you mention she was found very close to a residential area.'

He nodded. 'That's just it; the whole "death by natural exposure" thing never sat well with us, we always suspected there was something else at work—'

'Foul play?' Kennedy asked before MacDonald had time to finish his sentence which seemed to annoy him. Clearly he was a man who preferred others to listen while he spoke.

'Well, Detective, you tell me? How likely is it that a seemingly healthy young girl goes to sleep out in the elements and never wakes up? Surely the cold would have driven her for cover?'

'So how do you think she came to be there, sir?' Chris asked, trying to play up again to his sense of authority.

'Again, that is why I was almost certain she'd come from the hippy camp. We had several run-ins with them over the years, many reports of wild parties at the campsite. I recall picking up a couple of them walking down the center line of the main road once — bollock-naked and high as kites …'

'But the tox screen for Sleeping Beauty came back clean.'

'Depends on what they were screening for. We had no fancy GFU back then, remember, and of course the drink and drug culture amongst that crowd seemed very DIY, if you understand.'

Chris thought about it. MacDonald's theory that the girl could have wandered off from the encampment high on some homemade concoction, got lost and kept wandering the hills chasing fairies until she lay down to rest, eventually succumbing to the cold in her sleep made some sort of sense. It wasn't a bad theory — and actually gave them a new angle for the hit-and-run case. Perhaps this girl had also originated from such a group — hence the absence of a family member coming forward to identify her following the media release? He recalled too what Reilly had said about both girls being slightly at odds with the modern world.

'But even back then surely if she's been on the mushrooms or something psilocybin would have shown up in the tox report?' Kennedy continued, playing devil's advocate as he so relished doing.

MacDonald smiled; this was obviously something he'd considered too. 'That may well be, but the truth is there are plenty of potions or concoctions she could have taken that would have cleared the system by the time she died.'

He gazed down at the file picture of the girl and sighed. 'You've seen everything in the file. We chased every avenue we possibly could, the eco-warrior angle was the most likely one at the time, still is to my mind. The only problem being we couldn't prove it – I mean, why else has her body remained unclaimed and her absence unreported? She must have been some sort of drop out or runaway, one of those poor misfortunates who fall through the cracks every now and then.'

Chris nodded. 'I'm inclined to agree with you.'

But despite the parallels, their discussion with MacDonald

didn't give them anything more to work with on identifying either victim.

And as such, Chris thought as they left minutes later, MacDonald's case remained as cold as the dregs of the fancy coffee lining the bottom of his cup.

17

In the following days, and in an effort to move forwards in identifying either of the tattooed girls, the investigative team widened the net by searching through the database for all redheaded females, tattooed or otherwise, who had been found dead in mysterious circumstances.

And even more painstakingly, by trawling through every female missing person report from the last ten years.

There were dozens of potential matches from the outset, but the finer details had to be checked. While the system worked within certain parameters, the information on older cases was often incomplete or inconsistent. They therefore had not only to check all reported missing children with red hair, but also those in which hair color wasn't specified or was vague.

Apart from the angel-wings tattoo — which they had to assume had been done *after* the girls went missing — the only other distinguishing feature on either of the deceased was scar tissue on the radius and ulna of the hit-and-run victim, which Karen Thompson had reported as being indicative of a childhood broken bone.

Going through the files was chilling. Hundreds of children had gone missing in Ireland over the past two decades, and while many were runaways, plenty of other cases still remained unsolved, leaving thousands of parents and families wondering for the rest of their lives what had happened to their loved ones.

KENNEDY PARKED the car beside the aquarium that sat halfway along Bray promenade. Typically, given the recent brief flirtation with spring weather, it had been raining on and off all morning, a persistent drizzle that made it seem as though the very air itself had turned to water.

He groaned as he got out and tried to regain a fully upright position. Zipping up his windbreaker he raised his arms above his head in an attempt to further straighten himself up. He looked over at Chris who was getting out the other side.

'Do you not have a raincoat?'

Chris shrugged. 'It's barely spitting. I'll be grand.'

The beach along the seafront was stony and stretched from the imposing Bray Head at the southern end to a small pier at the North. The promenade was Victorian in design, Bray having been a bustling seaside getaway from Dublin in the times before two-euro Ryanair seat sales to more exotic destinations.

The wind blew ferociously from the North making Kennedy wrap his windbreaker even more tightly around himself. He and Chris hurried across the road to a pub called Molloy's, eager to be out of the damp air.

Kennedy brushed the rain off his coat, shook out his thinning hair, and looked around. The pub was quiet on this weekday lunchtime, just a few locals having a drink and eating sandwiches. The barman looked as though he'd been there when the pub was built. He was red faced, with long silver sideburns and a matching, luxurious mustache.

'Can I help you?'

Kennedy gave him his best smile, which was more than enough to demolish most men. 'We're looking for a guy called Rasher. Told you might know where to find him.'

The barman gave them a long look. 'He in some kind of trouble?'

Chris stepped forward and shook his head. 'No. We just need to ask him a few questions.'

'Only you don't look the types to be getting a tattoo, if you don't mind me saying.' He turned and shouted over his shoulder. 'Ralph? Come here a minute.'

Footsteps sounded from behind the bar, someone running down a flight of stairs. A fresh-faced boy of around nineteen appeared and looked at the older man.

'These people want to talk with Rasher. Can you show them where he lives?'

Ralph looked at the two detectives. 'No problem.' Outside, he led the way along the narrow street that went away from the seafront and turned into a cobbled alleyway.

'Just through here,' he said, pointing towards a courtyard that seemed to act as a service yard for several business premises that ran along the opposite side of the buildings. A rickety set of stairs ran up the side of a three-story Victorian building. 'That's Rasher's place up there,' Ralph announced. 'But you'll have to shout to get his attention — the old hearing isn't the best these days.'

'Thanks.'

Ralph trotted off as Kennedy and Chris carefully climbed. The wind howled around the fragile steps, blowing a squall of rain in their faces and causing the stairs to sway a little.

At the top was a wooden door, one glass panel replaced

with cardboard and duct tape. The yellow glow of a light shone through the remaining panes.

Kennedy looked around for a bell, but, finding none, he wound up rapping hard on the door with his knuckles. For a moment, all they could hear was the wind whipping against their ears. Kennedy rapped again, and almost instantly there was a response.

'Keep your hair on, I'm coming!'

The sound of heavy footsteps creaked towards them and the door opened. A man looked out at Kennedy and Chris, a curious look in his eyes. 'Whatever you're selling I'm not interested.'

Kennedy shook his head, sending a spray of raindrops cascading down his coat. 'No sir, we're detectives from Harcourt Street, and we're looking to talk to Rasher.'

The man turned his back before shuffling back inside. 'Well, you found him. Close the door behind you and keep the bloody rain out.'

He headed back across the room and Kennedy and Chris stepped inside. They were both caught off guard having expected a younger, trendy type. He was a big man, with a head of grizzled curls, the black long ago faded to white. His age was hard to guess — he could be almost anywhere from sixty to eighty — but judging by his movements, it was likely closer to the latter.

The room was small, cozy even, just a sagging couch in front of an old TV, a green recliner, and a table and chairs over by a sink.

'So who sent you, the bloody tax man I suppose?'

'Not at all. We're trying to get some artwork identified and we've heard you're the man to talk to.'

Kennedy was shaking the rain from his coat, looking around for somewhere to hang it. Even though he had his back to him, Rasher seemed to read his mind. 'There's a hook on the back of the door.' He found the hook, and duly hung up his coat. When he turned around, Rasher was gazing at them.

'So then, what's this artwork you mentioned?' he said as he lowered himself carefully into one of the wooden chairs, and waved them over. Kennedy sat in the chair next to him, Chris across the table. Kennedy took an envelope from inside his jacket and removed photos of the angel-wing tattoos. As he slid the pictures across the table, Rasher pulled a pair of glasses from the pocket of his cardigan, and perched them on the end of his nose.

The hand that reached out for the photographs was huge, with big swollen knuckles, and tattoos snaked down his arms to appear at his wrists when his sleeves slid up. He said nothing, simply studied them, one after the other, back and forth. Finally he set them down, then sipped at an open bottle of Lucozade that sat on the table in front of them He peered over the top of his glasses at Chris and Kennedy.

'Amateur,' he said eventually. 'But a bloody good one.'

The detectives leaned forward, waiting for him to continue.

'What type of ink did he use?'

'Pig's blood and soot,' Chris informed him, recalling the information on the GFU report, 'and some kind of alcohol.'

'Yeah, that's what gives it that lovely warm color — the wings almost seem to glow through the skin, don't they?'

'How does someone learn to do that?' Chris asked him. 'Or go about making his own ink?'

'Could have apprenticed at a tattoo parlor for a while, but just as likely to have learned it in the navy, or as a merchant sailor, maybe. As for the ink, well, that's easy enough; you can buy it at any stationer. As long as it's sterile, it's as good as any other.'

'Have you ever seen this particular work or design before?'

Rasher shook his head. 'No, definitely not. I'd recognize it if I had — it's very distinctive, not to mention he's a lefty, like myself, and in this game, we're like hen's teeth.' He took his glasses off and slipped them back into his pocket. 'Sorry I can't tell you more.'

Chris looked at the photo for a moment. 'One more question.'

'Fire away.'

'Any idea why someone would get a tattoo like that?' He paused. 'Especially a woman. It's so big…'

Rasher slurped as he finished his drink, setting the bottle down. 'I get what you're saying. Nowadays getting a tattoo is just a fashion, but it used to mean something.' He flexed his swollen knuckles. 'They originated as a way of signifying your tribe, your clan. Around these parts there are only two reasons to get an elaborate tattoo — other than those crappy Oriental things that the kids go for. I mean a proper, symbolic, tattoo.'

'Like what?' Kennedy asked.

'Well, one is a celebration — the birth of a child, getting married, winning a competition, stuff like that.'

'And the other?'

'To show you belong, that you're part of something.' The big man tapped a stubby finger at the photos still lying on the table. 'Those tattoos, those wings? A tattoo like that is all about being a part of something.'

ANGEL CULT IN WICKLOW HILLS

Gardai are currently investigating a bizarre case involving redheaded tattooed young women. The so-far unidentified women were each found with mysterious angel wings tattooed on their backs.

The discovery of a recent hit-and-run victim found with such a tattoo has been linked to another unsolved death of nine years. In both cases the dead woman had the same design tattooed onto her back.

Authorities are now trying to figure out the girls' identities and are working on the theory that they may both have been part of a cult which brands its members, and is potentially located in the Wicklow/Dublin Mountains close to where the bodies were found.

Anyone who recognizes the angel-wing tattoo (pictured above) should contact the newspaper directly at this email address ...

R eilly felt herself slump upon reading the article. Whenever the press got involved in a case like this it added complications and caused untold headaches. Not only did they have to spend time answering questions and run the gauntlet of photographers when they were out in the field but, there was the added pressure from Chief Inspector O'Brien, who was demanding a fast resolution.

'You've seen it then?' Chris stuck his head round the door of Reilly's office. He didn't wait for her reply. 'It's in all the tabloids.'

Reilly drew the paper closer, still shocked to see the photo of one of the angel tattoos beneath the headline.

'How the hell did they get their hands on that though?'

'Who knows? It's a lot easier these days when all this stuff is stored on the computer system. And all those journos have sources within the force — you scratch my back, I'll scratch yours et cetera.' The cynicism oozed out of Chris's voice.

'And the cult theory?' she asked hesitantly. 'Is that true?'

Cultism had been part of her studies at Quantico, and she'd worked firsthand on one particular case in North Carolina while still a rookie: the New Eden Cult as they had become known. Years later, she still had nightmares about it.

He shrugged. 'We have to explore every avenue ...'

Yet nobody had bothered to share this new avenue with *her*. She felt a pang of annoyance at effectively being sidelined in the investigation. She couldn't help herself respond. 'And you didn't think to tell me?'

'We were going to mention it at this morning's debrief.'

'But obviously decided that the press should hear it first,' she said, unable to conceal her annoyance.

He looked duly chastened. 'That's not how it happened, you know none of us tells those scumbags anything. James MacDonald raised the idea originally and it was late when we finished with the tattoo guy yesterday. He reckons it's a safe bet that the tattoo is indicative of some kind of membership. Of what, we're not sure. Sorry, we just haven't had the chance to—'

She cut him off. 'Fine. So what next? I take it you've heard from O'Brien about this?' She indicated the newspaper.

He nodded wearily. 'He was waiting in the office first thing when I arrived this morning. He's absolutely livid.'

'I don't blame him. This is going to raise hell.'

'It has already. Anyway, we'd better go. He's giving a statement at ten and wants us all there.'

She narrowed her eyes. 'Us?' She liked being part of the investigating team but could do without this exposure.

He nodded. 'It's an order.'

'Crap.' Reilly's day had started badly and clearly wasn't going to get any better.

'OK, the jackals are outside, I've got to tell them something. Bring me up to speed in two minutes. Now.' Chief Inspector O'Brien glared at Reilly, Chris and Kennedy, his deep red complexion and unusually unkempt flyaway gray hair giving away the depth of his frustration with the media reports. His assistant sat in the corner of his office, fingers poised over her laptop, ready to record every word they said.

Reilly spoke first. 'Hit and run four days ago — a seventeen-year-old female apparently wandering the country lanes around Roundwood in her nightclothes, no ID, nothing distinctive except a tattoo of angel wings on her back. And she was five months pregnant.'

Chris picked up the thread. 'We canvassed the immediate area with the help of the local police but nothing turned up. No one knows her, no one's ever seen her. However, on the plus side, we've since identified the vehicle that hit her and had the driver's father in for questioning. Seems it was a straightforward hit and run and he fled the scene. He is now out of the country but word from the Met is we should have him in custody imminently.'

'Well, that's something at least. But if it's a straightforward hit and run, where are the press going with this cult nonsense?' the chief asked as his assistant tapped down some notes behind them.

'We linked the tattoo with a cold case from nine years ago,' Reilly continued. 'Another redheaded girl, though older, pretty much the same tattoo design. Found dead in a patch of woods in the Wicklow Mountains. COD was listed as exposure at the time.'

Kennedy spoke next. 'We talked to a retired detective, James MacDonald, the chief investigator at the time. He believes this girl may have originated from a hippy commune or something similar.'

They all fell silent and O'Brien looked up, waiting for someone to continue. 'So is it a cult thing or not?'

'At this point, we can't say. However, the similarities in the girls' appearance as well as the tattoos suggests there may be more in play than our initial discovery. Based on these similarities, we're now working on the theory that they may well have originated from the same group — be it a group of New Age Travelers or otherwise.'

'Otherwise? Why do I get the feeling I'm not going to like the otherwise bit?'

Reilly spoke up. 'Well, like the newspapers suggest, there's the possibility that the tattoo is some form of … branding.'

The chief pinched the bridge of his nose. 'Christ.'

'Sir, it's just one theory at this point,' Chris said. 'We piece together shreds of information and, little by little, we form a picture. You understand that.'

'I understand that,' growled O'Brien, 'but the press don't. They watch *CSI* and think everything is solved inside an hour by a team of good-looking scientists, and comes wrapped up in a big red bow.' He nodded towards his assistant. 'Print that off for me.' She duly closed her laptop and hurried from the room. O'Brien perched on the edge of his desk. 'So what do I give them?'

'The cat's out of the bag now,' Kennedy said. 'We give the public what's helpful to us, and keep back the stuff we don't want them to know. It may be no bad thing, as sooner or later we'd have needed to launch a public appeal to try and identify these girls anyway.' He looked at Reilly, who nodded. 'The photo of the tattoo is already public, sir, so we focus on that, see if it rings a bell with anyone.'

O'Brien nodded. 'Fine.' He stood up, and looked them over. 'I suppose you lot look presentable enough. Let's go.'

Kennedy looked at him in horror. 'You want us all to come to the press conference?'

O'Brien nodded. 'Of course. It will look better if I have a team beside me, backing me up. Makes it look like we actually know what we're doing…'

Kennedy hitched up his trousers and straightened his tie. 'Josie will have a fit,' he said to Chris. 'She hates this tie.'

HALF AN HOUR LATER, Reilly stood behind O'Brien and gazed out over the assembled journalists, the cameras flashes half-blinding her.

Standing like this reminded her of prize-giving days at school, when the award-winning students were paraded up to pose with the principal and get a photo taken. It always struck her that it was much more about the school and how well it had done than actually celebrating the achievements of the individuals. She'd hated school, the cliques, the teams and had sought solace in her books. And Jess. She hadn't needed validation from anyone else but her back then.

O'Brien briefly outlined the facts of the case, referring to the notes his assistant had typed up.

'As you can see, our enquiries are ongoing.' He paused, turning on his most sincere expression. 'In cases like this we rely very strongly on the public to help us. We will therefore be distributing detailed pictures of the tattoo at the end of this briefing, and would ask anyone who recognizes it to please contact us on the information helpline. All calls will, of course, be treated with the utmost confidentiality.'

Chris sighed, and muttered under his breath, 'A thousand nut jobs a day, that's what we'll get.'

O'Brien stepped out from behind the podium and lined himself up in front of the investigative team. Reilly hoped deep down inside that the hassle they were about to go through as a result of going public with the tattoo might, just might, be rewarded with something useful.

The cameras flashed, blinding them for a moment, then O'Brien clapped his hands together and addressed the journalists. 'Now, ladies and gentlemen. Any questions for our investigators?'

The questions rained down, microphones were thrust forward and a scrum of eager faces swarmed around.

'Why is he branding them?'

'Is it a paedophile ring?'

'What are we dealing with here, some kind of religious nut job? Is it true you're looking at a cult? Is it a new Waco?'

Reilly sighed and discreetly flexed her foot to halt the onset of cramp. As usual the questions were piling up, but so far the answers were frustratingly elusive.

L ater that afternoon, Reilly was back at the lab. Before her on the workbench lay the remnants of what was left in the evidence box from the cold case: the dead girl's clothes and old, well-worn footwear.

'Can you come over here a sec?' she called out to Rory as he worked away at his own bench.

'Be right there, boss, just finishing up here,' he said, not even lifting his head as he delicately placed two sample slides into the 'Perkin'. The Elemental Analysis machine was used for determining mineral content and quantity from trace material. It burned the samples in pure oxygen and measured the elements present.

Following Reilly's direction, the GFU had embarked on a detailed reconnaissance soil map of the entire country, and it was hoped that in time any sample could be matched to within a small area with only basic analysis. There was already a general soil map dating back to the 1980s, which was far less specific but still useful in pointing them in the right direction.

Rory closed the door of the 'Perkin' before snapping off his latex gloves.

'You're testing soil samples?' Reilly asked.

He nodded. 'I'm running comparison tests on the mud Gary collected from the hit-and-run scene.'

She turned back toward the items on the bench. 'These shoes from the cold case; there's deep tread full of dried mud on the soles. I've scraped back some of the fresher stuff — most likely from the last few steps she took through the surrounding countryside — but there seems to be older clay and stone particles embedded into some of the treads.' Reilly indicated the shoe she had been examining. She had used tweezers to pick out some rock particles and placed them in a petri dish; alongside was another dish holding the clay.

'If we can compare the soil from the inner tread with the general soil map, it might help us get an idea of the terrain on her route before she reached the hillside.'

'What about the rock particles? You want me to run those too?'

Reilly nodded. 'Please.'

Rory carefully picked up the evidence bag containing the other trainer and carried it over to his bench where he gently placed it so as not to dislodge any of the soil. The computer screen attached to the Elemental Analysis machine had a message flashing. Rory moved the cursor and clicked print. The central printer sparked to life in the corner of the lab.

He opened a file on his desk and took out the analytical printout from the traces of clay collected from the hit-and-run site, the ones they'd suspected of having fallen from the vehicle involved on impact. He glanced at the document as he made his way to where the printer was frantically spewing out a complicated series of icons and letters.

As he watched, the results started to appear upside down, and he knew what to look for — the more unusual, rare elements that indicated that the samples were the same. Even before the printout was finished and despite being upside-down he already knew the answer.

'Good news,' he called over to Reilly, optimism in his voice, 'looks like we have another nail for our van driver's coffin.'

She smiled, knowing only too well the feeling of uncovering irrefutable evidence that would help put away the guilty party.

He started to recalibrate the machine by burning some benzoic acid in the combustion chamber. This would remove any interference with the tests he was preparing to do with the soil and rock samples from the shoes. As the machine was cleaning and adjusting, Rory set about separating the soil samples from the soles. Pulling on fresh gloves he flicked on the circular light and magnifier and pulled it across so he could take a closer look.

There was a fairly even coating of mud filling the treads, although a couple of them at the toe and heel were clear. Rory took a long slender tool — like a dentist's excavator — from a tray at the back of his desk. He began to gently poke at the soil, and when it started to crumble and flake, he took the shoe between his hands and bent it gently. This action allowed the hardened soil in some of the treads to come loose in one piece. He then placed a piece of tissue over the sole and turned it over so the soil came out and rested on the tissue paper. Now he was left with a couple of pyramid-shaped samples, the larger side of the pyramid being the newest soil and the point being the oldest.

Rory picked up one piece with a set of tweezers and held it under the magnifying viewer. Even with a naked eye he could see definite differences in the cross section. The older part of the sample was stony gray in color whereas the newer part appeared darker and more peat-like.

He then set about the difficult process of taking a separate sample from each end of the pyramid. When he was finished placing the four samples — two from each end of the sample — into vials, he proceeded to run the tests.

The beauty of analysis with the 'Perkin' was the speed at which it gave a result. Within the hour Rory had four reports giving him the chemical make-up of each sample.

Sitting down at his computer he opened a soil analysis program, input the two sets of data and waited while the on-screen hourglass icon indicated the search of their reconnaissance soil map.

After a few seconds the screen blinked and the message he didn't want appeared.

'No Match Found.'

He sighed.

He then manually inputted the details into the older general soil database, which would give him general non-specific pointers. The results came back almost instantly with three possible areas in which the samples could have originated: Sligo/Mayo, Donegal/Derry and Wicklow.

Rory gathered the printouts and headed for Reilly's office.

'I think we can safely say that the girl was local unless she walked all the way from Mayo the night she died,' Rory stated as Reilly looked up. 'The samples don't match anything on our own soil map, but the general map shows three possibles: two in the North West from Mayo to Derry, over three hundred kilometers away, and the other from where she was found in Wicklow.'

'Are the results consistent for all samples?' Reilly asked.

'No, there is a difference, both on visual examination and on further analysis. The older material is high in mineral content, it's almost 100 percent granite. Not solid rock, but more like compact granite dust, possibly sediment from a river or something like that,' he speculated.

Reilly nodded.

'Something else, too — traces of paraffin and petrol at a similar ratio to what was found on the other girl.'

Reilly's head snapped up. 'Same as what was in the swabs?'

'I think so.' He checked his files. 'Yeah, toenail swabs it says here.'

Her mind raced. It was small but it gave them strong reason to suspect that both girls had at one stage been present on the same terrain.

'That's fantastic, Rory, thank you!'

Rory allowed himself a smile. 'No worries, boss. Anything else you need before I get stuck into the mountain of paperwork on my desk?'

She shook her head, and picked up the phone to call the detectives. 'Hey, never let it be said that I'd stand in the way of officialdom.'

21

'Hello, I'm ringing about the young girl in the paper, the one with the tattoo ... it's terrible altogether, I've not been able to sleep thinking about the poor thing.'

The Garda tipline operator's voice was gentle and friendly. 'Thank you for your call, madam. What information do you have about her?'

'Well, I was just saying to the girls at bingo last night that she looks a bit like the Farrell girl that used to live at the end of my street. Nice family, would always give you a friendly wave when you passed. Mary said I should call the number from the news — it said any information might help.'

'Yes, anything that rings a bell might indeed be useful to our investigation. Is there anything else you can tell me?' the operator asked as she automatically logged the call detail into the system.

'I had to take half a Xanax to get off to sleep last night. It's just terrible that such a beautiful young girl was left alone like that, how could anyone ...?' The woman's voice trailed off.

'Can you give me an address for the Farrell family you

mentioned?' The operator knew from experience that this was yet another time waster, but she needed to be sure just in case. She tried to refocus the caller's mind.

'Yes, of course,' the lady continued with a sniff. 'They lived two doors down from me. Number 23 Woodside, Oranmore, Galway. They moved out a good few years back now, can't remember exactly when, but my Paddy was still alive so I'd say ninety-four or five — maybe even ninety-six. I really hope it isn't her though, lovely little thing she was, the youngest, can't remember her name, Aoife, I think ... she was probably around ten or so when they moved,' she babbled on, and the operator had to resist the urge to roll her eyes. 'I'm not sure where they moved to but some of the girls were saying the council might have a record of it. Do you think you'll be able to track them down?'

Doing the maths, little Aoife was in her late twenties now and the caller was typical of those who often phoned in these circumstances: elderly, lonely and fearful. They meant well but they didn't realize their calls were a hindrance rather than a help.

'We'll certainly try, madam. Thank you for your call, it's been most helpful,' she said, barely able to make a note of the details before the phone rang yet again.

22

Later that evening, Reilly pounded the dark streets, her running shoes splashing though puddles and scattering piles of windblown leaves. It was past nine when she'd got home, but some days she just needed to get out and run, clear her head, no matter how late it was. And tonight she'd felt the urge all the more.

It was stupid really. She'd long ago stopped caring and celebrating these things, but this was the first time she'd never received so much as a single card or phone call.

Even Mike was too caught up in his new romance to remember, she mused, feeling truly sorry for herself. Maybe she should stop resisting joining Facebook; at least then her 'friends' would automatically be reminded that today was her thirty-third birthday. She'd sort of hoped that Chris might remember at least, given that he'd wheedled the date out of her before, back when they'd shared such things. But obviously those days were gone.

Reilly slowed for a road crossing, briefly passed under the bright lights of a junction, then disappeared into the shadows of the pavement, shaded by a line of tall trees.

Self-pity was not an emotion she liked to indulge and so she forced her mind to focus back on the events of the day, particularly the new possibility of a cult being involved. Everything they'd discovered — the tattoos, the girls' mysterious lack of belonging and otherworldliness — could indeed suggest that both had once been part of a cult. Given the latest discovery of corresponding trace elements, it seemed the girls had almost certainly spent time in a similar area too.

But since there was almost a decade between the discovery of the bodies, if they had been members of the same cult, it would have to have been in existence for some time.

When Reilly had worked on the case involving the New Eden Cult back in the US, there had been some similarities. Two extended North Carolina families called Bullard, who owned a two-hundred-acre farm and woodland, decided under the leadership of Ruddy Bullard Snr that the world was gone to hell and it was time to sever all links with it. The group had moderate religious beliefs but were extreme survivalists. They had spent years gathering supplies and becoming self-sufficient. They had pretty much built a fortress and a small army by the time one of the younger Bullard boys came to the attention of the Greensboro PD for his part in an assault.

When they eventually tracked him down to New Eden, they were rebuked by Ruddy Snr, and when they came back with a warrant and reinforcements, the leader had called a code red. The families hunkered down in their fortress and a high-profile three-week stand-off ensued.

The FBI were called in within days, and Reilly's old mentor and friend Daniel Forrest had profiled Ruddy and three other senior family members. Reilly was one of the many officers stationed there for the duration of the stand-off, as well as the subsequent clean-up and investigation.

The clean-up was the part that still resonated with her; the faces of the kids in the barn, teenagers who looked so much younger and more innocent than their peers at the local mall or high school had ever done. They had discovered a small township inside the compound. The group had collected everything from generator fuel to tinned food; enough supplies to out live a nuclear winter, complete with bunkers where some of the clan — mostly the younger kids — were discovered gassed to death as part of a mass suicide. Sixty-three men, women and children dead, and four officers too.

But the reason the follow-up investigation had lasted so long was the kids. It seemed Ruddy had wanted to widen the gene pool so that when the outside world destroyed itself, they could flourish and repopulate, aided by the dozen or so non-family members who had been abducted and brought to the compound from as far away as Seattle. Tracking the children's identities had taken months; some of them had been missing for several years, and Reilly had helped match DNA from missing children's reports to New Eden victims.

Yet something about the cult theory for their current investigation didn't sit well with Reilly.

All too often, cults were about male dominance, sexual and otherwise. Yet, there was no evidence of sexual abuse — or indeed any kind of physical abuse — on either of the girls. They were both well nourished, healthy and indeed the lack of dental work suggested that they had had very wholesome diets.

Reilly glanced at her GPS watch. She was running an eight-minute-mile pace and barely out of breath.

And what of the algae? How did this fit in? Was the supposed cult's homestead situated somewhere near those lakes and mountain streams Chris mentioned were so prevalent in the area? And if such a group did exist and none of the locals seemed to know about it, how had it remained undetected for all this time?

Without context the very notion was simply another mystery.

She felt there was something more, something out there, a piece of evidence, a clue, something that would help the whole thing fall into place like the last tumbler that opens a lock. But what was it?

Despite the cold, the sweat was building up on Reilly's forehead. She wiped at it with her sleeve and picked up speed as she neared Ranelagh. Pushing herself harder, her feet danced over the wet pavement, the extra exertion pushing out every thought and instinct except the urge to suck in more oxygen. She rounded the last turn and sprinted all the way to her front gate before slowing down and dropping her pace to a gentle jog.

One more lap around the block to cool down, then she'd finally allow herself to relax and have some dinner. Pushing herself, driving herself, that was all she knew. She applied it to her work life *and* her personal life. If you work hard enough, push yourself — some might say punish yourself — enough, then eventually you will get what you want.

Did it work? She slowed to a walk as she approached her door, and slipped her key from a pocket in her sweats. Sometimes yes, sometimes no, but it was the only way she knew to assuage the guilt of failures past.

She slid the key into the lock and opened the door. Welcome home to an empty house, another night alone with just her thoughts and a glass of wine for company. Happy birthday.

Pushing hard may be a good tactic for work, she thought regretfully, but it sure wasn't doing anything for her social life.

She threw her running clothes in the laundry basket and stood in the shower. Time to try and forget about work for a few hours before it drove her crazy. Let the subconscious mind work on it while she watched ten-year-old repeats of *Friends* and tried to make a single glass of wine last all evening.

She was settling down to do just that when the shrill sound

of the phone made her jump. But the number on the caller display made her grin.

'Happy birthday to you … happy birthday to you ….' A familiar voice with an unmistakeable Virginia burr sang.

'Well, thank you, Daniel, but I'm glad to say it's nearly over,' she replied with a smile in her voice.

'Oh contraire, my dear. It's early in the day here.'

'And where exactly is "here" these days? I can't keep up with you since you retired.' The former FBI profiler now worked in a private consultation role and frequently traveled around the country.

'Clearwater, and forget retiring, I've never been busier. But enough about sunshine and easy living. How's the Emerald Isle treating you?'

'Great,' Reilly lied. They chatted a while about their respective work lives, Reilly feeling more than a little jealous of Daniel's beach house on Florida's Gulf Coast. It seemed his consulting practice was going from strength to strength. 'Todd is with the Tampa force down here too.' Reilly had met Daniel's son several times before — a fellow Quantico recruit who was shaping up to be a real chip off the old block.

'That's great. Tell him I said hi.'

'I will, and remember if you ever get tired of fighting crime in the North Atlantic, there's always an opening down here for you. Come for a holiday sometime, I'm sure you could use some vitamin D by now.'

'Thanks, I'll keep that in mind.'

As they said their goodbyes, and given the week she was having, Reilly already knew that the possibility would be very much on her mind.

23

I feel the weight upon me, the weight of expectation, of fear. I have failed once before, and now the specter of failure looms over me again. I have sworn to protect them, to shield them from a toxic world, but the fear has crept into our own world — the fear of uncertainty.

Our safety is everything, it is what defines us, what makes us who we are. We are complete, one family, one being, but now I see that our world is fragile. Like an egg, our shell is all too precious, and once it is broken it can never be repaired, things can never be the same.

Beyond the walls are cruelty and deceit, lies and pain, aging and death. As long as we are strong we can resist these things, but if we let our guard down, all manner of pestilence will enter.

But now I fear the walls may be breached, the shell cracked. Our family is cracking, fear and anxiety haunt our dreams, unanswered questions hover on our lips. How will we stay strong, stay together?

I have been here before, suffered through this once already — and this is a suffering too much for one man to bear. And so my failures haunt me.

I can see their eyes at night, shining in the darkness, accusing me *of my greatest failure, failure to protect those that I love. What more damning accusation can there be? How can I sleep not knowing where my darlings are, that they are gone because of me, that in their hour of need I was not there?*

But now I must again head out into the wicked world to find another, guide them to our home, welcome them to the bosom of our family.

STEPHEN AND JULIA DIGNAM entered the police station the following morning. Both were in their early fifties but looked older, the sleepless nights and worry taking their toll. Julia linked her husband's arm through her own and in her other hand she held a ring binder close to her chest.

Written on the spine in faded ink was one word: Megan.

The Dignam's daughter had vanished without a trace twenty years before and every new story of a missing child or unidentified body brought back a new flood of familiar emotions — fear, hope, the possibility of closure after so many years. But they were realists, and had long stopped hoping for the dream conclusion to their nightmare.

They longed now just to know what had happened to Megan, to have a final resting place to visit, a place to lay flowers — somewhere their beautiful daughter could rest in peace. Their lives had ended the day Megan disappeared and finding her was their only desire while they were still breathing.

Like so many others who'd made contact since the public appeal about the tattooed girls, the Dignams were compelled to come here, to have somebody listen to their story and to maybe find some truth — even if that truth meant hearing the worst news any parent could ever hear.

They gave the garda on duty all the details they could,

showed them photos and old documents from her missing person case.

And then the Dignams went home to continue doing the very thing they had spent the last two decades doing — wait.

24

All week the Incident Room was inundated with more false leads following the press release detailing the tattoo. At times it had resembled a trading floor on Wall Street, especially in the first twelve hours.

Ignoring the crank calls, they seemed to be divided into three categories: those who thought they might have seen angel-wing tattoos somewhere recently; those who seemed to remember once seeing a girl with a similar tattoo at some point in the past; and, most heartbreakingly, those who had a missing family member and were holding out hope that the remaining unidentified girl might belong to them.

Such cases were the hardest to deal with. Almost all of them were on record and already reviewed, but they still owed it to the families to at least give them a response.

They say hope springs eternal, but it also blinded some to reality. The people calling in about their missing relatives were not only from all over the country, but also went back decades, and included not just redheads, but blonds, brunettes and those whose hair 'looked sort of red in the right light.' Each got a call back, thanking them for their time and effort, but none produced anything useful.

Between them the investigative team divided up the leads and tried to follow up on them. O'Brien gave them some extra resources, but it was still a long, slow process.

As the calls continued to come in, the press stayed on the 'Angels' — and that meant that O'Brien stayed on their backs. For the first few days he'd called every morning for an update, but as the information they were getting from the public proved increasingly worthless his calls became less frequent but progressively more frantic.

'Isn't there anything?' he complained at the end of the week.

'I'm sorry, sir, but once again there's been nothing especially useful,' replied Reilly. She could hear him sucking on his teeth as he thought.

'And the evidence from the girls ... anything there?'

'Pieces of a jigsaw, sir. Until we have further information they are just tantalizing bits and pieces.'

O'Brien gave a deep sigh. 'Very well. I hope to hear from you.'

Reilly replaced the phone on its receiver. *I hope to have a reason to call you*, she thought.

Most of those who thought they had seen either girl could be ruled out quickly. Either their memories were so vague as to be worthless, or they had supposedly seen the hit-and-run girl her since her death, or the location was so far away as to be unlikely.

'Given what we know,' Kennedy said, as he and Chris sifted through another batch of notes passed on by the information hotline, 'I think we can rule out this report that our girl was seen last week on a beach in Ibiza.'

Reports of the angel-wings tattoo were again mostly too vague to be of any use. Most viewings seemed to be from some indistinguishable point in the past — on a beach somewhere, or a gym changing room. Nothing solid that would be of any actual use.

There was, however, one genuine lead from a social worker who called in to report that he had once dealt with a young boy who'd been tattooed in a similar manner. Reilly returned the call without delay.

'Simon Keogh?'

'Speaking.'

'Reilly Steel, GFU. You called our hotline in relation to our recent media request for assistance?'

'I did indeed.'

'You mentioned that you thought you'd seen a similar tattoo?'

'Yes. It was a strange case. A young lad about twelve, red haired like your girls. I remember reading something about a winged tattoo on the file at the time but didn't see it myself.'

'Do you have a name?'

He sighed. 'That's the problem. We never actually knew his real name, but we called him Connor.'

'Is there anything else you remember about the boy?'

'Yes. He was about nine years old, a bit wild, almost feral I'd say, and would only speak Irish. Listen, I'm sorry, I don't have the full details to hand. I'll go through my records at work tomorrow and call you back,' he promised.

'Thanks.' But Reilly guessed that this may well turn out to be yet another dead end.

25

Lucy picked up the coffee cup and took a sip before realizing it was stone cold.

'Damn,' she said out loud to the empty office at her third failed attempt to drink a cup. She kept getting sucked into the missing person reports in front of her and forgetting all about her coffee. The growing sense of urgency and frustration at the lack of progress was really starting to hit her hard.

Like some of the desperate families who'd made contact after the case had gone public, Lucy knew exactly what it felt like to have lost and to be helpless to do anything about it. Except now she could do something. She could try and help these people. But she was bone tired. Every day this week she'd come to work an hour early and left three hours late, yet they were still scratching at crumbs.

'Who are you, honey?' Lucy whispered, as she caught sight once more of the photo of the tattooed dead girl. These days she was seeing it even when she closed her eyes. Especially when she closed her eyes.

Lucy picked up another missing person file and opened it.

The picture of the little girl's face — so achingly young — immediately jumped out and she felt a lump in her throat.

Starting to read, she went through the details of the report. Statements from the family and neighbors, notes from the investigating officers, all so similar to the dozens of other cases she'd already reviewed.

But then she saw something in the medical notes and leaned forward.

Fracture to the radius bone, aged five.

It could be nothing; hundred of kids picked up similar fractures all the time. Still, she picked up the phone on her desk and dialed the relevant extension.

'Nikki, I need to order up a couple of x-rays.' Lucy rattled off the file number. 'Yes, it's very urgent.'

26

'I think I might have something ...' Lucy sounded breathless as she stood in Reilly's doorway.

Reilly immediately noticed how drawn the younger girl looked — her face was gaunt, eyes dark and sunk deep. She had obviously been burning the candle at both ends. Reilly knew only too well the obsession that took hold when working a case, and how trivial normal, everyday things like food and sleep could become, but she worried she was infecting her staff with her own crazy work ethic.

She was often haunted by thoughts of previous situations she'd been unable to control, the people she'd been unable to save.

The faces crept into her memory in a sequence of images: her mother, Jess, the children of New Eden, and Emily, the 'girl in the well' — a missing child that had been found much too late.

Reilly could still see her face, pale and dirt-covered, her little doll clutched to her chest — just the way they had found her. If only she'd run faster, if only she'd thought to look in the well sooner.

But she had been too slow, and the waters had risen inexorably, minute by minute, until…

Worse still, she didn't just recall what they found down that dark well, she also imagined what it had been like for Emily, trapped, lying still, paralyzed by horror as the water level rose higher and higher.

Obsession was not always a good thing, Reilly knew, but if managed correctly, it could sometimes be the difference between life and death.

'What have you got?' she asked Lucy now.

'From the missing person records. A red-haired girl that fits the description of our hit-and-run victim went missing in Navan ten years ago, aged seven. Her name is Sarah Forde.'

Reilly mentally ran the calculations. 'So she'd be seventeen now. The age seems right. What's the background? She was hardly a runaway at that age.'

'According to the report, the family maintained she was a bit wild but wouldn't just take off. She'd done it before though, taken off after a family row only to turn up at her gran's. It was called in, but reported as a false alarm as soon as she was found.'

'I'm guessing there's a reason it caught your eye …' Reilly urged her.

'Yes,' Lucy replied, pausing. 'She broke her right arm when she was five years old.'

'Do we have the x-rays?'

'Supposed to come through this afternoon.'

'Excellent. When they do, let's get Julius to take a look, him being the medical expert.'

Lucy groaned. 'Please don't let him hear you call him that — his head is big enough as it is.'

27

'What are the chances of this guy being at home I wonder?' Kennedy said, reaching into his inside pocket for a long overdue nicotine fix.

'Don't know but it's worth a shot.' Chris had been thinking about MacDonald's theory since they'd spoken to him.

If the retired detective had been right all this time, and the unidentified girl from the cold case had indeed been an eco-warrior type, someone who'd dropped out of mainstream society, it would explain a lot. It would certainly explain why nobody had been reported missing, and no one had come forward to claim the girl's body.

MacDonald had pointed out that they were a suspicious bunch that would not give the police the time of day, never mind answer questions about a potential member.

Kennedy leaned against the side of the car as he inhaled deeply on his quickly disappearing cigarette. 'Just because MacDonald thinks this "Van Winkle" guy is still around doesn't mean we'll be able to find him.'

'Look, if you don't fancy the walk just come out and say it.' Chris knew Kennedy wasn't particularly fond of muddy forest trails, or exertion of any kind for that matter, so his partner staying behind would save his legs. Not to mention Chris's ears. 'MacDonald said you can still make out the old bits of canvas from the road, so it can't be that far. I'll be up and back in five if you want to stay here.'

'Nah, it's fine, the fresh air will do me good,' Kennedy said, plumes of smoke escaping his nose and mouth as he stubbed the butt beneath his foot, propelling himself away from the car with his posterior as he did so.

Anybody who actually knew Rip Van Winkle's real name was either long moved on or dead. The name had stuck after local school kids had christened him back in the eighties because of his long gray hair and beard.

When a particular part of the forest earmarked for road development had turned into a battleground between the 'Friends of the Earth' and local authorities, Rip had been one of the senior 'warriors'.

MacDonald had been unable to shed any light on the man's actual identity; the only thing he could say for sure was that if the girl had indeed come from the hippy encampment, Old Rip would know. Whether he'd be more willing to help now, given how much time had passed, was another question entirely.

Chris and Kennedy followed a path between two way markers through a grassy area of picnic tables and beyond under a canopy of leafless oak trees, the indigenous trees that had been the source of all the confrontation years before.

'Think he'll talk to us?' Kennedy panted after a couple of minutes, as he struggled to keep pace with Chris.

'Looks like we'll soon find out.' Chris indicated up ahead to a collection of faded tarpaulin sheets, wooded pallets and plastic, just as MacDonald had described.

'Hello?' Chris called out in a cheery, unthreatening tone.

No response. Several signs were nailed to posts around the

camp, all with a decidedly 'green' message: *He who Plants a Tree loves Others beside Himself, This is YOUR planet, SAVE it.*

Mr Van Winkle clearly still strongly believed in the cause even if he was now fighting the battle alone. Chris and Kennedy stopped where they were, not wanting to intrude too much even though it was a public park. 'Good afternoon, anybody there?' Chris called out again.

'If you're calling about a television license, I don't have one.' The detectives both quickly whipped around at the sound of the voice behind them.

Walking towards them was an old, wiry-looking man dressed in shorts and a raincoat, pushing an ancient 'high nelly' bike. Trailing behind him was an equally aged black mongrel, its tongue nearly dragging on the ground.

'How can I help you two ... walkers?' the man asked, looking them both up and down suspiciously, his gaze resting on Kennedy who looked about as far away from a hillwalker as you could get.

'Hello there, Mr ...?'

There was a heavy silence.

Chris continued quickly. 'I'm Detective Delaney and this is my partner Detective Kennedy. We were wondering if we might ask you a few questions in relation to a case we are working on.'

The man eyed them both again and put his bike up against a tree, but he remained silent, waiting for Chris to continue.

'We are trying to establish the identity of a women found dead not too far from here several years back and we wondered if you might be able to help.'

'Should I be asking for a phone call or a solicitor, Detective?'

'No, no, not at all. We understand that you've lived around this area for some time, and so you might be able to help,' Kennedy assured him.

'I've seen a lot of people come and go through here over the years, that's for sure.' He poured some water into a plastic bowl and the parched mutt threw his snout in it. 'What makes you think I'd know this person?'

'I'll be honest, sir, we're not entirely sure. Our interest in this case has recently been revived because of a similar incident and we hoped...'

'Ah, I think I know where you're coming from. I might live in a hut with no television but I do read the papers,' Rip said, smiling at their obvious surprise. 'Your comrades called here many times, flashing pictures and asking questions about a tattooed girl.' There was a faint chuckle in his voice. 'And now all these years later you're back asking the same questions, because of another tattooed girl. Well I hope those two rest in peace, because if they're waiting for justice from you lot it might be a while off yet.'

'Sir, we are simply bringing ourselves up-to-date with the older incident to try and help with the latest,' Chris said, taking a photograph of the cold-case girl from his pocket. 'Some of the original investigation team believed, rightly or wrongly, that the girl may have been known to somebody from your community back then. We hoped to rule that in or out.' He handed him the photo. 'Could you at least take another look and tell us if you recognize the girl or the tattoo?'

Rip took the photo in his weathered hands and looked at the same image he'd been shown years before. 'I still don't know her, Detectives, and if there's another similar case ... well, take a look around here...' He indicated the surrounding trees, completely empty apart from the fading remains of long-abandoned encampments.

'The war is long over and there's nobody left but me and Bertie,' he said, nodding towards the dog lying with his head between his paws, his opaque aged eyes staring up mournfully at them.

There was no war left to fight, Chris thought. The motorway was long built but Rip had evidently fallen in love with the place and decided to stay on, long after the others had shipped off to some other battle ground, returned to college, or more likely, gone over to the dark side and got corporate jobs.

'What about the tattoo then? It's quite distinctive. Did you ever notice any of your people sporting something similar?' Kennedy coaxed.

'Look, this place here...' Rip scratched his head as if trying to explain something to people who spoke a completely different language. 'This place was never about *us*; we were merely protecting this place for our kids, for *your* kids.' His tone was completely sincere. 'People like us don't go in for collective ways of living, we're all about being individuals, despite having a common cause. Sure, some of the folks who fought here might have had various types of body art, but it was individual to them and who they were — nothing to do with the cause. It's not how we do things.'

He looked again at the photo. 'I'd remember that, and I'd remember her too. If you told me a name I couldn't be sure, a lot passed through, but a face ... I always remember a face.' He handed the photo back to Chris. 'We told your colleagues the same thing before. I hope for her sake this time you believe me. You're thinking that the tattoo might well be tribal, but believe me, this girl wasn't one of our tribe.'

28

'We've had a hit for a possible match on our hit and run,' Reilly announced to the lab team later that afternoon. Gary was inputting information into Pegasus while Julius was peering into one of the viewing lenses of the comparison microscope with Lucy close by. 'Medical records are just in. I'd like to get some opinions on these x-rays.'

She clipped two pairs of x-rays on to a light box and flicked a switch to illuminate the images.

'The set on the right are from a missing person report; the others recently taken from our hit-and-run victim during autopsy.' She turned to Julius, who thanks to his surgeon's training at Queen's University was the most medically minded of the team. 'Any initial thoughts?'

'Well...' He studied both sets of x-rays for a long moment before beginning his prognosis. 'The young girl's fracture is a closed fracture, probably caused by a garden variety trip and fall. It would have healed up nicely as it's transverse. I'd imagine it was in a cast for a few weeks.'

'By closed you mean simple, as in not a clean break caused by major trauma,' Reilly put in by way of clarification.

'Yes, looks like a minor injury, and I'm pretty sure it would have been classed by a physician as a Grade One.'

The team turned their attention to the x-ray taken from the hit-and-run victim.

'Looks like a match to me given the positioning,' Lucy said. 'I can see evidence of trauma in the same area.'

'Correct.' Julius picked up a pen and lightly circled the area along the bone belonging to the hit-and-run victim. 'There is an abundance of calcification in this area. When bones heal they overproduce additional bone, making the fracture site not only stronger, but also easier to spot in newer x-rays.' He stood back a little from the light box. 'If you compare where I've just traced that line halfway across that raised calcified bit, it certainly looks to be proportionately in the same spot as well as being the same shape on both sets.'

Reilly nodded. 'Pretty conclusive then.' She picked up the missing person file marked Sarah Forde and turned to look at the others. 'So it appears our first Fallen Angel now has a name.'

LATER THAT DAY, Chris and Kennedy peered over Reilly's shoulder as she inputted data into the PC.

Having discovered the matching x-rays, the detectives made their way to the GFU to oversee the final and possibly most decisive element of the identification exercise.

'So how does this work?' Kennedy asked her.

'Don't forget to explain it in one-syllable words for him,' Chris chipped in, 'and definitely no technical terms.'

'It's facial recognition software,' Reilly said. 'Using a photograph of someone's face, the software analyzes the person's underlying bone structure and projects what they would look like at different ages.'

Chris glanced sideways at Kennedy. 'We should put a photo of you in there, see what you'll look like when you're at retirement age.'

'Another few years working with you and we'll be able to see it already,' Kennedy muttered.

Reilly clicked on the program and a childhood photo of Sarah Forde from the missing person report appeared. They all fell silent as her sweet angelic features lit up the screen.

All this time she had been alive, so close and yet so far from those who'd waited in hell for some good news. Now, a decade later, when the breakthrough was finally made it would destroy any last hope they might have retained.

Reilly set the program to project what Sarah would look like at seventeen. Spread out on the desk alongside them were the photographs of the hit-and-run victim's face taken post mortem.

There were a few moments before an image of a beautiful woman with thick, long red hair appeared. As they waited for the program to finish, rendering the image, the room stayed silent.

'Well, there we have it,' Reilly murmured eventually.

'That's freaky...'

Looking at the images side by side, there could be little doubt that the elfin features of seven-year-old Sarah Forde had developed into the fragile beauty they had found lying on the road near Roundwood.

Chris straightened up. 'So now we know who our victim is.'

Kennedy nodded. 'I only wish that thing could tell us where the hell she came from that night, where she disappeared to for all that time, or what the heck that tattoo means.'

Chris looked pensive. 'I guess the next step is to break the news to the family.'

Kennedy's miserable expression showed what he thought about that. 'God, the thought of it — and after so many years. What must it have been like for them, wondering every day whether she was alive or dead, and what might have happened to her?'

'Well, if nothing else,' Reilly said, glancing sadly at the childhood photo of little Sarah Forde, 'at least now we might be able to give them some peace.'

29

Kennedy gazed out of the window at the rolling fields as he and Chris headed north up the M3.

'It's hard not to imagine it happening to you,' he said, eyes staring vacantly at the sky. 'I think of my two and wonder what I'd do if one of them went missing,' he added. He doted on his daughters Amanda and Jo, who were seventeen and fourteen years of age respectively. 'It would be living hell.'

Chris glanced across at him. It was rare for his partner to be so serious, but the prospect of telling Sarah's parents that after so long their missing daughter had been finally found dead was not an enticing one. Nor was the suggestion that while she was alive she may have been kept by some kind of cult.

To make matters worse, they would need to ask about the circumstances of her disappearance, rake over old ground at the very worst moment of their grief in order to attempt to find some kind of link to the other girl with the same mysterious tattoo.

'I'd move heaven and earth trying to find them. But have you ever looked at the statistics? Tons of young kids go missing here every year, and most never show up again.'

'I know.'

Although he didn't have any children of his own, Chris was very close to his two-year-old god-daughter Rachel, the daughter of his best friend, and he took the role seriously, having seen firsthand how having a child had changed his friend. He could only imagine what it must be like to have the incredible responsibility of a child yourself. Not to mention such unbelievable love. He wondered if he'd ever experience it himself.

Kennedy glanced across at him. 'Let me do the talking for this one,' he said suddenly.

Chris was surprised. It was generally agreed that he had the gentler touch in such situations, and was usually able to summon up more affinity than the often brusque Kennedy. 'You sure?'

His partner nodded. 'I think I'd rather be the one to tell them than just stand by, feeling helpless. Parent to parent.'

30

The Fordes lived in a small terraced house in the suburbs of Navan. According to the records, it was the same house they had been living in when Sarah had disappeared.

Chris parked four doors up from the house, while they waited for the Family Liaison Officer. The local station had called ahead to ensure that the Fordes were home and to arrange an FLO, but had not told them what it was about, simply that they had some questions. Protocol demanded that a professional be on hand to talk to the parents after the detectives had finished their questioning.

As he looked around Chris realized it would be hard to imagine a more boring place to grow up — small-town Ireland, endless rows of streets that looked the same. Had Sarah been happy in these quiet streets?

Kennedy was already out of the car, smoking his obligatory JP Blue, something to calm his nerves before they spoke to the Fordes. The breeze whipped the smoke from his cigarette and swirled it up past his face.

Spotting the FLO pull up behind them, Chris closed the car

door and locked it. The air was cold and went straight through his thin jacket. 'Let's get this over with.'

Kennedy dropped his cigarette, ground it beneath his heel, and walked towards the bereavement officer.

The man introduced himself as Jeff O'Neill. 'I've only just got the brief on this one.' He shook his head. 'Bloody tragic. Anything else I should know before we go in?'

'Not especially. The circumstances surrounding her disappearance are not exactly clear-cut, so we'll need to see what their reaction is like.'

Chris moved toward the Forde house, followed by Kennedy and O'Neill. As they walked up the path he noticed the front curtains twitch, and an air of foreboding settled over him.

They were expected. Anticipated.

Mr Forde opened the door; his wife was right behind him, peering over his shoulder. They were both in their early fifties, but looked far older. Gray hair, sunken faces, defeat and despair written in the lines and wrinkles.

Kennedy stepped forward and quickly made the introductions.

Mr Forde ushered them in. 'We were told you were coming.' Hope and anguish played across their faces and Chris didn't envy the task Kennedy had chosen to take on.

'This way.' Mrs Forde was a small woman. She wore a pair of gray tracksuit pants and a pink 'Pro-Sport' fleece top. She led them into the lounge where a small gas fire was on, along with a massive flat screen TV which looked far too big for such a small room.

'You will have a cup of tea, won't you?' she asked, her tone jittery as she ushered them to take seats.

'That would be lovely,' Chris replied smoothly when Kennedy hesitated.

While Mrs Forde bustled about in the kitchen, her husband

fussed around by the fire. 'Is it too warm in here for you? I could turn down the heat if you like …'

Chris shook his head as Mrs Forde returned to the room with a pre-prepared tray of cups, teapot and biscuits. 'No, it's fine. A bit wintry out there today.'

The man nodded. 'Wind from the east, whips in off the sea…'

They all sipped their tea. A decidedly uncomfortable silence settled. *Get a move on,* Chris mentally urged Kennedy.

His partner duly set his tea cup down on the table, and leaned forward. 'Mr and Mrs Forde, we're here about your daughter Sarah. I'm afraid it's not good news.'

Mrs Forde's hand went straight to her mouth, and her husband automatically reached for the other one, squeezing it tightly.

Chris knew that Kennedy needed to just keep talking, to move them through the shock, and not let them settle into their grief just yet. There would be plenty of time for that once they were gone and O'Neill had taken over with his training and bereavement pack.

'An unidentified young lady was killed in a hit-and-run accident in County Wicklow approximately one week ago. Through matching up medical records, we now believe the young lady was your daughter, Sarah.'

The Fordes looked at each other, completely lost for words.

Kennedy pushed on. He reached for the file that Chris handed to him 'This is your daughter, yes?'

He held out the photo of Sarah aged seven — the one from the missing person file that they had used for the facial recognition match.

Her parents both glanced at it, and nodded in unison.

'And she broke her right arm when she was five, correct?'

Again they both nodded. 'Fell off a swing,' added Mr Forde, clearing his throat.

'Barely even cried when we brought her to the hospital,' sniffed his wife. 'Always so brave.'

Kennedy reached into the file again, and pulled out a photo of the woman from the hit and run. 'Based on her medical records — the x-rays of the broken arm — and facial recognition software, we believe that this is how Sarah would look now.'

He held the photo of the hit-and-run victim — the adult Sarah – out to them.

For a second neither of them moved. Finally, Mrs Forde reached out a trembling hand, and took the photo.

The room was silent, just the quiet hissing of the gas fire, and Mrs Forde's faint sobs as they looked at the picture. Eventually Mr Forde looked up at Kennedy. 'You're sure?'

He nodded.

'You're absolutely sure?' the mother sobbed. 'There couldn't be some kind of mistake?'

'We can't be one hundred percent sure until—'

'So it might not be her then?' Her voice rose a little. 'She could still be alive?'

Chris spoke gently. 'Mrs Forde, the x-rays and facial recognition match mean it's very likely that the girl we found is indeed your daughter. However, we would also like to take away some personal effects today for DNA analysis in order to conclusively validate our findings.'

But Mrs Forde wasn't letting go of her hope that easily. She had, after all, held onto it for ten whole years. It had become her life, her reason to continue. 'I don't think it looks like her all, Pat, do you? It couldn't be—'

'Don't, Rita... Just don't...' Her husband cut her off and Chris was somewhat taken aback by the strength of his tone. He held the photo up in front of his wife and forced her to look at it. 'That's our Sarah. These men wouldn't be here if they weren't certain.'

For a second it appeared that she was going to protest and continue to fight, but with a sudden sob her will collapsed and she rushed from the room.

Pat Forde stared at the doorway, then stood up. 'I'll be right back.'

They watched him hurry from the room after his wife, and could hear the quiet cooing of his voice from the kitchen as he tried to console her.

'It never gets any easier, does it?' Kennedy said sadly. 'Those poor people ...'

Chris turned his attention back to the file and looked at the pictures of the tattoo on Sarah Forde's back.

'They won't know anything about that,' Kennedy said determinedly.

'Still, we need to ask.'

'What? And leave them fretting and worrying about it for the next ten years?'

Chris met Kennedy's gaze. 'You know we have to follow up—'

'And you always do what you're supposed to do, don't you?' countered Kennedy angrily. 'It's not right, Chris. Not now. I don't think they could handle—'

'Handle what?' Mr Forde had returned without them noticing, padding silently in his soft blue slippers.

'We had something we wanted to ask you — something about your daughter...' Chris looked past him but his wife was nowhere to be seen.

'She's gone to lie down.'

'It's a long shot ...' Kennedy interjected.

Pat Forde perched himself back on the edge of the couch. 'We have waited years for news of Sarah, thinking about all sorts of possibilities,' he said. 'We want to know absolutely everything.'

Chris slipped the photo from the folder and handed it to

him. Despite his assertions to Kennedy, he did have sympathy for the man. Bringing up the tattoo was one thing, but the pregnancy was a different matter entirely.

Sarah's father gazed at it silently for a moment. 'What is it?' he asked finally.

'That's what we're wondering. We've got two girls, bodies found ten years apart, both with red hair, both with that same tattoo. Have you ever seen it before?'

Pat Forde gazed at the photo for a few seconds more, then slowly handed it back. Chris watched him closely for a reaction but his expression was blank. Kennedy was right; it meant nothing to him.

'I'm sorry, Detectives, I've never seen anything like that in my life. What does it mean?' Then the thought struck him. 'Oh my … is that, is it Sarah …?'

'Mr Forde,' Kennedy continued quickly, 'we're so sorry to have to bring this up now, but we need to talk a little about Sarah before she disappeared.'

Pat Forde nodded, but Chris thought he noticed something other than grief pass across the man's face.

'Was she a difficult child?' he asked, and noticed Kennedy give him a surprised look at the directness of the question.

The man sighed heavily. 'She was the sweetest girl you could ever imagine. I adored her, we both did.'

They talked some more about Sarah, and what her childhood was like, before touching on the circumstances surrounding her disappearance. 'She never came home from school one day,' he told the detectives. 'We were distraught … didn't know what to think.'

'Yet she'd run away before?' Chris said, referring to the incident in the file about her turning up at her grandmother's house.

'It wasn't quite like that. Like most children of her age — any age, I suppose – there were some … discipline issues.

There was an argument one time, and Sarah fled to her grandmother's. Happens in every family, doesn't it?' Forde met Chris's gaze.

'Of course,' Kennedy agreed. 'My own are the same, I can't keep up with them most of the time and ...' He trailed off, reddening at his poor choice of words.

'What kind of argument, Mr Forde?' Chris pressed.

He shrugged. 'It was so long ago. Something about homework as I recall ...'

Something about homework? If it were Chris he was certain he'd remember every second of that argument, go back over every word, terrified that what he'd said might have been the cause of her disappearance. Yet Pat Forde didn't seem to remember much about it at all.

'I see.' Chris stood up suddenly. 'Mr Forde, again, you have our deepest sympathies.' He indicated to the FLO who, up till now, had remained silently in the background. 'Officer O'Neill will answer any questions you might have from hereon, but before we go, could we possibly have an item of Sarah's with which to compare DNA? A hairbrush would be ideal.'

'Of course.' Sarah's father duly shuffled away again to another room of the house.

When he was gone, Kennedy frowned at Chris. 'What's with the attitude?'

'What attitude? I was simply trying to draw out whether there were any family issues related to her disappearance.'

'It hardly matters now, does it?' Kennedy retorted, and Chris guessed he was projecting again. He could hardly blame him, but unlike his partner, he wasn't going to let the tragic circumstances color his thinking.

Mr Forde returned with a hairbrush that had once belonged to his daughter.

Kennedy went to shake his hand. 'Thank you again, Mr Forde, you've been most helpful. Please pass on our sympathies again to your wife. Officer O'Neill will be able to make the necessary arrangements for you both to see your daughter soon.'

Pat Forde nodded. 'Thank you, Detectives. The last ten years have been … a living nightmare, to say the least.'

Chris was deep in thought as he shook the man's hand. It all sounded fine on the surface, but for some reason he didn't believe that everything had been hunky-dory in that household.

He'd interviewed enough grieving families over the years to spot the signs.

Sarah Forde's father was hiding something.

But what?

31

How did the infection come in? That is the question that haunts me. The outside world is always trying to find a way through our defenses; I must remain vigilant, watch constantly for attempts to breach our walls, to get among us, to spread poison.

I have my suspects, those close by who have cast covetous eyes upon us. Do they think I didn't see the way they looked at her, the lust and longing her beauty provoked? Her long limbs, her proud gait, her flaming hair, all these things and more they wanted.

I tried to keep them away, but I cannot be everywhere at all times. Did one of them turn her head, whisper poison in her ear, infect her mind with thoughts of the other world, the one we have sought to keep from us?

She had everything here, but like Eve, honeyed words made her want more, want something beyond love and happiness. And so she left us.

So now I must again head out into the wicked world to find another, guide them to our home, and welcome them to the bosom of our family.

. . .

REILLY PHONED Chris's mobile while he and Kennedy were on their way back from the Forde house, explaining that she had a new theory.

'I was thinking again about the whole cult angle. Right from the start I was never convinced it had legs. However, I did have another thought.'

'Go on.'

'It struck me when I was going through Sarah Forde's file after you left earlier. Sarah was reported missing in early 2002, yes?'

Chris nodded, momentarily forgetting that she couldn't see him. 'According to the records, yes.'

'And the body of our cold-case victim was discovered late the previous year — end of October to be exact.'

'Right ....' Chris frowned. 'What of it?' he asked, trying not to sound short, but it had been a very long day, and he wasn't really in the mood for one of Reilly's famous theories.

'So what if Sarah was some kind of replacement for the girl who died?'

'Replacement ...' An automatic chill ran down Chris's spine.

Alongside him in the driver's seat, Kennedy frowned at his reaction. His mind reeling, Chris took a moment to explain her theory to him.

'Holy shit ...'

'I'm not sure I like the implications of that,' Chris said to Reilly.

'I don't like any of it, but you have to admit it has a sort of warped logic to it,' Reilly continued.

'You make it sound like someone's collecting these girls.'

At this, he heard Kennedy emit another low curse.

'Sarah went missing when she was seven years old. There's no way she would have ended up in a cult ... or hippy camp or whatever ... of her own accord at that age. So we can only conclude that somebody else was involved, somebody responsible for the tattoo and perhaps the pregnancy too. Which means that we need to be looking at an abduction situation.' Reilly took a deep breath. 'Viewing it from that perspective, I'm having a hard time believing the date correlation is just coincidence. It would make sense if losing one girl would prompt whoever is behind this to find another for the camp or cult or whatever.'

'But that's exactly it — for *what*? What would an abductor want them for?' he said, asking the obvious question. 'There were no signs of sexual abuse or anything like it on either girl.'

'No sign of abuse, but at least one of them was sexually active, and may have been for some time,' Reilly said, truly hoping that they weren't talking about some kind of paedophile ring. 'It's already been suggested that the tattoo could be viewed as some form of branding. Your hippy friend insists that this doesn't happen amongst them, that any such collectiveness is anathema to their way of life.'

'I get what you're saying but—'

'And I had another thought.'

He gave a deep sigh. 'Go on then, this day is shot to hell anyway, why not ruin it further,' he said, his tone softening. She truly was like a dog with a bone. And that was part of the problem between them just now. 'What else has been brewing in that brain of yours?'

Chris could see that Kennedy was trying his utmost to keep his eyes on the road and not be distracted by the conversation, and was almost tempted to tell him to pull over. But it was late, and they were still a good hour away from base.

'Well, if we go along with the notion that somebody is abducting these girls for whatever reason — is it one at a time, or are there several?' Reilly posited. 'Remember all those missing person hits that fitted the pale skin/red-haired description?'

Chris rubbed his face at the idea of a full-blown abduction

scenario. 'Ah hell ...' The very idea was turning his brain to ice. Yet he had to admit, it made some sense.

'We can't overlook anything. So I'm thinking, instead of going back over missing person files,' Reilly continued, 'we need to narrow it down a little more, and concentrate on searching for missing *children*. If, like Sarah, red-haired pale-skinned girls are being abducted when they are young, it means our cold-case girl would have gone missing back in the nineties.'

'Which means this has been going on for a long while ...'

'Too long. And he may well be on the hunt for the next addition.'

'Doesn't even bear thinking about,' Chris replied, deeply unsettled by the notion. 'But for the moment, it all comes back to the same thing — where did Sarah and the other angel come from?'

'Or to put it another way,' Reilly said ominously, 'if there are more, where is he keeping them hidden?'

32

The following morning, Kennedy stood at the back of the queue at Starbucks.

He watched the various characters in front of him, all desperate for an early morning caffeine hit before heading off to various cubicles in office buildings around the International Financial Services Center.

As he daydreamed he became aware of the car horn beeping outside. He turned to see Chris with one hand holding a phone to his ear and the other beckoning him back to the car. Whatever it was, it better be important, he thought, reluctantly giving up his place in the queue; going without his morning fag and cuppa was not the way he wanted to start the day.

'What's up?' he asked, opening the car door. Chris held up a hand to silence him as he finished the phone conversation. 'On our way now, we'll be there in five.'

Hanging up the phone, he turned to look at Kennedy. 'Guess who walked into Pearse Street station this morning?'

'Enlighten me.'

'Young William Connolly. Looks like the old man came through. He's been charged and remanded.'

Nice one, Kennedy thought, as God only knew how long it would have taken the UK authorities to track him down and escort him back. 'Is he on his own?'

'No, his father showed up with him for moral support.'

They breezed through the early morning traffic using the siren and lights, taking only a couple of minutes to travel the short distance to Pearse Street station. Inside Fitzmorris, the senior officer on duty who had made the formal arrest, greeted them and led them up to the interview room where Connolly was being held.

'No solicitor?' Chris queried.

'Not present, but they've indicated that they had consulted with one during the arrest. He knows his rights.'

'OK, let's go.' Chris nodded to Kennedy before turning back to Fitzmorris.

'Have you got the video set up?'

'Everything is ready to go. Brady here will take the notes so you can get him to sign the statement afterwards.' He indicated a young female officer who waited outside the interview room as they approached.

William and his father stood up nervously as they entered and Chris was taken aback at how young the kid looked. His complexion was pale and tired, acne scars still visible across his cheeks a reminder of his young age, and the black lines under his eyes telling of recent sleepless nights since he'd run poor Sarah Forde down.

Kennedy walked across and pulled out a chair without saying a word. Chris and Brady did likewise. Saying nothing, they made a great show of shuffling through file notes that had been sent over from Harcourt Street.

It was a practiced move; they wanted him to feel nervous. It would be easier to get a clear and concise statement that way. Chris suspected that he didn't need to try too hard. The kid looked petrified already.

Chris was still unsure what the kid's version of events would be — would he claim to have no knowledge of hitting Sarah, that he'd thought it was an animal or something?

And if so, would he be telling the truth?

Chris could feel Connolly's discomfort and out of pity he told him to take a seat. It was obvious that this was not a kid used to being in this type of position.

He and Kennedy had often walked into an interview room containing some scumbag who'd sit, feet up on the desk, issuing demands and acting like they owned the place. This boy was not one of those.

'William Connelly,' he began, his tone neutral. 'I'm about to commence the interview. It will be recorded by video and in writing. You have already been advised of your rights so we'll get straight to it. Any questions before we begin?'

'No,' Connolly replied in a croaking voice. Chris hit the record button on the camera as Kennedy read out the file number, date and charges relating to the hit and run. Connelly remained seated, his head slumped as the charges were read out for the record.

'Mr Connolly, do you admit to being the sole driver of the vehicle, registration number 08-MH-3457 on the night of the fourteenth of March last on the R134 road in Wicklow?'

'Yes,' Connolly confirmed, sitting uneasily in the chair.

'Can you describe in detail what happened that night?' Kennedy asked in an authoritative tone.

Connolly took a deep breath. 'Umm ... I was driving home from Blessington. I'd just helped a friend move his stuff from a flat he was moving out. It was dark, a bit drizzly. I put the wipers on...'

'Can you approximate the speed at which you were driving?'

He kneaded his forehead. 'I was well under the limit ... I wasn't in a hurry. I was listening to the Chelsea game on the radio. I was probably doing thirty, maybe forty, tops.' Chris noted to himself that this tallied with the iSPI projection.

'I came around the corner and there it was … something just standing there looking at me through the mist. I hit the brakes, but it didn't even try to get out of the way. It was just standing there in the road as if it was waiting for me …'

'When you say there "it", what exactly are you referring to?'

'Look, I know it sounds stupid, but I thought I was hallucinating. It looked like a ghost. As the van slid closer, I saw it was a girl and all of a sudden, she turned her back to me …'

Chris bit his lip, tempted to interrupt and ask what kind of ghost would leave a couple of grand's worth of damage to the front end of a van, but he knew the importance of letting Connolly describe events in his own way.

But it was interesting that he'd said Sarah actually turned her back to him.

'You say she "turned her back to you". Can you elaborate for us?'

'Like I said, she made no attempt to jump out of the way. I mean, she must have seen the headlights before I came around the corner. She just folded her arms and turned around, calm as you like. I didn't know what to do. I panicked, I didn't want some suicidal nut job to ruin my life.'

Connolly fell silent, and the detectives let it hang, giving him time, hoping he'd feel the need to fill the empty silence.

She turned her back … Chris thought about his observation. Perhaps it was no surprise Connolly had thought it odd, but maybe he wouldn't find it such strange behavior if he'd known Sarah was pregnant and that she had turned her back to the van in a last ditch attempt to save her unborn child.

'Why did you drive away when you hit her, William?' Kennedy said. 'If it was an accident as you say, why didn't you report it, call 999? By leaving the scene you deprived her of any chance she may have had.'

'I don't know … I just panicked,' Connolly said, holding back a sob.

'Well, from what you're telling us here, it seems this was very much a straightforward accident,' Chris put in, 'but if that's the case why did you then leave the country in what could be argued was an attempt to avoid detection when the van was discovered?'

'Look, I didn't just take off, OK,' Connolly shot back in a first display of conviction since the interview began. 'I was due to go to London for a football match, I was still in a state of shock … To be honest, I didn't know whether I was coming or going.'

Chris sensed this response sounded like something he'd rehearsed in his head a hundred times, perhaps something he'd even discussed with the solicitor beforehand. 'I made a mistake … I was in shock,' he repeated. 'But I came back and came here as soon as Dad called me.' He looked to his father for reassurance.

There was little doubt that his stance had been well thought out. Connolly had had time to rehearse, so Chris figured the moment had come to shake things up a little.

'Can you tell us a little more about how you spent the evening prior to the incident?' he asked.

Connolly looked at him, confused. 'I don't know what you—'

'Did you consume any alcohol in the hours leading up to the accident?'

'No, like I said, I was helping a friend move house…'

Chris knew from experience that the most likely event was also the most probable. Connolly had no reason to run from the scene unless he had something to hide; unfortunately the majority of hit and runs involved alcohol or somebody driving who shouldn't be.

Connolly had been driving the van on small secondary

roads when it would have been easier and quicker to use the main route. He was young and seemingly an avid supporter of Chelsea who were playing a big Champions League game that evening.

In short, one and one made two.

'Mr Connolly, I want you to think hard about the responses you've given here today. Our investigation will be thorough, we will be following every line of enquiry and questioning those you claim to have spent the evening with. If it is discovered that you consumed alcohol that evening, and we can prove it, it will be very difficult to find a judge who will look kindly on your position.'

Kennedy let the full impact of Chris's words sink in before continuing. 'Any judge faced with a hit-and-run case involving a drunk driver and a slaughtered pregnant woman will be itching to drop a heavy hammer.'

Connolly closed his eyes briefly but remained sitting in silence and stared at his clammy hands in his lap. Eventually he spoke again. 'I'd like to consult with my solicitor now.'

Chris indicated that they should pause the interview, after which Connolly had a thirty-minute meeting with his father and their solicitor.

When the interview recommenced, Connolly admitted to having three or four drinks earlier that evening. His final account eventually matched most of what the GFU had deduced from the scene. He hadn't jammed on the brakes as first asserted. In fact he had barely had enough time to react before he'd plowed into Sarah at full speed. He had gotten out to have a look, which would have given opportunity for his almost empty MegaCoffee cup, an attempt to sober up, to fall out of the van. He had made the decision to run, claim he'd hit a sheep, and hope for the best.

The best he could hope for now was less than ten years.

33

L ater that afternoon, Lucy called out to Reilly as she was headed down the hall for a coffee refill. She poked her head into the lab. 'What's up?'

Lucy was hunched over her laptop. 'Based on those new parameters, the missing children instead of missing persons ...'

Reilly hurried over. She'd heard from Chris that the driver who'd hit and killed Sarah Forde had turned himself in that morning, and an arrest had been made. So it felt in some small way that in finding both her identity and her killer, Sarah's case had been laid to rest.

However, if her theory was correct, Sarah and the other girl had been abducted and there may well be others.

Lucy spun the laptop around for her to see. 'Jennifer Hutchinson. She went missing almost twenty years ago.'

Reilly glanced through the information. The little girl was another redhead who'd been reported missing from the Tallaght area when she was ten years old. She did a mental calculation. Given that the age of the cold-case girl was listed as being between twenty and twenty-four years old, and was found ten years ago, if it was this girl it sounded about right.

'She fits the profile in a few ways — appearance being the obvious one,' Lucy went on. 'Just like Sarah Forde, similar age, no major behavioral problems, simply went missing on the way home from school one day — no leads, no one saw anything, she just vanished.'

Reilly stared at the little girl's face on the screen — once again the pale, delicate features, the mass of red curls. Her heart sped up. 'They could almost be sisters...'

'That's what I thought. Makes what you said about Sarah possibly being a replacement for the other girl seem more and more likely.'

'Why would somebody want to collect little girls who look so alike?' wondered Reilly out loud.

'I can think of lots of reasons,' Lucy replied quickly. 'None of them nice.'

'Of course. But let's eliminate the sexual abuse angle for a minute,' Reilly said thoughtfully. For a moment they both fell silent, gazing at the picture of young Jennifer Hutchinson. Immortalized in time. 'But why?' Reilly finally asked.

'Maybe they reminded their abductor of someone?' Lucy suggested.

'Possibly. Who?'

'Someone from his childhood maybe — assuming we're talking "he". A friend, a sibling, even a rival, something like that?'

'That's possible.'

'Or,' Lucy added suddenly, her voice breaking a little, 'a family member. Someone who died ... or disappeared.' Her voice trailed off.

Reilly shot her a glance, picking up on the emotion in her tone. 'Dig deeper and see what else you can find on this girl — once again we'll need to try and compare her medical records with our cold case, and see if we can confirm a match. If it looks good, then we'll take it from there.'

Lucy nodded. 'Will do.'

Again, Reilly looked at her closely, sensing that there was something else on her mind. 'You OK?'

The other girl said nothing.

'Lucy?'

Her dark gaze finally met Reilly's. She took a deep breath. 'I suppose, going through these files, I can't help thinking about Grace,' she said finally.

The room suddenly seemed very quiet. Reilly could hear the ticking of the clock, someone's footsteps as they hurried along the hallway past the lab. She mentally cursed herself for not making the connection before now.

Lucy's older sister Grace had gone missing almost fifteen years before. She had never been found. And since they had now been tasked with going through missing children reports, how could it not have brought it all back? Reilly was horrified. How could she be so wrapped up in the smaller details to forget that such a case would have such a huge significance for those around her – especially Lucy? Perhaps it was for the best she had very few friends here, she thought miserably. Clearly she wouldn't be a very good one.

'Oh Lucy, I'm so sorry, how thoughtless of me not to realize. If you want off the case, just say the word...'

'No no, it's not a problem.' Lucy waved her hand absently to try and alleviate Reilly's obvious mortification.

'I don't know how I didn't—'

'Forget about it, honestly. But I guess ...I've been waiting for something like this,' Lucy continued. 'It's kind of the reason I'm here, the reason I chose this career.'

Reilly immediately thought about her own history, the events that had shaped her, and made her the person — the investigator — she was today. She looked at Lucy and saw the same fierce determination in her eyes.

Her sister's disappearance would have been a defining event in Lucy's life, and had shaped much of her relationship with her father, Jack Gorman, another senior GFU investigator who already disapproved of his daughter working in the same field.

Still, Reilly could now appreciate why Lucy was even more dedicated than usual, and had become so consumed by this case. She reminded her of herself in ways, how back at the beginning of her career her own personal circumstances had driven her forwards, as if she somehow needed to atone for everything that had gone wrong with her family. While she'd thrown herself into work, her father had thrown himself into drinking. And her sister had chosen an entirely different way to work through her own demons.

Reilly hadn't known about Grace when she'd first started at the GFU and while she and Lucy's father, Jack, had got off to an inauspicious start, with the older man seemingly resentful and suspicious of her presence, the discovery of his family circumstances had softened her opinion of him.

How could losing a child not affect you as a father and a man? There wasn't a day that went by when Reilly didn't think about Jess, and she was sure it was the same for Jack and Lucy.

Now Lucy's determination was no longer just about the unidentified girls, it was about Grace and identifying with something that had haunted the Gorman family for so many years.

'It's hard not to draw comparisons, especially when dealing with something like this,' the younger girl said gently, indicating the lengthy database, lists and lists of other families' heartbreak.

Reilly wanted to curl up and die. 'I'm sorry. I really should have thought. I'll get Rory to go through them ...'

Lucy shook her head vigorously. 'Absolutely not. Notwithstanding that, I'm a professional and we need to confirm if this girl is our cold case.' She looked up at Reilly, her tone heavy with emotion. 'And if nothing else, I'd love to be the one to help bring Jennifer home.'

34

In the trees right beside the playground, the man could hear a group of teenagers talking. Their conversation excited him.

'Ha, Jade doesn't even know what a blow-job *is*,' one of the boys sitting on top of the roundabout shouted, and the others began to laugh.

'I do too!' a much younger girl protested as her face reddened and gave away the truth.

'Go on, what is it then? Better still, *show* me,' the older boy chided, evidently enjoying her discomfort.

As he listened to their chatter, the man held a mobile phone to his ear and pretended to talk into it, waiting for his chance. Perhaps today was the day, and with luck, maybe he'd have the opportunity to do more than talk.

Ninety-nine times out of a hundred that was all he could do: watch and listen. Today, though, felt different. This one was being isolated, taunted. Maybe if the dogs drove the lamb away …

He tried to dampen down his excitement.

'I'm going home; anyone coming?' The girl called Jade tried

once more for some support but there were no takers. The spring-loaded playground gate slammed shut with a clatter as she stomped out.

The man swallowed hard as he walked in the opposite direction behind the cover of the tree line before doubling back after he'd finished his cigarette.

She might need a friend, he thought, as he made his way towards the parking area close to the path, a preferred place for his fishing expeditions.

Increasing his pace, his pulse quickened as his and the young girl's paths started to converge.

Today could be the day.

35

'How's your Irish?' Reilly asked, approaching Chris's desk at Harcourt Street with a definite spring in her step.

He looked up, somewhat perplexed. 'Bit rusty. Why?'

'That social worker I told you about called back earlier with the kid's details.'

'The one with the same winged tattoo?'

'Yes. According to the social worker, a guy called Keogh, the child is currently in state care, in a children's home in Inchicore. His name is Conn – apparently that's about all they could get out of him originally, but it definitely seems that Conn has a set of wings too.'

Chris stood up and called out to Kennedy who was standing over by the coffee machine, deep in conversation with another officer. He finished up and hurried over, hitching his trousers up as he went.

'Morning, blondie. What brings you to our lowly slum this morning?'

'Oh, I like to mix with the peasants from time to time,' she replied. 'It helps keep me grounded.'

'Seems we've got a location for another kid with the same kind of tattoo,' Chris told him, ignoring their banter.

'Only trouble is, he doesn't speak English – only Irish,' Reilly added. She looked from one to the other. 'And seeing as it's all double-dutch to me...'

'Hell, it was part of our Garda exams and it's still double-dutch to us,' Kennedy said, shaking his head.

'Speak for yourself; some of us remember the basics.' Chris grimaced. 'Although how much at this stage remains to be seen.'

He explained that while all members of the force were required to be able to speak the native language, it was mostly those stationed in Irish-speaking 'Gaeltacht' areas that used it day to day.

'Well I know I won't have a clue what's being said, but do you think I could tag along?' Given that the kid was her lead, Reilly was interested to see if the tattoo was indeed the same as the others.

If so, it would be the first time they'd encountered it on a living person, and have the opportunity to question them about it.

36

Maggie Molloy, the director of the children's home, was a tiny woman in her mid-fifties. She wore a woolen skirt and cardigan, and had an air of busy professionalism about her.

She shook hands with all three of them on arrival; a firm, crisp handshake which belied her stature. 'You've come to speak to Conn?'

Chris nodded. 'Thanks for taking the time to see us.'

'Not a problem.' She led them down the hallway. The building was brightly lit, with rooms on either side: a canteen, an art room where several children were busy gluing leaves onto a huge sheet of paper. 'I believe you were talking to Simon about him. You do know Conn won't speak English, don't you?'

'I speak some Irish,' Chris told her. 'Enough to converse, at least.'

'That's good but even so there are no guarantees. We've brought Irish speakers in before but to no avail. Doctor Marsh, the psychologist, says Conn has selective mutism. He spends a lot of time in his own world, and seems oblivious to what's happening around him.'

'So he is able to speak English?' Kennedy asked.

Maggie nodded. 'He certainly understands it,' she said. 'It's just I personally have never heard him speak anything other than Irish, but I know some of the staff have heard him mutter a word or two of English.'

'How long has he been here?'

'Two years, on and off. We try to find placements for the boys, families who can foster or adopt them, but Conn defies us.'

'Defies you?' Chris enquired.

'He's been with three foster families, all Irish-speaking, but each time he rebels and is back with us within days. The families say he is unmanageable, almost feral.'

The sound of someone playing a piano came from a room up ahead. Maggie indicated for them to look inside.

A young boy was sitting at the keys. There was no recognizable tune, yet the music was not discordant. Reilly thought it had a wistful, haunting air to it.

'He'll play for hours,' Maggie said. 'It's the only thing that really calms him down. It's obvious he's had lessons at some point, but mostly he just plays his own compositions, like now.'

They listened as the plaintive notes swirled around them. Maggie stepped into the room. 'Conn? You have some visitors.'

Reilly looked at the boy. He was around eleven years old, small for his age, with the same distinctive mass of red curls and pale Celtic skin as the dead girls. He played gently, caressing the keys, appearing not to have heard, but at the same time his eyes gave a quick glance towards the doorway as she spoke, and she noticed his shoulders tighten slightly.

'These people would like to talk to you,' continued Maggie.

The music picked up pace, becoming more frantic; Conn's obvious anxiety seeped into his music. The tempo was building, his hands moving faster, striking the keys harder — a determined effort to keep the world at bay for a little while longer while he lost himself in the music.

Maggie nodded for Reilly and the detectives to go in. They all stepped into the room and the music picked up again, the boy's hands moving rapidly across the piano keys, the melody becoming lost in a frantic effort to make noise, enough to block out the visitors, block out the world.

There were chairs against the wall and Maggie indicated that they should sit. Kennedy and Reilly lowered themselves into the chairs, but Chris remained standing alongside the piano, a little way away from Conn. Maggie started to say something else, but Chris motioned for her to stay silent.

'*Dia duit Conn,*' he began. '*Chris is aimn dom.*' Hi Conn, my name is Chris.

Instantly the music got louder and faster. Conn's discomfort with the intrusion was patently obvious. The boy shifted on the bench, turning his body away from them. Chris looked at the others and nodded towards the doorway. Reilly, Maggie and Kennedy obediently followed him back out into the corridor.

'Maybe I should try to have a word on my own for the moment,' Chris suggested as the music flooded out into the hall. 'Less intimidating for him.'

The others now a safe distance away, he returned to the room and tried again.

'*Is maith liom do chuid cheoil - an déanann tú do amhráin féin a scríobh?*' I like your playing — do you write your own songs?

For a second Conn did nothing, then he looked up at Chris with some interest.

Chris indicated the keyboard. '*An féidir linn seinnt le chéile?*' Can we play together?

The boy considered the question for a moment before looking around the empty room. Then he slowly stood and closed the piano lid before turning and walking towards the window. Eventually, he started to hum a tune, not one Chris recognized, but more a random tune of discomfort.

Chris waited in silence for few moments more, but still Conn refused to acknowledge him.

Eventually, he rejoined the others in the hallway.

'I'm sorry, Detectives. Clearly he's not up to talking today — he can be like that sometimes.'

'Perhaps it's best if we leave it just now, and call back in a day or so,' Chris suggested. It was frustrating, but realistically all they could do for the moment.

In the meantime, he had to try and think of some way to get this enigmatic boy to talk.

I dreamed of a haven, a place of infinite peace, of eternal beauty and everlasting happiness, and I found it — not in my dreams, but in reality. It is a place of wind and earth, grass and water, horses and birds. But what good is heaven when you are there alone?

And so I became the guide...

I often wonder why I was chosen. Is it my gifts, my ability to talk to a child, to calm their troubled mind? Or that I can recognize the lost souls, the ones that have been battered by the winds, damaged by the cruelties that we hurl at the young?

And so I gather them in, the lost children. I bring them here to a place where they can heal. A place without fear, without evil, a place of infinite tranquility, where they can remain children for ever.

They do not fear me when I find them — they know that I mean them no harm. They understand that my words are true, not honeyed invitations to a darker world — the world of adults, the world of pain — but rather, an invitation to a better life, a life without hardship.

And so I have gathered them here with me, have created this place we call home, this magical, mystical land across the water. They are my family, and I am their protector, their father, and though some may disagree, ultimately their saviour...

.   .   .

THE DETECTIVES WERE on their way back to the station from the children's home when the call came. Reilly had driven her own car, and had early on left them far behind.

'Clondalkin station just called in an attempted abduction,' a younger officer told Chris over the phone. 'Guys in the responding squad car remembered us and called it in because the girl has red hair.'

Chris looked at Kennedy. 'You said "attempted" — the girl got away?'

'Yeah. Apparently she started kicking up blue murder when he tried to snatch her. Some other kids nearby noticed, and seems the guy panicked and took off.'

Chris's pulse quickened. 'Give me the address.'

SPRINGFIELD WAS an anonymous estate in Clondalkin just off the N7 heading west out of Dublin.

Chris parked the Ford by a quiet row of former local authority houses and double-checked the address. 'Number forty-seven, this is it.'

Kennedy climbed from the car, and looked up and down the street. 'It's quiet,' he said.

'Maybe that's why our guy picked it.' Chris slammed his car door and held the gate open for Kennedy as they walked through.

The front door of number forty-seven popped open before they had time to ring the bell. A blond woman in her mid-thirties, dressed in jogging pants and a *Guess* T-shirt, was waiting for them. 'Are you the guards?' she asked shakily.

'That's right.' Chris quickly made the introductions. 'We believe there was an attempted abduction on your daughter earlier?'

The woman who introduced herself as Tracy Carney nodded. She ushered them into a narrow hallway littered with kids' toys, the hall table stacked with a few weeks' worth of junk mail.

'Sorry about the mess,' Tracy called over her shoulder as she led them down the hall towards the kitchen. 'Four kids; you know what it's like.'

As they passed the doorway to the living room, Chris glimpsed a gaggle of children sprawled out on the carpet, eyes glued to the television.

The kitchen was not much better. The counter tops were littered with dirty dishes, the table showed the remains of lunch — a bowl of baby mush, plates with left-over bread crusts, and empty crisp packets. Tracy grabbed the plates and the bowl, pitched them in the sink, and ran a dirty tea towel across the stained table.

'Can I get you anything — a cup of tea maybe?'

'No, we're fine, we've just had lunch,' said Kennedy hurriedly. One look around the kitchen had been enough to discourage him.

'Suit yourself. How about you, Sergeant?'

Chris managed not to grin at being called sergeant. 'A cup of tea would be lovely,' he replied.

Before she could begin to organize the tea, there was a scream from the living room followed by loud shouting. Tracy groaned heavily. ''Scuse me a minute.'

She hurried off down the hall, shouting at the kids as she went.

Chris stood up, found the kettle and tried his best to fill it with water from the cluttered sink.

'Jesus, do you have a death wish or something?' Kennedy whispered.

'Wimp,' Chris teased. 'Home interviewing 101; always accept a cuppa. Puts people at ease.' He switched the kettle on, and sat back down at the table. 'Of course, in your case it's too late for redemption. She'll have already labeled you as stuck-up.' He looked up and smiled as Tracy came back in. 'I put the kettle on.'

'Oh, you're a love...' She scowled back towards the living room, which was decidedly quieter now. 'Little brats. I don't know what to do with them sometimes.'

'Could you tell us what happened today with your daughter?' Kennedy asked, getting straight to the point.

Tracy ignored him, addressing her reply to Chris. 'You just can't imagine that kind of thing happening in an area like this ...' She sniffed and shook her head sadly.

'We never like to think of these things happening in our own backyard,' Chris sympathized. 'Your daughter — what's her name?'

'Jade. She's twelve.'

'OK, so where was Jade when it happened?'

'At the playground — she was home today with a little snif-fle, didn't seem right to send her to school I thought,' she said, apparently missing the irony of letting the kid hang around in a playground instead. 'Anyway, she says this man came up and started walking with her as she was coming home. I'm always warning them not to talk to strangers, but you know what it's like, in one ear and out the other...' She rolled her eyes.

Just then, the decibel level started to rise again from the living room. 'Luke, don't make me come in there again!' Tracy roared. Chris winced and she turned back to him. 'Sorry, where was I?'

'Jade was walking home from the playground...'

'Yeah, and this fella came up and started talking to her. She says he tried to get her to go in his van with him.'

'How did she get away?'

'Done what I told her,' said Tracy proudly. 'I said to her, any man ever tries to grab you, you kick and scream till he lets go.

And that's what she done. Then of course she came running home here bawling, and told me what happened.'

'You've obviously taught her well,' Kennedy said.

'Too right. You've got to teach them to be tough these days. No room for shrinking violets around here, and not many fellas you'd want to be grabbing you either,' she added dourly.

'Where's your daughter now, Mrs Carney?'

'In the living room. And it's Miss,' she added with a smile and a pointed look towards Chris, who visibly gulped.

'Could we talk to her, please?'

'Jade,' Tracy screeched. 'Jade! Come here for a minute!'

They heard footsteps approach, and saw a young girl walking slowly down the hall towards them.

'Hurry it up, they haven't got all day, you know.'

Jade came and stood before the detectives. This, thought Chris, was a girl who was used to being in trouble. Her whole demeanor suggested that she was expecting to be told off.

Tracy busied herself making the tea. 'Answer their questions, all right?'

Jade nodded, keeping her eyes fixed on the floor.

'Jade,' Kennedy began, his tone kindly. 'Your mum has told us a little bit about what happened earlier. We know you've already answered some questions but we have a couple more, OK?'

The girl nodded as she wiped her runny nose on her sleeve.

'You were at the playground, yes? Was anyone else there with you?'

Jade nodded.

'Can you tell me who?'

'Britney Burke, Ethan and Robert Halley, and Molly Cowen.'

'Do they all live locally?'

'Some of the local kids,' said Tracy, setting Chris's tea in front of him with a smile.

'Do you know where they live?'

'Britney and the Halley boys live on this street too,' said Tracy. 'Molly lives with her gran, just around the corner.'

Kennedy turned back to Jade. 'Jade, when you were at the playground, did you see the man there?'

The young girl nodded, and finally looked up. 'I think I noticed him one time ... kind of walking around in the field behind.'

'Did it seem like he was watching you?'

'Don't know. But he was definitely there.'

'So when you left the playground,' he continued, 'where was he?'

She shrugged. 'Not sure. He was just suddenly walking next to me near the car park.'

'What did he say?'

She shrugged again. 'Asked me about stuff I liked. Games and stuff.'

'Anything else?'

'And sweets,' she added. 'He said he had some sweets in his van.'

'Not very original, is it?' snorted Tracy. 'That one was old when I was a kid.'

'It's often the simple things that work,' Chris said. He turned back to Jade. 'Do you remember anything at all about the man? What he looked like or anything about his van?'

She looked thoughtful. 'He was kind of old.'

'Kind of old?'

'Yeah, not like real old, but you know, kind of old...'

'How old? Like me?' Kennedy pointed to himself, 'or him?'

'Definitely old like you and fat too,' Jade replied and Chris tried to hide a smirk.

'And his van?'

She screwed up her eyes, trying to remember. 'It was a dark color.'

God, it was like pulling teeth, Chris thought. 'When you say dark, do you mean black, brown, blue even?'

'Maybe dark blue … I think.'

'Anything else you remember about it?'

Jade thought again. 'When he opened the door it was one of those sliding ones like the knackers have — there were no seats in the back.'

'Jade!' her mother scolded. 'I told you we don't use that word. Those people are called travelers.' She looked at Chris and rolled her eyes.

'That's great, Jade. Your answers have been really helpful. Is there anything else you remember about the man or the van? What he wore, his hair color, what he smelled like, anything at all…'

'His hair was kind of dark, but had those silvery bits at the side.'

'That's good.'

'And he didn't smell nice.'

'Did the smell remind you of anything?'

Jade shook her head. 'Just not nice.'

fterwards, Kennedy and Chris walked down the street from the Carney house. The field and the playground could be seen at the end of the road.

'What do you reckon?' Kennedy asked.

Chris made a face. 'She's not really a redhead, not like the others.'

'More like a strawberry blond,' Kennedy agreed. 'And not exactly pale either. But if he's desperate …'

'It's possible, I suppose. Still, she seems like a bit of a handful and much older than Sarah and the other girl when they were likely first abducted,' Chris pointed out.

'I can't imagine anyone trying to brainwash that one. She'd soon tell you to fuck off.'

He chuckled. 'I hear you. That's the problem with interviewing kids though. They are such unreliable witnesses, and usually so desperate to please they'll say anything just to be helpful.'

Kennedy gave a bitter laugh. 'In my experience, that's not so different from adults.'

They had reached the field. The playground was to their left

— a set of swings, a merry-go-round, a small climbing frame and a slide. Two boys sat side by side on the swings, barely moving. They were both in their early teens, and both had a mop of dark hair.

'What did Jade call them again?' Chris said. 'Ethan and Robert Halley, wasn't it?'

Kennedy nodded. 'Two likely lads if ever I've seen them. We should have a little chat – I wouldn't say the kids around these parts miss much.'

The boys looked up as the detectives walked in to the playground. Kennedy was right — the boys had the wary look of a pair of foxes ghosting through a suburb late at night. There was little doubt in Chris's mind that they would bolt at the first sign of a threat.

The boys' eyes never left the detectives as they walked over to them.

'Cops are you?' said one of them.

Chris raised an eyebrow. 'What gave us away?'

'The smell,' said the other under his breath and the first one grinned.

'What did you say?' Kennedy said, stepping forward, a menacing look in his eyes.

The two boys looked at each other, taken by surprise. 'Nothing, just messin' is all,' one of them replied.

'Well, cut the lip, quick as you like or you'll both be marched home for your parents to sort you out.'

The two of them shrugged, acting as though the prospect didn't bother them.

'What's in your hand?' Chris indicated to the older one, who wore a Manchester United tracksuit top. He looked to have his fist clenched around something.

'Smoke,' he replied, opening his hand to reveal the burning end of a cigarette.

'You're too young to be smoking. Does your mammy know about it?'

The two of them grinned nonchalantly. 'She doesn't give a fuck what I do,' the smoker replied with increasing bravado.

'Hey, watch your language and put that out, you little shit,' Kennedy ordered.

The boy took one last drag from the cigarette then flicked it on to the grass. Exhaling deeply, he aggressively blew out the smoke.

'You're pushing your luck, mate. Quench that out and put it in the bin. This is a playground,' Chris barked, losing patience with the two troublemakers. These kids had no regard for authority of any kind, and being disrespectful — especially to the cops — was a badge of honor these days.

'Right, quit the messing, lads, do you know Jade Carney?' Kennedy asked, trying to move things on.

'Yeah. What of it?'

'She was playing here earlier,' he continued. 'As she left a man tried to grab her and get her in his van.'

The boys were silent. This was not what they had expected.

Chris pushed on. 'Jade said the man was walking around the field earlier when she was playing here. Did you two notice anything?'

They shot each other a glance.

'Could you describe the man?' Chris continued, realizing that they had seen something. Move right through the question of *if* they saw him, let them know that you already know they did.

'Bobby said he looked like a paedo ...'

'What made you think that?'

'He thinks *everybody* looks like a paedo, he's worried they might fancy him or something,' the older brother teased.

'Could you describe him for me?' Chris asked again, trying

to focus them. 'Then we might forget about the smoking, littering and vandalism down at the local school,' he added, bluffing.

The two boys seemed to know they were on a hiding to nothing so they decided to play ball.

'He was a nasty-looking shit — kind of greasy gray hair, wore one of them blue suits like a mechanic.'

'A boiler suit? Like an all-in-one?'

The older one nodded. 'Yeah. Bloke at the garage wears one like that.'

'Anything else?'

The other brother chipped in. 'He was watching. You know, like when you're trying to watch someone but look like you're not? That's what he was doing. Over there, by those bushes.'

Chris looked over. There was a clump of bushes about twenty yards away from the playground. 'That's more like it.'

'Whatever. Can we go now?'

Chris and Kennedy watched them as they slouched away, their jeans hanging almost off their backsides. Just as they reached the merry-go-round, the younger one turned back. 'He was smoking too, yer man I mean. I was dying for a fag, but he,' he nodded towards his brother, 'wouldn't give me his last one.' He chuckled. 'I said we should go ask the guy for some but Ethan said he'd probably only want a blow job in exchange.'

When the boys had left the playground, Chris and Kennedy walked across the field towards the bushes. Kennedy peered at the ground on the far side of the shrubbery. Chris joined him, studying the surroundings. 'Find a cigarette butt, get some DNA?'

'That's the theory. Get Miss Baywatch to work her magic.'

They both fell silent as they scanned the muddy ground. Kennedy saw several old butts, but it was Chris who struck gold. 'There. Looks fresh,' he said, pulling a plastic bag out of his inside pocket. He proceeded to pick up the butt like a responsible dog owner would pick up their pet's droppings. 'If this is our man's, then we might just have caught a break.'

'Not before time too,' Kennedy added.

.

39

'So what's this plan of yours to break the ice then?' Kennedy asked Chris as they drove back towards the children's home the following day in the hope of getting Conn to open up.

'Check the glove box.'

Reilly leaned forward in the back seat to get a better view of Kennedy pulling Chris's so-called ice-breaker from the glove box.

'A book?'

'Not just any book. It's *'Ceol na hÉireann'* — the music of Ireland, one of my old schoolbooks. One of the tunes Conn was playing yesterday is in there, but he was playing from memory.'

It was definitely worth a shot, Reilly thought. The kid seemed to find comfort in music. So typical of Chris to find such a gentle, non-invasive way of breaking down someone's defenses. Which merely made his own pigheadedness about his medical condition all the harder to take.

At the home they were once more greeted by Maggie

Molloy who led them again towards the day room where Conn's music could be heard.

'OK, here goes nothing,' Chris said, walking into the room with the music book in his hand, the others having agreed to keep a safe distance this time.

'*Dia dhuit arís Conn. Cén chaoi a bhfuil tú?*' Hello again, Conn. How are you?

The boy glanced up briefly before looking back down at the piano keys.

'*Fuair me rud éigin agus ceapaim gur thatnóidh sé leat.*' I found something you might like.

Conn glanced up again, this time his gaze landing on the book in Chris's hand.

'I used to play piano in school and this was one of my favorite books – I think you might recognize some of the tunes. Do you mind if I sit down?'

After a beat, Conn moved over slightly on the bench, making room for Chris beside him without taking his eyes off the book.

Chris opened it at one of the few songs he could play well, and placed it in the script holder. Loosening up his fingers, he then placed them very deliberately on the piano keys, and began to play.

For the first few seconds he was hesitant, finding his way, but then he relaxed into the flow of 'An Chailin Alainn', filling the room with his graceful swirls.

Conn kept his attention on Chris the whole time he played, watching his hands as they danced across the keys.

Finally Chris finished, then said in Irish: ' My mum made me learn when I was young. Do you know that one?'

Conn shook his head.

'I heard the tune you were playing when I came in. Was that one of your own?'

The boy nodded.

'Could you play it for me?'

Conn thought, then nodded once more. He closed his eyes, then slowly began to play, his fingers caressing the keys.

Reilly watched from the hallway, fascinated to see Chris finding a way to get through to the young boy. It was a paternal side of him she had never seen before and she had no idea that he could play the piano, never mind communicate in Irish. But once again she felt a growingly familiar sense of being very much on the outside looking in — today both literally and figuratively, given that she had to stay out of the room and couldn't understand a word.

When Conn played, his face was calm, lost, almost beatific. She tried to reconcile it with Maggie's description of him yesterday as feral. Not feral, she thought, but wild, wild and untamed like the ocean. Wherever the boy had been, whatever he had done, she guessed that discipline had been minimal, and freedom virtually unlimited.

Conn continued to play, glancing repeatedly up at Chris, then down again at the keyboard.

She saw Chris watching him carefully, trying to gauge his mood. Did Conn want Chris to play with him now?

Chris obviously deduced the same thing and tentatively he joined in, his eyes still on Conn.

The boy gave a barely imperceptible nod, then closed his eyes as the melody took over. Chris gradually picked up the pace, slow at first, then with increasing confidence. As he played he followed the melody that Conn had established, adding to it, embellishing it.

The sound filled the room, creating a safe, warm environment, yet in amongst the grace of the music Reilly could also hear echoes of wild places, stormy waves crashing on the shore, winds whipping the trees, dark, dangerous nights and long, lonely days.

Now that Chris was playing, Conn allowed the music to

becoming wilder and wilder. Chris stayed with the basic melody, but the young boy roamed far and wide, at times returning to the heart of the music, at others wandering far away.

Then, the music stopped.

Conn sat very still for a moment, then looked over at Chris with wonder. '*Seineann tú go hiontach,*' he said, his voice barely perceptible. You play great.

Chris smiled. 'Thanks. You too. I'd like to play some more in a minute, but I need to ask you some questions now. Is that OK?' he asked in Irish.

Conn looked carefully at Chris, then looked around the room. Reilly and Kennedy stayed out of sight.

She knew Chris had established a crucial bridgehead, but was it strong enough to withstand the questioning, or would it crumble as soon as he moved away from the safety of the music?

'*Tá tú Gardai?*' Conn asked.

'*Sea.*' Chris nodded.

Conn looked down at his hands; those long elegant fingers, perfect for playing the piano. He mumbled quietly. 'What have I done? Am I in trouble?'

'No, not at all,' Chris assured him. 'But when I was your age, I always assumed I was in trouble too,' he chuckled.

Conn was still looking down. 'What do you want to ask me?'

Chris spoke softly. 'It's about your tattoo. About where you got it, and where you were before you came here.'

Conn looked up at Chris again. He gazed at him carefully for a moment, as though weighing things up, measuring his trust, then finally nodded. 'OK.'

At first the boy answered slowly, but gradually he seemed to become more comfortable with Chris's questions, and the replies became more animated.

His demeanor was one of patience, Reilly thought, as she listened to Kennedy's rough translation of the conversation in a low whisper for her. This was a boy used to waiting for things to happen, comfortable with his own company, someone who had learned to survive on his own.

It also amazed Reilly how Chris had hit on exactly the right method to lower the boy's defenses and also how comfortable and at ease he was in dealing with Conn. Especially for a man who didn't have any children of his own. The notion of what a good father he would make automatically popped into her mind, and she banished it immediately and tuned back into the translation.

'They say they found you wandering the streets? Do you remember how you got there?'

Conn shook his head. 'It was cold. People out here are so mean – I didn't like it, I just wanted to go home.'

Chris frowned. 'Out here — here at the center, you mean?'

Conn shook his head, and Chris continued. 'You were found in Dun Laoghaire. Where is home?'

Conn went very still. The only movement came from his hands, fiddling compulsively in his lap, one stubby fingernail picking at another. Reilly noticed his jaw muscles clench and unclench. Finally, he almost spat the words out. 'They didn't want me any more.'

'They? Who were "they"?'

Reilly could see from Conn's eyes that he was remembering. He would have been nine years old when the police picked him up. How much did an obviously traumatized nine-year-old remember? 'He said I was too disruptive, that I had to leave.'

Reilly strained her ears even though she couldn't possibly understand. She felt frustrated. She was good at languages and spoke near-perfect Spanish, the primary language in many of the southern states back home. The Irish language had a very different air — it sounded less rhythmic and more guttural — much closer to the Nordic languages than the lyrical cadence of Spanish and Italian.

'Who wanted you to leave, Conn?' Chris asked gently.

Conn looked troubled. The past was evidently painful for him to recall and to explain. His voice came out in a whisper, a faint expiration of sadness right from the heart. 'Father,' he sobbed. 'He was...' Then he stopped and looked quickly away, gazed out the window at the trees whipping back and forth in a fierce wind, their leaves being ripped loose, swirling and scattering in tormented gusts.

She saw his fingernails digging into the palms of his hands and knew that Chris could lose him at any moment, that Conn could clam up in a flash, and bring down the veil that had protected him.

But if he didn't keep going and take advantage of the connection they had shared, they might never have another chance. Reilly wanted so desperately to ask Conn some questions herself, but knew she had to trust Chris, trust the rapport he had established with the young boy. She understood how fragile the process was, how easily Conn could close up, how deftly Chris was steering him through evidently heartbreaking memories.

'That must have hurt. Being told to leave by your father.'

Chris's words pierced Conn's defenses. Somebody understood. He nodded, the tears running down his cheeks. 'I only wanted to stay there. Be with the others. Just be with the family...'

'You must have loved your family very much,' said Chris softly. 'How many of you were there?'

Conn sniffed, wiped his nose on his sleeve. 'Six. There were six of us. Me, the father, and the girls.'

Reilly noted how the reference was to 'the' father not 'my', as Kennedy continued to translate. Her mind automatically flicked to the widely reported incidences of Catholic child abuse. Worth considering?

'Four girls?' said Chris jokingly. 'And just you to keep them in line?'

Conn smiled. 'I dream of them still, wonder if they dream of me...' His eyes were fixed upwards on the ceiling and she could see him gulp back tears.

'You said you were a family. Were the girls your sisters?' Chris asked.

'Not my real sisters, but we were all a family.'

'Where did you live, Conn? Did the place have a name?'

He nodded. 'Of course. It was called Tír na nÓg.'

'Tír na nÓg?' Chris repeated, and Reilly saw Kennedy frown, evidently confused.

Through the stories Mike used to tell them as kids, Reilly was somewhat familiar with the legend of Tír na nÓg — it was the Gaelic equivalent of Nirvana, or Valhalla. Had Conn lived in a house called Tír na nÓg?

'Can you describe it for me, Conn, the place where you lived, this Tír na nÓg? I've always heard that it was incredibly beautiful.'

Conn looked nervous. His hands skittered across the keyboard, tapped random keys. Painful memories were surfacing again, and he was struggling to deal with them. 'Maybe tomorrow. I'm tired now,' he said wearily.

The toll the questioning had taken on the boy was obvious. His hands were red from the constant squeezing, and he was visibly exhausted. Reilly guessed he had given as much as he could give for one day.

Chris seemed to feel the same way, though he couldn't mask the disappointment in his tone. 'OK, Conn. I'd love to hear more about it sometime. And I'd like to maybe play the piano together again. I could bring you some more books.'

Conn smiled but said nothing, and then simply resumed

playing. This time there was no invitation for Chris to join in. He was retreating back inside his world, losing himself once more in the safety of the music. But Reilly felt certain that another time, another day, Chris would be able to cross the bridge once more, and get a further glimpse into Conn's secret world, into Tír na nÓg.

Chris slowly headed towards the door before turning back to the boy.

'Conn, maybe the next time I come I can bring you a music player and some CDs so you can play some music in your bedroom. And maybe you might show me the angel wings on your back?' he added, in the hope Conn would have time to think about it.

But as he walked towards the door, Conn stopped playing and spoke again. 'They're not angel wings; I'm not a girl,' he scoffed, as if this was obvious. 'They're the special wings father gave us — our swan wings.'

40

Outside the home, Kennedy lit his cigarette, battling against the fierce wind as it whipped around them. 'No wonder social services thought he was nuts.' Chris glared at him.

'I'm trying to understand what he said at the end, about the tattoo,' Reilly said. 'About them being not angel wings but swan wings.'

'I don't even want to begin to think about what that means,' Kennedy groaned.

Chris nodded to a café across the road from the home. 'Let's talk about it somewhere warmer.'

'Good idea.' Reilly wrapped her coat around her as a squall of rain appeared and she and Chris scampered across the road. Kennedy followed at a more leisurely pace, trying to squeeze in as many puffs of his cigarette as he could before they reached the café.

It was fuggy inside, with hot air steaming up the windows. The place packed with workers grabbing a late breakfast or an early lunch — a full Irish, buttered toast, fried eggs.

Reilly and Chris settled for a cup of tea, but Kennedy couldn't resist the lure of fried meat. 'Josie won't let me have the good stuff at home,' he grumbled. 'It's all bloody muesli and wholewheat toast these days.'

Reilly cursed her keen sense of smell as the appetizing whiff of fried bacon swirled beneath her nose as they waited in the queue. Her diet was becoming poor these days — way too much convenience food — and she really needed to get out running more. Getting the time to train for the marathon she'd mentioned to her father might be a stretch, but she had to find a way to nip in the bud her slowly thickening waistline. Or at least find somewhere local that did good sushi. But the cold weather seemed to make her crave greasy stodge, like fried potatoes and bacon, or 'rashers' as they called them.

'You did a great job getting him to open up like that,' she said to Chris after they sat down at a corner table. 'And you knew exactly when to stop.'

'I was just afraid of losing him, to be honest.'

Kennedy pulled up a chair and set his steaming plate on the table. He dove straight in. 'What I thought was interesting,' he said through a mouthful of sausage and beans, 'is that what seemed to bother the kid was not what happened at whatever place he was in, but the fact that they threw him out.'

'Sounded like Conn felt safe there; it was his home,' Reilly said. 'Tir Na Nog you said he called it?'

'Yes.' Chris frowned. 'I feel like I'm going back to my childhood – Tír na nÓg and the Children of Lir.'

Kennedy dabbed at his mouth with his napkin. 'Yeah, I used to read those stories to the kids years ago.'

'It's referenced in Irish mythology and folklore,' Chris told Reilly, toying with his teaspoon. 'Translated, Tír na nÓg literally means "Land of The Young".'

'It was said to exist off the edge of the map, on an island to the West,' Kennedy continued. 'There's no sickness, no crime, no worries, heaven on earth.'

'Like some kind of earthly paradise,' Chris agreed. 'Conn actually used the word "paradise" when I asked him where he was from.'

'So if it's a myth,' Reilly asked, 'why does he think he was there?'

'Good question. I didn't get the chance to ask him that. But in the stories you needed a guide to get there.' Chris sipped his tea and looked at Kennedy. 'As I recall, there was some magical horse who could gallop across the water and carry you there.'

'It's all a bit hazy to me, to be honest.'

'Across water...' Reilly mused out loud, instantly thinking about the algae in Sarah's hair.

'But what about this guy he mentioned,' said Kennedy. 'The father.'

'I know what you're thinking, but I get the feeling he was being metaphorical.'

'We can only conclude that this person somehow brought Conn there and either arranged for the tattoo to be done by somebody else, or did it himself,' Reilly posited. She frowned. 'So if this is connected to our girls, and it certainly sounds that way, are we looking at a cult or an abduction – or both? But why the mythology? And the tattoo ...the swan wings, what is the significance?'

'Part of another Irish legend, actually.'

'Ah come on,' Kennedy said, looking balefully at Chris. 'You're thinking the Swans of Lir?'

Chris nodded and turned to Reilly to explain. 'There's another story, taken from the same mythology, called the Children of Lir.'

She leaned back in her chair. 'Go on.'

'The story is about a wicked stepmother who turns her stepchildren into swans. The curse lasts for nine hundred years, and they live on a lake, in the sea, different places for three hundred years each.'

'More water ...' she mused.

'And more children living for ever — or at least a long time in solitude.' Chris cradled his tea in his hands. 'Based on that scenario, I'm leaning towards abduction.'

'This Conn seems to want to go back though,' Kennedy pointed out.

'Stockholm syndrome? He wouldn't be the first to fall under the spell of his abductor,' Chris suggested.

'So he takes them when they're young and the fairytales are being presented as truth as the kids grow older,' Reilly said, trying to get her head around it all. 'There,Tir Na Nog is good, paradise even. Out here — the real world — is bad.'

'Conn said there were four girls at Tir Na Nog when he was there, including Sarah presumably. So that suggests there are at least three others still there.'

'Assuming he's not added any more in the meantime,' Kennedy said darkly

'But our cold case, she was found dead when Conn was just a toddler. Which means there are two possibilities here: either Conn was abducted, possibly to replace the first girl. Or he is actually the biological son of this guy.'

They were each lost in their own thoughts. Finally Reilly sighed. 'I think we'll need to go back through all the missing person files again, focusing on males as well this time, to see if one matches Conn's profile.'

'The biggest question still remains,' Kennedy grunted, wiping his mouth, satisfied with his feed,'where the hell is this supposed Tir Na Nog place? And how come Conn is no longer there?'

Chris shook his head. 'Looks like we're dealing with a nut job here. The guy took Conn at some stage then presumably, and for whatever reason, got rid of him. Let's just hope he doesn't decide to get rid of any of the others he might have.'

Reilly shook her head. 'I don't think so. Based on what Conn described, it doesn't sound like a threatening place.'

'I agree,' said Chris. 'Whatever is going on at their version of Tir Na Nog, Conn was happy there. His sadness comes not from having been there, but from being cast out.'

'So what happened with Sarah?' Kennedy wondered. 'If she was there in this place, how did she end up on the side of the road that night? Was she thrown out too?'

Chris nodded. 'Because of the pregnancy perhaps. Which begs the question ...'

Kennedy stood up. 'I need another fag.' He pulled the packet out of his pocket, and looked down at Reilly and Chris. 'I don't know about you, but all this stuff is frying my brain.'

As Kennedy worked his way through the tables to the door, Reilly turned to Chris. 'When do you think you might be able to talk to Conn again?'

Chris shrugged. 'Soon, I hope. At this point he's the best chance we have of finding this place, wherever it is.'

'I'm guessing it must be reasonably close to where Sarah was found, and the region of the cold-case discovery. In the mountains somewhere?' she suggested. 'But with a body of water in the vicinity too, given the algae.'

Chris shook his head. 'But the same question applies as when we were considering a cult: how could such a place go unnoticed? We've had three rounds of door to doors in a twenty-mile radius of where Sarah was found, and drawn a blank. I'll see if we can set up another — give the local police this new information and extend the radius.'

Reilly looked thoughtful as they got up to leave. 'Well, given the mythology angle, I'm wondering if we should talk to O'Brien about bringing Reuben in...'

'Are you serious?' Chris glanced outside to where Kennedy was huddled under the café's awning, trying to light his cigarette in the wind and the rain. He pulled a couple of coins from his pocket and threw them on the table. 'Irish mythology and Reuben Knight,' he said, shaking his head in resignation. 'A match made in hell.'

41

L ater that day Rory tracked Reilly down with an update on a potential match for the remaining unidentified angel.

Or swan actually, Reilly corrected herself. She was doodling; trying to allow her right brain to kick in and make sense of all the facts and details that were emerging. She put her pen down and looked up at him.

'I've gone through the files and what's left of the corresponding evidence from the cold case. Unfortunately, we don't have a lot of comparative DNA. The dress she was found in has perished over the years. We *do* have some interesting information on the missing girl Lucy thought might be her though. Jennifer Hutchinson was listed as having a distinguishable strawberry-shaped birthmark on her back when she went missing.'

'OK ...'

'This reminded me of those slight differences in the second tattoo which we'd explained as deterioration, but I'm wondering if the wings might originally have been an attempt to disguise the birthmark?' He handed Reilly the cold-case photos once again.

She squinted as she studied the photo, but couldn't make out any such skin irregularity amongst the design.

Inconclusive.

'Did Lucy follow up on the missing girl's family?' she asked.

'No next of kin in Ireland apparently. Her mother died of cancer two years later, and her father was killed in a car crash a few years after that.' He read through the case notes. 'Jennifer was an only child; her parents moved here from the UK before she was born. We have traced down a sister of Jennifer's mother who lives in Hertfordshire in the UK. She is willing to help in whatever way possible,' Rory continued.

'Well, that's good news at least.'

'So what do you want to do next?' he asked.

'Something I was hoping we wouldn't have to,' Reilly said with an air of resignation. 'I'll need to talk to the coroner's office.'

She had been hoping it wouldn't come to this, but given that this now appeared to be a full-blown abduction case, and their cold case was a major part of it...

'So how does the exhumation process work?' Rory asked when she explained her line of thinking. 'I've never been involved with one before.'

'This will be my first in this country too. Initially, I'll need to convince the coroner's office to reopen the file. We'll need to apply for a license through the courts, but it should be quick and unobjected, seeing as she was a Jane Doe. And if we can get the aunt on board...'

No doubt it would raise all sorts of hell, but with the possibility of other missing kids involved, further investigation of a corpse from ten years before might not only confirm the girl's identity, but could also help them discover more about exactly where she'd been before her death.

Tir Na Nog?

At the very least, Reilly thought, if they could confirm an ID, then after ten long years, the poor girl would be able to get a proper burial and at least one family member would be able to say goodbye.

42

S hortly afterwards, Reilly stopped by the lab to see how Lucy was.

After their recent conversation about Grace, she was concerned, not only about the younger tech's ability to remain objective, but also from a personal point of view. She cared about the girl and was worried about the effect all of this might be having on her.

Lucy was just hanging up the phone when Reilly approached. She had a tired look in her eyes.

'Are you doing OK?'

Lucy gave a half-hearted shrug. 'Surviving.'

'We're making progress, you know.'

'Do you think so? Rory told me about Jennifer Hutchinson. I hope it doesn't lead to a dead end.'

Reilly put a hand on her arm. 'That's just the nature of these cases — for every promising lead there are a hundred dead ends, you know that.'

'I know that. I just feel for all these people...waiting, wondering...'

Reilly looked at her closely.

'Of course you do. For us it's professional — usually. For them it's personal, as personal as it can get. You too, because of your own experience.'

'A loved one, a child missing...' Lucy said croakily. 'How do people cope with that?'

'People do what they have to do,' Reilly replied, trying not to sound trite. 'Just like your own family did.'

Lucy looked away, tears in her eyes.

Reilly reached across the desk, grabbed a box of tissues and slid them towards her. The younger girl grabbed one and dabbed at her eyes. 'It's the first time I've cried about it in years,' she said.

'Well, maybe it's about time.'

Lucy sniffed, and continued to pat her eyes. 'It just feels so hopeless, Reilly. But at the same time, you can't help but feel that they must be out there somewhere. I scan faces when I'm out shopping, wondering if I'd still even recognize Grace if I saw her.'

Reilly said nothing, just allowed Lucy the chance to say the things that must have been playing on her mind for years.

'I know firsthand how busy the authorities are — we are,' she continued, 'how little time there is for missing person cases. I mean, unless there is evidence of foul play, unless there is a reason to think they have been killed or abducted, there are just too many of them, aren't there? And just no time to investigate them all properly...'

She looked up at Reilly, her eyes red.

'Are you talking specifically about Grace now, or all these other cases?'

'Both,' admitted Lucy. 'I've never been able to look at Grace's case file; my father won't allow it. But I can't help but wonder...'

Reilly could see the question in her face. She took a deep breath. 'I'll take a look at it if you want...' she offered.

Lucy's face brightened. 'Seriously?'

'I can make no promises about what we might find,' she continued, 'but I will promise to have a look and see if anything stands out.'

But as she encircled the girl in a reassuring hug, Reilly felt a sinking sense of dread about what she might be getting herself into.

43

Kennedy's reaction to the suggestion of consulting Reuben Knight had been predictable.

'What do we need that gobshite for?' he grumbled when the team assembled in a conference room the following morning. 'It's a bit late in the day now, since we have Conn, the dead angels – I mean swans — and potentially some DNA from another attempted abduction. What the hell can he add?'

'I still think it would be helpful and O'Brien agrees,' Reilly pointed out. 'We're only starting to build up enough of a profile of the abductor, and based on what we know, Reuben can help us move forward.'

'Well, don't expect me to talk to him ...' said Kennedy.

'Deny him your famous insights, you mean?' Chris mocked. 'You know how much he values what you have to say.'

Kennedy's response was considerably less polite.

Fortunately, O'Brien was willing to sanction such an expense to help them move forwards on the case — but only to the point of a telephone conversation rather than bringing the profiler in on the ground.

In any event, Knight was away working on a case in Italy.

'Italy!' said Kennedy as they sat around the conference table. 'All right for some.'

Reilly looked at him while they waited for the conference call to go through. 'I thought you didn't want to be here for this?'

'Couldn't trust you two not to screw it up,' he told her with a grin. 'We need someone with a bit of maturity in the room.'

'OK, we're connected,' Chris announced. 'Reuben, I'm going to put you on speakerphone.'

There was a moment's silence, a quiet click, then Reuben's nasal voice filled the room. 'Hello all! So who's there? Detective Delaney, of course. And the lovely Reilly?'

'Hi, Reuben.'

'Always so wonderful to hear your voice. What are you wearing today? I hear the weather has turned cool — not that lovely dark blue McQueen?'

'It's none of your business,' Reilly replied with a smile. She wasn't about to let him know he had guessed correctly.

'As I thought, the McQueen. And is Detective Dinosaur there, too? Oh I do hope so ...'

'Let's get down to bloody work,' Kennedy growled.

'I heard that guttural rumbling in the background, so I'll take that as a yes.' Reuben paused. 'I won't even begin to imagine what *he's* wearing; it will quite take away my appetite for lunch and I'm planning on feasting on a good baccala. So, on to our agenda...'

There was a quiet rustling of papers.

'I've read through the information you sent. Fascinating...' Somehow he made the word last several seconds. 'I do so love it when people confuse myths and legends with everyday life. And, Detective Delaney, seems you got to show off your ability to speak Irish? I bet *that* impressed the lovely Reilly ...'

'Reuben,' said Reilly somewhat impatiently, 'can we move forwards?'

'Oh? Am I detecting an atmosphere there?' he added excitedly. 'Has something finally happened in the ongoing will they/won't they saga? Do tell all...'

Chris clenched his jaw. 'For Christ sake...'

The profiler sighed. 'Well, I do hope you allow more foreplay when—'

'Reuben ...'

'OK, so what do we know?' he said, suddenly all business. 'Our man seems to be fixated on pale, red-haired children. He kidnaps them, keeps them at some unspecified location, tattoos them. Anything else that we actually know?'

'The two girls seem to have escaped the location, or perhaps even left of their own accord,' Reilly pointed out. 'The boy, Conn, it seems that he was made to leave.'

'Yes, that's rather interesting, isn't it?'

The room was filled with a strange clicking noise – Reilly could picture Reuben, tapping his beloved Mont Blanc pen against his teeth. 'So first of all, why is he taking them?'

'Could he be replacing someone?' Reilly said, thinking of Lucy's suggestion. 'Maybe trying to recreate a family that he lost?'

'Darling, when you do decide to lift your head up from those test tubes and microscopes of yours, you're really quite bright. Yes, based on the boy's interview, and multiple mentions of family, I thought that too. So let's assume for a moment that our kidnapper has lost a family.'

'Lost can mean lots of things,' Kennedy pointed out. 'They could be dead, or it could be a divorce and the wife's taken them.'

'Correct indeed, Detective Dinosaur. But it still might be worth checking people who have suddenly lost entire families in an accident — a car crash, something of that nature. Perhaps he has found a way of successfully isolating himself from reality, from the world.'

'What about the boy?' Chris asked. 'What do you make of that?'

'You said in your case notes that what seemed to make him sad was not what happened in Tír na nÓg, but the fact that he was expelled, that he was no longer there.'

'No doubt about that. I'm sure if he was given the chance to go back he would jump at it.'

'So that could suggest very strong brainwashing.'

Reilly thought for a moment. 'Of course, it could be that he has, indeed, created a paradise on earth.'

'Ah, Miss Reilly. A little too simplistic, I fear.'

'What do you mean?'

'You imply that the boy must have really loved it there, so *ipso facto*, the place must be really delightful.'

'Right.'

'But you ignore the role of persuasion, of manipulating the mind to create that feeling,' Reuben pointed out.

'Enlighten me.'

'Of course.' He gave a little cough, preparing to go into lecturer mode. 'I'm not suggesting that you can make something out of nothing,' he began. 'As the alchemists finally discovered, gold cannot be created from base metals. However, what you can do is build on something that already exists, make it so large in the mind that it excludes all other things.'

'And in this case?'

'So in this case, Detective Delaney, our man has obviously created an environment that is safe and nurturing for these children, one that allows him to play out his fantasy of the family he lost — or maybe never had which is another option. But he has not actually created paradise. The only place you can create paradise is in the mind.'

'Cut the mumbo jumbo,' growled Kennedy. 'What are you actually saying here?'

'Ah, Detective Dinosaur has once again awakened from his slumber. What I'm saying, my dear man, is that while these children may indeed live somewhere that is peaceful, delightful, idyllic even, to create somewhere that looms so large in the mind of a child that two years later he still wants to go back there comes not just from the physical surroundings, but from the mental real estate his captor has created.

'Your man has clearly spent a considerable effort persuading these children that they live in an earthly paradise, that it is the most wonderful place they could possibly be, and that the outside world is a dangerous and dissolute place.

'He has taken what is already there — the place they are living — and blown it up so large in their minds that they struggle, conceptually, to look beyond its walls.'

Kennedy thought about this for a moment. 'All right, clever clogs. So if this place is so wonderful, why did the girls leave — or escape or otherwise?'

'Why indeed?' replied Reuben. 'That is the mystery at the heart of this particular enigma, isn't it?'

'One of them was pregnant,' Reilly reminded him. 'So she had presumably found forbidden fruit that tasted sweet.'

'What a perfect metaphor. Forbidden fruit indeed.'

Chris reached for his coffee and swirled the dregs around in the bottom of the cup. 'But what about the cold case? *She* wasn't pregnant. She froze to death on a lonely hillside...'

'Any type of brainwashing of this sort is going to be an uneven process,' Reuben pointed out. 'And it may well be that she was the first ... the experiment even.'

'I worked on a case in North Carolina. We found the same thing there,' said Reilly. 'The level of acceptance was uneven, even among devotees who believed in the basic dogma.'

'But,' Reuben added, 'the fact that you've only discovered

two potential runaways in over ten years, and that the boy, Conn, would go back now if he were permitted to do so, suggests that our unsub is something of a master manipulator.'

'Which brings us back to one of the unanswered questions,' Reilly reminded him. 'Why was Conn expelled from paradise?'

'One could speculate endlessly...'

'Isn't that your job?' Kennedy said.

Reuben ignored him. 'However, it is my *experience*,' he emphasized the word strongly, 'that in cases like this, boys are much less pliable than girls. My guess is that the young boy was too rebellious, that he rocked the boat. And when you are creating a powerful fantasy, something that you have to sustain amongst several people across many years, you cannot afford a disruptive influence. If you pushed me,' he concluded, 'I would have to guess that Conn was expelled solely for being male...'

They were all silent for a moment.

'What about the pregnant girl, Sarah?' said Kennedy belligerently. 'You make this sound like a paradise, but if she was pregnant, maybe he's responsible for it? Maybe he is abusing them ....'

Reuben tutted. 'What a sordid mind you have, Detective Dinosaur.'

'You work as many of these cases as we have, you assume the worst, you know that,' Kennedy replied quickly.

Reuben's loud sigh came down the line. 'I'm afraid I can't deny the truth in what you say. I've learned to expect the worst, and still not be surprised when it's even worse than I imagined.'

'I've never suspected that,' Reilly added quickly. 'If these are replacements for his family — his children — then maybe there's nothing sexual in this.'

'I concur,' said Reuben firmly. 'While I could be wrong – I seem to recall being so once before, in the eighties I think,' he added devilishly, 'I would be very surprised if there were any sexual element, any abuse at all in this scenario. I think he loves these kids like his own children.'

There was a long silence.

'So how do we move forward?' asked Chris finally.

'Like I said, I would begin by looking for men who have lost a large family, in a car crash, something similar. And I would also be on the lookout for new abductions or missing children. I think he will want to replace the latest escapee, Sarah.'

'We actually had another attempt a day ago,' Chris informed him. 'Unsuccessful.'

'Oh, I do love it when I'm proved right!' Reuben crowed.

'Still, it's only a matter of time before he tries again. How do we get to him first?' Chris demanded impatiently.

'Go back to the boy, see if you can get more details from him, and think carefully about how you might locate where he's hiding them. After all, there can't be too many places in the area that could double for an earthly paradise.'

'Anything else?' Reilly asked.

'Well for starters, my dear, don't forget this place isn't actually mythical. Do what you do best … follow the breadcrumbs. Allow them to lead you right along the path to Tir Na Nog.'

44

I t had not escaped Jack Gorman's notice what his daughter was working on. When Reilly returned to the GFU after the conference call with Reuben he collared her in the hallway, a scowl knotting his bushy dark eyebrows together.

'You're not helping, you know,' he said by way of introduction.

His comment caught her by surprise – Gorman rarely said anything to her unless they were directly consulting on a case. 'Not helping?'

'Lucy,' he barked. 'This case you've got her working on. It's not helping her.

She still thinks she's going to find her sister, after all these years...' His voice trailed away. 'But she's gone. There's no way around that, and raking over old coals won't bring her back.'

Reilly looked at his dark eyes, half hidden behind his thick glasses. Were his eyes moist, tears lurking at the corners? 'Jack, I'm no psychologist—'

'No, you're not.'

'But I know this is important to Lucy,' continued Reilly.

'Grace disappeared when she was just a child. Lucy feels help-less about what happened. I think she's trying to understand it better, come to terms with it in her own way. And perhaps by helping others who have gone through a similar experience …'

Gorman stared down at his feet, pulled a handkerchief from his pocket and wiped fiercely at his nose. 'No good will come of it,' he croaked. 'Grace is gone, and that's all there is to it. Do you not think I've used all the tools at my disposal over the years to try and find her?'

Reilly watched him as he shuffled away, his head bowed. Oddly she felt that the conversation hadn't been about Lucy but about himself, the demons playing inside his head, and the thoughts that tortured him in the small hours of the night.

CONN WAS SITTING in the lobby of the children's home when Chris and Kennedy returned the following day.

'He's been waiting out here since I told him you were call-ing. He said something about a music player?' Maggie said as she ushered them inside. Chris told her about the player and the disks and checked that it was OK for Conn to have them.

'Of course. That's very decent of you, Detective.'

'You came back!' Much to Chris surprise, Conn immedi-ately walked up to him, his eyes scanning for the promised CD player.

'Here you go — just like I told you.'

The boy's face broke into a rare smile and he uttered a shy thank you. 'I know you want to ask me some more questions,' he said in Irish, 'but can we play together a bit first — you know, like last time? Nobody else here can play.'

'Of course. I've been practicing a bit myself too, want to make sure I can keep up with you.'

Conn glanced back over his shoulder at Kennedy, who was

walking behind them with Maggie. 'Where's your girlfriend today?'

Chris laughed. 'She's not my girlfriend. And she's busy with other stuff.'

They turned into the music room, and Conn led Chris straight to the piano. 'Listen. I made this one up.' He laid his hands on the keyboard, almost reverentially. 'It's about Tír na nÓg.'

Kennedy hung back and pretended to be busy on his phone.

Chris was heartened by the boy's obvious delight at seeing him again, the rapport now established between them. Hard fought but worth it. He tried to imagine what it must be like to be trapped inside yourself for this long, not connecting with anyone, not trusting anyone, wondering why the world would play such a cruel trick on you.

Conn began to play the piano. It was a haunting melody, half developed, but almost the better for that. He wandered around it, leaving then returning, drifting at times, but always coming back to the same core.

Following their discovery and the consultation with Rueben, the team had heavily researched both Tír na nÓg and the Children of Lir. It was Reilly who'd pointed out that both stories shared a theme of immortality — or eternal youth at least.

The Swans of Lir were innocents who had been punished for no good reason — evil had been committed against them. The tale of Tír na nÓg, on the other hand, was a story of sanctuary from the evils of the world, a place where music and beauty were celebrated and happiness lasted for ever.

Chris had enjoyed discussing the stories and their potential bearing on the current case with Reilly. Since the discovery of his circumstances and his determination to keep things hidden, it had felt as though she'd thrown up a wall around her, no longer willing to be open with him. If he was going to hide things, then so was she.

But the two had spent the previous evening pouring over texts to try and figure out how best to approach the investigation from hereon. It had been a rare opportunity to try and rebuild bridges, little by little, and regain some of the closeness they'd once shared.

Conn was lost in his music, his eyes sometimes closed, sometimes gazing out of the window, occasionally turning to Chris. Finally he slowed and the notes gradually faded away. He was almost breathless. He turned and gazed at Chris, the unasked question in his eyes — did you like it?

Chris nodded slowly, then began to play. A smile engulfed Conn's face – Chris was playing his melody. Not quite the same — his own variation, his own interpretation — but unmistakably the same tune.

Even though he didn't have kids of his own Chris liked to think that he had a way of connecting with them that came naturally. He was using every ounce of that here with Conn.

As his hands caressed the keyboard he looked at Conn. 'This is what Tír na nÓg is all about?'

Conn nodded.

'I don't think I'd want to leave either.'

Chris played for a moment more, then gently rested his hands on the keys. 'Can I ask you a few questions now, then we'll play some more?'

Conn said nothing and gazed out the window. Chris looked at the side of his face, wondering what passed through his mind when he played the piano — was it conscious thought, or was it simply emotions racing around, forcing their way out through the music?

He caressed the keys, not really playing, just letting Conn's melody guide him, slowly, gently circling it, creating the mood, the feeling that Conn's playing had evoked. Without stopping playing, Chris began to question him.

'When we talked the other day, you told me about the man who brought you to Tir Na Nog. Did he have any other name?'

'Athair,' said Conn.

Chris's pulse quickened. 'Anything else? The girls ...did they ever call him anything else?'

Conn shook his head. 'Athair mostly, and sometimes Setanta. He was our father, but he was sort of our mother too — he did everything, like real parents should.'

Real parents ...Chris touched the keys and repeated Conn's melody again. 'What kind of things did he do?'

'I don't know — all the things your mum and dad would do, I suppose — he fed us, looked after us, tucked us in at night, read us stories about the bad places beyond Tír na nÓg. Places like this,' he added sadly.

Chris thought about his next question. He found his hands guiding him, and changed from Conn's tune to an old Irish folk song. Conn looked at him sharply.

'You know that one?' said Chris.

'Sarah used to play it.'

Sarah ... Chris tried not to look too excited. Repeating the melody, he kept his voice light. 'Do you remember anything before Tír na nÓg?'

Conn furrowed his brow. 'Little bits of stuff come into my head sometimes, you know, like when you're not sure if it's real or from a dream?'

Chris smiled. 'I get that a lot. Is it something I remember, or a story I heard, or did I dream it?'

'Yes. Father said we were special, that we were chosen but that our dreams would try to trick us sometimes, and we should ignore them.'

'Can you tell me about any of them? The dreams?'

Conn looked thoughtful. 'I kind of remember my

minnie, she shouted a lot when I did things she didn't like.' He gazed up at the ceiling. 'But I remember a really old lady mostly. She played the piano, old songs like you just did, I remember her face had so many cracks and lines on it.'

'Who was Minnie, was she your sister or something?' Chris asked.

Conn smiled. 'No, stupid, my minnie was my mother. Before I was chosen.'

Chosen...

Chris changed to another old song, one he himself had learned from his grandmother.

Conn smiled. 'That's another one.'

'Did you have a piano at home? In your first home I mean, not Tir Na Nog.'

'I don't think so – I can't remember...'

'But you remember this old lady, maybe your gran, playing the piano. Anyone else you remember?'

Conn sighed. 'Father told me to forget them. Said I was better off away from them.'

That makes sense, thought Chris. Focus them on the here and now and forget what they might have left behind.

'There's a man I see sometimes in my dreams. He always makes me wake up, he isn't very nice. Father said that he took me away from there because of him, and that I'd always be safe with him and the others in Tír na nÓg...'

He went quiet.

Move on, thought Chris, move on before you lose him. He quickly changed his playing back to Conn's melody, bringing him back to Tír na nÓg. 'So what else can you tell me about Tír na nÓg? It sounds like a very special place.'

Chris could almost feel Conn's mood lift as he brought him back from the dark place. 'It was lovely,' he began. 'But I never realized how lovely it was till I got stuck here.'

'Did you ever go anywhere else away from there, to school or anything like that?'

Conn shook his head. 'Father said the land would be our teacher. We would often walk through the woods or play down by the beach in summer, but he also made us do some stuff inside the house — times tables and reading. We did lots of reading.'

A house ... beach ... the woods Chris looked at him with interest. 'Did you have a lot of books there in the house?'

'In the kitchen there was a whole wall that was just books, and we were allowed to read any one we wanted.' He looked at Chris. 'Sarah used to read to me a lot.'

'Was she the oldest?'

'I guess so,' said Conn with a shrug. 'She must have been, she was kind of like a mum. Used to look out for the younger ones, help us with our chores and stuff.'

'You had chores to do?' laughed Chris. 'I thought you said it was paradise.'

'It was fun, though, the stuff we had to do.'

'Like what?' Now that Conn was talking about Tír na nÓg, his words were coming quicker, and Chris desperately wanted to keep him talking, keep the flow going.

'Cooking, washing up, and looking after the animals — that was my favorite.'

'You had animals there?'

Conn smiled. 'A few.'

'Like what?'

'Sheep, goats and chickens. The chickens were funny; they were my job mostly, wandering around everywhere. They used to come into the kitchen looking for scraps and Sarah would chase them out. But they weren't scared, they used to chase the dogs too.'

'It sounds fun.'

Conn smiled, the happy memories flooding back to him. 'It

was brilliant. I used to get the eggs every morning, still warm they were.'

'So did you get most of your food from the land?'

Conn thought for a minute. 'Most of it, I think. We had a big vegetable garden — that was hard work — and lots of fruit in the summer and autumn. Father would be busy working on his *crois*, I would help him sometimes but it was very noisy and the dust used to make me cough.'

Chris was puzzled. 'What's a crois?'

'Oh they were beautiful, he made them from the giant rocks he'd bring home in the van. Sometimes he'd get even bigger ones — a big truck would deliver them or we'd get smaller ones from the mountain or woods. He shaped them in the barn,' Conn said, pride in his voice.

Chris thought about the trace evidence, Sarah's silicosis ... Rock dust?

'So these crosses, what did he do with them?'

'Every so often he'd have to take a trip, he said if he didn't make them and deliver them up to Balor we would no longer be safe from the demons that hid out beyond the woods and the water. Balor would no longer protect us,' he said solemnly and Chris recalled that in Celtic mythology, Balor was the god of death. He could hear Conn's tone change as he spoke. He obviously was still affected by what he perceived as a real danger from this demon.

Chris was beginning to understand a little better how the children were controlled. Fear was a powerful tool when used against the immature minds of innocent kids.

'Can I ask you a question about Tír na nÓg?'

Conn nodded.

'You mentioned the beach. Was there water nearby?'

'Yes, a big lake.'

Which of course tied in with Reilly's freshwater algae, Chris thought, feeling somewhat guilty for dismissing it so readily before. 'And it was big, this lake; you could swim in it?'

'You could. But the others were afraid of Kelpie. I wasn't though; I knew Balor would protect us from him like Father said, but I can't swim so I just splashed about along the shore in the summer.' He was lost in his thoughts for a moment. 'I always wondered what it was like on the other side,' he said. 'Sometimes we'd see things from a distance. But then when I got lost — when Father took me away – I just wanted to go back...'

Tír na nÓg'Who is Kelpie, Conn?' Chris asked.

'Kelpie is a sly demon who lives above and beneath the water,' Conn said with apparent disbelief that the detective didn't already know this. 'We could hear his cries at night as he galloped above the water. Sarah saw him once and cried for days. Father said he was far more cunning than any being and could even turn himself into a handsome man to trick the girls into falling for him so he could steal them away and consume them.'

'Yes, girls can be scaredy cats sometimes,' said Chris, his mind racing. Was this 'kelpie' the one who had impregnated Sarah perhaps? An outsider that had somehow managed to find his way into paradise?

'I would have fought him though,' Conn continued, all bravado. 'I wanted to but Father wouldn't let me.'

'Conn,' Chris said, remembering something Reuben had said the day before. 'You said that your father banished you from Tir Na Nog. Why? What did you do?'

Like a sunny day suddenly turning to a thunderstorm, Conn's face changed in an instant.

'I'm sorry, I didn't mean to upset you.'

'I'm tired of playing now. I want to go back to my room.' And with that Conn got up and was gone.

45

Later that evening, Reilly was perched on a stool looking into the comparison microscope when Chris stopped by her office to update her on what he had learned from Conn. 'Have you got a minute?' he called out.

She nodded. 'Of course, come on in.'

He walked behind her, leaned over her to get a better look at what she was doing. He could smell the subtle scent of lilac in her hair, and had to resist the urge to reach out and touch it. He missed her, missed the easy relationship they'd once shared, yet had no idea how to restore it. Focusing his mind, he looked at the slide she was studying. 'What's that?'

'I had some water samples taken from a bog and a small pond on National Forestry land near where Sarah was hit. I just wanted to run some comparisons to the algae found in her hair,' she said.

'Did you find anything?'

'Yes, unfortunately there was similar algae present in all of the samples.' Of course conditions in that particular area at this time of year are perfect for spread and growth. Open up a bottle of mineral water up there and you'd probably have the stuff growing in the bottle before you've finished drinking it,' she added, sitting upright on the stool.

'So there's no distinguishing between the growth of it in one area to another?' Chris asked.

'Well, the water samples themselves will have different content in relation to location, but we only have the algae itself, not the water source. The chemical make-up is identical, so there's no way of pinpointing a particular area.'

'Pity,' Chris said. 'Even a rough idea would've been some way helpful. In any case,' he continued, 'I spoke again with Conn this morning. Seems they were definitely being held near water; a big lake according to him, though I'm not sure what constitutes "big" for a ten year old.'

He lowered himself into a nearby chair and gave her a brief rundown on what else he'd learned. 'Conn mentioned a couple of things, old Celtic fairytales … monsters that he said he and the other kids were scared of. He spoke like they were something he'd actually witnessed himself, genuinely feared.' He sat forward. 'He said his father made crosses out of stone to ward off Balor. First thing that jumped into my head was rock sculpting...rock dust...'

'Sarah's silicosis,' Reilly said and Chris nodded.

'This Balor is some sort of mythic monster that lives in the darkest depths of water. He also mentioned that if Balor was not kept happy, they would not be safe from all manner of demons that roamed the woods and mountains.'

Reilly bit her lip. 'Fear and love …'

Chris nodded. 'These are no ordinary abductions, Reilly. This guy's a clever fucker — he takes them young, brainwashes them and has them want for nothing. It's the perfect recipe for Stockholm Syndrome.'

'Perhaps, but if he's really that clever why did he let our two girls go?'

'I thought we were working on the assumption that they had escaped?' he said, trying to see Reilly's angle.

'Exactly – it was an assumption, mostly based on the fact that Sarah was pregnant. We have no idea how the other girl ended up where she did.'

'That reminds me of something.' Chris explained the bit about Kelpie, the outsider who'd supposedly made Sarah cry.

'You're thinking a third party might be responsible for Sarah's pregnancy?'

'Why not? We keep saying that it's unlikely the guy himself is responsible, and if he's not abusing them, then it would have to have been an immaculate conception.'

'Perhaps, but regardless of who the father of the baby was, the abductor would have known that a pregnancy would be a major threat to him. Unless you know what you're doing, childbirth requires outsiders, help … complications he doesn't need.'

'And it's not as though he hadn't cast one of his swans out before,' Chris said, taking up the thread. 'So maybe after learning about the pregnancy our guy took control, took Sarah somewhere far away from base, somewhere she wouldn't draw the heat.'

'Yet she wasn't showing,' Reilly pointed out, remembering that she herself hadn't spotted any visible signs of pregnancy on Sarah's body.

'There are other signs though: morning sickness, cravings …' Chris scratched his stubble. 'So what are you thinking? He pushed her into the path of the van?' He thought back to the interview with William Connolly. 'The driver did say she'd just appeared from nowhere, like a ghost …'

'I don't know but I don't think we're seeing the full picture. She was struck from behind while walking away from civilization, dressed in minimal clothing on a cold, damp night. If she'd just escaped from somewhere she'd surely be heading towards the lights of a village or another house for help. Yet she wore no shoes and her feet were in good condition.'

Then Chris thought of something, something he hadn't remembered until now.

'She was hit from behind because she turned around,' he told Reilly, telling her about the interview with William Connolly. 'The way he described it, it sounded to me like an attempt to protect the baby.'

They both paused, thinking about it.

Reilly shook her head. 'I don't know. I guess until we find the place, all we can do is surmise. But my instinct is that, paradise or not, Sarah escaped. The fact that the van driver saw her turn to save the baby suggests that even more. Like Reuben said, maybe as she got older she realized that paradise wasn't all it was cracked up to be, and was hoping to take her chances with the baby in the outside world.'

'And look how that worked out,' Chris added sadly.

'I know.'

'So it seems the more we dig the further we seem to get from the truth.' She went over to her desk, picked up an official-looking document, and laid it in front of him. 'What's that?' he asked.

'The exhumation license for Swan number one, aka Jennifer Harrington,' Reilly told him. 'More digging, but of the literal kind.'

46

I stare into the lake. It is our protection, it gives us life, its green depths providing food and safety. It moves constantly, gently, pulled by the moon and caressed by the winds, kissing the shore like a hand gently rocking a cradle.

In summer, it is a place of fun, the water retreating to offer a beach for play in the shallows. In winter, it rises high, claws at the bank, seems to threaten us, its fingers longing to crawl up the land and invade our home as we huddle round the fire, listening to the storms raging outside.

The swans fear it, as they should. They know it protects us, but there is also a place in their hearts that senses that this is how we arrived in the first place, born on magic hooves across the cold depths. And if it is the entrance to our world, it is also the escape, a way to leave...

Is that what called to her? Did the water call to her? It is a spirit, has a life of its own, not malicious but capricious, a bringer of life and a protector, but also a bringer of death, and a weakness in our other-wise impregnable stronghold.

Did the water call to her that night? Was it seductive, offering an escape to her troubled mind, already turned by the worms that had *crept within? Did she succumb? Was she dragged down, her cold eyes staring upwards through the green murk to the world she had left behind?*

Does she lie there still, a prisoner for ever?

ON THE EVENING of the exhumation Reilly and the GFU team made their way out to the cemetery.

'Ever done one of these before?' Gary asked her from the passenger seat of the van.

'Not here but a few in the States,' she told him, visions of the excavation work on the burial plots at New Eden flashing into her head.

Over a period of many years, twelve family members had died and been buried on the ranch. Reilly had been part of the team that had spent weeks exhuming and examining their remains.

The memory sent a fresh chill down her spine.

There had been a wide cross-section of remains from the very old to still-born babies. The corpses were buried simply — no caskets, no embalming, just a hole in the ground and a coating of quick-lime to prevent odors or disease. Reilly had been tasked with collecting DNA to cross-reference with missing persons. It had been a grim undertaking, and in truth the prospect of facing similar horrors with Jennifer Hutchinson today filled her with dread.

'They're pretty straightforward,' she said. 'We just need to be careful and ensure as much as possible remains intact and in good condition.' She was unwilling to elaborate on the finer details so as not to unsettle him.

'Do you think we'll find much at this stage though?' Gary asked. 'She's been down there for a long time.'

'It's hard to say.'

The girl's burial records didn't state whether or not she had been embalmed.

If she had, any tox screens they wanted to carry out would be pointless, notwithstanding that the deterioration of the corpse meant they would be pretty difficult anyway.

Reilly looked out the window at the world around them as the GFU van went by. Life was carrying on regardless: bin men collected rubbish, mothers brought kids home from school and commuters made their way back from work, all oblivious to what was about to happen.

In the back lay a box of protective clothing and face masks, two five-gallon drums of disinfectant, and an oversized plywood casket.

The casket was tarred and lined with zinc. It was in this that the remains would make their next journey; a journey that Reilly hoped would end in justice and a proper reburial in the presence of her only living relative who'd flown in from the UK earlier that day.

'What I'm really hoping for is sound DNA, so that at least we can confirm whether or not she is Jennifer Hutchinson,' Reilly said.

They would also be able to use DNA analysis to compare the remaining personal effects and, depending on decomposition, further investigate the tattoo.

'So who else will be here this evening?' Gary asked as the traffic lights turned green.

'Well, the aunt of course, a couple of suits from the Environmental Department along with the excavation operators, I would think.' Chris and Kennedy would be making an appearance too, as well as a representative from the Press Office, anxious that what was typically considered a ghoulish process would not cause a public relations stir.

Gary turned the bend so they could see the entrance to Glasnevin cemetery.

'Looks like there's a good turn out; doubt there were as many around when the poor girl was buried,' he said, indicating the line of vehicles parked either side of the road outside the gates.

Reilly's heart sank as she saw photographers and journalists crowding round the entrance as they passed.

'Damn, that's all we need.'

They approached the entrance which had a large tarpaulin screen ready to be pulled across to give some privacy and security. A uniformed officer stood out on the road and, recognizing the GFU van, waved them on through the gates.

'Just pull in over here,' she instructed, spotting Chris waving for their attention a little further down.

'So much for low key...' he said, by way of greeting. He looked back towards the gate where already lenses were being trained on them. 'They're still calling it an Angel Cult. Maybe we should put them right — tell them the tattoos are actually swan wings. That might soften their coughs for them,' he said, as Kennedy walked toward them, a small officious-looking man trailing him.

'What's up?' Chris asked. His partner's bright red face gave away the fact there was some kind of problem.

'Ask Mr Fucking Self-Important here,' Kennedy grumbled.

'George Mullins. I was sent as overseer by the DOE. Are you Ms Steel?' he asked, directing his question to Reilly.

'Yes. I have the paperwork from the coroner's office right here,' she replied, retrieving the documentation from her kitbag.

'The paperwork is not an issue. What *is* an issue is the security cordon, or should I say lack of,' he blustered. 'I simply cannot allow this to proceed in full view of all these people. As our directives clearly state, our obligations are to the deceased and next of kin.'

'And I have told the *gentleman*,' Kennedy barked, suggesting that Mullins was anything but, 'that once the screen is pulled across and your van parked across the entrance, we will have enough privacy for a Royal visit.'

'Look, Detective, I am merely doing my job,' the official continued. 'Such matters are very sensitive, and I would be in a world of trouble if the front page of tomorrow's papers carried photographs of a muddied coffin being pulled from the ground, especially relating to such a high-profile investigation.'

'Ah, for feck's sake...' Kennedy started, but Chris cut in.

'Mr Mullins, we understand your position, but please consider ours. This exhumation may well be pivotal to an ongoing abduction case. What do you need from us to make this happen?'

'Well, can't you get rid of them?' he asked, referring to the journalists. 'Even with the screen and van in place there are still several vantage points where those snappers and their big lenses can clearly see the grave plot.' Mullins indicated the sides of the graveyard, one sharing a boundary with a church and the other a sports ground.

They all stood looking around, searching for a solution.

'I have a suggestion which might work,' Reilly offered eventually. 'We have several tarps and a tent in the van. We can surround the plot with them and back the van up when removing the casket. That way the grave will be shielded at all times.'

Mullins nodded reluctantly. 'Sounds good in theory but I will need to see it in practice before I can sign it off.'

'OK, let's get it done then.' Chris walked away, beckoning Kennedy to do the same before he said anything else to upset the guy.

'Where's the aunt?' Reilly asked, the presence of Jennifer's next of kin unsettling her a little. If she'd had her way, the woman would be waiting for results back in the warmth of her hotel. But when the coroner's office originally sought out the woman's consent for the exhumation, she'd been insistent about attending.

'In the back of the squad car.' Chris indicated a parked garda car a hundred yards from the main entrance.

Reilly decided to introduce herself and familiarize the woman with the lay of the land.

'Ms Rogers, my name is Reilly Steel.' She offered her hand through the open window to a nervous-looking middle-aged woman, who seemed shaken by the sight of the machinery and heavy police presence.

'Hello.'

'I believe my colleagues at the coroner's office explained the process to you, but just so you know, you aren't expected to do anything today,' Reilly said gently, hoping to put her at ease. 'We'll take care of everything and when it's done, you'll be taken back to your hotel and we will be sending anything we find to the lab for analysis. We should have the initial results back very shortly and then we'll be in touch again to discuss the outcome and next steps. Did you fly over on your own today?'

The woman nodded. 'My husband flies in tonight. He can't get off work until later. I wish Lisa were here,' she added, referring to girl's mother. 'It was Jenny going missing that killed her really.' She took out a handkerchief and blew her nose. 'I just hope it is her down there so we can bury the poor little thing with her mum and dad where she belongs.'

Reilly swallowed the lump in her throat. 'Me too. You take care for the moment and I'll talk to you again soon, OK?' She patted Dawn Rogers's hand before heading back to the GFU van.

Some time afterwards, the tent and supporting concealments were erected.

A large tent had been set up with one end open to allow the small digger access. The GFU van was parked with its rear doors facing the open end of the tent, with two sets of privacy tarpaulin screens either side of the van. This gave Reilly and Gary enough room for the zinc-lined shell into which they would maneuver the casket once it was out of the ground.

The press and photographers had to make do with pictures of a white forensic tent and the GFU van which would surely not be graphic enough for the front pages.

This was enough to satisfy the DOE officer, who retreated to the comfort of his car while he waited to verify the casket number and finish his paperwork.

Any other police and officials on the scene stood off to the side, leaving room for the mini-digger, which proceeded to peel back the first few layers of soil. A workman with a shovel would carefully uncover the rest.

'So what are you hoping to find once you get her up?' Kennedy asked, blowing out cigarette smoke, while they waited for the heavy digging to finish.

'Hopefully, a casket in relatively good shape and a corpse that will, at the very least, enable us to confirm ID,' Reilly said, raising her voice over the churning noise of the excavator.

And if they were lucky perhaps a few more clues that would help them figure out where she, Sarah and Conn had been held.

The machine noise stopped.

They all stood back and waited as one of the workers continued unearthing the layers of soil immediately above the casket. He needed to be more careful than the excavator for fear of damaging anything, but the sound of the shovel scraping through the soil in the falling darkness of the cemetery was still bone-chilling.

'Looks like he's reached the coffin,' Chris said, when eventually the worker stopped and shouted something to one of his colleagues above the grave.

All turned and looked back expectantly into the hole.

'Excuse me, Detectives?' one of the corporation workers called out. 'I think you need to come and look at this.'

'Have you found it?' Kennedy asked.

The man shook his head. 'That's what I'm trying to tell you,' he said, a little uncomfortably. 'Come and see. This grave is empty, there's nothing to find.'

47

A little while later, Reilly and the detectives reconvened back at the incident room, trying to make sense of what they'd just discovered.

Or not. The interment records for the cold case clearly showed the date and time of burial, as well as a casket number. As there was no record of a family member coming forward to claim the body or request removal to a family plot, they could only conclude that the grave had been tampered with. The task of telling Dawn Rogers that her niece had not, after all, been located, and that her visit had been in vain would be awkward to say the least.

'Somebody dug her up,' Kennedy said, stating the obvious. 'But who? And more to the point, why?'

'With regard to who at this stage we can only conclude that it's him,' Chris replied, referring to the abductor.

'Agreed, but why, and where's the body now?'

Chris breathed out deeply. 'Maybe we'll find the answer to that when we find Tir Na Nog.'

Reilly rubbed her eyes. Taking into account the information Conn had given Chris about his former 'home', she'd spent the last few hours on Google Earth studying the topography of the area closest to where both dead girls were found, in the hope that she might be able to figure out the location. She talked as she typed on her laptop. 'I've been trying to pinpoint a possible location for Tír na nÓg,' she said. 'Reuben set me thinking before when he said that there couldn't be many places in Wicklow that could be considered *anyone's* private heaven on earth.'

'I think he was just being a smart-ass about Wicklow,' Chris said.

'Of course, but he was also right in a way. And based on the geographical information we already have, the location of the girls' bodies, and what Conn told us about it being close to a body of water, I've narrowed it down to a few possibilities.'

'How many possibilities?'

She clicked on the mouse, and turned the screen so the others could see. 'Look, here's Sarah's hit-and-run location and ...' She made the area map bigger. 'The cold-case body was found here.'

The two detectives followed along as Reilly pointed out the locations.

'I started within a five-mile radius of the accident, where you had the locals canvass for information the first day,' she explained. 'Like we said, Sarah was barefoot, so she couldn't realistically have traveled far.'

'Assuming she did indeed walk to the location.'

'Well, let's just say for a second that she did walk, irrespective of whether she' escaped or, like Conn, had been cast out. Her feet were not badly damaged yet her clothing was still wet — not from the drizzle, but from swimming through a water source, hence the algae in her clothes and hair.' Reilly zoomed into a specific area on the map. 'So I concentrated on lakes – big enough that you'd have to actually swim across it — which were also close to fertile land, possibly farmland, given what

Conn told you about them growing vegetables and raising chickens.' She zeroed in on the area a little more. 'This place struck me first.'

'Glen of the Two Lakes,' Chris mused, as he looked at the screen.

'What?'

'That's what Glendalough means in English,' he explained. 'We used to go there on school trips for geography class. Don't you remember learning about U-shaped valleys?' he continued to Kennedy. 'That place is one of the best examples in the country. Like you said, steep cliffs and a lake, and not only that but the Glendalough area is also teeming with history.'

'So if our guy has a real obsession with Celtic history and mythology, this area would be right up his street.'

'Far from private, though,' Kennedy pointed out. 'Up there you're more likely to encounter a busload of tourists than some kidnapper who is trying to keep kids hidden away.'

'I thought that too.' Reilly moved the screen again to show a wider cross-section of the surrounding landscape. 'There are other lakes nearby. Sarah's feet may not have been badly damaged if, say, she traveled over land like this...' She circled her finger around some brown and green parts on the screen which indicated grassy areas.

'Then she may well have traveled further than we had considered,' Chris said.

'Exactly. These lakes are not too isolated, they're all good-sized, have farmable land close by, and yet are all somewhat remote.' She clicked on a map icon that switched the screen from the satellite image to a more traditional map which made viewing surrounding roads, rivers and lakes easier.

'So from east to west we have the Roundwood reservoir, Lough Dan, Lough Tay, then the Glendalough lakes before finally the Blessington lakes to the west.' She used her pen to point to several areas on the map where the lakes were located.

'OK, so which of these do you think is most likely?' Chris asked, guessing that she had no doubt already considered them all.

'Well, if it were me, and I wanted to keep away from outsiders and at the same time make it difficult for anyone to escape, I'd choose here,' Reilly said, pointing to a secluded valley surrounded by forest and a sheer, unclimbable cliff-face, bordered by a large glacial lake. 'It's surrounded by steep rocky slopes, woodland and more interestingly ...' She zoomed in a particular area. '...what looks like a patch of strand.'

Chris stood back. 'Or as Conn called it, a beach.'

'Exactly.'

'And not just a beach but plenty of rocks and boulders to use to make offerings to this "Balor" fella.' Kennedy indicated the visibly rocky western shore of the lake. 'Good work, Miss Baywatch. We'll make a detective out of you yet.'

'Cheers,' she replied drily.

'Those fields pretty much front onto the lake,' Chris observed. 'Farmland?'

'Possibly.'

He peered closer at the satellite image. 'It's difficult to make out, but it looks like there's a fence or stone wall on this side...' He traced an outline round the northern end of the property.

'That's quite a lot of land,' said Kennedy finally. 'You'd need a few quid to be able to afford a spread like that.'

'Could be a family owned place, or maybe this guy gets more than protection for all those sculptures Conn was talking about.'

Chris took out his phone. 'I'll ring the station and get someone chase Land Registry to find out who the owner of that place is.'

Kennedy nodded. 'Better check with the locals in that neck of the woods too — see if they know anything about who lives there.'

He sat back down.

Reilly stared at them both for a moment. 'And that's it? We just wait?'

'Well, what do you suggest?' Chris replied. 'We can't just call the cavalry and go charging up there. You know as well as I do that our hands are tied until we get a better sense of what we're dealing with. We can maybe have a look around sure, but—'

'Hey, I'm all for protocol, and I know what happens when procedures aren't followed, but this is different surely. We can't just sit on our hands when we know there may well be other children being held there.'

'Like Chris said, we'll go and check it out, have a scoot around the area,' Kennedy told her. 'In the meantime, it's not like the kids are in immediate danger, seeing as Conn seemed to have nothing but good things to say about the place.'

'We'll just have to tread carefully on this one, Reilly,' Chris reassured her. 'First, let us check it out, see how the land lies.'

'Fine,' she concurred. 'But if you're going up there to check it out, I'm coming with you.'

48

I sat by the water yesterday, simply watching them play. Their laughter rang out, clear as a bell, carried by the wind across the fields from a distant church. Their joy was untempered, unrestrained, no thought of tomorrow, no cares for what might happen in the future — they live in the here and now, in the eternal beauty of youth.

The days have been difficult since she left us, but they are strong, my little swans, they are slowly recovering, finding their security again in the daily rhythm of life, the tending of the animals, the preparing of the food, the games and songs and laughter that fill their days.

Today the sun shone, the world smiled upon us, and the children played. What else would they do? What else should they do? Childhood is for playing, for laughing, and that is what they do.

We have created between us a place that is everything they need and nothing more. What better description of paradise could you find?

The nights are harder, though — the young ones miss her the most, she was always there, always calm, always the comforting pres-

ence when they woke in the night with dreams of dark terror haunting them. At night they fall asleep remembering her, and fear rushes into the void that she left.

She haunts my dreams too: her radiance, her aura of beauty. I offered her love, safety, security, eternal youth and beauty. What more could she have wanted?

KENNEDY DROVE hard around another corner on the country roads of Wicklow, picking up speed on a short downhill as the road snaked its way up along the course of one of many streams and rivers.

They had decided to travel on the N81 which would take them past the Blessington Lakes, and onwards through the Wicklow Gap passing Glendalough on the way.

Reilly sat in the back, gazing at the passing scenery. As they drove through the Wicklow Gap she was struck by the isolation of the area — dense forests had given way to heather-blanketed boglands, interspersed with varying sized boulders of granite — perfect for offerings to Balor. With Conn's mention of his captor's profession in mind, she took note of various rough-hewn Celtic crosses dotted along certain parts of the landscape.

As the car swept around another corner, a stunning panorama opened up. To the right, a large waterfall plunged toward the valley floor, exposing the earth's granite heart, while the mountain seemed to soar into the heavens, and Reilly was reminded of Tolkien's portrayal of Middle Earth in *The Lord of the Rings*.

Yes, this was indeed a suitable landscape in which to re-enact a mystical fairytale.

Kennedy continued to drive as fast as the narrow roads would allow, seemingly oblivious to the surroundings.

'Trying to impress me with your macho cop driving skills?' Reilly teased.

'Tell me again why she's here,' he said to Chris, feigning annoyance. 'Shouldn't you be staring into a microscope in your lovely white coat, and leaving the real detective work to the professionals?'

'Well, seeing that it was *my* real detective work that got us this far, I thought I'd come along for the ride, make sure you don't arrive here like a bull in a china shop.'

'Yes, subtlety is not his forte,' Chris said, joining in.

'Thanks, mate, you're supposed to be on my side,' Kennedy shot back. 'Then again I should have known better with you two. I keep saying to Josie we could do with a good day out. When are you two kids going to stop pretending you weren't made for each other? I don't think I can handle the tension any longer, and Josie wants a new hat.'

'Very funny, smart arse,' Chris shot back, while Reilly shook her head and stared uncomfortably out of the window. 'You're like a teenager sometimes.'

'That's what Josie says.' Kennedy strained his neck to wink at Reilly in the mirror.

'Speaking of the lovely Josie, how is she doing these days?' Reilly had picked up on Josie's health issues via the usual office gossip channels. Another detail Chris obviously hadn't seen fit to share with her.

Kennedy's face clouded. 'She's OK. Doctor's sending her for some more tests,' he said, and by his expression Reilly knew it was a difficult subject and immediately wished she hadn't brought it up.

'Well, give her my best, won't you? I haven't seen her since … Christmas drinks last year, I think it was,' she said, amazed at how quickly the time had passed.

'Yeah, it's been a while, and I'll tell her you were asking for her. Will I also tell her to buy a hat?' he added, mischievously lightening the mood as he always did when things turned difficult. They drove on past the sugarloaf mountain and turned off at the village of Roundwood, which, according to the sign, was Wicklow's highest village in terms of altitude. Chris told Reilly about a house the drug squad had raided there a while back in which they'd found eighty grand's worth of cannabis plants, leading to the inevitable newspaper headline 'The Highest Village in Ireland.'

A few miles later the road narrowed and they approached a junction. 'OK, which way from here?' Kennedy asked.

Reilly checked their GPS location on her iPhone.

'Go right. According to the map there's a forestry road just up here. We might be able to park the car and go on foot from there.' She pointed up the hill towards a thick pine forest.

'What's all this about walking? You know I don't do walking.'

'We know,' Chris replied drolly. 'Calm down, we'll get out at the forestry road and have a look around. You stay in the car and keep in touch with base and see if they've come up with anything from the Land Registry,' he said as the car bounced along the pot-holed surface.

'Sounds fair.'

When they reached the entrance to the road, Reilly got out of the car and stretched. Then she reached back into the car, pulled out her kitbag and slung it over her shoulder. She wore a dark blue North Face jacket and chunky hiking boots.

Chris was wearing his usual leather jacket and T-shirt. He shivered. 'I feel under-dressed.'

Reilly pointed towards the stile they had to climb over to get onto the forest path. 'Don't say I didn't warn you; there are only two kinds of weather in the mountains — raining or about to rain.'

As if to validate her point, it began to drizzle, light drops splashing onto the damp grass. Reilly paused halfway over they stile, and looked back at him. 'You can always wait in the car with Kennedy, you know…'

He looked back at the car where his partner was already lighting a cigarette, then peered up at the rain clouds. 'Actually, I think I'd rather get soaked to the skin.'

'You may well get your wish.' She climbed easily over the stile and followed the worn path across the field; Chris fell into step beside her.

From the Google Earth images and soil profile maps they had looked at, it was clear that this particular area was perfectly located for anyone wanting privacy. There was only one track leading in and out, and no other dwellings nearby. The lake, which protected the western side, was only accessible via a rambling path, which skirted the opposite shore of the lake. It was about a half-mile climb in from the road, enough to deter anyone except keen hikers.

The route was wet and muddy from recent rainfall, and Chris soon found himself sliding about in his slick shoes. Reilly set a fast pace, stomping along in her hiking boots, seemingly oblivious to the mud underfoot or the rain overhead.

She had the iPhone in a weatherproof holder, but she didn't need to refer to the GPS – she had a good idea where they were going from her research. The path crossed a rocky field, then skirted another, before crossing a small ditch, half hidden in a thick hedgerow. On the other side of the ditch the land climbed slightly, obscuring their view of the lake until they were almost upon it.

As they rounded the corner, they heard a rustling in the bushes. Startled, they both stopped and looked at each other. Chris moved past Reilly and edged slowly toward the noise. Before he could react, a man with wild hair and dressed like a mannequin from an outdoor pursuits store strode into the path in front of them.

'Ah *guten morgen*, lovely day for tramping, yes?'

'Erm, hello, good morning to you too,' Chris stammered.

'This is the way to Roundwood, ya?' the hiker enquired.

'Yes, just back that way,' Reilly confirmed.

'*Danke. Auf wiedersehen.*' The man smiled as he confidently marched past them.

'Holy shit...' Chris turned to Reilly with his hand on his chest. 'He frightened the crap out of me.'

She smiled. 'C'mon, Bear Grylls, let's attack that hill. Looks like we should get a good view down to the lake from it.' She pointed in the direction of a hill covered in granite rock, heather and tough mountain grass.

As they made their way to the top, the misty rain seemed to be coming from every direction as the wind forced the air upwards against the steep cliff face that fell away down into the lake.

The lake itself was shrouded in fog, but parts became visible from time to time as the air swirled around, giving glimpses of the inky blue water below.

To the left was the sandy shoreline that they had seen on the satellite images, and in the field beyond several visible buildings.

Chris slipped and slithered along behind Reilly, the misty rain falling more steadily now, and he felt his damp jacket stick to his shoulders and his hair plaster itself to his forehead. He wished he'd been more prepared as right now he felt like an idiot while Reilly took off like some kind of girl-scout leader.

The lake was roughly oval shaped, and on three sides was bordered by boulders and rocks that had been slipping down the steep sides since the last Ice Age.

On the other side the river had carried sediment into the

lake, creating the beach and fertile flood plain where the fields were.

'What do you think?' he asked her.

'It's within a ten-mile radius to where both of our girls were found, and it certainly matches Conn's description. Also, I checked the soil analysis reports, and the samples we have are consistent with this area,' She began biting her lip. 'I'd so love to get some samples from that beach though,' she added, straining her eyes through the thickening mist.

'Agreed, but unless you've got a hand glider in that kitbag of yours there's no getting down there from here.' Chris wiped a water droplet from his nose. 'I don't want to jump the gun but this feels right to me too. Let's let O'Brien know what we've got and take it from there.'

Reilly went to work taking some soil samples from the grass verge as well as some other gravel and rocks for trace comparison. It wasn't ideal; what she really wanted was some samples directly from the beach and farmland to compare with the trace they'd taken off the old shoes and from beneath Sarah's toenails, but for now this would have to do. 'How do you think O'Brien will approach it?'

'With kid gloves, I'd imagine. The last thing we want is some kind of Waco-style standoff,' Chris said as he tried to retrace his steps without looking like he was going to fall on his backside at any second.

They continued to speculate on tactics as they made their way back to the car. As they approached, they could see that the driver's window was open and cigarette smoke was escaping.

'Anything interesting?' Kennedy asked, as they both climbed in.

'Bad enough that we're wandering around in that weather and then having to come back to a bloody smoke-filled car,' Chris moaned.

'Jeez, what a nag...' Kennedy turned the ignition key, so the electric windows would work and let his down fully. Reilly left the door open on her side to let some fresh air in.

'It looks interesting,' she told Kennedy as she peeled off her wet jacket.

'Yeah, I've been looking at the map,' he said, taking a folded OS map from the dashboard. 'Looks like there's only one road in and out of that property.'

'Did you talk to the locals about it?' Chris asked.

'Owned by a local family according to the guy I spoke to. They're not terribly well known or active in the community though. Interestingly, a squad car called and spoke to the owner when they were investigating the hit and run. He said he'd seen nothing but would let them know if anybody else in the house had. There was no answer at the front gate on any of the follow-up calls.' He looked at Chris. 'The local guy said they reported it to Harcourt Street but had heard nothing since.'

'Jesus, what's the point of wasting man-hours canvassing if the reports don't come back to us when alarm bells should be going off?' Chris said, frustrated.

'What about Land Registry?' Reilly asked.

'Slow as a funeral. I rang base and asked them to call a solicitor, see if we can get them to use their online system to get a quicker response,' Kennedy said, winding up the window now that the smoke had cleared. He switched on the ignition.

'Could we just take a quick ride up to the gate before we go?' Reilly asked. 'We'll just drive down and do a U-turn like lost tourists so as not to spook anybody. I'd really like to try and sneak in some samples.'

'We could chance ringing the bell for a chat while we're there,' Kennedy said as he maneuvered back onto the narrow road.

'Chances are if there was no answer for the local officers there will be none for us either, and the last thing we want to do is throw a cat amongst the pigeons if we have indeed found our Tír na nÓg,'

'Cat amongst the swans, you mean,' Kennedy quipped.

The gates to the property were tall and imposing, hung on impressive granite pillars with granite stone-clad walls in each direction making access to all but the invited very difficult. A wooden pole rose up behind the wall with three CCTV cameras on top spanning 360 degrees.

'Seems a bit excessive if it's just an ordinary family living there,' Kennedy commented. 'If it's the gateway to a mystical land, however ...'

'It's not actually that rare for large country estates to have such a high level of security,' Chris said. 'I've seen it before; people out in the sticks often feel more of a need to take self-protection into their own hands.'

'Fair enough but all those cameras?' Kennedy reversed the car around, trying not to linger too long and risk arousing suspicion. 'It's way OTT and weird. A bit like *Jurassic Park* or something. These people are either trying to keep somebody out or somebody in — or both.'

'Well, either way, the local boys better sit tight on this place,' Chris said. 'If things ends up going pear-shaped I'd hate to be the one explaining to an internal investigation how it was called on four bloody times. Hey, where are you going?' he called out, as Reilly opened the door and stepped outside.

'Trying to get a sneak peek inside paradise.'

She approached the entrance, and looked through a crack between the pillars and the gates. Inside the first set of gates was a second set — an intermediate zone between the entrance and the property itself.

Then looking through the gap from a side perspective, she immediately understood its purpose — to her left was a huge tank for fuel oil and a generator house. She could hear the generator rumbling away inside its small shed.

Follow the breadcrumbs, Reuben had said. Her mind racing, she turned and walked back to the car.

But as she made to leave Reilly stopped in her tracks. She'd just noticed something else. Delicately sculpted into the stone on the pillars was an elaborate Celtic-style pattern with a winged horse at the center of the design.

The gateway to Tir Na Nog?

49

Much later, back at the GFU, Reilly slumped into her office chair.

Various items of post were stacked on top of her desk. There were some familiar external envelopes, and a couple of jiffy bags she did not recognize but no doubt heralded more items for her ever-increasing to-do list.

One piece that did catch her attention was an inter-departmental padded envelope marked as being from Phoenix Park HQ.

Unsure as to what headquarters would possibly be sending her, she ripped open the seam and slid the contents out onto the desk. A green bulging file was bound together with an elastic band, and written on the front of the cover were several pieces of information, but catching sight of a name she soon realized exactly what this was.

File Number: IIRGSmk24
   Name: Grace Olivia Gorman
   Date reported: 14/8/1997

Reilly felt a pang of guilt. She'd ordered the file a couple of days ago and in the middle of all the drama surrounding the current investigation, she'd almost forgotten her promise to Lucy.

She looked closer at the folder. It was covered in small notes and official stamps that represented its removal and resubmission to file storage at headquarters in the Park. There had been plenty of activity with this file, she noted, although not surprising given it related to the daughter of a senior member of staff.

Reilly removed the elastic band and opened the folder. Removing the order of contents sheet she was immediately drawn to the last entered record, a printout from the online missing children's website.

Most modern missing person cases were now listed online, which enabled click-through from independent missing person websites or social networking pages, and thus easier access for anyone with a potential sighting or useful information.

The printout that Reilly was looking at was a relatively updated version compared with the original report paper-clipped to the inside cover of the file. Grace's case had origi-nated at a time when investigations were far less interactive.

Her gaze fixed on the first of two photographs, a smiling image of a happy teenager in her school uniform, and immedi-ately she felt a lump in her throat. If she didn't know better she would have sworn it was Lucy as a child staring back at her. The resemblance was striking.

Reilly tried to put aside any background knowledge she'd already gleaned from Lucy; she wanted to have a clear head as she looked through the file.

The second photo was a computer-generated image of what Grace would possibly look like today, similar to the one they'd recently created of Sarah Forde.

The image was haunting, surreal. Reilly wondered about

Lucy and Jack Gorman – did they ever look up the missing person website? What did they think when they saw the CGI version of Grace? Had fourteen years of not knowing dulled the pain, made it any easier? She read through the initial case notes.

Name: Grace Olivia Gorman
Case Type: Missing From Home
Missing Date: 14-Aug-1997
Missing City: Dublin
Missing County: Dublin
Missing Country: Ireland
Case Number: IIRGSmk24
Circumstances: Grace Gorman is missing from her home at 23 Marley Court, Rathfarnham, Co. Dublin since 14th of August 1997. When last seen she was wearing blue denim jeans, a white 'Boyzone' embossed T-shirt and brown suede boots, and a silver necklace with a distinctive star-shaped pendant hanging from it.

The low level of detail was striking, and while Reilly knew that this was a basic information sheet, and more details would be found in the rest of the sizable file, she had expected more.

She read on through the remaining details under the Age Progression CGI image.

Gender: Female
Height: 5' 3" (160 cm) approx.
Weight: 125 lbs (56.7 kg) approx.
Build: Teenager
Hair Color: Sandy
Eye Color: Blue

As Reilly started to leaf though the assorted documents she began to get a clearer image of what had happened.

She read the report of the officer who'd called to the family home after Grace had failed to return from a friend's house on an August evening that summer.

The statement from Gorman's wife Joan, who was described by the officer as 'distraught', reported that she'd allowed her daughter go to a friend's house that afternoon, expecting her back by six p.m.

The officer had gone on to describe how Joan had phoned the friend's house and spoken to her mother, only to be told that Grace had left at five p.m. The statement had been taken at eight p.m., three hours after Grace had last been accounted for.

The initial report listed Gorman himself as 'absent for work reasons but en-route home.'

Reilly could imagine the panic: no mobile phones to keep in touch, a husband desperately trying to make his way home from a job somewhere.

And all the while, she couldn't help imagining a fresh faced, blue-eyed teenage girl, wondering what was happening around her, not realizing her life and the lives of those around her would never be the same again.

There was a lot of activity over the first couple of days of Grace's disappearance. Senior members of the Missing Persons Bureau, which had been set up only five years earlier, had become involved almost immediately and a nationwide campaign had been launched with ads in newspapers as well as appeals for information on the main evening news.

Reilly leafed through more documentation, copies of ads from the paper, details of numerous so-called leads that had ended up going nowhere. The case even featured on *Crimecall*, a national TV show seeking information from the general public. The program had re-enacted Grace's last known movements in the hope of jogging somebody's memory. Reilly could sense the frustration from the file — dead ends and false hope. Multiple leads being chased up fruitlessly. The Irish authorities had been quick to link up with international counterparts in case she had absconded or been taken abroad but to no avail.

She read through several interviews with Grace's friends, which seemed to paint her in the same light as Lucy had: a happy, loving girl with absolutely no reason to run and every reason to stay.

There was a transcribed interview with a 'boyfriend' whom the parents had evidently known little about, but her friends had spoken of.

Fifteen-year-old Darren Keating was interviewed twice, and it seemed was high on the investigating team's suspect list. He had a weak alibi, but had remained steadfast in his own defense that he had not seen Grace much since the school holidays and that they had just 'shifted' a couple of times. Reilly guessed that 'shifted' was a local term for 'snog' rather than anything more intimate.

Keating's involvement had eventually been dismissed when two friends and a surveillance camera placed him in an amusement arcade at the time of Grace's disappearance.

Leaving the file aside, Reilly got up and went to the coffee machine, lost in thought.

She wondered what, if anything, she could bring to this case but she had made a promise to Lucy and she intended to keep it.

There was no physical evidence, in fact there was little evidence of any sort. Grace Gorman had vanished into thin air, and the investigation that followed for years afterwards was broadly based on appeals for help from somebody who might know something. The person or persons who might have were clearly not willing to help, and until they were, the trail was cold.

Returning to her desk, coffee in hand, she resolved to

temporarily put aside thoughts of poor Grace Gorman and tried for the moment to turn her attention back to the investigation she *could* bring something to.

She was still thinking about what she'd seen at the entrance to the property in Wicklow and was almost certain that the place was indeed the location Conn had described.

She was also thinking about the generator, and specifically the traces of paraffin and petrol they'd found on both girls. The running of generators on this fuel combination would have been very common years ago but was unusual now. Which meant that the generator was old. It had certainly looked it and, given its age, she guessed that such apparatus was notoriously unreliable, and would need specialist attention when it came to servicing or repairs.

Turning to her computer, she brought up a list of relevant mechanical engineering companies throughout the Wicklow/Dublin area. It was a long directory, and Reilly's to-do list was even longer, but she had a sneaking suspicion the answer lied in it.

50

Later that afternoon, Chris and Kennedy pulled up to the large hangar-sized building just outside Blessington. The gates were open and a van was parked outside.

Getting out of the car, they made their way to the reception hatch, trying to avoid the spilled oil and puddles on the way.

'Lakeside Engineering?' Kennedy asked loudly to the overall-clad figure inside.

'Yep, what can I do you for?' The voice was jocular, easygoing. 'Mick Wilson.'

'Detectives Delaney and Kennedy from Harcourt Street station.'

Wilson's face changed immediately. 'Never a good start to a morning ... what's going on?'

'We just wanted to ask you a question connected to an ongoing enquiry. We believe you hold the service contract for a generator near Roundwood, owned by one David McAllister?'

'Oh right, somebody phoned this morning about that. Yeah, we've been looking after that antique for years. Dan is the man to talk to about that, he usually does the callouts for it. Was out there several times last year as I recall. Ended up custom making parts for it; it's so old.' There was a brief pause. 'Like I said, it's ancient and well past needing replacement, but your man wouldn't hear of it. So if anything's gone wrong with it …'

'No, it's nothing like that,' Chris put in quickly. 'We'd just like to talk to your service engineer about what he might have seen while he was out there.'

Wilson shook his head. 'A weird place. Been up there myself in the past. All those fences and cameras. Always wondered what was going on, thought it might be some kind of government place or something.'

Kennedy looked at his watch. 'What time does Dan get in at?'

'He's supposed to be in five minutes ago, so I'd expect him in another ten, at least.' He rolled his eyes. 'You know what young lads are like these days.'

'Right.' Chris stepped inside the workshop. There was a long bench running down the middle of the floor, laden with generators and motors in various stages of disassembly. He could see the questions in Wilson's face. 'Don't worry. I meant what I said. He hasn't done anything wrong.'

The owner looked relieved. 'Oh good. He's a nice kid, works hard. It's not easy getting help these days — not anyone worthwhile, anyway.' He led the detectives through the workshop towards the back.

'Ah, speak of the devil …'

A young man of about twenty-five walked through the front door with a backpack slung over one shoulder.

'Dan, these two gentlemen want to have a chat with you about that place up near Roundwood with the old Briggs & Stratton,' Wilson told him. 'They're detectives.'

The engineer's face automatically reddened, and Chris glanced sideways at Kennedy to see if he, too, had caught the reaction.

'Oh ... right yeah, that place. What do you want to know?' he stammered as he laid his bag down on the bench.

'We are currently investigating some suspicious activity in the surrounding area, and would be grateful for your assistance. What can you tell us about your time there?'

Dan looked like he'd been punched in the stomach.

'Look, it was a mistake, all right?' he blustered. 'I didn't want to get involved and things just ... got out of hand.'

What the ...? Chris was completely taken aback by man's reaction.

His boss frowned. 'Involved in what? What's going on?'

'Mr Wilson, do you think we might have a minute with Dan alone?' Kennedy said.

'Sure, call if you need me,' he said reluctantly, before retreating outside.

The engineer stepped out from behind the bench and placed his hands deep into his pockets.

'So spit it out,' Kennedy demanded. 'What happened up there?'

'Look, she said she was eighteen, OK? I believed her, she looked it... and acted much older ... I didn't want to get involved, I have a girlfriend and a daughter ...' He looked crestfallen. 'She won't find out, will she? My girlfriend, I mean,' he added, his head still bowed.

All of this was so unexpected that Chris wasn't sure how to proceed. What girl was he talking about? 'That depends on you. Tell us everything. And start at the beginning.'

'I only started doing servicing out there about two years ago after Jimmy left. I thought it was strange at first, all the security, and rules.'

'Rules?'

'Yeah. Like there was a certain way things had to be done. I'd have to be there at twelve o'clock on the button, he opens the outside gate but that's as far as I get. I do my work on the generator, and then I leave.'

'He – you mean the owner?'

'I suppose. He wasn't much of a conversationalist, if you know what I mean. I know he's some weird artist type; he'd sometimes have statues and things on pallets inside the gate. He told me he sculpted them himself when I asked him — pretty cool, they were.'

'So you go in, work on the generator. How does he know when you're ready to leave?'

'There's a bell on the inside gates,' explained Dan. 'I ring that then he opens the outer gates again.'

'So what about this "mistake" then?' Chris prompted, not wanting to give him too much time to pick his words.

A look of shame crossed the engineer's face. 'That genny should have been long retired, it wasn't designed to run multiple power outlets, especially not on that fuel combination. Last summer I ended up having to call nearly every other week after it shut down completely, then had to make up some parts here and install them because Mick wasn't able to source new ones.'

Dan gazed around the yard, gathering his thoughts. 'I told your man that it would be cheaper and quicker to just replace the stupid thing, but he wouldn't hear of it. He seemed a decent sort but a bit of a hippy type – I reckoned he just wouldn't spent the cash on a new one.'

He paused for breath. 'So anyway, a couple of times I'm out there I can hear a couple of kids whispering in the bushes beside the gate.'

The hair on the back of Chris's neck stood up and he glanced discreetly at Kennedy. 'Kids? You're sure?'

Dan shrugged. 'Yeah. I figured there was a family living there. But the kids wouldn't talk back when I spoke to them, so

I ignored them until one day she got brave and started talking to me.'

Was he referring to Sarah? Desperate as he was to get to the point, Chris decided to let Dan ramble on. They needed to let him tell his own story.

'Anyway, to cut a long story short, she was nice, a little bit shy, always asking me questions, but she would never answer mine. I didn't mind, she was cute and it was someone to talk to while I worked. Sometimes she'd ask if I wanted to hear her sing which was a little weird, and at first I thought she might be a bit ... you know... *special*.' He said the last word in a low whisper.

'Because she sang?' Kennedy asked skeptically.

'No, no, not just that but the way she acted. It's hard to explain really, she just wasn't like any other girl I knew, kind of innocent, you know?'

'Until you came along like Prince Charming.' Chris said, guessing that they'd made an unexpected breakthrough in finding not only the father of Sarah's baby, but also the reason she had decided to fly the nest.

Dan shook his head. 'It wasn't like that. When the genny broke I spent a couple of weeks back and forth working on it. So anyway over the course of that time I'd call and sometimes she would answer the buzzer to let me in. I thought he must be out, delivering his sculptures or something, but didn't pay much attention. So instead of talking to me from behind the fence, this time she would come out and sit on the grass beside the generator while I worked, asking me constant questions like a three-year-old – where did I live, could I dance ... all sorts of random stuff. I enjoyed it and she was funny; not all self-obsessed like most of the girls you meet nowadays.'

Chris could hear genuine fondness in his tone.

'Go on. I'm guessing we're getting to the part where you tell us how you showed her to tango.' Kennedy was clearly getting impatient.

'Look, what do you want me to say? I've got a steady girl-friend, it was a mistake, it just happened.'

'You're saying she came on to you?'

Dan took a deep breath. 'Kind of. I went out there one day and again she opened the gates, and sat beside me while I worked, but saying nothing this time. It was unusual, because she'd been getting chattier each time I called. I asked her why she was so quiet, and she just burst into tears.' He moved away from the bench that he was resting against. 'I felt sorry for her, I put my arm around her to calm her down, she was in quite a state, talking about how she wanted to leave and would I take her with me. I asked her what was stopping her from leaving herself and she started talking about being afraid that the beasts would get her and all this weird stuff. Anyway, she was shivering, so I gave her my jacket and told her she could sit in the van if she wanted. She asked me to sit with her for a while and I did, I was just finished working anyway...' Dan took a gulp of air. 'So we were in the van still talking, when out of the blue she just plants one on me. One thing led to another and it just ... happened.'

'Did you use protection?' Chris asked, already guessing the answer.

'No offense but I don't bring condoms out on jobs with me. I'm not some kind of Casanova ...'

'OK, so you had sex. Then what?'

'Well, it's not everyday a girl like that throws herself at you, but then right after we got into it she got all crazy, started sobbing and yelling, telling me to get off her, calling me weird names and stuff. I stopped straight away, honestly, I would never rape anyone, you have to believe me...' he said, sounding desperate.

'Is that why you think we're here, because you're being accused of rape?'

'It wasn't like that, I swear. She ran back in and I didn't see or hear from her again. I was shitting it, but then when nothing happened after a few weeks I started to forget about it. Then when the next service call from there came in, I gave the boss some excuse and he said he'd get one of the other lads to do it. I didn't rape anyone, I swear.'

Chris exhaled deeply.

'OK, Dan, calm down, that's not why we're here,' he said, putting the man out of his misery. 'But the information you've given us may prove very helpful with our investigation. What else can you tell us about the property? And how many children were there?'

51

'So now we know for sure that it's the right place,' said Chris.

The team had reconvened in the incident room for a meeting with O'Brien to update him. 'And more importantly, we also know that this guy is holding more kids captive.'

Following extensive questioning of the engineer, and based on his account of events, they'd learnt of the existence of at least three other children at the property, all redheads.

O'Brien peered at the image on his computer screen, then scowled. 'Last thing we want is a stand-off like at Ballycastle.' He was referring to an incident from a few years back whereupon some local detectives had called to ask a young farmer a few questions about a recent fracas outside a nearby pub. Taking exception to their presence on his land as well as their questioning, the farmer had threatened them and tried to force them off with a shotgun. The armed response unit were called out, and a long stand-off ensued, resulting in the farmer being shot dead after firing a bullet into the air in a fit of rage. There had been a huge outcry and it had all ended up a public relations disaster for the force as a result. The ensuing internal inquest had changed the manner in which all similar investigations had been handled since.

Reilly, Chris and Kennedy stood in a semi-circle around O'Brien, looking over his shoulder.

'We have no reason to believe that there are any weapons there, sir,' Reilly pointed out.

'And no reliable intel to say that there aren't either,' he growled. 'Everyone seems to be armed these days, and if this guy is as serious about security as you say... I mean someone like this, who has created his own little fortress — we have to assume he is armed. So what *do* we know about this guy?'

'Land Registry details just came back,' said Chris. 'He's a self-employed sculptor, headstones mostly but some bespoke pieces too. Tax records are minimal as he's a registered artist and benefits from tax exemption, so has remained out of the net for the most part.'

'He's originally from Glasgow, but has been living here since the late eighties,' Kennedy added. 'But the big news is that his family died in a car crash a few years back.'

And this crucial piece of information, Reilly thought, was what made this farm most likely to be the place.

'According to the locals, they were a family of redheads,' she said, 'so Knight may well be spot on about our guy trying to recreate such a situation.'

'So this McAllister sounds like our man then.' O'Brien stood up and gazed out of the window. 'I read Knight's report too. Someone like this can be unpredictable.'

'For what it's worth, sir, he doesn't sound like some Fritzl-type who keeps kids locked up in a cellar; in fact he seems more your garden variety psycho, fencing them in with fear instead of walls.'

O'Brien nodded. 'Knight mentioned that the abductor may himself have come to believe these scare tactics he's using on the kids to keep them in check.'

'Yes, sir.'

'So I don't want us to go knocking at the door with a bunch of uniforms, getting him all riled up.'

'We have reasonable cause though, based on what the engineer told us about there being kids in there,' Kennedy pointed out. 'I vote we bring the Armed Support Unit and get in and out before the guy knows what's happening. It'll be like pulling off a plaster.'

O'Brien glared at him. 'I think you've been watching too many Jerry Bruckheimer films, Detective. There are children there, we don't know the layout, and certainly don't know how this fella will react. The last thing we want is him holed up somewhere in there, the kids held hostage, and the press all over it. Before we know it, we'll be the stars of Sky News's latest reality show. No, initially we'll just have to make a low-key approach and see if we get a response.'

'I can't see him opening up for us if he's already had four opportunities,' Kennedy argued. 'The locals reckon that he's a bit of a recluse. Incidentally there are no kids from that address registered in any of the local schools.'

'No surprise there,' Reilly said.

'Makes you wonder how he's pulled this off for so long though, doesn't it?' Chris ventured. 'What happens when the kids get sick?'

'Maybe they don't,' Kennedy said. 'My two only started picking up bugs when they started school. And clearly these kids don't mix.' He was distracted by an incoming call on his mobile.

Chris shook his head. 'I don't know. The more I think about this, the stronger I'm leaning towards tactical forced entry.'

'Absolutely not,' O'Brien retorted. 'I say we give McAllister one more chance to talk to us, but no uniforms this time.' He looked at Reilly. 'You don't look anything like a cop, and I mean that in the nicest possible way. What would you say to approaching via the front gate with Detective Delaney to see if he'll talk?'

'Happy to,' Reilly agreed immediately.

Chris looked horrified. 'With all due respect, sir, that is not in the GFU's remit. A direct approach could be risky, especially when we don't know what we're up against.'

O'Brien shushed him into silence. 'Steel's not in the least threatening, and it would be good to get an idea of who we're dealing with before we go barging on in there.'

'And what if he doesn't take too kindly to us?'

'Chris, I'll be fine. I'm happy to do it,' Reilly insisted, eager to be a part of the action. She turned back to O'Brien. 'Sir, how about if ASU back us up but stay back, and out of sight? They could discreetly inspect the surrounding area in the meantime, and see if they can confirm the presence of any children inside. Then if McAllister does decide to get hostile, we're covered.'

O'Brien looked at them all then slowly nodded. 'All right. But don't foul it up. I don't want this to turn into a stand-off, you hear me?'

Kennedy hung up the phone. 'That was the station. Seems one of the neighbors in Clondalkin called in this morning with a tip-off on the van from the other day.'

'The one from the abduction attempt on Jade Carney?' Chris asked. 'Did the neighbor get the registration? Was it McAllister?'

'Seems she only got a partial on the plate, but they're checking CCTV cameras for around that time, see if they can find anything that matches the description. With luck, we might pick up the reg then.'

He looked at O'Brien. 'Still want to go ahead with a softly softly approach, sir, or should we wait until we get confirmation on the van?'

The inspector was thinking hard. 'I think we go ahead now, see what the response is.'

'And what's the plan if McAllister answers?' Chris asked.

'I think you're going to have to play it by ear, see if it feels threatening or not.' The inspector looked back out the window. 'We'll move first thing in the morning, give me a chance to get ASU into the mix.' He nodded, indicating that the meeting was over. 'And good luck,' he threw at them as they closed the door.

'We're going to need it,' muttered Kennedy. 'There are so many ways this can go wrong...'

BACK AT THE GFU, Reilly was heading towards her office when she heard footsteps behind her in the hallway. Hanging up her coat, she turned around to find Lucy waiting in the doorway.

'Come in,' she said, guessing what was coming.

Lucy slipped into the room, and closed the door behind her. 'I heard about tomorrow and—'

Reilly cut her off. 'I know what you're going to ask, and I'm not sure it's a good idea.'

'How do you—'

'You want to come up there tomorrow — to the McAllister place.'

Lucy gazed at her hands, restlessly rubbing at them. 'But what if—' she whispered softly, unable to get the words out.

Reilly exhaled. 'Lucy,' she said gently. 'I understand that this has all been very difficult for you, and has brought back a lot of painful memories but the chances—'

'I know what you're thinking, but I'm not stupid,' Lucy interjected. 'I don't think Grace is there. For one thing the age profile is all wrong...' But Reilly guessed that there was still a tiny part of her that held out a faint glimmer of hope, futile or otherwise. 'It's just ... I've practically memorized every missing children's file there is since all of this began. If there's a chance that even one of those kids is in there, and could be saved ...'

Reilly looked at her dark, intense eyes and understood. 'The operation is strictly limited in scope,' she said. 'It's just a small team going out there to make initial contact. We have no idea how this guy is going to react. If our information about this place is sound, and McAllister is holding kids in there, then things could get messy.' She looked at Lucy.

'You don't have to tiptoe around me, Reilly. But I know I have to be there.'

Reilly wrestled with herself. A GFU van would be needed on standby anyway, just in case everything went to pot. She nodded reluctantly. 'OK, you can be part of the unit tomorrow. But you stay in the van and follow the rules.'

Lucy face brightened. 'Thank you.'

'I mean it; it's the only way,' Reilly said firmly. 'We have one shot to get McAllister to talk to us. If we spook him, who knows what he might do? As self-sustaining as this guy seems to be, he could dig in tighter than a tick if we get him rattled.'

How can you replace a mother? What do you do when the one you turn to, the one you rely on, is no longer there? Permanence is part of the essence of motherhood — you know that she is always there, you know that she always has a comforting word, arms to hold you, time to heal you.

A mother is a balm, a lotion, an ointment for whatever ails you.

So what do you do when she is gone? Who can take her place? Who amongst the swans is ready to take that role, try and fill the space left by her departure?

She was just seven years old when she came to us — yet stronger than most adults could ever aspire to be. For her, motherhood was not something to take on, something to try, it was her destiny, her calling. How could she ever be anything else?

And yet now, inconceivably, inconsolably, she is gone. To what? She had everything — what more could she want?

'PULL OVER HERE,' said Chris.

The following morning Chris, Kennedy and Reilly were on a narrow country lane, not far from the McAllister place. He was pointing to a battered gate half-off its hinges, leading into a field. 'The entrance is just up ahead,' he continued. 'I don't want to drive up there and alert him to our presence too soon.'

Kennedy eased the car into the narrow space — they were far enough off the road for other cars to get by.

Reilly eased the door open and squeezed out in the space between the car and the gate. Chris and Kennedy climbed out the other side.

It was a typical Irish March day, the wind gusting, the air damp.

'I don't want to spook him,' Chris explained. 'It seems obvious that he has a fear and mistrust of the modern world and of outsiders, so the two of us banging on his front door is almost guaranteed to have him battening down the hatches.'

'So what do you suggest?' asked Reilly.

'Plan A is to try and make contact, but we'll have to check on plan B before we stroll on up to the gate.'

He indicated to the four Armed Response Unit vehicles that had just pulled into the side of the road. Two patrol cars also blocked the road a hundred meters either side of the turn in to the lane way where the entrance was located.

'Let's go and get the lowdown,' Chris said, and headed for the van marked ARU command unit.

Inside they were greeted by O'Brien and head of the ARU, a man called Nolan, who beckoned them over. They were gathered around a table looking at aerial maps of the homestead.

'Come in, we're just setting up.'

'How accurate are these images?' Chris asked.

'Very,' responded O'Brien. 'We requested a high-level fly-by from the Air Corps late yesterday.'

All buildings on the plot were outlined in highlighter pen and given a representative number. There were five buildings in total, although some bordering the lakeshore looked to have a series of lean-tos and extensions which meant they were virtually all joined up.

'So I take it the heavy hardware is part of plan B?' Chris pointed to a nearby trailer with officers unloading tools, motorized cutting equipment and ladders.

'The paperwork is in place. I spoke to top brass this morning; we're getting in there today, either by carrot or stick,' said O'Brien, sounding a lot more gung-ho than the previous afternoon. Clearly head office were putting on the pressure.

'So why bother announcing our presence and lose any element of surprise by knocking on the gates first?' Kennedy asked.

'Haven't you been reading your procedural notes?' O'Brien replied sarcastically. Ever since the Ballycastle Tribunal there were strict protocols for such situations, the first one being announcement of intent.

'OK,' said Chris, 'so the plan is, we ring the buzzer a couple of times and give McAllister say, two or three minutes to answer, then your lot cut the gates down and move in?'

'That's pretty much it,' O'Brien confirmed. 'The ARU has been divided into two teams, and each have been fully briefed on the layout. You and Kennedy will join a team each as soon as the word to go in is given. We want to move fast and sweep each building before this guy knows what's hit him.'

'Sounds good to me.' Kennedy was already feeling a twitch of adrenaline at the prospect of Plan B.

Having finalized the details, Chris and Reilly made their way back along to the lane way, leaving Kennedy with the difficult task of finding an ARU vest that could fit around his middle.

The lane was in poor condition underfoot, full of bumps and puddles, probably intentionally to deter unwanted visitors. Or visitors period, Reilly thought. She and Chris started picking their way between the potholes.

'You heard what O'Brien said — this ends today,' said Chris. 'I just hope it doesn't get messy.'

'You and me both. There's no telling what this guy is thinking.'

Echoes of New Eden pushed their way into Reilly's mind. She knew all too well just how messy things could get in these situations, and not just for those inside the property.

Many had lost their lives in the final takedown that day in North Carolina – innocent kids forced to live their lives to the tune of some psychopathic hardline survivalist, as well as the people tasked with saving them.

Reilly didn't know three of the officers that died that day but the fourth – Bradley Jones – had been a good friend since their training days.

After the terror and carnage had raged, when cult members had opened fire at the surrounding officers and themselves, there had been an eerie calm as everybody crouched in a state of shock, gunfire still ringing in their ears.

Bradley had been part of the first response team, checking for remaining hostiles and then for survivors. Reilly was being briefed on the unit's next move when she heard the explosion; the four-man team had walked straight into an improvised boobytrap.

She and Chris walked in silence now along the rest of winding track toward the first set of gates, the wind whipping at them, gray clouds scudding overhead, the misty rain ever-present.

Finally they reached the gates. They were not the friendly farm gates with three bars that you would expect to find at the end of a country dirt road-,these were industrial gates, the sort you would find on a trading estate, designed to keep people out, day or night. Over three meters tall, they completely blocked their view of what lay beyond.

Having pressed the intercom buzzer on one of the pillars,

the two waited by the gates, looking through the gap to the inner area to see if there was any movement.

After a beat, Chris pressed the buzzer again and looked at his watch.

'Two more minutes and I'm making the call.'

'If he's lost a family before and gone to such lengths to create and hold onto this fairytale he's living I can't see him giving them up quietly,' Reilly said. 'I fear this guy would rather die, and I don't even want to think about what might happen to the kids.'

Chris shrugged then pulled out his phone and pressed the redial button. 'It's a no-go, sir, send in the cavalry.' He put his phone back in his pocket, 'Well, I guess that's it. You might as well head back to your crew and start getting ready to process the compound.'

Three vehicles approached and Nolan climbed out, followed by Kennedy who wore a focused no-nonsense expression that Chris had only witnessed in similarly tense situations. He handed Chris an ASU vest.

'You ready for this, mate?' he murmured out of Nolan's earshot. 'Cos I don't want a repeat of the last time something like this went down ...'

Chris stopped short at the unexpected remark. He'd thought that what had happened during a takedown on an earlier case was over and done with, and that his partner had long forgotten his brief lapse in which — due to his condition — he'd failed to take control of a crucial situation.

It unsettled him.

'Course I'm ready, don't worry about me,' he replied testily.

'OK, listen up,' Nolan began. 'You all know the drill, this is first and foremost a sweep and secure mission. Red Team, Detective Kennedy will be with you, and Blues, Detective Delaney. We suspect one adult male and likely three or four minors inside.' With this, Nolan gave the order for an advance team to scale the first set of gates with ladders, and start cutting the inner gate hinges while at the same time the first set were being removed.

It went ahead swiftly and seamlessly and the two teams methodically maneuvered through the entrance. As they passed it, the generator that had effectively betrayed McAllister kicked into life with a load roar.

'Holy shit, what's that?' one of the ASU guys shouted.

'It's an electricity generator,' yelled Chris. 'This place is off the mains grid.'

Which meant that right then, someone or something was using power.

53

Reilly picked up the pace as she headed back towards the GFU van.

She heard the noise from the angle grinder stop and knew that it wouldn't be long before the entire scenario was played out — for good or for bad.

Either way her team was about to run a crime scene, so she needed to focus on that.

'What's happening?' Lucy had started to speak before Reilly had the door open. She jumped into the seat.

'Tactical entry,' she replied, closing the door. 'He wouldn't answer at the gate.'

'So what's next then?' Gary asked.

'We wait. It could take an hour or more to secure the compound. In the meantime will you start getting the equipment and suits sorted out in the back?' she asked Lucy, knowing that she needed to give the younger girl something to take her mind off what was unfolding.

'Where are you going?' Lucy asked when Reilly opened the door again.

'To check with O'Brien. I'll be back shortly.'

Reilly made her way to the ARU central command van. She knocked and entered before waiting for a response. Inside Nolan, O'Brien and two other men stood around the table.

Loud crackling from the radio headsets of the two team leaders inside the property played mostly static, apart from the occasional low-key instruction.

The tension in the room was as thick as the smell of sweat and humidity. The men shuffled through maps and took notes. O'Brien lifted his head to acknowledge her.

'Everything OK?'

'Yes, sir, just prepped my team. What's the status?'

'No visual on the suspect or any children yet. There is a single vehicle in the driveway — a white Fiat van. Main building has now been swept and is secure,' O'Brien said casually, Reilly thought, as he flicked through some maps. His tough exterior was often hard to read, especially in these situations.

'Any sign of life at all?' Reilly asked.

Doorway straight ahead ... clear... building secure, over. The radio continued to relay a shorthand acount of events inside the grounds.

'Heating and lights have been used very recently, somebody is home.'

Reilly felt a knot in her stomach when she heard the tinny, crackling sound of Chris's voice. *'Mr McAllister, please make yourself known.'*

Silence.

'Mr McAllister, please make your location known. We need to ask you some questions.'

Between Chris's announcements you could hear a pin drop in the van, everybody straining for some new development.

'Proceed to outbuildings — on my mark,' came a whispered command from another voice Reilly didn't recognize.

She looked at the map with the highlighted buildings. McAllister would be running out of places to hide. The fact that he was unwilling to respond was not a good sign. Was there anybody in that place at all?

54

Kennedy stood with his back flat to the wall of the outbuilding. His team had been detailed with trailing the others who were sweeping the buildings from the outside in case the suspect tried to make a dash for it.

The only sounds they had heard so far were their own and those of the internal team. Then suddenly, in the distance, Kennedy heard what sounded like a muffled sob. All senses on high alert, he indicated to the team leader beside him, who nodded to confirm he'd also heard it.

'Audio confirmed — building E,' he whispered into the headset.

Building E was a wooden-clad outhouse near the lake that sat right on the water's edge. It looked as though it had one time been a standalone shed, but was now connected to the other buildings by a network of cheaply built lean-tos and extensions.

One of the ASU officers named Hagan moved up beside Kennedy. He squeezed as close as he could get to a window on the side of the boathouse.

'Mr McAllister, we need you to acknowledge your position,' the officer called out. 'We need you to talk to us, sir, we can hear you. We are police officers and need to ask you some simple questions then we'll be on our way.'

Again, a faint sob broke the silence.

Finally, a deep voice spoke. 'Leave us be. You're not wanted here. By the Wrath of Balor I command you to go now while he allows it.'

Christ, Kennedy thought. This was the place. This was the guy.

Hagen looked at Kennedy with a questioning look.

'The guy has built up some makey-up world of fantasy to keep the kids in check,' he whispered. 'We're not sure whether or not he believes it himself. Just keep him talking.'

'OK, Mr McAllister,' Hagan continued. 'I'm going to tell my men to fall back. We are not here to harm you, but can you please just confirm that the children are OK?'

Silence.

'Mr McAllister…'

'Be gone, snake, do not poison my ears with your venom and lies. Your tricks and spells are no good in this place; no demon can hide its putrid face or mask its slithering voice. Your invasion is a smite to Balor, and you will all pay a dear price.'

With that, a loud motor suddenly roared to life from within the building, making the wall vibrate behind them.

'What the fuck is that?' Kennedy spat. The AMU officers stared at each other, nobody quite sure what to do next.

They relayed the information back to control hoping for some external guidance, but the sound grew louder and Kennedy jumped away, expecting a bulldozer or tank to smash down the wall at any moment.

Suddenly a loud gunshot rang out above the cacophony, and the two ARU officers dived for cover.

'*Fall back! Fall back!*' Kennedy heard Nolan shout over the radio.

Before anyone could say or do anything, the roaring noise grew deafening and a RIB with a large outboard engine burst out of the building on the lake side.

The full-throttle engine forcing the nose into the air, the boat started to skip across the water like a flat stone. The team looked on open-mouthed as they saw a tall man at the controls, and alongside him the huddled shapes of two small children clinging onto one another while the third stood sentry, her back against the boat's only seat for balance, and a shotgun held in the comfortable fashion of a person who knew how to use it.

'Holy shit ...' Kennedy gasped.

The swans had taken flight.

It took several minutes for the team to locate the source of the gunfire. An agricultural scare gun used for crop protection from birds had been set up in some bushes to the left of the building. McAllister had obviously spent time planning for such a day.

The initial scramble to pursue the boat had been chaotic.

Squad cars rushed to the forest road at the opposite side of the lake, but by the time they reached the shore, all they found was an empty boat with a cooling engine. McAllister had evidently moved onto phase two of his escape plan, and they were one step behind.

A further call went out to set up checkpoints on all possible escape roads, but O'Brien already feared the worst.

'Shit, shit, shit!' he yelled at himself as much as anybody else, when everyone reassembled in the CC van. 'Why the fuck was that forest access road not on the maps we have?' he demanded.

Nobody answered.

'Sir, what do you want us to do next?' Chris asked, eager to do something, anything to rescue the situation.

O'Brien snapped out of his daze.

'Get on to traffic, I want McAllister's details run again — see if he has another vehicle registered to his name. Try all variations of his name, and check this address as well.' He shuffled through the maps. 'I want a second set of checkpoints in place within twenty kilometers on all roads — this guy is not getting through the net.' O'Brien was starting to get his thoughts in order. 'And we need an up-to-date photograph — make sure the GFU know that finding one in the house is a priority.'

'I must warn you,' Chris replied, 'having been in the house, it's very olde worlde. We're more likely to get a canvas painting than a photograph.'

'Just see what you can fucking get,' the inspector spat. 'Look for a driver's license or something; we need to let these checkpoints know who they're looking for.'

'Sir, there were three kids. All redheads. All under twelve, I'd say,' Kennedy told him. 'That's pretty hard to miss.'

'True, but this guy has had time to think. Chances are he may well have some means of concealment.'

THE GFU TEAM moved slowly and methodically through the McAllister house dressed head to toe in their white dust suits.

Reilly remembered sitting on the couch at home with Jess watching *Little House On The Prairie* and *The Waltons*, and right now she half expected Laura Ingalls to walk into one of the rooms.

The world McAllister had built up for the children was a simple one. There were no obvious mod-cons, and Reilly knew she was unlikely to find anything like a laptop or X-box here.

The room she was examining now had obviously been the main family room. At its center was a solid oak table with six matching chairs. Set into the wall beyond was a large open fire and two boxes with cushioned folding lids that acted as storage for fuel as well as a place to sit by the fire.

On each side of the fireplace were shelves covered with books. There was quite a collection but they were old and tatty.

A glance at the nearest shelf suggested considerable insight into McAllister and the life he had created here. There were titles Reilly had never heard of, but names like Cu Chulainn and Fionn mac Cumhail jumped out at her as being related to the same mythology that McAllister had used to brainwash his captives with.

Reuben would have a field day here, she thought, fighting the urge to take down some books and start reading through them, knowing there were far more pressing issues at hand.

She looked over at Gary and Lucy as they slowly worked their way through the room, collecting and tagging items of interest as they went. She had been impressed by Lucy's strength. When the news came through about McAllister's escape, and that it looked as though he had only very young children with him, she knew that whatever faint hope the young tech might have had for finding her sister here had been very quickly dashed.

Given her emotional state of mind, Reilly had given her the opportunity to sit this one out. But no, Lucy had insisted that it was business as usual as she collected trace for DNA analysis and any evidence to cross-reference with all those missing children cases that included her own sister.

'Hey, boss,' Gary called out, startling Reilly from her thoughts. 'I'm pretty much finished with this room now, want me to start on the kitchen?'

'Just make sure Rory is done dusting in there first. Anything interesting?'

'Well, it's certainly a nice change from the usual mess; not a drop of blood anywhere. Plenty of hair though, mostly long red strands but some gray ones too, possibly animal, and belonging to those, I'd imagine.' He indicated out the window to the driveway where McAllister's van was parked. Inside were two nervous-looking collie dogs that had begun chewing and clawing the glass angrily when the team had first parked up. McAllister must have had another form of transport waiting at the far side of the lake.

'We'll get the ISPCA in to secure the dogs before we sweep the van,' Reilly said, picking up a pair of knitting needles and some wool that looked to have been hurriedly tossed into the corner.

'Reilly, you might want to take a look at this...' Rory called out from the kitchen, and she went to join him. 'I was just checking the back of this,' he pointed to one of the kitchen cupboards. 'There seemed to be a lot of fingerprints there,' he said, standing aside to let her see. 'I gave the back cover a little nudge, and it came loose.' Behind the false back were two shoe-boxes filled with invoices, receipts and other documentation.

'Excellent. This could tell us something about McAllister's movements and, with luck, give us some clue as to where he's heading next,' she said, examining an invoice for a Celtic cross headstone, listing the address and phone number of one of McAllister's clients.

She flicked through the papers to see if there was anything of interest from a forensic point of view.

Next, Reilly moved on to the bedrooms. As she did, she spotted something through the bay window overlooking the lake. On a grassy area beside the water was a large erratic rock standing up in the earth. It looked to have some sort of carving on the front, and at the base grew an array of small shrubs and spring flowers.

She stopped in her tracks as the thought dawned on her, and quickly unzipped her coveralls to find her phone.

Chris answered immediately. 'What's up?'

Reilly pulled her face mask away from her mouth, as she quickly explained what she'd found. 'Looks like we're going to need our friends with the grave excavator again.'

56

Later that evening, back in Dublin, the meeting with O'Brien was stormy to say the least.

'We should have had the Water Unit in support — it was pretty obvious that McAllister wasn't going to just ask us in for tea,' Kennedy said, looking tired and dejected.

'Yes, well, you know what they say about hindsight, Detective,' O'Brien said, sitting back in his swivel chair, as they dissected the events of a very long day. 'But let's move on — there will be plenty of time for post mortems later; the Park have already been on looking for explanations,' he added, referring to the Garda HQ in the Phoenix Park. 'Let me worry about that, you lot just concentrate on finding this guy and getting those kids back, whoever they are.' He turned to Reilly. 'Anything from the house that will help track McAllister down?'

'We found a passport for him amongst the documents, none for the kids unsurprisingly. The photo is old though, as the passport was issued several years ago, but it's the best we've got. Chances are he'll lose the beard in the meantime.'

'Any clues as to where he might be hiding?'

'We have all hands on deck going through the two boxes concealed in the kitchen, but nothing jumps out just yet.'

'This guy may sound cuckoo but he's certainly not stupid,' Kennedy put in. 'He planned his escape with the boat, so no doubt he's also planned his next move.'

The door opened, and O'Brien's secretary appeared carrying a tray of coffees, a little jug of milk and a bowl of sugar cubes. She hurried in, set them on O'Brien's desk, and scurried out.

Reilly reached for a cup, blew on it to cool it, and took a quick sip. 'If I were him I'd be looking to get as far away as possible as fast as possible, or I'd have another place to hide.'

Chris sighed. 'Well, the ports are covered, his Scottish background might make fleeing the country an option for him. Other than that, we have to hope the vehicle check or the evidence collected from the house yields something.'

'There were some invoices related to his stonework issued in McAllister's name,' Kennedy said. 'He seems to have carried out regular work for one company in particular, called Mount Leinster Memorials.'

'That'll be your next port of call. Steel, any helpful forensic trace from the house?' O'Brien asked, rubbing his bloodshot eyes.

'My team is currently working on that, sir. We've also ordered cadaver dogs to search the property.'

And while Reilly guessed the dogs would find the corpse they'd dug for once before, she sincerely hoped that was all they'd find.

I HEARD them plotting their invasion. The children knew this day would come, that evil wasn't to be kept from our door eternally. Once one had fallen for Kelpie's charms the seal of paradise was broken, and soon the festering waters of that pitiful world beyond our borders would pour in, their stench preceding them.

It is the turning of the season, when the winds blow and the trees begin to blossom, and all God's creatures feel the earth moving beneath them; restlessness is in the air. We have left our sanctuary but together we are strong, the bells have not yet tolled.

This is merely an interlude. I must protect the flock and I must grow them too — for strength lies in numbers.

Change is in the air, the herd is restless. Our paradise may be lost but another awaits ...

57

In the GFU lab, Reilly and the team stood around the trays and bags of evidence they had collected from the McAllister place.

'OK, priority goes to anything that might give an indication of where McAllister could have gone with those kids. Let's see if we can outsmart him.'

She tasked Gary with going through the mats from the van, hoping to isolate material common to the house, and then see what they were left with: natural or unnatural, plants, minerals, rocks, soil or any chemicals/synthetics.

'No problem, boss, I'm on it.' He sprung to action with surprising gusto for a person who'd had little more than a couple of hours' sleep.

'Rory, I want you to process the prints and partials — check if they happen to match what's already on file.'

'Will do.'

In the hope of identifying the children McAllister had with him, Reilly then tasked Lucy with cross-checking anything found in the house with the current missing children files. It would be a painstaking and likely fruitless process but they had to try.

For much of the morning, the team busied themselves collecting various evidence bags and equipment to launch into what seemed from the outset a mammoth task.

Reilly went over to where Julius was sifting through the books. She thought about the complexities of McAllister's brainwashing and how he had created an elaborate belief system to keep the children in check. However, he had not accounted for the fact that childish fear was not a lifelong fear. Children grew into adulthood and began to question everything, no matter how sterile and controlled the situation around them.

But the question now was what would McAllister do next?

She was startled back to reality by her phone ringing.

'Hey, Chris.'

'Some good news. We just got word on a registration on that van in Clondalkin.'

It took Reilly a moment to figure out what he was talking about. 'The attempted abduction?'

'The very one. A neighbor reported a blue Volkswagen van cruising their street right around the time that Jade Carney's mum called us. One of our guys here checked the CCTV cameras and managed to pick up a plate.'

She sat forward. 'You have an address?'

'Yes, we're headed straight there now. With any luck that's where we'll find McAllister, and hopefully the kids too.'

'Well, if it is the place, we're ready to move.' She looked up as Gary entered the room, a thoughtful look on his face.

'Great. Will keep you posted.'

Hanging up the phone, Reilly shared this latest piece of news with the team.

'Did Detective Delaney happen to mention where the house is?' Gary asked, reading from a report.

Reilly recognized his tone.

'No – why?'

'Pegasus has just thrown up a strange result from the mats, and I was wondering if McAllister might have been spending time in Eldorado.'

She frowned, completely confused. 'Eldorado?'

'Yes, you know … the city of gold.'

58

Chris and Kennedy waited patiently while the locals jimmied the front door of the house that matched the registration of the van.

'There you go. You're in,' said the officer with the crowbar and stood back.

The front door swung open and Chris poked his head inside. 'Gardai. Anyone home?' His voice echoed in the empty house.

The hallway contained nothing but a pair of wellington boots and an umbrella — no photographs on a side stand, no pictures on the walls, nothing.

'Cozy,' muttered Kennedy, following him inside.

There was an archway through to a dining room with similar décor, which then led on to the kitchen. Chris opened the fridge — all it contained was half a packet of stale butter and some out-of-date eggs.

Kennedy rummaged in the cupboards — tins, packets, simple no-recipe food. 'Not exactly homely ...'

'Let's check upstairs.'

The stairs creaked slightly as the detectives ascended. The

upstairs of the house was as devoid of personality as the downstairs. There was a small bathroom — avocado bathroom suite, no shower — and two bedrooms. One contained a double bed, neatly made, and a wardrobe of obviously charity shop clothes. The other was set up as an office — a desk against the wall, bookshelves and a small radio, though no computer or other electronic equipment.

'This is beyond spartan,' Chris said, shivering. He didn't think he had ever seen a house so austere. 'It's downright creepy. If it weren't for the lack of dust, you'd think no one had lived here in years.'

'Whoever does live here doesn't like to move with the times, that's for sure,' Kennedy agreed. He shook his head. 'No sign of McAllister here anyway. I'll go get the forensics, see if they can dig anything up.'

As Kennedy clomped back down the stairs Chris gazed around at the bookshelves. They were mostly empty apart from a few books including *Salem's Lot* by Stephen King, another nameless novel with a torn cover, and a couple of textbooks on physiology and anatomy. Something about them sent a fresh shiver down Chris's spine.

There was definitely something off about this place.

THE MAN RAISED the binoculars and scanned his front garden. One of the cops had come back out — there were also several others in uniform, and then two figures in white suits entered with bulky toolboxes.

Forensics.

He watched as one of the cops, in a crumpled jacket and tie, called them in. They would violate his house, their dirty shoes on the carpet, their sticky fingers in every corner. It was no longer his. It was time to move on.

Again.

He lowered the binoculars, slipping them away in the daypack he wore, and walked quickly to his van, taking the keys from his pocket.

He would have to disappear, cover his tracks. He had stayed out of sight for too long to allow them to catch up with him now. He would have to be more careful though.

Two close calls in a few days was cutting it fine.

He slid into the driver's seat and cranked the engine. It purred into life. He had maintained the van himself, kept it running perfectly, but like everything else, it was now expendable.

He knew exactly where he was going, had planned for every eventuality; there was nothing left to chance. Everything would go exactly as he had foreseen it.

When he was back in control, he would build another world in which to fulfill his desires and fantasies. Where he would go and who he would become he had not yet decided. What he had decided, though, was that he would go for blonds; not your trashy peroxide types, but pure Aryan blonds.

Hard to find but worth the hunt.

The roads were quiet, but he drove carefully, exactly at the speed limit as he always did. He couldn't help but smile as he passed a squad car racing the other way, lights flashing, on its way to some petty crime, the officers unaware of what they had missed, and who they had passed, his nice new number plates unnoticed.

A little while later, he rolled to a halt, then climbed out, taking care to avoid the puddles. He lifted a broken latch and slid the gates open.

Inside was an abandoned warehouse — it had stood deserted for many years, just another empty building on a quiet country road, another anonymous place that no one ever visited.

He drove in through the gate, then stopped to close it

exactly as it was, before driving the van in through the open loading bay and all the way to the back of the warehouse.

He climbed out and looked around. No one in sight, but he couldn't take any chances. He stood very still and listened — not just for ten seconds, as an amateur might, but for a minute, two minutes, three minutes.

The only sounds were the ticking of the engine and the exhaust as they cooled, a branch from an overgrown tree worrying the wall of the building.

Satisfied that no one was around, he opened the back of the van.

Stacked inside were three large cans of petrol. He lifted them out, set them on the floor, then walked around and opened all the doors. There could be no trace, nothing to link the vehicle to him.

One by one, he emptied the cans of petrol over the van, thoroughly and meticulously, making sure to cover all the surfaces, soak the seats, the steering wheel ... and the floor in the back where he had scrubbed so assiduously to remove the bloodstains.

When all three cans were empty, he placed them back inside the van, and pulled the box of matches from his pocket.

He paused, took a moment to analyze his feelings; they were a mixture of something he was familiar with. Fear and excitement, horror and delight? Yes, he was used to mixed emotions. On this occasion though, it was satisfaction at executing his plan so competently, as well as regret at having to give this one up and start over with a new one.

Then just as quickly he kicked back into action — lit a match, dropped it into the box, watched as the whole box flared up into a large flame, then tossed it into the van.

Poof. The petrol lit instantly, almost sucking the air out of his lungs as the flames roared into life. Blue and yellow, they raced around the van, inside and out, like a starving animal searching for food, and within seconds the entire van was alight, the flames dancing, devouring.

Then the man turned on his heel and walked calmly away, the smell of burning petrol and rubber in his nose, his plan becoming clearer in his mind.

It was time to assume a new name, move into his new kingdom, which was already prepared and waiting for a day such as today.

It was time to begin again.

59

Chris, Kennedy and Reilly took seats in front of O'Brien's desk for a debrief.

Chris spoke first. 'We followed up on the van from the attempted abduction in Clondalkin. It was registered to a house in Whitestown in the name of Martin O'Toole. Turns out he's been dead for eight years, although he has somehow managed to drive the van and keep drawing disability benefit, which is quite a trick.'

'How does this still happen in this day and age?' O'Brien said, rolling his eyes. 'The left hand never seems to know what the right hand is doing ...'

Kennedy looked at his notes. 'He had a co-signatory on the disability benefit. His carer is listed as Clive Farrell. He's come up a blank though — doesn't seem to exist, so it's likely to be a scam.'

'Anything linking the place to the Wicklow house?'

Reilly sat forward. 'No, sir, the place is clean, too clean. We think it was used as a safe house. However, my team's initial examination was only preliminary; we would like to have a closer look, but the order initally was to fall back and keep surveillance in place.'

'Which begs the question, if this place is indeed McAllister's safe house, why didn't he use it?'

'Maybe it wasn't remote enough or wasn't suitable to prolong the Tir Na Nog fantasy,' Chris suggested.

'Or maybe he just abandoned the kids — or worse — before taking off alone,' said Kennedy gruffly.

'I doubt it,' Reilly argued. 'Based on what we already know about McAllister, he seems to care for these kids.'

'Or maybe it's just the fantasy he cares for,' Kennedy replied. 'The guy is off his rocker. The stuff he was sprouting yesterday when we tried to talk to him ... Personally I wouldn't be surprised if he believes everything he's told them.'

'And if he does, then we need to worry about what happens next. In the fairytale you wither and die if you leave Tir Na N'og...' Chris pointed out.

At this, the room fell silent, as they each tried to comprehend the implications.

'Right,' O'Brien said, refocusing. 'It's almost twenty-four hours since we last had a visual. Time is moving on, our resources are stretched to the limit and as yet we've had nothing of any real value.'

'There's still a lot to get through,' Reilly told him. 'We're continuing with the missing person cross-referencing. Granted, there's nothing yet, but it's only a matter of time. My team are also going through the documentation, hoping to find something that might pinpoint to McAllister's whereabouts.' She cleared her throat. 'But there is an interesting development. We've picked up some specific trace material from the van. Lots of sulphur and metallics, including traces of chalcopyrite.'

When the others looked puzzled, she continued. 'You may know chalcopyrite as fool's gold. Its chemical composition is copper, iron and sulphur. Initially we thought that it may have something to do with McAllister's stonework, and that he used some sort of metallic paint for the inscriptions on his sculptures or headstones, but nothing matched from our analysis of the trace from his workshop. But what we did find from both the van and on some gardening tools in the workshop, was ochre.'

'And what's that?' Kennedy asked, unashamed to admit ignorance.

'Hydrated iron oxide, also known as yellow or gold ochre. It's basically an earth pigment that was used for centuries before modern dyes were invented. Many older cultures including Australian Aborigines, Maoris and Celts used it. But the point is, it's not something that just sticks to your shoe when out walking the dog. It's specific to certain areas.'

'Specific to the immediate surroundings of the McAllister place?' Chris asked.

'Based on our soil database, we've identified it as being mostly prevalent in the Avoca River Valley,' she told them.

Chris nodded. 'As the crow flies, that wouldn't be a million miles from the lakeshore. There may well be some off-the-beaten-track mountain routes that lead down that direction. It may even be within the checkpoint radius, which could explain how we missed him...'

'This might be promising.' O'Brien was all business. 'Get a team on the ground in that area focusing on possible sightings, knock on a few doors. We need to make sure there are no slip-ups the next time we get near this guy, OK?'

Reilly pushed her chair back and stood up. 'I'm going to head down that direction myself and see if I can confirm a match to our trace.'

'Very well, I want to be kept informed of developments at all times,' O'Brien said determinedly. 'If this *is* fool's gold, let's make sure we're not the ones being made fools of this time.'

60

As they drove through the city and headed south towards Avoca, Reilly sat in the back as Kennedy moved through traffic with full lights and sirens.

She scrolled through the information she'd uploaded to her iPhone earlier — mineral maps and records concerning the history of the area.

Avoca actually sounded like a little bit of home, and Reilly was surprised that she hadn't heard of it before.

Like California, there had been a mini gold rush there in the 1800s. Eighty kilograms of gold was panned from the river, including a one-and-a-half-pound nugget, the largest ever discovered in the British Isles.

'Whether or not this is where McAllister is heading, he has definitely spent time there. The mineral make-up from the area is unique,' she told the others.

'I visited there many times as a kid,' Chris said. 'The place would have been beautiful before the mining started. Sadly it's been an ecological mess ever since — the run-off from the mines killed the river, and not much can grow on the ugly slag piles.'

'I can imagine; open-pit mining is cancerous to the environment, very toxic.'

'So what's the plan, comrades?' Kennedy asked.

'We'll ask around the shops in the village first, see if they've seen or heard anything. Where do you think is best for sampling?' Chris asked Reilly.

'The river valley, mainly the slag heaps I would think. The ochre trace was in high concentration, not what you'd expect from topsoil, so by concentrating on the places where the subsoil and slag are visible we're more likely to be following in McAllister's footsteps, so to speak,' she said, reaching for her phone which had begun to ring. 'Steel. When? No, I don't want it disturbed, I'll have a team sent up right away.' She hung up and made a face. 'Looks like we're going to be doing an exhumation after all. The dogs have sniffed out at least one body in the grounds of Tir Na Nog,' she told them, dialing the lab to arrange a team.

'Jennifer?' Chris asked.

'I hope so. Poor thing might finally be reunited with her own name, if nothing else.'

Sitting back in the seat, Reilly rubbed her eyes until she saw stars, the fatigue hitting her as the car journey took its toll on her barely rested body.

Some minutes later, they reached the village of Avoca, after passing some of the mines and slag heaps that blotted the landscape on the way in, and along the course of the river that looked like flowing cola.

'It's very pretty,' Reilly commented, as they pulled into a parking spot in the center of the village. 'Looks kind of familiar...'

'Ever hear of *Ballykissangel*?' Kennedy asked.

'Sure, my dad used to watch it back home. It was filmed here?'

'Yep. Do you want to take the car back out to the river,

while we ask around?' He tossed her the keys.

'Just don't go wandering off into the hills. I know what you're like when you get a hiking trail in front of you,' Chris added, and Reilly smiled, pleased that they seemed to be on better terms since having to work in closer proximity. As the case's tension began to escalate, it was as if they'd automatically settled into their usual familiar rhythms.

'No girl-scouting for me this time, I promise.' She got into the driver's seat and fumbled around for the adjustment lever that slid the seat forward from Kennedy's near-backseat position.

On the way in, Chris had pointed out a slip road that led up to the old mines. A good place to start.

Heading directly for the road, Reilly drove along what seemed at first to be a pleasant country lane, but after a few minutes the tarmac disappeared and gave way to an unkempt dirt track with industrial wire fencing either side of it.

Along the track was yellow-colored gravel that matched the loose banks of mining waste inching its way down the slopes. Dotted along the fence were warning signs: *'Danger, keep out, land reclamation in progress. Land prone to slippage.'*

Reilly drove along slowly, the car bouncing through the yellowish mud and puddles splashing up onto the car. Kennedy will kill me, she thought, as a particularly deep splash sprayed across the windscreen as if somebody was shooting at her with a paintball gun.

She pulled into a gateway, grabbed her kitbag and got out to take a proper look around.

Shame to have this ugly blight on such a naturally beautiful place.

There was no sign of any residential properties immediately nearby, only a couple of old buildings that looked like outhouses and a hay barn.

And while the area was certainly not a place for raising a

family, Reilly mused, it might not be a bad spot for hiding one.

She already guessed that the trace they had found could only have been from this area — it was as unique as a fingerprint.

But it begged the question: what had McAllister been doing down here? Was it work-related?

Reilly walked up the road a few yards to take a better look at an old building with chimney stacks that had caught her eye.

On closer inspection she figured it must have been the old smelting house attached to the mine. Nearby were several similar outbuildings from subsequent mining eras that had also sprung up, and since been abandoned.

She supposed it was a ghost town of sorts, and immediately remembered a childhood trip she'd taken with her parents and sister to a place called Bodie near the Sierra Nevada.

Expecting it to be scary, Reilly hadn't wanted to go there at first, but ghost towns were different in the US. They had restaurants and gift shops and people dressed up as cowboys, prospectors and burlesque dancers.

This place was different though, and Reilly could almost smell the history in the air. Commercialism had stopped the day the last pick had been swung, and all that was left now were some old buildings and scars in the earth that would never heal.

FASCINATED, the man watched her, hunched over, picking up bits of soil and rock.

She flicked a loose bit of blond hair behind her ear. He liked blonds, though had always considered red to be the purest hair color.

He had been teased in school because of it — called names like carrot and ginger. It didn't bother him now, of course, but back then they were only kids, and didn't know any better.

That was the problem though, too many incestuous inbreeds around these days without the intelligence or ability to raise a rat, never mind a child, a pure precious child.

It angered him to see society's workshop of disfunction, churning out bastard children who would be poisoned and polluted only to go on to raise the next, even more sick, generation.

But he had been called on to build a haven, to protect.

And now as he watched the blond woman and recognized her face, he feared he'd be forced to run again.

He questioned his strength and resolve; the flood waters of sin and greed were rising around him, threatening everything he had given his life for.

He started to breathe more easily as the blond lady made her way back to her car. But as she reached it, he saw her turn and look in his direction, and then walk towards him. He held his breath.

'Excuse me?'

He was torn — should he pretend he had not heard her and walk away, or talk to her and put her off?

'Hello there, miss, lovely day for a ramble,' he replied as casually as possible.

'Yes, it is indeed. I wonder if you could help me. I don't suppose you know who owns these lands?'

He hesitated a little, and the woman smiled. 'Allow me to introduce myself, my name is Reilly Steel, and I work for a company mapping the soil and geology of the Irish countryside,' she said, holding up her sampling bag.

Liar...

'Ah, I'd wondered what you were up to. To be honest, I'm not sure, I just walk through here mostly, but I do share your love of rocks,' he said.

'Yes, nature is truly amazing, especially in places like this. Sadly, here the beauty of nature is side by side with the destruction of man,' she said, indicating the ugly remains of decades of mining.

He smiled. 'Never a truer word spoken. They destroyed this place for a few pounds of precious metals, not realizing that it was the place itself that was precious. Few people see the irony.' He chuckled. 'Even more ironic that one of those few who do is a lady named Steel.'

She smiled at his joke. 'I suppose it is. Anyway, thank you for your time.'

'Thank you, Miss Steel. It's nice to know there are souls out there who still care for the precious things in this world.'

Reilly deliberately slowed her pace, and tried to make herself relax as she walked back to the car. She could feel her heart beating faster in her chest.

The moment she had stood in the gateway, she knew this was the place. The industrial gates were chained and padlocked from the inside, and recent tyre tracks had passed through, but the thing that stood out the most was the small pool of motor oil that lay in the gateway.

She could picture the van stopping, McAllister getting out to unlock the gate, while several droplets of engine oil had left a smaller version of the larger oil stain photographed near the boat he had escaped on.

When she had seen his face, even without the wild beard he'd sported in the only photo they had of him, she knew.

Reilly started the engine and raced back towards the main road. As she drove she tried first Chris's then Kennedy's phone … Damn, no reception.

As she re-entered the village she spotted Chris standing outside the local newsagent talking to a man.

Blowing the horn twice to get his attention she waved him to the car in a manner that let him see she was flustered.

'What's up?'

'It's McAllister. We've got him.'

'I'd like to introduce you all to Steve Jacobs.'

Having quickly returned to base after learning about McAllister's whereabouts, the team wasted no time in planning their next strategy. A local unit had been installed to keep watch on the area and O'Brien was about to advise them of the next steps.

Now, the inspector entered the room and nodded towards the man behind him.

He was around six foot three, well built, with a strong jawline, and blond hair just starting to recede. He looked a bit like a middle-aged surfer, Reilly thought.

'Jacobs, meet Detectives Kennedy, Delaney, and our GFU head, Reilly Steel.'

Nodding as they exchanged greetings, Jacobs gave each a bone crunching handshake. He paused as he held Reilly's hand, his challenging blue eyes resting on hers.

'Mr Jacobs is a hostage negotiator,' O'Brien told them. 'I thought it was best to bring in an expert this time.'

He ushered them around the meeting table.

Jacobs sat next to Reilly, and stretched his long legs out in front of him, looking at the mass of maps and documents gathered on the table.

'I'm aware that you've handled this very sensitively at all times so far,' he began, 'and I don't want to tread on any toes. But if the situation is as the inspector describes it, then maybe I can help.'

Reilly could tell that Jacobs had immediately put Chris's back up. He was used to being the alpha male around here, the tall, attractive, masculine one. Chris looked at O'Brien. 'With all due respect, sir, I'm not sure why this is necessary. Kennedy and I have extensive hostage negotiation training.'

'Perhaps, but Mr Jacobs has a doctorate in psychology,' O'Brien replied, 'and comes with the highest recommendation of the Chief Inspector of the UK Met.'

Jacobs sat forward. 'Detective Delaney, wasn't it?'

Chris turned quickly towards him. 'Yes.'

'As I said, I don't want to tread on any toes – I think the chief just wants to make absolutely sure that everything runs smoothly this time. I'm here to support you guys.'

'I think it's a sensible move,' Reilly put in. 'At this point all that matters is the safety of those kids.'

Jacobs turned his surfer's smile on Reilly. 'Graciously put, Miss Steel. I'm here purely to help the team achieve the best resolution possible.'

Kennedy seemed to be watching all of this with wry amusement. 'So if we're finished getting to know one another,' he said impatiently, 'time is running out and we need to move quickly. Is Mr Jacobs going to head up the operation in Avoca, or what?'

'Please, call me Steve,' Jacobs said smoothly.

'Mr Jacobs will be responsible for negotiating with McAllister for his surrender and for the safe release of his captives,' O'Brien said. 'You will support and assist him in any way you can. Given that there's little time to waste, I'd suggest the four of you immediately agree a path forwards.'

He looked at all of them, his gaze resting on Chris the longest. 'Any questions?'

There was silence.

'Good.'

'Steve,' Reilly began, 'we appreciate you stepping in to help us, you've obviously read the file so you have some background – I thought it would be best if Chris brought you up to speed on where we are at this point.'

Chris looked surprised and Reilly knew she'd spiked his guns by forcing him to engage with 'Steve'.

Out of the corner of her eye, she saw Jacobs gave her a subtle nod of approval.

Chris tapped the end of a pencil on the table. 'We already know McAllister is intelligent, a meticulous planner as he demonstrated at the lake house. But in my opinion, this time will be different. Now he's angry, he wasn't expecting to be cornered again so quickly after executing his escape plan.'

Jacobs nodded. 'What's your take on where we stand now?' he asked, and Reilly liked the way he was so easily, almost offhandedly, making sure that the detectives didn't feel like outsiders in their own back yard. Clearly he was used to this.

'He's holed up in there now,' Kennedy continued. 'He has the advantage of an elevated position, and can see everything coming up that drive. We could send in the heavies again, but with three, maybe four children at risk, and the mood he's in, plus the fact he seems to have nowhere to run …it could get nasty.'

'You mentioned his mood; do you think he'll be too hostile to talk to us?'

'For a guy who is so paranoid about the dangers of the outside world,' Reilly put in, 'we've so far been living up to the reputation of these so-called "demons" that he seems to fear. I think his mood will be predominately hostile, yes.'

'So we need to build some trust, but in order to do that, we need to open some line of communication first,' said Jacobs.

'He'll be a tough nut to crack,' Reilly said, recounting the conversation she'd inadvertently had with McAllister earlier. 'The whole nature of what he has done is built on paranoia, mistrust of the outside world. It's hard to know what he actually believes, though he seemed almost normal when I spoke to him.'

'You think the charades are for their benefit to protect the illusion?'

'According the profile, he may have a natural affinity towards women.'

'His wife was killed in a car crash,' said Jacobs.

'That may well be crucial, the trigger for the creation of this elaborate fantasy, but I'm not sure if this alone would make him withdraw from the world. I wonder if he's got a deeper rooted reason for shunning modern society.'

'I think it's simply his way of keeping dangerous influences away from the children,' Chris said.

'So that means no TV, no radio, no computers, nothing that would let them have any contact with the outside world,' said Jacobs.

Reilly nodded. 'There was nothing like that at the lake house — the only modern thing I've seen is the CCTV system he had to monitor the fence line and the gates, and that was locked in his study — away from little eyes.'

'But he's plucking those kids from the real world, so they know those things exist,' reasoned Jacobs. He thought for a moment, then turned to Chris. 'What else can you tell me about the boy, Conn?'

'Apart from the fact that he would go back there in a heartbeat?'

'Yeah, that's interesting, isn't it?' The negotiator eased back in his chair.

'The way he spoke... if you didn't know otherwise you would think that in Tir Na Nog he had a happy, loving family,' Chris said.

'So McAllister's created what the boy wants, a surrogate family.' Jacobs gazed at the ceiling absentmindedly. 'He plays upon the power of a child's imagination. Kids grow up in a world that's half reality, half fantasy. Santa Claus, the Easter Bunny, the Tooth Fairy. For them they are as real as Mum and Dad, aunts and uncles ... What McAllister has done is taken that natural affinity of children — their inclination to believe in magical, fantastical places — and turned that to his advantage. He has created a mythical world, and the kids have bought into it.'

'Our profiler is in agreement,' Reilly said. 'He used the analogy of the Catholic Church and how it exerts control by fear of mortal sin and damnation.'

'Look, all this is very well but how does it help us to get him to come out?' Kennedy asked impatiently.

'That's the question, isn't it, what does McAllister believe? When he lies in bed at night, is he David McAllister, child kidnapper? Or is he Setanta, spiritual guide of Tír na nÓg?'

Reilly raised an eyebrow. 'You make it sound almost charming.'

Jacobs leaned forward, his face full of fire. 'It is, Reilly, it is, at least to McAllister and those kids. In his mind he has created something wonderful, something precious. We have to figure out how to get him to give that up.'

'We could play on that fantasy,' Chris suggested.

'The Celtic mythology?'

'Yes, the Children of Lir is a complicated story, full of jealousy and double crossing, but I think the crucial part is whether McAllister chooses to believe this is the end of one of those periods, or the absolute end. In the story, when the kids were finally released from the curse, they withered and died.'

'Well, we need to coax him along to believe that this is not the end, and certainly not the place the children should spend the next period of their lives,' Jacobs said. 'Something about the effects of keeping the children there, that they have to leave eventually, and what happens to them then. We know that the boy Conn was rebellious or too difficult to control as he got older like all maturing males — why else would he cast him out? And we can only assume that the other two—'

'Sarah and possibly Jennifer, we haven't been able to confirm her identity yet.'

'Right. We have to consider that they too were rebellious, that they had a hankering for greener pastures. Why else leave?'

'Sarah was pregnant of course,' Reilly reminded him.

He nodded. 'Guess it was first hormones, and then maternal protection that kicked in there.'

Kennedy stood up, eager to get going. 'So how are we going to play this?'

Jacobs looked around the room at each one of them. 'Look, you all know what I do. I try and talk people out when they're dug in like fleas on a hound. I'm not always successful, but most of the time I can get people to walk out without blood-shed.' He paused. 'But one of the reasons I am successful is that I use whatever help I can get — and unless any of you have any thoughts to the contrary, I think the biggest asset we have right now is Reilly.' He turned to face her. 'You're the only one who's actually been up close and personal with this guy.'

She frowned. 'I'm not sure what you mean …'

'I wouldn't be fooled by that spiel in Avoca earlier. You recognized McAllister, but he may have known exactly who you were too, possibly saw you in the CCTV cameras at the gates last time.'

She closed her eyes, cursing herself for how stupid she'd been in not considering the possibility that McAllister had made her.

'So chances are, he knows we're coming and he'll be ready. However,' Jacobs continued, 'the fact that he conversed with Reilly and didn't attempt to harm her is a good thing. From what I've read about him from the files and the profile, he seems reasonably well disposed towards females.'

'So what's the plan then, Jacobs?' Chris asked.

'I'll want Reilly on hand to start with. You're the only one he has spoken with, maybe you can introduce me and see where we go from there.'

'How do you think it will play out?'

He grimaced. 'I hope to be able to speak with McAllister myself to get some kind of real feel for the situation,' he said, 'but I have little doubt that we'll have to tread softly with this one. Get him spooked, show any force, and we'll lose him again. We already know he has issues with reality. Who knows what he's liable to do?'

Back in Avoca, a command post had been set up amongst the trees near the perimeter of the outbuildings, but well out of the visibility of the occupants.

On the journey back to the village, Jacobs riding up front alongside Kennedy, Reilly could feel the tension radiating off Chris, which she wasn't entirely sure was justified. They needed an expert this time, especially when things had gone so easily out of control before despite their own team's best efforts.

The quiet country lane had been transformed by the time they got back. Unfortunately, it wasn't just the presence of emergency services vehicles; once again, the press had got wind of the story.

Since the initial lurid headlines about the Angel had appeared, the media had resorted to speculating wildly due to the lack of further detail, or any more bodies. A story was only news when something was actually happening — but now the reporters had the taste of fresh blood, and were circling like a pack of hungry hyenas.

Reilly and Jacobs had to run the gauntlet of TV vans and

parked cars lining the narrow lane, while the detectives headed to the CC command post. They arrived just in time to see O'Brien addressing the gathered reporters.

Reilly groaned as she saw the media scrum ahead of them. 'How did they find out?'

'How does anyone ever find out anything,' Jacobs replied quickly. 'It's human nature — a secret is only really interesting if you can share it with someone who shouldn't know about it. There has got to be at least a hundred people who know about this — that's a hundred people with the chance to make a buck and feel important.'

They climbed slowly out of the car, grateful that O'Brien was garnering all the attention. 'Are you going to have to say something?' Reilly asked him.

Jacobs grinned, and shook his head. 'Not in the contract. My name isn't mentioned, and I don't do press interviews.' He was wearing a Gore-Tex rain jacket –he pulled the hood up tight around his head, and grabbed Reilly's arm. 'Let's leave O'Brien to do what's in *his* contract...'

Reilly followed his lead, and they skirted around O'Brien and the media, sticking to the grass verge, mostly hidden by the line of parked vehicles.

They reached the police cordon, and flashed their IDs to get past. Jacobs paused a moment. He turned back to the officers blocking the road. 'Who's in charge on the ground here?'

They nodded up the road to a tall cop talking into a radio. 'Stokes.'

Jacobs nodded and they strode over to the man. He saw them approaching and gave Reilly a nod of recognition — their paths had crossed previously. He finished speaking on the radio and turned to them. 'Reilly, nice to see you again.'

She smiled. Daniel Forrest had taught her to always go out of the way to be polite and friendly to people whose help you need — secretaries, maintenance workers, the often unrecognized people who make things happen. She had added uniformed officers to her list when she'd started in police work. 'Hello, Sergeant Stokes. Good to see you too. How are you?'

'Great, thanks. That being said, I always know things are going to be, how shall I say…interesting when you're around,' he replied with a grin.

'I'll take that as a compliment.' She turned to Jacobs. 'This is Steve Jacobs, our hostage negotiator. He's going to be working with us to try and resolve this and get those kids back safely.'

'What can we do to assist, Mr Jacobs?' Stokes asked.

Jacobs looked around. 'Press are out in force here. Is the perimeter sealed? I gather it's quite a big site.'

'It's good and tight. The fact that it backs onto the old quarry and is surrounded by the old slag piles means there no getting in or out from the west or north end of the site.' He pointed in each direction. 'The rest is bordered by the fence and we have a cordon set up at each end.'

'Excellent. How close are your men to the gateway?'

'As per request, we've tried to keep the men at least seventy yards away, and behind any natural cover,' Stokes informed them.

'Great. Just one more question — who's my liaison?'

'Sergeant Lee should be inside waiting for you.' He indicated a small white trailer nearby.

Jacobs led the way to the trailer. Several uniforms were inside, drinking tea and chatting. One of them jumped up when they entered.

'Which of you is Sergeant Lee?' Jacobs asked.

The liaison officer was clean shaven, with dark hair graying slightly at the temples.

'Tell me what we've got.'

'This guy is going to take some convincing,' Lee said, looking toward the building. 'We've been talking options, and feel it would be best to try and get him a radio. We've a short wave rig — the base is here, we can give McAllister a handset. You too.'

Reilly looked — there was a bank of radio handsets plugged in and charging on a counter at the back of the trailer.

'We've also got a handful of mobile phones,' Lee continued.

'They all call into the same number?'

Lee nodded. 'That's the only number they can call. Everything else is blocked.'

Jacobs looked at Reilly and raised his eyebrows. 'Will we load up?'

Lee started busying himself grabbing phones and radio receivers. 'There's also some more vital equipment here,' he informed them, pointing to a kettle and some tea bags. 'Could be a long night.'

'Are you ready?' Reilly nodded as she and Jacobs started to move closer to the gateway, picking their way through the puddles.

'So you walk just in front of me, and let him see you first,' he said.

She swallowed hard, her throat dry at the realization that what she was doing was fraught with danger. One wrong move and she could mess up everything. 'What do I tell him?'

'Tell him that your bosses are insisting that you talk to the kids, just to check on them. Don't give him any deadlines, no pressure. We want him to think, not panic.'

'What about you?'

'Don't say anything. He'll ask.'

Reilly looked up at the negotiator's face. He looked calm and relaxed, as though they were a couple out walking the dog in the country on a weekend afternoon. 'Will you tell him why you're here?'

He nodded. 'If he asks. Never lie to people, they always find out. We have to establish trust — build on the familiarity he already has with you and try and extend that to me.'

Reilly let out a sharp breath. 'OK, let's do it.'

He smiled at her. 'Trust me. You'll be just fine.'

They reached the gateway. Reilly stood before the gates with Jacobs slightly off to one side — simply having him with her gave her confidence. He was one of those people who exuded positive energy.

'How long do we stand here?'

He stayed focused on the gates. 'As long as it takes.'

'Do you think he's watching us?'

'We have no way of knowing, but my hunch is, yes. He's a smart guy, I'm sure he'll want to check us out a little before he shows.' They had now been waiting for around ten minutes. 'Either he's testing us, waiting to see if we persist or...'

'Or?'

'Or he's trying to decide what to do.'

Any further speculation was cut short by the sound of footsteps approaching on the gravel.

'Here we go,' whispered Jacobs. 'Showtime.'

McAllister slowly walked into view with a grim look on his face, and much to Reilly's horror, a shotgun nestled in the crook of his arm. He stopped a few yards from them, gate in between like a safety barrier. 'Your friends may think they're being very clever out there, hiding behind the trees and bushes,' he began, 'but they stand out like blood on snow.'

'They are there to keep people out, not you in,' Reilly replied shakily.

He looked puzzled. 'People? *What* people?'

'The press.'

The scowl on his face deepened. He thought for a minute. 'Tell them they can stay — but don't get any closer.'

'I'll let them know.'

He peered at Jacobs. 'Who's that?'

'My name is Steve Jacobs.'

'I don't give a damn what your name is, what are you doing here?' he growled.

Jacobs stayed quiet, forcing McAllister to dictate the encounter. As long as he was still there talking to them, Reilly thought, they were making progress.

He glared at Jacobs, then back at Reilly. 'You lied to me, you said you were checking soil and rocks, you said you wanted to protect the beauty of this earth from men.'

Reilly hesitated a moment. 'That was no lie. I've dedicated my whole life to protecting the beautiful things from the evil you and I know this world contains.' She was thinking on her feet, trying to appeal to his way of thinking.

He didn't respond, and she thought he looked tired, weary from trying to protect his crumbling fairytale. 'I would like to see the children,' she continued. 'My boss says I need to see them, make sure they are OK.'

'They've been "OK" for years without your help,' he snapped, 'so why do you need to see them now?'

'Ms Steel is simply doing her job,' Jacobs quickly replied.

He turned his attention back to the negotiator. 'What did you say you were doing here?'

'I'm just here to talk, to help.'

'Ah ...' McAllister gave a bitter smile. 'So I'm the crazy guy holed up with a bunch of prisoners, and you're here to talk me out of it, is that it?'

Reilly held her breath, wondering how Jacobs would reply.

'You're the one holding the gun,' he pointed out calmly.

'What do you expect?' McAllister snapped. 'There's an army of people harrying me for simply doing the right thing, and they are just waiting for me to relax my guard.'

'Who do you think they are more likely to shoot?' responded Jacobs. 'An unarmed man, or one pointing a gun at two officers?'

McAllister considered this for a moment.

'Why don't you just place the gun on the ground at your feet?' suggested Jacobs, 'so that we can have a polite conversation.'

'Show me you're not armed.'

Jacobs slowly unzipped his rain jacket, held it out above him, turned a slow circle in front of McAllister. 'I'm not a policeman. I just talk to people.'

He looked past Reilly and Jacobs, nervous glances darting in every direction. Finally he seemed to relax. 'No tricks?'

'No tricks,' Jacobs reassured him in a steady voice. 'You have my word.'

McAllister gave a last suspicious glance around them, then slowly set the shotgun down at his feet. 'Now what do you want?'

'Now we talk,' replied Jacobs. 'We talk about whether we can see the kids.'

'And if I say no?'

'Let's cross that bridge if we come to it.' McAllister was focusing his attention on Jacobs now. Reilly was impressed at how the negotiator had used her to bring McAllister out, then deftly taken the focus away from her. 'If we wanted to use force, we could have done so already. We could have ordered up a sniper to shoot you the second you pointed that gun at us, or sent in a team in the early hours of the morning to overwhelm you … that's not what we want.'

'So what *do* you want?' He was still suspicious, but Jacobs had got him thinking.

'To talk,' Jacobs answered. 'To check on the kids and reassure the boss that everyone is safe.'

For a moment Reilly thought McAllister was about to agree, then suddenly he bent and picked up his shotgun. 'I need to think about it.'

Jacobs nodded, his face a picture of understanding. 'Of course. It's a big step for you.'

He glanced back towards the buildings. 'I need to go and see how the children are. They have been through a lot this last few weeks. They miss me when I'm gone.'

'Of course they do,' said Jacobs. 'But before you go, can I give you something?'

McAllister hesitated. He was getting twitchy. 'Give me something?'

'So you can call us when you want to talk more.'

'What? I don't like phones. Nasty intrusive things.'

'How about a walkie-talkie then, a radio?' suggested Jacobs. 'No one will call and bother you, but when you want to talk, you can contact us from inside the house.'

He nodded, keen to be on his way. 'Throw it here then.'

Jacobs pulled the walkie-talkie from his coat pocket, and took a few steps forward.

McAllister instinctively raised the barrel of the shotgun.

'Can I show you how to work it?' asked Jacobs.

He nodded at Reilly. '*She* can show me.'

Jacobs handed the radio to Reilly. She stepped forward slowly, and held it out towards the abductor. 'You turn it on there, and press this green button to talk.'

McAllister peered at it, glanced around one more time, then darted forward. Grabbing it out of her hand through the gap in the gate, he then scuttled back up the driveway to the old smelting house.

R eilly and Jacobs walked slowly back towards the trailer to debrief O'Brien and the rest of the team.

'Taking the radio was a big step,' Jacobs said. 'It will make him feel in control of the agenda.' He looked at Reilly. 'He seems to trust you more — that's why he took it from you. Either it's a female thing or you struck a chord with him with what you said before about caring for beautiful things.' He smiled. 'Either way, I suspect you may be key to getting us in there – I'm afraid you might have to stick around until this thing ends.'

She smiled lopsidedly. 'I wouldn't miss it for the world.'

Her confidence faded somewhat as they approached the trailer – O'Brien was pacing around outside, looking like a caged animal. He hurried up to them as soon as he saw them. 'Well, what did he say? Is he coming out?'

Jacobs gave him the type of smile you would give to a child when you were explaining something difficult to them. 'Sir, we've just made initial contact.'

'But you gave him a deadline though? How long does he have?' O'Brien's eyes were full of impatience.

'No,' explained Jacobs. 'I did not give him a deadline – I gave him a radio.'

They had reached the trailer. Jacobs paused by the door. 'He can call us when he wants to talk. And I didn't give him a deadline because people like him get antsy and make rash decisions when they feel pressured. He's in there with multiple kids and a shotgun — do you want him to make a rash decision?'

O'Brien scowled. 'No, of course not, it's just that—'

Jacobs opened the door of the trailer. ' We need to be in here, ready in case he calls us.'

O'Brien looked crestfallen. 'So how long will this take?'

'As long as it needs to, to get those kids out safely…'

'THIS LOOKS COZY,' Chris said, poking his head round the door of the trailer. Reilly was sitting at a small desk working on her laptop, and Jacobs was on one of the benches going through the case report.

It looked like they were settling in for a long night.

'So I hear you got to talk to McAllister,' he said to Reilly. He looked at Jacobs. 'I thought that was your job.'

'Regardless, we spoke to him,' Reilly replied. 'Steve reckons he won't call until later, when the kids are in bed or asleep. It's more likely we can talk sense to him when he's out of character and doesn't have to maintain the fantasy.'

'So what happens now?' Kennedy asked, entering behind Chris.

'We sit tight,' Jacobs informed him. 'McAllister has the radio. He'll use it.'

'You sound pretty sure,' Chris challenged.

'I've done this a couple of times before,' he said, eyeing him levelly. 'The crucial step was getting him to take the radio. Now he's got it, he'll use it, sooner or later.'

'So he calls,' says Kennedy. 'Then what do you do?'

'This guy understands the game. He knows we are camped outside. There's nowhere to run this time, and he hasn't planned on staying here long, that's for sure. Unlike Tir Na Nog, those outbuildings aren't homely, so clearly this place was intended only as a temporary stopover for him — somewhere for him and the kids to lie low for a while.' Jacobs looked determined. 'There's nowhere to run this time though. We are moving towards an end point. Now it's about negotiating the terms of his surrender, letting him feel as though he can control the way his fantasy ends.'

'Seems like you've got it all sewn up,' Chris said, his skepticism obvious.

Jacobs shook his head. 'Not at all. There's always a real danger with something like this — when a guy's cornered like a rat — that he decides to end it on his own terms.'

'Sounds ominous,' said Kennedy. 'What does it mean in plain English?'

'Think about it, McAllister's under pressure. He and the kids are all crammed into this tiny space and the net is closing in on him. The pressure gets too much and he decides to kill the kids, or turns the shotgun on himself,' Jacobs said, his voice grim. 'And they all live together happily ever after in whatever after-life he believes in.'

Was I wrong? Did I love you too much? For so many years I have kept the world at bay, brought my lost ones in to protect them from the vicissitudes of a cruel world, but now the world has come knocking at my door, and I can keep it out no longer.

What will become of you, my little swans? They will break you, shape you to be just like them, with their wickedness and their ways, and you will change and grow, and eventually forget that once there was a place where you were safe, happy, eternally young.

When I look in the mirror I see that time has caught up with me. There are lines on my face I don't remember; my hair is changing, receding, the bright color of youth replaced by the dull gray of age.

My body, too, rebels; what was once easy, taken for granted, now requires thought, effort. I must rest when tending the horses, the cows, can no longer keep up with you when we play our games of chase in the woods.

But you, you my loves, are unchanged. You are still fresh, young, unsullied by the world outside. Would that I could preserve you like this for ever, but there is only one way to do that.

Every minute their cries grow louder, their voices more shrill, *until finally they enter our nest whether we like it or not. They violate our garden with their heavy feet, invade our quiet spaces with their loud, hectoring voices.*

And so I will call you all to me one last time, hold you, love you, remember you this way for now and all eternity, my beautiful, beautiful swans...

AFTER CHRIS and Kennedy left the trailer, Jacobs and Reilly discussed the case so far over cups of coffee while they waited.

'There was another attempted abduction I see?' He nodded to the case file.

'Just last week.'

'You think it was McAllister?'

Reilly looked thoughtful. 'I'm not sure. We did at first, but with him so busy planning his escape around that time, it doesn't feel right that he'd be looking to increase family members. Also the circumstances didn't seem anything like the others. It could just be a nasty coincidence.'

The sudden chirping of the radio stopped them. 'Hello?' McAllister's voice cut through the static.

Jacobs nodded to Reilly. 'You should answer it.'

She grabbed the handset and clicked a button to respond. 'Mr McAllister, this is Reilly Steel.'

'Hello, Miss Steel.' There was something in his voice, something different. Reilly glanced at Jacobs – he'd heard it too. McAllister sounded exhausted, drunk or both. He gestured at her to keep talking.

'I'm glad you called,' she said.

For a moment there was nothing but static. Reilly wondered if he had disconnected, but suddenly he was back. 'They're growing up so fast,' he said suddenly. 'My little swans...'

'I'm sure they're a credit to you.'

Jacobs hurried over to sit beside Reilly, a notepad in his hand and pen at the ready.

'They're growing up so fast,' McAllister repeated, sounding incoherent and uncertain. Reilly was almost certain he'd been drinking. 'And then they'll want to fly the safety of the nest I've provided. Like Sarah.' He gave a little sob. 'Lisa will be next. Her mind already wanders beyond our borders, I can tell.'

'I went through something like that with my father. I wanted to fly the nest too. It's natural.'

Jacobs nodded furiously, mouthing, 'Good.'

'You seem to have turned out OK,' McAllister slurred.

'Thank you. But my father didn't want to let me go, didn't think I would survive.' She paused, waiting, but McAllister said nothing, so she continued. 'I've always thought that the true test of how well we are raised is not through hiding from the evils of this world, but in facing them and emerging victorious.'

'Miss Steel, I almost feel like I know you from another place or time. I felt it right from the start. You have wisdom for one that lives amongst today's self-obsessed world. Your family must have been good people.'

If only you knew, she thought.

'But my swans are too innocent for this world,' he said, his words garbled. 'I fear their pain in a future without my sanctuary.'

Jacobs scribbled frantically on the pad. Reilly read his words. *He's tired. Maybe on the verge of giving up?* She nodded.

'Let us work together then,' Reilly suggested. 'I will help you bring your swans to a place they can thrive and learn. Learn to become strong, to face the world and be triumphant.'

There was no reply and for a moment she worried that she'd pushed him too quickly.

'I don't know…' he said eventually and Jacobs gave a nod of satisfaction.

'Are the children asleep now?' Reilly asked.

'They always slept like little angels back home, all the fresh air and hard work, but they've been restless here. Where else could they live a life like the one I gave them? Where else will they be surrounded by fields and trees and animals and sky every day?' His voice had a distinctive catch in it; he was close to sobbing.

'It's been a wonderful experience for them, something that will stand them in good stead for the rest of their lives.'

'But it's time to move on — is that what you're thinking?'

'What do you think will happen?'

'One way or another it's finished,' McAllister said sadly, and Jacob's eyes widened. He scribbled again on the pad and held it up to Reilly.

'So how can we ensure that the children's experience remains positive?' she said. 'That their memories of their time with you are happy, without a shadow over the ending?'

Jacobs wrote some more.

'You have created a beautiful life for them, a beautiful story — can we give it a happy ending?' Reilly pressed.

McAllister sniffed. 'I can't see their faces any more.'

'Their faces?'

'My wife and every one of our children. I thought I'd never forget any of them, that they were imprinted on my heart forever, but now, when I try and picture them, I can't see their faces.'

Reilly sat forward. 'My mother died when I was young. For years, when I tried to picture her, the only image I could see was the last one I had of her, an image of her dead. I thought I was a terrible person, I couldn't even remember my own mother's face when she was alive.'

Jacobs was staring at her, a curious expression on his face.

'You sound as though you've come to terms with it ...' McAllister said.

'It took a very long time, then one day I realized that it

didn't matter. Her face was just a tiny part of the memory. What mattered was the way I felt when I remembered her, and by focusing on not seeing her face I was robbing myself of everything else. My real memory of her was her laughter, the fun things we did, the way she made me feel.'

'And how did she make you feel?'

'Loved. Happy.'

McAllister seemed to ponder her words. 'Will you work with me?' he asked eventually. 'Will you work with me to ensure that my swans are treated right?'

Jacobs was on tenterhooks, perched on the edge of his seat. He nodded furiously.

'Of course.'

'Do you have that power?'

She looked at Jacobs. 'Yes.'

For the first time, she could hear warmth in McAllister's voice. 'Your name suits you. I hope you can give some of that steel to my children. Help prepare them for the challenges out there.'

'Mr McAllister,' Reilly continued. 'Could we talk in person? I can come to you now if you'd like?'

Jacobs' eyes widened. That last bit hadn't been his suggestion.

There was a long silence. Finally McAllister's radio crackled back to life. 'No commitments, no promises. Just talk — and come alone this time.'

She nodded. 'I promise. I'll be there in a few minutes. Just give me time to get my coat.'

'I'll be looking out for you.' With that, McAllister disconnected.

Reilly looked at Steve. 'OK?'

He shook his head reluctantly. 'I don't know. You're sort of doing my job for me, but ... his defenses are definitely down at the moment, so it might be best to roll with what he wants, at least for the moment.'

'So what do I say?' Reilly asked, already regretting her impulsiveness.

'Like McAllister said, no commitments, no promises, just talk.'

'About what?'

'He's starting to move forwards,' replied Jacobs, 'thinking about leaving. You have to help him to find a way to voluntarily walk out of there.'

She nodded. 'That's what I'm hoping.'

'Just remember he sounded vulnerable, and that combined with liquor and firearms is a toxic mix.'

She gave a watery smile. 'Jeez, thanks for putting my mind at ease…'

Steve grabbed a mobile phone off the counter top. 'Trust me. You'll be fine, he's already opened up to you. Take this and try and keep us updated as much as you can. We'll have a team in place to act quickly if things get sticky.'

Reilly slipped the phone into her pocket. She knew what she needed to do, her FBI hostage training had taught her a few things about situations like this.

She knew the golden rules: keep him talking and observe. Then she went through a checklist of what she needed to do once inside: establish the children's whereabouts, draw a mental picture of the layout of the room, and assess the weaponry and threat level posed by McAllister. And most importantly, keep all communication lines open.

She sighed. If McAllister didn't kill her, O'Brien surely would.

It had been a long time since she'd had to draw on this part of her training, and even then it was more geared towards hostage-takers with specific demands. McAllister seemed different, his only demand was a simple 'leave us alone'.

She glanced at her watch. 'It's after seven thirty. I'll try and call in by eight, whatever happens.'

'OK, I'll be waiting. Be safe — and remember, Reilly, you don't have to resolve this now, tonight,' Jacobs told her. 'It's enough to just get McAllister thinking about it, and talking about how to end it. Drawing him out of his fantasy is a major first step. Keeping him there is another.'

She gave a grimace. 'I'll see what I can do.'

L ucy looked around the empty house. Given that McAllister was holed up in a completely different hideaway, it seemed clear that the attempted abduction of Jade Carney was not carried out by him, but by somebody else entirely. Someone who had been using the identity of a man that had died many years ago and had been spooked enough to take flight.

The GFU had been called back to the house after the discovery of a burned-out van that had nearly caused a major fire at a local industrial estate.

Whoever had been living here was not coming back. The question now was, how could they identify him?

'Where do we even begin?' Gary looked over Lucy's shoulder into the living room. 'It's like a time warp in here. My gran used to have those ducks flying over the mantelpiece.'

'Everyone's gran used to have those,' Lucy replied drolly. 'That still doesn't help us figure out where to start. A fresh scene we can handle; there are usually some obvious things to start with.'

He grinned. 'You mean like a body or a big pool of blood?'

She shook her head indulgently. 'Be serious for once.' She picked up her tool kit, and headed towards the stairs. 'I'll get the upstairs.'

'Suit yourself.' Gary stepped into the living room. 'Welcome to the nineteen seventies...'

All was quiet in the house as the forensic techs continued working in their own little bubbles, methodically examining each room, identifying trace and collecting evidence, hoping that something they found would help them to unlock the true identity of the person who'd lived there.

Gary had started with the couch. He liked couches, they collected the detritus of people's lives — not just loose change and missing remote controls, crumbs and old tissues, but hair, skin follicles, useful things with DNA attached.

He pulled out the cushions and stared at the couch in disbelief. He had never seen anything like it. 'Who the hell keeps their couch *this* clean?' he muttered to himself in wonder. Either the guy never sat on the couch, or he vacuumed it every bloody day of the week.

Dropping down on the floor, he peered under the couch — his other favorite place for finding the debris most people left as part of the residue of everyday living. Nothing. No old pens, no lost keys, coins or odd socks. This guy had the cleanest, most unlived-in home he had ever seen.

Which begged an interesting question — did he actually live there, or was it just a useful address, somewhere to get his mail, to visit from time to time to keep up the appearance of living there? Or maybe he knew to expect a visit and had had time to wipe it down?

Lucy was experiencing a similar situation upstairs. The bathroom was immaculate, the bedrooms clean, the bed unslept in, not even a toothbrush or hairbrush to be found.

Like Gary she peered beneath the furniture, in the backs of the closets, all the usual places where they might find trace. Whoever he was, he wasn't leaving any signs of his existence.

She focused on the bathroom again — her father would love it. Jack Gorman was fastidious about cleanliness in the home, and liked nothing better than a gleaming bathroom that smelled of bleach. He would be right at home here, she thought as she turned back into the hall.

And it was right there and then that something caught her eye. Was that a stain on the bathroom floor?

Lucy paused, moved back into the room, and stared. Wrong angle. She stepped back again, paused in the doorway, and this time she could see it. A faint shadow of a stain on the tiles. She dropped to her knees and sniffed. The smell of bleach was especially potent in the flooring.

'Nice view.'

Lucy peered over her shoulder at Gary who had come up the stairs.

'Stop gawking at my ass and hand me the luminol,' she ordered.

'Think you've got some blood?' Gary pulled out the spray bottle and handed it to her.

'There's a faint stain, there and there,' she pointed to the places she had seen, 'and a strong smell of bleach.'

Gary watched as she sprayed luminol across the floor, up the tiled wall and the side of the bath.

As the fine drops of liquid settled they stared — slowly but surely, in several places on the wall, a bluish luminescence glowed in the brightly lit bathroom, the tell-tale sign of blood.

'Camera.'

Gary handed it to her, and she took several pictures of the gleaming patches before the luminescence faded. Finally she stood up and handed him the camera.

He scanned back through the shots she had just taken.'Well spotted.'

Lucy smiled, quiet satisfaction on her face. 'If that isn't blood spatter, I don't know what is…'

As they said it, the implication sunk in for both of them. Gary met her eye. 'Better call it in. I'll go check the rest.'

While Lucy was on the phone, Gary got out a stepladder and positioned it on the landing beneath the hatch to the attic. He climbed halfway up, and took out his dusting kit. Setting up a tool tray on top of the stepladder, he placed dark fingerprint powder, a brush, some print tape and a knife into the tray. Then he gently dipped the brush into the powder and used light, short brushstrokes to apply the dust to the door.

'You beauty …'

Almost immediately several good fingerprints started to appear as the powder stuck to the oil and grease left behind by whoever had been accessing the attic.

There were lots of them too; the attic had obviously been frequently used. Unusual in itself, perhaps.

He took the tape and cut several strips, placing them over the fullest prints collecting as many variations as possible before storing the samples away in his kitbag.

Then he climbed a little higher and placed two hands squarely onto the hatch itself, not sure if it opened up or down.

He pressed against the door as one edge lifted and the other stayed fixed on a hinge, then pushed the door all the way until it stayed upright on its own. Inching higher on the ladder, he twisted his body so he could reach the inner ledge and stuck his head though the attic opening.

The first thing that struck him was a musty smell; the odor of long-dead mice he thought, unable to see a thing in the darkness. As his eyes adjusted he reached for his pocket torch, lifting it up while using his other hand to keep his balance on the ladder.

Flicking on the beam, he reeled back in terror. His heart pounded in his chest and his heavy breathing through the dust mask caused a mixture of sweat and condensation to build up around his mouth and nose.

What the fuck...?

Dozens of eyes were staring back at him.

R eilly could feel the butterflies in her stomach as she made her way down the lane way towards the old smelting house. The van had been ordered, but would wait by the trailer until she called and okayed it.

While everything sounded good in theory, she knew from her previous conversation with McAllister that he had an ever-changing grip on reality, so she only hoped that by the time she got there, he wouldn't have changed his mind about talking to her in person.

No, Reilly thought, dismissing any doubts. She would convince him, she was confident of that. The children were going to come out safe and sound, and she was going help to reunite them with their families.

She moved past the last turn before the gate, and just as she did so, something in the darkness caught her eye, a movement.

A man darted from the bushes and scampered across the muddy ground onto the driveway. His camera bounced against his chest as he ran.

'Who the hell are you?' Reilly demanded, her voice a low hiss.

He held his hand out. 'Paul O'Connor. *Sunday News.*'

Reilly's heart thumped. 'I don't give a damn which rag you work for, you shouldn't be here!'

He shrugged, as if such abuse was part of the job.

'Get out of here now! You'll ruin everything ...' Reilly shoved him away to the side, out of view, terrified of the implications. Had McAllister seen him?

If he had, what would he do? She pulled out her phone to call Jacobs – the best thing to do was try and get rid of the photographer.

She pressed the call button, all the while berating O'Connor. 'Get the hell out of here — *now,*' she repeated hoarsely. 'Do you hear me? Better get out of my sight if you don't want to spend the next seventy-two hours in a jail cell.'

'Oh come on, give us a break ...'

'For Christ's sake, there are *children* involved here!'

It was as far as Reilly got — one glimpse at the guy's face told her that her plans for a smooth resolution had already gone to hell. She looked round — standing in front of them was David McAllister, his shotgun pointing right at them.

'I thought we had an arrangement, Miss Steel. I thought I could trust you. But you are the Leanan Sidhe, whispering all I want to hear while plotting against me.'

Leanan Sidhe ... Reilly had gleaned the name from the Irish mythology books they'd taken from the lake house. Right then she couldn't remember the details but knew it wasn't good.

O'Connor looked worried, but he kept his wits about him. 'Ah it's not her fault, boss, blame me, I tried to sneak in.'

The shotgun didn't move. Reilly could see that McAllister now looked tense, edgy — dangerous.

'I'll just stay here,' the photographer offered, 'and you and the lady go right ahead with what you were doing, all right?' He took a step backwards, his hands up to signal his intent.

'Don't move.'

O'Connor froze in mid-step with the shotgun aimed right at him.

'Mr McAllister, please, just let him go and you and I can talk,' begged Reilly. 'It's as he says — he just sneaked up behind me.'

'Liar. You're all a bunch of liars.' McAllister flicked the shotgun to indicate that they should move towards the building. 'Come on, let's go. The only way to stop a beast is by taking its head.'

BACK AT THE HOUSE, it took more than a few seconds for Gary to realize that the deadened empty stares weren't alive or even human, but dolls.

No, not dolls, he realized then — mannequins.

Mannequin heads to be precise. They reminded him of a toy his sister got for Christmas once; just a disembodied head with all this hair she used to spend hours arranging in different hairstyles. He shone the torch around; there must have been two or three dozen heads with hair, all of varying lengths and colors.

'Anything interesting up there?' Lucy called out.

'You are not going to believe this. Here, take a look,' he said, descending the ladder and handing her the torch.

'What is it?' She looked uncertain.

'You tell me — some weird shit that's for sure,' he said, as Lucy climbed the ladder and shone the light around inside.

'Oh God, that's seriously creepy! It's no wonder dolls always freaked me out when I was small. They're evil-looking.'

'I'll put the ladder up through the trapdoor so I can get in there properly. I got some prints from the hatch; we might get more up there than we did in the rest of the house.'

'*The Diary of Edmund Harold ...*' Lucy mused.

'Who?'

'One of the books I saw downstairs — it's about a wigmaker.'

'You think that's what the guy does for a living?'

'Either for business ...' Her eyes widened, and she got back up to take another look. 'Oh Jesus, Gary...'

'What?'

'The hair ...there's some skin attached.'

Gary felt sick. 'You're not suggesting ...'

'It's definitely human,' Lucy confirmed. 'I'm sure of it.'

'But where the hell would anyone get that much hair?' Gary asked. But already afraid of the answer, Lucy didn't reply.

Reilly and O'Connor edged forwards into the old smelting house; it smelled of mildew but there was a fireplace, a makeshift kitchen and a door off to one side. She wondered where the kids were, but couldn't make out much detail. Only a thin trickle of light came through the windows due to the security grille on the outside and layers of dust on the inside.

'On the ground, now!' McAllister was wound up tight, his tone of voice leaving no room for discussion.

Reilly and the photographer threw themselves down on the damp floor. She could feel the cold against her cheek, through her clothes. She tried to keep an eye on what McAllister was doing, but he stepped quickly round behind them.

'You're a cop,' he snapped at Reilly, 'do you have any handcuffs, restraints, in your bag?'

She lifted her head slightly to look at him, and shook it. 'I'm a forensic scientist, not a police officer.'

She could see him thinking — this had taken him by surprise, and he was not sure what he was going to do next.

'Listen, mate,' began O'Connor again, 'just let us go, that

will be the easiest thing for you.' He began to climb to his feet and turned towards the door. 'We'll get out of your hair and—'

It was a bad decision, and helped make up McAllister's mind. As O'Connor moved, a loud blast echoed off the bare walls.

In the time that it took Reilly to realize what had happened, the photographer had slumped forwards, his wide eyes staring at Reilly as he hit the floor. He scrunched his face up in pain. 'He fucking shot me!' he cried.

McAllister loomed over him. 'I told you to lie down.'

Reilly looked up, horrified. 'What have you done?'

The older man looked almost as shocked as O'Connor. 'What I had to do.' He looked down dismissively. 'He'll be all right. It's only a seat full of pellets.'

The photographer groaned. 'Oh God, oh God...'

She glanced up at McAllister. He was watching her carefully. 'I'll need to call in now,' she said, 'and let my team know what's happening. They'll have heard the shot; they'll want to send people ...'

'You call in — but you tell them exactly what I say.'

'I won't lie.'

'You'll do what I say.'

He hurried over, reached into her coat pocket for the phone, and shoved it in her hand. 'Call them. Tell them everything is fine. Say there's an idiot intruder here and I'm not happy about it.'

'And what do I say about the shot?'

'Tell them there was an accident, but everything's fine.'

Reilly looked at his wild eyes. She could see how the pressure was mounting on him, how he was changing. The earlier trust they'd built up was disintegrating.

She took out the mobile and called Jacobs, putting him on speakerphone.

There was an almost immediate response, the negotiator's

calm voice filling the room. She felt instantly better, reassured. 'How are you doing?'

Reilly kept her eyes on McAllister. He hovered over her, so tense it almost seemed that he was holding his breath too. 'Everything is fine.'

'That's good.' Jacobs's voice was warm, but she could hear the hint of enquiry.

'We have a problem though.' McAllister's jaw muscles tensed as she said this but she hurried on. 'A photographer got through the police cordon somehow, he sneaked up to the house alongside me.' She stopped, wanting to give Jacobs time to absorb the information, give him time to think.

His response was measured. 'I see. That is … awkward.'

She could imagine him back at the trailer, trying to figure out what was going on. 'Inspector O'Brien is with me now. Is there anything else we need to know?'

There it was, in the question. He had heard the gunshot, but Steve was smart enough not to ask about it directly. And O'Brien also now knew she had gone rogue. She felt her throat go dry.

'I'm fine,' she answered quickly.

'That's good to hear.'

He had understood. Reilly was fine, but not necessarily everyone else. 'Is there anything you need?'

'David understandably isn't happy about the photographer being here,' she said, using his first name to suggest familiarity. 'It has complicated things.'

'Of course,' replied Jacobs. 'I'm sure he feels betrayed, even though you knew nothing about it and there was nothing you could do.'

Clever. Express McAllister's feelings, but exculpate Reilly. 'David and I need to make the photographer more comfortable for the moment,' Reilly informed them, 'then we'll call you back.'

'Very good. We'll listen for your call within fifteen minutes.'

Exactly what she needed — a commitment, a deadline, something to get McAllister to understand that this could not continue indefinitely.

He was picking up some of this, and looked angry. He grabbed Reilly's arm, and chopped his hand across his throat to indicate that she should end the conversation.

'OK, I have to go now. I'll update you in a little while.'

'Good talking with you, Reilly.'

The line went dead. McAllister grabbed the phone from her, and slammed it down on the table. 'I suppose you think that's clever?'

Reilly pointed at the photographer, lying on the floor, eyes scrunched shut in pain. 'Look at him. He needs proper medical treatment, we need to get him to a doctor ...'

'Not yet we don't.' McAllister stepped back. 'OK, on your feet both of you, move into the corner.'

Reilly helped O'Connor to his feet — he was panting, wincing, blood seeping through his pants. He limped, leaning heavily on her, groaning the whole way.

As soon as they stopped he collapsed to his knees and looked up at McAllister, who still held the shotgun. 'I need a doctor.'

'You'll see a doctor when I say so,' he growled. He circled around them. 'If you're a scientist, then you can treat him.'

'I'm used to examining dead bodies,' Reilly told him, 'and unless you want him to become one, you need to let him go.'

'Treat him. Tell me what you need. We have supplies here.'

Reilly sighed in exasperation. She had medical training, yes, but was not exactly experienced in treating gunshot wounds. 'OK, put the shotgun down — believe me, neither of us is about to run out of here.'

He looked dubious, but after a moment placed the gun down by his side.

'OK,' Reilly continued. 'Help me to get him up onto that,' she said, pointing to a nearby table.

McAllister quickly cleared the table, then grabbed O'Connor under one arm while Reilly held the other. Together they manhandled him up onto the table, the photographer groaning in pain the whole time.

'We'll have to get your clothes off,' Reilly told him.

She slid the trousers down — they were quite bloody, and he looked to have at least a dozen pellets in his legs and back-side. She tapped the camera bag he wore and slid his pack off — it was dripping wet. She set it down, looked inside, and raised an eyebrow as she pulled out his dripping thermos. 'Saved by your tea.' She held the thermos up for O'Connor to see — it had four holes in it.

Now he could see the damage he had caused, McAllister looked contrite. 'So what do you need?'

Reilly quickly examined O'Connor's injuries. 'I can't get the pellets out — he'll need a hospital for that ... I guess water, a couple of clean cloths, then whatever you have for these wounds — dressings, tape...'

He nodded to another door to the right. 'Running water's in there, and some towels in that box by the door.' As he spoke he rummaged in the bottom of a larger box just inside the entrance. He retrieved a large biscuit tin. 'First aid kit,' he informed Reilly, setting it on the table.

She ran some water in a bowl she'd found amongst the supplies, grabbed two towels, and returned to the table. She looked down at O'Connor. 'You all set?'

He nodded, and closed his eyes.

Reilly set to work cleaning the wounds.

As she did so, she thought about what would happen next – O'Connor's appearance had completely changed the rules. Where did they go from here?

'Jesus Christ. You let her go out there *alone?*' Chris had returned to the trailer with Kennedy and O'Brien and was outraged to discover that Reilly had been sent to talk to McAllister. God only knows what that madman could do to her ...

Jacobs gave him a cool, detached look. 'Detective, I understand that you have strong feelings for Miss Steel—'

'You're damn right I do! Strong feelings that she shouldn't be alone with an unstable lunatic!' he shot back, anxiety dripping from every pore.

'Together we made an informed decision,' Jacobs went on smoothly, 'and we both felt that given the trust established—'

'I thought *you* were the negotiator — how come she's out there doing your job for you?'

'Like I said, McAllister trusts her,' Jacobs replied. 'She understands that, and is keen to do anything she can to get those kids out of there safely.'

'Including risking her life?'

'There's a plan in place should she encounter hostility. And I'm sure you know she's no fool.'

O'Brien had held his tongue so far, but he clearly wasn't happy either. 'What the hell did all that talk on the phone mean?' he asked Jacobs.

'You sent her in there, and now it sounds like it's all gone pear-shaped!' Chris reiterated.

Jacobs managed to stay calm. 'You heard her. We've got a situation that none of us could have foreseen.'

'A damned member of the press in there?' Kennedy raged. 'Somebody's screwed up.'

'That's one for you to deal with,' Jacobs continued. 'What we have to do now is help Reilly get things back on track.'

'She said she was OK though, didn't she?' Chris said, sounding desperate. 'So that's something at least.'

'She said she was OK – but there's that shot...' O'Brien liked plain talk, none of this trying to read between the lines bullshit. 'So what are you saying? Is she or isn't she OK?'

'I would say that Reilly is OK, but I wouldn't count on the press guy being unharmed.'

'That's it,' O'Brien declared. 'I'm sending in the Armed Response Unit. If he's shooting people, we need to end this situation right now.'

'Wait a minute.'

'There's no time to waste, Jacobs; we've got Reilly and the kids to worry about.'

'And she's given herself a clever way of keeping us up to date with how things are going,' he argued.

O'Brien looked at him impatiently. 'How so?'

'She said she'd check in within fifteen minutes. Let's see how she's doing then. The ARU is on standby, they're ready to roll, but first give Reilly the respect of allowing her to rescue this situation. It's our only chance to end this thing peacefully.'

Chris paced the room. 'Peacefully? The guy is a maniac!'

'The angle that we're using,' Jacobs continued, 'is to get McAllister to consider the welfare of the kids — the ones he's already lost have got him thinking about the futures of the others, whether he can cope, whether he can continue looking after them. Reilly's alluded to the fact that if he lets them go we'll take proper care of them – I think we need to be clearly seen to be doing that in order for him to trust us.'

'What does that mean in practice?' O'Brien barked.

'I'd suggest that we offer a van with blacked-out windows to get him and the kids out of there,' Jacobs said. 'He knows the press are sniffing around.'

'He's a criminal,' snapped Chris. 'We can't have him just riding away free in a van. They're still digging up at the lake house, we could well have another Fred West on our hands here.'

'If we leave him, there's a danger that he could stay holed up in there after the kids are let out,' Jacobs pointed out. 'He could be suicidal.'

O'Brien snorted. 'Frankly, once we have the kids out safely, I don't care what happens to him.'

'We might need him, though,' Kennedy said. 'He's the only one who knows where these kids came from, their real names and backgrounds, and like Chris said we'll need to talk to him about what else we find up at the house.'

O'Brien gave him a sharp look. 'Surely the kids will know?'

'If he abducts them when they are young, then brainwashes them for years, they might not remember anything about their former lives,' Jacobs pointed out.

'So we just let him come out a free man?'

The negotiator shrugged. 'You're the boss. I'm just suggesting what seems the most likely way to get everyone safely out.'

BACK AT THE GFU LAB, Julius pulled on a fresh pair of gloves and got to work.

Inside the boxes were some of the items removed from Tir Na Nog, McAllister's house by the lake. An old biscuit box caught his attention, and a memory from his own childhood filtered into his brain. USA biscuits to him meant Christmas and happy memories of eating all those chocolate rings with the jellies on while leaving behind the boring Rich Tea ones.

What memories did this particular box hold? He was out of his comfort zone with this type of evidence — it was the smaller stuff that he preferred, a piece of glass, a strand of hair …

Breaking things down, using the smallest molecule to build a bigger picture, that was Julius's forte.

Here with boxes of everyday stuff that had been tucked into a cupboard years ago, he wasn't sure how to start to build any picture. Old books, little knick-knacks, he knew they told a story, but he couldn't see it.

He opened the biscuit tin and pulled out the contents. Lots of individual items, documents, receipts, family photographs of McAllister's family in happier times. He glanced at one of the photographs. It was a typical family scene, happy, smiling people on a warm sunny day.

McAllister held his wife from behind with his strong, sun-tanned arms and a young redheaded child was in front of them both, grinning broadly.

How would it feel for a man to hold all that was dear to him in his arms on a perfect summer's day, then have it all stolen away with a swipe of Fate's hand? If it was him maybe he'd end up creating a fantasy world too, Julius thought, empathizing.

He tried to look at the photo differently in the hope that it might yield something interesting, but it was hard to pull focus away from the happy faces. He looked at the background; where was it taken? The lake house probably — he could make out trees from the forest behind, and they may well have been standing on the shore of the lake.

He set the photo aside, and hearing noises from the doorway, turned and saw that Gary and Lucy had returned from processing the house in Whitestown.

'How'd it go?' he asked as Lucy set her kitbag down and dropped into the chair beside him.

'Great. If you think finding an attic full of creepy mannequin heads is fun…'

He raised an eyebrow. 'Mannequin heads?'

She sighed, and waved him away. 'Don't ask. Any word from Avoca?'

'Nothing yet, but we need to be on standby, just in case.'

'Bloody hell, it's nearly eight o'clock on a Thursday evening. Why did I ever think a job like this was a good idea?' She rolled her eyes. 'So what are you up to?'

'Just sifting through more of that stuff taken from the lake house.' Julius picked up the photograph and showed it to her. 'Who'd have thought a normal-looking guy like that would turn out to be such a nut job?'

She looked at it. 'It's sad, isn't it?'

'Even sadder for the poor misfortunates he kidnapped,' Julius said.

'He really was trying to replace them,' Lucy said sympathetically. 'His little girl is the absolute image of Sarah Forde.'

Julius looked again at the girl in the photograph, who looked to be about nine or ten years old.

'Hold on,' Lucy said, sitting up straight. 'I think that *is* Sarah Forde.'

'What? How could it be? Didn't he only start abducting kids after his family was killed?'

Lucy was shaking her head. 'I've spent the last week practically memorizing those files, and I would know that little girl's face anywhere, especially that gap in her teeth.' She looked at Julius. 'It's Sarah Forde; I'm telling you. Which means …'

Nodding, he quickly reached for the phone. 'I'll call Reilly.'

eilly sat in a rickety chair, watching McAllister looking lost and helpless.

But the sight of O'Connor lying on the table was a reminder that while the abductor may be struggling to know what to do at this point, he could still pack a punch.

She looked at him. 'The kids, they must be scared by what's happening,' she said gently. 'Where are they?'

He glanced over at the photographer lying on the table. O'Connor looked as though he was asleep, but his occasional groans suggested otherwise. 'I don't want them anywhere near him.'

'Are they in the next room? I could go and talk with them; I'm sure they must be scared ...'

'I'm not stupid!' he snapped.

'I wouldn't do anything to—'

'Right now I'm not sure what you would or wouldn't do.'

Reilly fell silent, thinking, trying to regain his trust.

'You don't understand what it's like out there,' he continued, sounding exhausted, 'why I brought them to me, why they need my protection.'

She sat forward. 'I understand entirely what it's like out there. I'm just not sure that I agree with your solution.'

He looked puzzled. 'But if you understand … if you know what a hateful, wicked world it is out there, how can you not see that the one I created was right, the best possible thing for these poor souls?' His voice was full of passion, brimming with emotion. He nodded over her shoulder to the outside world. 'Out there they would be chewed up, devoured, defiled. I can protect them. You saw the lake house. Our Tir Na Nog is truly a paradise, a Nirvana.' He leaned towards her, the fire burning bright in his eyes. 'Tell me, Miss Steel, be honest with me. Have you ever seen a better place for children to grow up?' His face was bathed in missionary fervor as he gazed at her, his eyes like glowing blue chips in the gloomy air.

'It's beautiful, yes,' she began, 'so much care and love, that's easy to see on the surface. But all swans eventually want to fly the nest,' she went on, 'and what then? What happens when the children want to leave?'

His beatific smile faded, to be replaced by a scowl. 'Why would they want to leave? They have everything they could possibly want.'

'Except freedom.'

He gazed at her for a moment, then looked away. She watched him carefully as she delivered the next piece of news.

'I've met Conn.'

Her words caught him off guard and she heard a sharp intake of breath. 'Where? How is he?'

'He's in a children's home. They can't find a family for him.'

McAllister nodded, as if this made sense. 'He was always a wild one. Always challenging me, challenging everything. Miriam would have been better at getting through to him. When I rescued him I hoped I could change him, but in the end he was just too disruptive for our family, and I had to admit defeat…' His words faded into nothing.

Miriam... Reilly's ears pricked up at the mention of the name. One of the other children?

He sniffed, and wiped his nose on the back of his hand. 'We were so happy. We loved caring for the kids, giving them a home, a place to feel safe.'

Reilly frowned. What was he talking about? Who was 'we'? Was there somebody else involved in this too?

His voice had fallen very quiet. 'My favorite time has always been tucking them in at night. It's a magical time. All the energy and excitement of the day has passed, they're all clean and soft and tucked up in their beds, smelling of soap and toothpaste ... The way it's supposed to be.' He suddenly looked up at Reilly. 'You don't have kids, do you?'

She shook her head.

'They are such a gift. Miriam always used to sing a wee song, and I'd tell stories. Ellie's favorite was always the Swans of Lir.'

Reilly's mind was racing. She wasn't sure whether McAllister was mixing up actual reality with the one that he had created since the death of his family. But now with the way he was talking, she was wondering if Miriam might have been his wife and Ellie – had that been his daughter's name?

'I'd sit on her bed and tell her the story, listening to her breathing as she slowly drifted off to sleep.' He looked up again. 'She loved that story so much she wanted wings of her own.'

Wings of her own ...

'The tattoos,' Reilly asked. 'I wanted to ask you about those. Do all your swans have them?'

He looked at her. 'Only the older ones, if they want them. Conn was a bit young but insistent because Sarah had hers. I only gave them to her because ... I was afraid they would take her, like they took Ellie.'

So Ellie must have been his daughter. 'Tell me more about Ellie.'

McAllister shook his head, smiling. 'She was the first to come to us. So troubled, so afraid and suspicious of everything and everyone. The only thing that seemed to calm her was stories, especially the story of the swans.' He smiled. 'I suppose that's why she got the tattoo.'

Reilly frowned. His daughter had had the same tattoo? 'You didn't tattoo Ellie yourself?'

'Oh no. That would have been frowned upon. I think that's why they took her away, but I don't know. I just know that shortly after she got the wings, she never came back. Ironic really.'

Never came back …

'And then of course, they let her die all alone like that. It was barbaric…which is why I brought her back, brought her home.'

Reilly's mind was struggling to make sense of it all. She needed to be very careful here, given his muddy perception of dreams and reality. 'Ellie and your wife … you lost them at the same time?'

'Of course not. How could that be? Ellie was taken from us long before … that. If it wasn't for Sarah, I'm not sure how we'd have coped, especially when they wouldn't give us anyone else.'

Now Reilly was seriously confused. Who were 'they'? She could see he was deep in thought, deep in memories, so she said nothing further, hoping he might offer some insight into what he was talking about.

'After losing Miriam, Sarah was my rock, all I had left in the world. I was so afraid of losing her. After all, it was my job to protect her.'

'But you did lose her, David.' Reilly braced herself for a reaction, not knowing if she was talking to the deluded fanciful David McAllister, or the weary broken man who'd lost his family once before and was now trying to surround himself with a world he thought he could control.

'It's time to end it, you know that,' she said. 'You've done your very best to offer these children a haven from a world gone mad, but in the end you can't protect them from themselves. They have to be allowed to change, to grow, to have the freedom to find their own place in the world, and you can't give them that. It's what Sarah wanted.'

When he didn't reply, she decided to press further, hoping her words were striking a chord. 'Sarah flew the nest. And I think you know the time has come for the others to do the same. What happened to her doesn't have to happen to them. We can help them.'

'What do you mean?' he asked suddenly. 'What happened to Sarah, where is she?'

She paused, not sure what to say. Of course, McAllister would have no clue that Sarah had died on the road. Should she use this, she thought, maybe it would help draw him out...

'She's safe and waiting for you,' she lied.

He shook his head. 'Not out there. She'll never be safe with him around.'

Reilly frowned. Never be safe with who around? The father of her child, maybe?

Just then, the photographer called out in pain, and Reilly went over to check on him.

He was complaining of pain in the region of his left kidney, and she was worried about how deep the pellets had gone. Whether it was from the pain, or from an infection setting in from the wounds, she couldn't tell, but he was starting to drift off. 'I could do with a drink,' he murmured. He was still lying face down on the table — with the pain he was in, there was no chance of him sitting or lying on his back.

Reilly got him a glass of water, and handed it to him. 'You doing OK?'

He sipped the water awkwardly, and looked over at McAllister, who was still sitting gazing at the empty fireplace.

'He doesn't expect me to get my assignment in today, does he?'

The comment caught Reilly by surprise. 'Assignment? What are you talking about?'

O'Connor nodded towards McAllister. 'My editor. He's a real stickler for deadlines usually, but I was hoping that getting shot in the ass would give me a little leeway...'

Reilly took the empty water glass from him. 'I'm sure you'll be given time to get better first. Why don't you close your eyes for a bit?'

'Be the first time if he does...' He laid his head back down on the table. 'Think I might close my eyes for a few minutes — wake me up if he starts getting shirty, right?'

As soon as O'Connor looked settled, Reilly moved over to rejoin McAllister. He had his back to her — wild thoughts crossed her mind — maybe she could grab something heavy and beat him over the head with it?

But what looked easy in the movies was a lot harder in real life. She doubted her own resolve, and worried what would happen if it didn't knock him out — what if he fought back?

He was close to the edge. Reilly attacking him might be all it took to push him past the edge of reason — and if that happened they could all wind up dead. No, she had to work with what she had — words, her ability to keep him calm, and the trust they had built up.

'About your family ...'

'Take a look at this,' McAllister said, handing her a large book, worn from years of gentle handling. She opened it slowly, McAllister peering over her shoulder, his alcohol breath engulfing her as he talked.

'This is of all our swans, going back over the years...'

He pointed to the first page — a little child's picture was glued there, a mass of squiggles and colors, the kind of thing only a parent finds fascinating. 'That was Ellie's first picture,' he informed Reilly. 'She said it was the swans.'

He leaned over closer, and turned the pages for her. 'Ah, look at that one.'

This was slightly more identifiable — a lumpy brown animal with four legs, green grass below, blue sky above. 'Conn drew that — the pony we used to have...' He thought for a moment. 'What was that pony's name? I can't remember.'

Reilly looked up. 'They're lovely.' She searched for the right words — the ones to move him forwards. With the photographer getting worse and McAllister moving back and forth from fantasy and reality, there was little time to waste now. 'But you can't live forever in the past. Children aren't butterflies, you can't pin them to a board and expect them to stay there.'

He swayed slightly as he looked down at her. 'We should not be blinkered by society. Just because the world operates a certain way doesn't make it right, only those who choose their own path can truly live a blessed life...' He clasped his hands together and looked into Reilly's eyes. 'The world beyond the reality my little herd knows is lost — it was already lost to them before they came to me. The only chance an innocent child has is by being protected from its cancerous touch. That's my calling, and I've seen and heard in you something that tells me it was no mistake that you came to us.' He suddenly grew very serious, and crouched down level with Reilly, stared into her eyes. 'It's not me who has to make a decision, Miss Steel, it's you. Look into your heart and find the answer ... you know these swans will be safest with me. Like Sarah's mother knew it was better to get her away from the leering eyes of her so-called father.'

'I don't understand,' Reilly said, completely confused. 'You knew Sarah's mother?'

'Of course,' McAllister replied as if it was the most obvious thing in the world. 'She's my sister.'

71

K ennedy nodded towards the door of the trailer to indicate for Chris to follow him.

Outside he puffed at his freshly lit cigarette. 'Well, what do you reckon on surfer boy?'

Chris snorted. 'Let's say we agree to disagree.'

'So he's running the show, and we're shut out?'

'Something like that.'

'Was it his idea for Reilly to go in alone?'

'His, hers. You know what she's like when she's got the bit between her teeth. Thinks she can save the world.'

'She's pretty hard to say no to once she's made up her mind, that's for sure.' Kennedy dropped his cigarette after only three or four long pulls, and stubbed it out with his foot. 'I don't like it though.'

'Me neither, and I really don't like sitting around waiting for—'

They were interrupted by the ringing of Chris's mobile. 'It's the lab,' he told Kennedy, answering. 'Delaney here. Hi, Julius. No, she's … unavailable at the moment. Anything I can help you with?'

He listened for a couple of minutes and then looked at Kennedy, his face changing. 'Are you absolutely sure?'

His partner gave him a questioning look.

'OK, thanks. I'll follow up on it.'

When he clicked off, Kennedy spoke. 'So what was all that about?'

'I'm not sure what it means yet,' Chris replied, frowning, 'but it seems our information is bad ... we've got the timeline all wrong on this somehow.'

'What do you ...' The rest of his sentence was cut off by a shout from one of the officers nearby.

'Heads up, somebody's coming out of the building!'

Chris ran down to the perimeter, closely followed by Kennedy.

Staggering down the drive was a man wearing no trousers, blood running down one side of his left leg, as he limped and looked around, confused. Several times he lost his footing on the loose gravel as he tried to pick up the pace.

'The photographer ... Reilly must have convinced McAllister to let him go,' Kennedy said.

Chris breathed a relieved sigh. 'Which hopefully means this is almost over.'

72

Back in the trailer, Steve Jacobs reached for the radio and pressed the answer button.

'Mr McAllister, how is everything?'

'This is not a social call, Jacobs, just do what I say,' McAllister bellowed down the radio, clearly irate. 'Listen very carefully. I want you to have one person drive a van up here, back it up close to the door, and leave the keys in the ignition. No games, I'll have my sights on it. My family and I are leaving now, and we do not expect to be followed. My little swans don't like it here. We want to go home...'

Jacobs's voice was calm and measured. 'We'll get somebody working on that right now. It'll take a few minutes though. Can you put Reilly on the line so we can organize the details?'

The radio clicked off.

'Damn...'

'What did that photographer say, what's happening up there?' O'Brien demanded as Kennedy and Chris reappeared in the trailer.

'We haven't been able to talk to him,' Kennedy said. 'Paramedics are with him at the moment, and he looks in poor shape.'

'I want somebody out there now to see what they can get out of him. And then I want him arrested and charged!' O'Brien spat, venting his anger and venom at the easiest target.

'Have you heard anything from Reilly?' Chris asked Jacobs, who shook his head. Chris turned to O'Brien, his jaw clenched. 'Sir, this has gone on long enough. We need to get a team in there.'

'Detective, might I suggest we buy some time, play along, tell him the van is on the way?' Jacobs said, holding the radio.

'Chris is right, the time for talking is over,' Kennedy agreed, looking at Nolan, the ARU chief, hoping he would step in with a suggestion.

Nolan nodded. 'I have to agree with the detectives. This has gone on long enough. We need to act.'

'Any suggestions about how we should act?' O'Brien blustered. 'We have a senior investigator in there as a hostage.'

'Sir, can I make a suggestion…' Jacobs began, before getting abruptly shot down by Chris.

'Stay out of this, Jacobs, the talk shop is shut. All you've done is sit around here talking crap, and sent one of us in to do your job.' Chris's face flashed angrily.

'What's your suggestion, Jacobs?' O'Brien asked, ignoring Chris.

'Reilly and the children's safety is our ultimate priority now, and if we just charge up there, who knows how it will end? So I was thinking… we give McAllister what he wants.'

'That's it? That's your brainwave?' Chris yelled, and Kennedy put his hand on his arm to calm him down.

O'Brien shook his head. 'We give him the van and then what? He takes off home…back to the lake or Tir Na Nog or wherever the hell he thinks home is… we'd be back to square one.'

'Not quite,' said Jacobs. 'My thinking is that we send him a Trojan horse. Give him his van but with a surprise inside.'

They all contemplated the suggestion.

'It's the only way to get my men up there safely without arousing any suspicions,' Nolan agreed. 'We put a four-man tactical team in the van, back it up good and tight to the door, and use two men on the flanks with two others in the back. When we get a visual we either take him down, or get him out.'

O'Brien massaged his temples. 'OK set it up. Jacobs, get back on the radio. Tell McAllister his van is on the way, and ask to speak to Reilly again.'

It was risky and a lot could go wrong, but right then it was all they had.

73

Reilly could feel the water churning above her.

Few women surfed at Maverick's; it was a potential graveyard. The ocean swell that had charged thousand of miles through the ring of fire and then crashed into the sharp continental shelf south of San Francisco made it a must for elite surfers.

Or those with a death wish.

Reilly fell into the second category. Witnessing so much suffering, so much death had left a void, a chasm that would temporarily vanish when faced with her own mortality. Life or death.

It was just her versus nature, and as the gurgling monster of the Pacific ocean hammered over her, her board was dragged one way and her body the other as her tether cord reached its elastic limit.

More water pounded in — which way was up, which way was down, Reilly didn't know, but she also knew there was no point in panicking.

The next wave struck, sending her board back towards her like a bullet, the rear edge hitting her on the head with all the force the ocean could muster. The pain struck first, then silence and finally the blackness. Mother Nature was winning. Her body was limp and relaxed, floating. She felt a tight grip on her arm, tugging, shaking her …

'Come on, time to go. You have been chosen to help me.'

Reilly's head throbbed as she came to. Where was she? She struggled to open her eyes, but it was as though they were made of lead. Searing pain shot through her temple.

'Miss Steel, wake up now, the time has come for us to return. You can come with us; you will have true peace.'

Reilly slowly remembered what had happened. She kept her eyes shut.

How long had she been out? What had happened to O'Connor? She remembered him trying to make a run for it while she and McAllister were talking ... but everything had happened so fast after that she wasn't sure … Had he got out? Or had McAllister …?

Jolted upright by a strong grip, she opened her eyes and groaned in response.

'Ah good, you're awake.' McAllister returned to the window and the radio crackled to life.

'Mr McAllister, the van has arrived.' Reilly heard Jacobs's voice but wasn't sure what was going on … Was McAllister surrendering? 'We are going to cut the chain on the gate so the driver can drive up.'

He reached for the radio. 'OK, but remember I can see everything from here, don't try to trick me.'

'What's going on, where are you going?' Reilly asked as she stood up for the first time.

Blood immediately rushed to her brain and stars appeared before her eyes. She bowed her head, thinking she would faint. A wave of nausea hit, and she vomited on the floor beside the table, unable hold it in.

McAllister walked towards her, seeing her knees tremble with the weakness.

'Come, come, sit, I'll get you a drink.'

He hooked her under the arm to support her, placing the gun on the table. Reilly saw it through watering eyes. It was now or never. She took a deep breath, and wiped her eyes.

'Here, let me—'

Then summoning every ounce of energy she had, Reilly charged into McAllister, catching him completely by surprise. He lurched sideways, trying to keep his legs under him but became entangled with a chair and crashed to the ground.

Reilly grabbed the gun from the table.

'Don't move,' she commanded, as he tried to get back on his feet. 'It's over, stay right there. I will use this, don't let the children bear witness to your death. I *will* fire …' she warned again.

He looked up at her, got slowly to his feet then put his hands in the air.

'Move over there towards the door,' Reilly said as she reached for the radio. Outside, the bang of the van door startled them both.

Jacobs's voice cracked through the radio. 'OK, Mr McAllister, the van is outside, the driver's on his way back. Now we need something in return, let me speak with Ms —'

She grabbed the radio. 'Jacobs, it's me, I have him, get somebody up here!' she cried breathlessly.

'Are you OK?'

'I'm fine, just get somebody —'

There was a loud crash, then a bang and Reilly felt herself sailing through the air.

She heard the ARU officer shouting something in the distance. 'Team Trojan, go! Suspect disarmed, secure and confirm!'

The back doors of the van burst open as the armed unit

flew out and charged the door. The first two officers entered, guns raised.

Coming into the room they saw Reilly on her back struggling to sit up from where she'd landed after McAllister had charged.

'The gun...'

One of the officers secured the weapon while the other stood over the injured McAllister. He unclipped his radio and called the trailer. 'Suspect down and injured, officer injured, send in paramedics.'

Just then, Chris and Kennedy rushed through the door.

'Reilly, are you OK? Jesus... are you hit?' Chris asked, helping her to her feet.

'I'm OK, he charged me ... I think the gun went off ... is he ...?'

'Don't worry about that, here, sit down.' Chris ushered her to a nearby chair and she was grateful for the strength of his arms around her.

'Ms Steel, can you confirm the suspect was alone?' one of the ARU officers asked.

'Yes, there was a photographer here as well ... I don't know where he is now. He tried to get out, and McAllister went ballistic. He cracked me in the head with the gun, I think. I don't know what happened after that.'

'Where are the kids? Have you seen them?' Chris asked.

'Out back somewhere, I think. I'm not sure,' Reilly said, as she sat forward on the chair, her hands starting to shake as the adrenaline began to wear off.

'I'll go take a look.' Kennedy walked towards the other door.

The paramedics rushed in to check on Reilly and treat McAllister.

'Was he hit?' Chris asked.

'Yes. He's lost some blood, but the pellets seem to have

missed any major organs or arteries,' he confirmed as McAllister let out a loud groan and tried to move.

'I want him sedated.'

'I'm not authorized to do that, sir.'

'Well then, I'll sort it while you get authorization,' Chris growled, as he bent down and unceremoniously pulled McAllister's hands behind his back. The man screamed out in pain as the pellets embedded in his shoulder rubbed against bone.

Chris's gaze rested again on Reilly. 'Are you sure you're OK?'

'I—'

Right then, Kennedy hurried back into the room. 'Reilly?' he said, looking perplexed. 'There's nobody else here.'

While all the outbuildings were being searched to try and locate the children, McAllister was taken to the nearest police station for questioning. The bare walls of the holding cell were painted a dingy yellow, the camera lurking in the corner the only decoration of any kind.

McAllister barely moved when Chris and Kennedy walked in. His eyes were still red-rimmed, and he had a fierce anger inside.

'Where are the children, McAllister?' Chris sat in the chair across from him, Kennedy in another chair to the side.

McAllister considered the question for a moment. 'I'm thirsty.'

'The game is over,' Kennedy said. 'I suggest you start cooperating. Where are the kids?'

'My children are safe; away from prying eyes and wickedness.'

'They are not your children,' Chris shot back angrily. 'You abducted them, brainwashed them. You attacked a member of the public as well as an officer. You're in a whole word of trouble, McAllister, so I suggest you start answering some of our questions.'

McAllister gazed up at the camera. 'Are we on tape?'

'All interviews are recorded. McAllister, where are the girls? For the sake of their families ...'

'They have a family, I am their father,' he snapped. 'You people, in your wisdom, decided that the family they already had didn't fit your narrow definition of what was acceptable.'

'Forget the word games,' Chris said. 'Those children have families, real parents who love them, who miss them ...'

'Don't talk to me with your foolishness, you don't know what you speak of.'

Kennedy crossed his arms across his chest. 'OK, we have all the time in the world here. We can wait as long as it takes for you to start cooperating, but I'm not sure the children can,' he said, trying to switch the focus to them.

'It's only a matter of time before our people find them,' Chris said, hoping he was right. 'No matter what happens, this is over, there's no going back now, and once we find them, we will find their parents too. You not cooperating does nobody any favors, least of all the children ... their time with you is over. We need to return them to—'

'Their families?' He lifted his head, and spat the word at them. 'Their families? Do you have any idea what their families were like? Why don't you ask Lisa about the beatings she got from her father when he was drunk? Ask Eve about all those "uncles" sneaking into her bed when her mother was passed out on the couch? Or Julie – running around without a coat in winter, hanging out at the playground instead of going to school because she was too embarrassed about not having a clean uniform to wear?'

He sat up, eyes blazing, and stared at both of them. 'You

think I picked these children at random? You think they were happy little things who missed their mummies and daddies? I've spent my life helping children like that, and my wife and I did great work until people like you decided to take it all away from me.'

Chris met Kennedy's eye. What was he talking about?

'I did them a favor, I was called upon to save them, and now you with your self-righteous meddling are trying to take them away from the only happy, safe family they've ever had.'

McAllister's words had Chris floundering.

He had seen what he had created. Yes, it was a fantasy built on lies, but it was serene, peaceful, and in any other circumstances would be a wonderful place for kids to grow up. But when all was said and done, it was not reality, and it could never last.

'What do you mean, you and your wife? I thought your family was dead?'

There was a flicker of something across his face. 'My wife was taken from me. We were never blessed with children.'

What the ...?

Chris stood up. Kennedy nodded. The background information they'd been given by the locals was wrong. This coupled with what Julius had said about Sarah Forde needed immediate investigation.

'Tír na nÓg was a paradise,' whispered McAllister. 'Those children have everything they could ever need, and now you're trying to return them to this cesspit.' He spat the word out, looking around the bare room, its dirty linoleum floor, and cheap plastic chairs.

'I don't know what their families are like,' Kennedy was saying as Chris left the room. 'But they are not yours to lock away. There is someone else out there who loves them and misses them...'

When McAllister looked at him, his gaze was one of

sadness, tears brimming in his eyes. 'There is indeed someone who loves them, someone who misses them, Detective. And you will have to live the rest of your days knowing that you succeeded only in taking them away from that one, perfect place.'

75

R eilly had remained in Avoca in an attempt to try and locate the children. She couldn't believe it when they hadn't been in the adjoining room of the smelting house. She'd naturally assumed that McAllister would want to keep them close to him.

A detailed search was being made of the outbuildings and surrounding area but to no avail.

She was frantically hoping that they could figure it out without having to rely on Chris and Kennedy to get the information out of McAllister. Who knew how long that would take. Especially when he was so reluctant to give the kids up.

'I think I have an idea.'

'What are you thinking?' she asked Steve Jacobs now. She'd been searching through one of the old outhouses when he phoned her with a possible theory.

'The driving force for McAllister's world ...' She heard him flick through some papers back in the trailer. 'It's all based on this mythology, the story of Tir Na Nog. So why should that be different now? Yes, he might have had to move them from the lake house – from the enchanted land if you like – but think about how he did it?'

Reilly frowned, impatient. 'In a boat … how is that significant?'

'I've been going through the text again and according to the legend, you can only travel to and from Tir Na Nog over water. If you touch the ground, you will immediately wither and die, or like Oisin, become an old man. So I'm thinking,' Jacobs continued, the words coming quickly, 'that McAllister's hidden the children somewhere their feet won't touch the ground.'

Reilly's brain raced. Won't touch the ground? But where could …? Then it hit her, and she raced out the door and headed straight for the hay barn.

For the second time in as many weeks, Chris knocked on the door of the Forde household in Navan. Mrs Forde answered, her features ghostly.

'Mrs Forde? You got my message.'

She nodded and looked and down the street as if her husband would arrive home any minute.

'Would it be better if we went somewhere else?'

'No. It's OK. Pat has his poker game on a Thursday night. He's usually not back till after midnight. We won't be disturbed.'

She shuffled through to the living room, and Chris followed, closing the door behind him.

He'd since heard from Reilly that the kids had been located. Three young girls of various ages, approximately six to eleven, had been hidden away in a nearby barn, huddled together up in the old hayloft.

According to her, they seemed in good health, but were understandably very frightened and asking for their 'father'.

As much as he disliked the man, Chris had to give credit to Steve Jacobs for figuring that one out.

But now there was one more puzzle to solve.

He looked up as Sarah Forde's mother sat across from him, her hands fidgety. He had refused the obligatory cup of tea, this time ignoring one of his own rules. This was not a time for relaxing; he wanted to get straight to the point.

'Mrs Forde ...'

'Please, it's Rita.'

'Rita, like I said on the phone, I believe you haven't been exactly truthful with us about the circumstances surrounding Sarah's disappearance.'

She refused to meet his gaze. 'I'm sorry ... I didn't mean—'

'Your brother David was just arrested in Wicklow. He's in a lot of trouble. You need to tell me what was going on, Rita. Are you involved in these abductions?'

She looked genuinely shocked. 'Abductions? What are you talking about?'

Chris wasn't giving anything away. 'He's been arrested for abducting and holding three young children at his farm in Wicklow, a place he refers to as Tir Na Nog.' The mention of this meant something to her, he thought. 'We were working on the assumption that your daughter Sarah had been one of abductees, but recently escaped. However, we now have reason to believe otherwise.'

She rubbed her sweaty hands on her thighs. 'I don't know anything about any other children, I swear. I haven't seen David for years. I haven't been able to ... '

'Mrs Forde, Rita – your brother told one of my colleagues that you asked him to take care of Sarah some years ago, that you wanted to get her away from her father. Is that correct?'

Like Reilly, Chris had been gobsmacked by the revelation and had no idea what it could mean. Had Rita Forde lied about her daughter's disappearance to not only the authorities but her husband too? And if so why?

Granted, on his recent visit, he'd suspected that there was

more to the family dynamic than met the eye, but he could never have anticipated something like this.

Tears filled Rita Forde's eyes. She had the defeated look of a person who'd been carrying a heavy burden for a very long time. 'It was when Miriam was alive,' she said with a sob. 'Pat was ...' She took a deep breath, struggling, 'I didn't want to believe it, but Sarah came to me one day and told me what was going on. I didn't want to believe it. I talked to David and Miriam about it, probably because they had experience with this kind of thing ...'

Chris frowned. 'How so?'

'Well, with all the kids they used to take in ... many of them were abused, some mentally, others physically ... like Sarah.'

'I don't understand. Are you saying that your brother and his wife used to act as foster parents?' Chris asked, bewildered. Why hadn't this come up on McAllister's background search? But thinking about it, they'd only checked with Land Registry and motor records. Tax records were minimal because of his artist's exemption, and there was nothing of a criminal nature in the system. Notwithstanding that such information would have been with the Health Service Executive, a completely different department. Good old public service records. Like O'Brien had said, the left hand never seemed to know what the right was doing ...

'They were so good at it' Rita Forde continued, 'and so good with the kids. It was such a shame they'd never been able to have any of their own...'

Chris was baffled. 'But I thought your brother lost his wife and kids in an accident many years ago?'

'No, it was only Miriam. None of the kids were in the car at the time, the foster kids I mean. Although I'm not sure if they had any with them at the time. There was a bit of a problem after Ellie and the tattoo...'

'Who's Ellie?'

'She was one of the girls who used to come to them on and off. She was the oldest, and was definitely David's favorite too. He used to tell her all his stories, the ones about Oisin and Tir Na Nog.' She smiled. 'He was always fascinated by them, even as a child, and he passed a lot of it on to Ellie over the years. But then one day she turned up with this huge set of wings tattooed onto her back, and the social services people weren't happy. They blamed David for it, and wouldn't let Ellie go back to them after that. The poor child, she was devastated. I don't know what happened to her; if they got her another family or something. I doubt she'd have settled, she adored Miriam and David and the place in Wicklow.'

Suddenly the pieces were beginning to click. Chris realized he knew exactly what had happened to Ellie.

And once again he realized that they'd got it all wrong. Ellie – their cold case — hadn't been trying to escape from Tir Na Nog; she'd been trying to get back, despite the authorities.

And had died alone on the Wicklow hillside on the way.

Rita Forde was still speaking. 'It wasn't long after all that, that I confided in Miriam about Sarah. I didn't know what else to do, she was only seven and …' Her voice caught and she looked away. 'I had to protect her. Miriam offered to take her in, at least for a while until I figured out what to do. I made up this story to Pat about her disappearing, he phoned the police and somehow it all seemed to take on a life of its own.' She sobbed loudly. 'I'm so sorry, I never meant things to go that far …'

'So you just left your daughter with your brother's family?'

She looked at him. 'It was better than having her here — with him.' Her eyes filled with tears. 'You don't understand … I had to do what was best for my child. I knew she'd be safe with David and Miriam.'

Chris's voice was gentle. 'Rita, if what Sarah said was true, why didn't you report it?'

She looked at him as if he were mad, and he was immediately reminded of Brian McGavin's wife and how she too was reluctant or more likely afraid to let the authorities deal with her husband. It was the same story the world over.

'As the weeks went by it just seemed easier to let Pat think that she'd disappeared,' Rita continued. 'He never had much to do with my family anyway, would never have even suspected …' She wiped her eyes. 'But it went on for too long, and then a few months later, when Miriam was killed…'

'You couldn't very well just bring Sarah back.'

She looked pained. 'I couldn't even comfort David back then, in case Sarah saw me. She was only small, and David insisted she was fine, she was happy. I couldn't take her back here, back to him.' She cried openly, remembering. 'I knew my brother would take good care of her. And Sarah was fine; as far as she was concerned she was on an extended holiday at her uncle's house. She'd always loved spending time there anyway. I had to be careful when I kept in touch, but a little while afterwards I got the impression that there were more children there, so I just assumed he'd started fostering again.' She looked up at Chris. 'Are you sure that's not what happened? Why would he abduct children when all he's ever done is look after them, protect them?'

Chris thought about McAllister's words back in the interview room, about the children's' supposedly dysfunctional backgrounds.

Protect them? Granted it was a strange way to go about it. But in truth, perhaps it was *exactly* what the man had been trying to do.

I felt myself in the bosom of the waters, gently held, the light filtering through, green, translucent, slowly rocking me, washing my fears away. The cold seeped into me, calming my nerves, soothing my tired limbs, singing to me like the sirens, sleep, sleep...

I close my eyes and sink, drifting downwards into the depths, surrendering to the cold allure, the chance to sleep and never wake — and then I felt its grip, its icy grip, pulling at me from below. Down in the murk it waits, ever vigilant, always hungry; death incarnate, ready to wrap its fingers around you, hold you with an iron fist, never let you go.

I tried to fight, tried to force my limbs into motion, to fight the fierce hold it had over me. My eyes burst open once more, peered through the gloom to the light above, so far away now, fading with each thrashing stroke as I was dragged lower and lower, until finally all light was gone, and there was nothing but darkness — eternal darkness.

My eyes opened from the dream, the nightmare, and I blinked at the darkness, grateful to be alive. Is that what happened to you, my angel? Did our protector turn on you as you lay in its cool embrace?

The lake is our barrier, our shield, our defense against the violence, ugliness and decay that lie on the other side, but it is also a protector with a mind of its own. The dark depths of the lake hide their own secrets, their own desires. Our isolation, our protection, come at a cost, and we must respect those.

Did you betray that trust? Did you yield to temptation, try to leave the family and discover what lay on the other side? I close my eyes, try to sleep once more, but when I do, I see your cold, green eyes staring up at me from the murky depths.

O'BRIEN SMILED as the following morning, several microphones with the logos of TV and radio stations were thrust at him. 'Ladies and gentlemen, I'm delighted to report that thanks to the courage and bravery of various departments of the Garda Siochana, three young abductees have been liberated, and their captor is now in custody.'

A cacophony of voices called out all at once. 'Can you confirm there was a gun battle?' asked one tabloid journalist.

O'Brien's face was the picture of calm. 'There were shots fired from a recreational gun, but no officer discharged their weapon, and nobody was seriously injured.'

'Have you identified the abductees?'

'The investigation is still ongoing, and—'

'Was it a paedophile? Did he harm the kids? Were they abused?'

'The children are uninjured but have been taken to a secure location for medical and psychological assessment with the assistance of Child Services. We would ask for some privacy for them while we endeavor to reunite them with their families. As you can imagine, it has been a very tough ordeal for all concerned.' He held up his hands. 'Thank you; that's all we have for you just now. The press office will be issuing full details and further information as it becomes available.' The chief walked away from the media scrum and back toward the CC van for the debrief, breathing a visible sigh of relief as he went.

The children had been kept together following medical examination and spent the night under close surveillance. Special allowances were sanctioned given the strange circumstances surrounding their captivity, and their likely view on reality.

Three senior social workers and a child psychologist had been fully briefed and had spent the preceding evening assessing and trying to reassure them.

The team, including Steve Jacobs, were gathered at the incident room for a final debrief, with the exception of Chris who'd gone directly to the Health Services Executive offices first thing to try and speed up access to their records.

Based on the information he had received from Rita Forde, he was trying to access David McAllister's fostering history, as well as that of the various children who'd been in his and his wife's care.

The couple's qualifications to foster would have automatically ceased after his wife's death, and Reilly guessed that losing his wife, coupled with the loss of his ability to care for disadvantaged children, would have been enough to trigger his eventual descent into fantasy, and the creation of a 'safe' world he could control.

'How are the kids doing?' Kennedy asked Reilly, who'd called to the center earlier that morning to check on how they were doing.

'As well as we could expect, really,' she said. 'They've been through a lot. The older girl, Lisa – assuming that's her real name — is very much in charge and decidedly hostile, and they're all very suspicious. They keep asking for McAllister – their father, as they call him.' She supposed that this was to be expected given that they'd been brainwashed into thinking all strangers were not to be trusted. 'The psychologist reckons gaining their trust will be a huge challenge. I'd imagine the two younger ones will be easier, but for now they are very much under influence of the older one.'

Kennedy nodded. 'Well, the sooner we know who they really are, the sooner we can locate their families and set them on the road back to normality.'

Reilly wasn't so sure. McAllister's words suddenly flashed in her mind: *Why don't you ask Lisa about the beatings she got from her father when she was drunk? Ask Eve about all those 'uncles' sneaking into her bed when her mother was passed out on the couch...*

Had they done the right thing here? Or would it have been better if they had not figured out where Sarah had been, if McAllister and his little swans had been left in peace at Tir Na Nog, their earthly paradise?

'They certainly have a long road ahead, even after their families are found,' Jacobs ruminated. 'Especially since they already think they are a family, and think McAllister is their father. I suspect it will be a long time before they are ready to go home to their real parents, whoever they are.'

McAllister certainly seemed insistent that the children he'd 'saved' were from dysfunctional backgrounds. If so, chances were they were already in the social services system.

The department were also currently trying to track down any records of Ellie in order to see if they could confirm her as being the unidentified girl found in the mountain, trying to find her way back to paradise.

Given the remains found at the lake house, McAllister had obviously become aware of her death at some point after the investigation and subsequent burial, which prompted him to uncover the grave and bring her 'home'.

The investigation was as such effectively over, but for her part Reilly didn't take any comfort in it.

For whatever reason, Sarah Forde had wanted to escape Tir Na Nog.

Perhaps she'd understood that things at the lake house weren't quite right, and the stories her uncle were spinning weren't healthy. Her pregnancy may well have been what prompted her to make the break ... either to make a new life for herself and her child, or even to try and make her way back to her own mother. At this point they could only speculate.

But as Reilly was beginning to discover, the true definition of 'home' wasn't just about location, it was about people, and being with the ones you loved.

And like Conn, she also knew that the other children didn't feel liberated now because of their efforts, they felt imprisoned.

Reilly couldn't deny that lately, she could almost understand the feeling.

She thought back to Chris's rough-handling of McAllister at the house the night before, and figured that while he may have been somewhat reserved towards her recently, evidently he was still concerned about her welfare.

That thought, at least, heartened her, although it didn't do much to counter the feeling of not belonging that she was experiencing.

As the meeting broke up, Steve Jacobs caught up with her outside in the hallway. 'Again, I'm sorry you ended up in that position yesterday,' he said. 'It really should have been me in there.'

She gave an embarrassed half-smile. 'I'm sure you would have handled it very differently.'

'Not really — we got everyone out alive which is always the best possible outcome. But it was a very difficult situation nonetheless. You have great natural instincts, Reilly. If you ever fancy a change of career, let me know.'

She shook her head. 'No thanks, way too stressful. To be honest I much prefer the lab.'

As she and Jacobs said their goodbyes, she thought back to the case she'd been working on just before this one.

Based on her evidence, Brian McGavin had been arrested and charged with attempted murder for leaving his wife in a pool of blood on the kitchen floor. Following her examination of the house and the bloody fingerprint she had found, the local police had since uncovered the bloody end of a milk bottle underneath a patch of shrubs behind the house.

That felt like a win, and technically it was no different from following the evidence from the hit-and-run site and winding up with McAllister in custody and the girls in the hands of Social Services.

She tried reminding herself of what she had been taught from day one — her job had nothing to do with the morals of each case; nothing to do with right and wrong. She just followed the evidence, and let the judges and the courts decide who was guilty and who was innocent.

So why did it all feel so pointless?

As it was, the events of the last week had convinced her of one thing — she needed a break, needed to put some distance between herself and the job for a while, be it to join Mike and Maura on their trip back home next month or maybe take Daniel up on his offer of a visit to the Gulf Coast.

The question was, could she do it? Was she actually capable of turning her back, albeit temporarily, on the only thing that seemed to give her life meaning?

Reilly took a deep breath and got in the van to head back towards the GFU, where it seemed another conundrum awaited, this one at the home of a man who made a living out of making wigs out of human hair. Whether the donors were willing or otherwise was yet to be determined.

One investigation over, another already in the pipeline.

Story of her life.

The following day, Reilly stood outside the small terraced house. She had driven out there on her own, the windows of the car rolled down, the throttle pushed hard despite the slick, wet roads. In truth she was glad to get back to the 'normality' of working a crime scene, even though it was still a mystery as to what crime had taken place.

The others would be along soon, but until they arrived she had a few minutes to herself. A uniformed officer opened the door for her, and she stepped inside.

As she looked around, as she breathed in, she felt everything else slowly wash away. Sarah Forde, Ellie and the other children ... a possible vacation ...Daniel's offer ... Chris ... all of it just disappeared. She was ready.

The house was cold — it had stood vacant for a couple of days at least — but there was more to it than that. There was a cold that had seeped into the walls, a coldness of spirit. It was unloved, and despite its immaculate, clean condition, was also uncared for. Everything that had been done here had been done in a precise, clinical fashion.

Reilly stepped down the gloomy corridor, flashlight in her

hand. She shone the beam down at the skirting boards. Gary was right — dust free. It was the cleanest house she had ever been in.

The strangeness of the scene that Lucy and Gary had described in the attic meant it would have to be her first port of call.

She climbed up the ladder that had been left in place, and seeing a hand lamp beside the hatch opening, she flicked the switch.

Even though their findings had been described in great detail by the others, it was still unsettling, the blank expressions and dead eyes of the heads making her feel uncomfortable.

She looked around and noticed something strange. The mannequin heads seemed to have been arranged in order of hair color: brown, blond and red from top shelf to bottom. Her eyes lingered on the bottom shelf, and her mind again turned to the three frightened red-haired girls now in state care. Reilly reached out and touched the hair on one of the heads, holding it between her latex-covered fingers.

It was indeed human.

Where had the hair come from, who had it come from, and why was the house practically wiped clean and yet the wigs left behind? If this guy knew they might come he must also have known they'd find these ... his trophies?

She left the attic and headed downstairs to the living room, although that was a misnomer. No one had lived here for a very long time. Most houses took on the personality of the owner, but it was hard to see it in this one. Whoever this guy was, he had left little trace of himself here — no pictures, no CDs, or movies, just a couple of old books and magazines.

But in abandoning the house like this, he had also inadvertently left his imprint all over it. His cold and clinical hand was in every clean surface, every empty shelf, every bare cupboard.

The door opened and Lucy and Gary tumbled in, laughing at something or other — but as soon as they were inside, their laughter stopped.

The house did that to you.

They stepped into the living room, quiet, eager. 'So what do you think … have you been up in the attic?'

'Yes and I've taken some pictures. We'll bag and tag each head separately so we know exactly their position on the shelves, just in case they're in a specific order aside from the color. I just wanted to check out the rest of the house before starting into that.'

'So what are we looking for?' Gary asked. 'We've already been through it and, like I said, it seems pretty clean.'

'The things he doesn't want us to find,' Reilly replied, her face grim.

He raised his eyebrows and she looked at him. 'Don't you feel it?'

Gary didn't reply but Lucy nodded.

'Something happened here,' Reilly continued, 'even without the blood splatter Lucy found, we would have known that. This house has secrets, secrets it doesn't want us to know about.' She looked around the living room. 'Just look at it. It's not bad décor, but it's deliberate, a deliberate attempt by somebody to separate himself from the house, from the things he did here.'

Lucy shivered. 'I felt that too.'

Gary looked less convinced, but he knew Reilly well enough to trust her instincts — the fine attunement that had come from her experience and training. She was seeing things he wasn't, even if she couldn't yet identify what they were.

Somehow, at a subconscious level, the little things present in a house like this spoke to her. 'So where do we begin to find the things like that?'

'Under the floorboards, the cupboard under the stairs, the

back of the wardrobes — where would you hide something in this house if you didn't want people to find it?'

Gary nodded. 'I'll start in the kitchen.'

Reilly turned to Lucy. 'Why don't you show me the bathroom?'

Lucy led the way up the stairs, happy to show off her good work. They stopped in the doorway — there was a faint light coming in from the thick opaque window.

'It was mostly up that wall,' she said, 'as though someone had hit their head on the sink, maybe?'

Reilly nodded. The photos Lucy had taken of the luminol were still clear in her mind, she could see them almost as clearly as if the blood was there, splattered up the tiled wall. 'Thanks. Why don't you help Gary downstairs? I'll check out the bedrooms.'

Lucy duly trotted down the stairs and Reilly gave the bathroom one more glance before heading into the bedroom.

It was as bland as the rest of the house, faded wallpaper, sun-bleached curtains with a faint flower pattern on them, the small bed messed up where Lucy had already checked it for residual body fluids.

She opened the small wardrobe, empty now that all of the clothes had been taken away for processing. All that remained was the smell of mothballs. She touched the back panel, tapped lightly up and down, side to side. Nothing untoward. She checked the bottom of the wardrobe in the same manner; again nothing stood out.

Little by little she carried out her examination — checked for creaking floorboards, the underside of the bed, lost in the world she preferred most of all, thinking, assessing, searching...

Gary's heavy footsteps disturbed her from her reverie. 'Nothing in the kitchen, just like before,' he reported. 'Lucy's checking the living room – I was wondering, should I check out the garage?'

Standing on the stairs, Reilly nodded. 'Sure, why not. And at some point, when it's not so wet, we'll need to check the garden too.'

'OK.' He bounded off.

He stopped halfway down the stairs and looked back, something catching his eye beside where Reilly was standing.

'Hey, that power socket beside you, it looks pretty clean … new, almost.'

She looked at the electrical socket.

'And the screw heads are a little 'used' for a new socket.' Gary came back up and took a flip-out screwdriver from his pocket.

Selecting the Phillips head, he gently started to turn the first screw anti-clockwise, and Reilly noted that the grooves in the head of the other screw was indeed damaged from either overuse or an incorrect driver being used.

He unscrewed the second screw and then gently gripped the double socket to pull it back, expecting to feel the resistance of the attached wires.

Instead it came away in his hands.

He set the socket cover down and tugged the carpet back further so that Reilly could see — there was a panel cut into the stair with a small metal handle recessed into it. Gary reached for it.

'Gloves …'

He grabbed the gloves that Reilly tossed him, and waited while she repositioned herself and took several photos of the covering.

'What have you guys got?' Lucy stood in the doorway of the living room looking up at them.

'A dummy socket on the landing,' Reilly explained quickly. She leaned over the hole and shone her flashlight inside. Then she reached in and pulled out a clear plastic bag with items inside.

Gary was smiling. 'Nice one...'

Lucy hurried up the stairs and stood behind them, eager to see what they had found.

Reilly opened the bag. It looked like a collection of various bits and pieces, perhaps nothing all that interesting after all.

Then, quickly realizing what she was looking at, she paused. 'Looks like we were wrong about the wigs being trophies.' She began sifting through the hidden items — a hairbrush, a mobile phone, a bracelet, a necklace ...

But catching sight of one item in particular, she felt a cold shiver run down her spine. And just then Reilly wished she were anywhere else but here, looking at anything other than what she was seeing. Although ironically this very discovery meant that any vacation plans would have to be put on the back burner for a while.

Lucy was watching at her. 'Reilly? Are you all right?'

Gary, too, was giving her strange looks; he had never seen her look so rattled. 'What's wrong?'

And as the details of the missing person document she had only recently read burned through her brain, she struggled to comprehend the implications of what she was holding in her hand.

A distinctive piece of jewelry ...

'Reilly?'

Her heart heavy, Reilly stared at the thin silver necklace, a single star-shaped pendant attached.

The same kind Grace Gorman had been wearing the day she disappeared...

ALSO BY CASEY HILL

ABOUT THE AUTHOR

Casey Hill is the pseudonym of husband and wife writing team, Kevin and Melissa Hill. They live in County Wicklow, Ireland.

Translation rights to the USA Today bestselling CSI Reilly Steel series have been sold in multiple languages including Russian, Turkish and Japanese.

Made in the USA
Columbia, SC
08 August 2022

64831330R00236